Praise for Rich Larson's
CHANGELOG

"*Changelog* is perfect for fans of *Blade Runner* and *Black Mirror* with stories that span across biopunk, military sci-fi, space opera, the cosmic, exploring addiction, trauma, and the webbing of relationships through narratives both quiet and action-packed. Gritty and raw, Larson brings us tales reminiscent of classics like *1984* and worlds eerily palpable in their depictions of our far futures."
— Ai Jiang, author of *Linghun*

"Rich Larson is among the very best authors of his generation. He skillfully creates sunny dystopian end-of-the-world-as-we-know-it stories, hard-hitting thrillers, and chilling off-world tales. Characters like the mother and child in "You Are Born Exploding" and the violent central figure in "Painless" are beautifully drawn. Rich's stories are often taut and terrifying, but they also reveal his compassion and humor."
— Sheila Williams, award-winning editor of *Asimov's Science Fiction Magazine*

"Rich Larson is one of the most versatile short story writers I know. He's equally at home creating believable characters and worlds in space and on Earth. What I especially love about his stories is that I never know what he's up to until I begin reading. He's an editor's and reader's dream."
— Ellen Datlow, multi-award winning editor

"Within the astonishing short stories contained in *Changelog*, the wonder-inspiring visions of technological possibility that lie at the heart of science fiction's appeal exist simultaneously with a deep concern for the marginalized, the destitute, the powerless, and what future shocks will have in store for the least of us. Rich Larson's talent never ceases to awe me, whether he's sketching in only a few words characters that leap off the page, or taking age-old SFNal tropes and tweaking them in ways that will surprise the most jaded reader. You will be thrilled. You will be frightened. You will be moved to tears."
— Mike Allen, author of *The Black Fire Concerto*

"Rich Larson starts these stories with his foot on the accelerator and never lets up. They race through dark alleys on Earth and soar to spaceships orbiting distant planets. His people get things done, not always in accordance with the laws of their worlds and sometimes with catastrophic results. *Changelog* is a showcase for one of science fiction's most inventive writers."
— James Patrick Kelly, winner of the Hugo, Nebula and Locus awards

"Rich Larson is one of the best and brightest writers working in science fiction today, and has been since he burst onto the scene nearly fifteen years ago. His smart, sharply observed fiction is always compelling and entertaining, and I'm always looking forward to what he's going to do next. *Changelog* is the best of his recent work and it belongs on every reader's to-be-read pile and on next year's awards lists. Highly recommended!"
— Jonathan Strahan, award-winning editor

"Larson kills it again. Vivid, poignant, driven. Chilling as they are, his far-flung, dark futures never descend into hopelessness or the mere cautionary tale; they're agentic dystopias where you can make things happen. His futures ask no permission. PS. Someone please option 'Quandary Aminu vs the Butterfly Man.' I need to see this as an animated film."
— Ted Kosmatka author of *The Flicker Men*

"Rich Larson's new collection, *Changelog*, is further evidence that the prolific and talented Larson is one of the best short-form science-fiction writers in the field today. In this masterful collection of stories previously published in top markets, he offers us everything from flash fiction to novelettes, all of them perfect in their length. His ideas are wildly inventive, his plots are deftly handled, his characters are delightfully strange but all-too real, his storytelling can be touching and angry and violent by turn, and his vivid powers of description bring the setting to life, whether on a colony ship in deep space or a near-future Cape Town that reminds us of our lives today. This is superb science fiction, written by a master of the trade. Highly, highly recommended."
— Rick Wilber, author of *Alien Morning*

"Rich Larson's *Changelog* is an exceptional collection of some of the best of his recent short fiction. The focus is mostly on the fairly near future, dark visions of promising technology often misappropriated for horrific ends. It is full of fascinating ideas, and convincing extrapolations of the social effects of technology. There is propulsive action in places, and moving, even wrenching, characters stories in other places—or sometimes both at the same time."
— Rich Horton, *Strange at Ecbatan*

ALSO BY RICH LARSON

CHANGELOG

CHANGELOG
RICH LARSON

FAIRWOOD PRESS
Bonney Lake, WA

CHANGELOG

A Fairwood Press Book
September 2025
Copyright © 2025 Rich Larson
All Rights Reserved

First Edition

Fairwood Press
21528 104th Street Court East
Bonney Lake, WA 98391
www.fairwoodpress.com

Front cover art by Tithi Luadthong
Cover and book design by Patrick Swenson

ISBN: 978-1-958880-33-3
First Fairwood Press Edition: September 2025

Printed in the United States of America

For Immie Larson,
who wrote me into the story 33 years ago—thanks, Mom

CONTENTS

INTRODUCTION
BY SAM J. MILLER

R ich Larson is my Amadeus.

Like Salieri discovering Mozart, I adored the work before I met the maker. I swooned at the sublime aching hard-boiled lyricism of his stories, and I fell for every one of his broken protagonists.

And then—like Salieri—I was shocked when I first made the acquaintance of the artist.

I don't want to neg Rich in the introduction to his own book, so I'll be clear: my gut response to meeting Rich was problematic and ageist. Because HOW the ENTIRE FUCK had this CHILD achieved a level of craft and power that it had taken me decades to (maybe) (almost) (sometimes?) achieve? How had someone so young come by such astonishing insights into human pain and loss and redemption? Where had he learned so many marvelous storytelling tricks?

Writers are readers first. Love of words and stories is what starts us down this road, and that never really goes away—but the experience of reading gets complicated once words and stories become a profession as well as a passion. Because suddenly your heroes are also your competition! Not on an economic level, not really, but in terms of craft: how are they so good? How did they do that? AND MORE IMPORTANTLY WHY CAN'T I

When I read Ted Chiang or Karen Joy Fowler or N.K. Jemisin, I feel joy and wonder and heartbreak and pleasure—but I don't feel jealousy, because those authors are following a star that's super different from the one I follow. What they're doing is several galaxies away from what I'm trying to do. I can read their work without feeling personally attacked.

But the star Rich Larson follows—apparently—is located DIRECTLY in front of my own. When I read his stories, I feel my face flushing and my fists clenching, because, *gah, fuck, how, the, fuck, did he just fucking do that*? His stories go for the jugular; his characters punch you right in the heart. His sentences ache with tough raw muscular poetry—the caustic, un-self-aware, slightly-self-loathing, unshowy poetry of his alienated protagonists, beautiful beings in a world that hates their awesomeness, struggling (and often breaking) under the weight of masculinity's toxic gifts.

Rich Larson is Ray Chandler by way of Ray Bradbury, Philip K. Dick as seen through Sarah Pinsker's scanner darkly. He's a prodigy, turning out stories at an astonishing pace, and the insult added to the injury is that they're all fucking great.

This collection has what you need. Whatever you need. Smoky rooms and glitchy screens and broken people whose operating systems are crashing slowly—then all at once. I don't know how it happened, but Rich has been to the dark places. Young as he is, Rich Larson has been through the electric-blue flames of a razorblade cyberpunk narcotic hell—and he's emerged, still smoking, bleeding hands cupped, cradling this gift he brought us.

PAINLESS

Mars stands in the middle of the highway, knees locked, head tipped back. *The sky overhead is choked with harmattan dust. There is so much dust he can stare directly at the rising sun, a lemon-yellow smear in the dull gray. There is so much dust it looks like everything—the scraggly trees, the sandy fields, the road itself—is disappearing, as he often wishes to disappear.*

He used a pirate signal to monitor the progress of the autotrucks coming from the refinery in Zinder, loaded with petroleum. He watched them snake along the digital map. Now he can feel them coming: Their thunder vibrates the blacktop under his feet. They move fast and their avoidance AI is shoddy. In the low light, they will not see him until it is too late.

Mars takes a breath of cold, dry air. He bows his head, shuts his eyes. He can hear the first autotruck now: roaring, squeaking, clatter-clanking. He imagines it as a maelstrom of metal hurtling toward him. His heart thrums fast in his chest.

When the truck flies around the curve, Mars realizes he still wants to live. He tries to dive aside. The impact splits his world in half.

Dusk falls and Mars is still waiting beneath a twisted baobab for Tsayaba, the old woman who claims she can find anybody in this city, anybody at all. So far only the stray dog he met this morning has shown up. It sits in front of him, panting expectantly, tail thumping the sand.

"You again."

The animal is gaunt, with fat black ticks studding its neck and shoulders, burrowing deep into matted fur. It has cuts on its backside from wriggling under some jagged fence. But it is luckier than some of the other strays here. Mars saw a man with an infected eye implant roving the streets with three skeletal dogs chained to his waist, intending to sell them down in Nigeria to a tribe that still eats dog meat.

Mars takes out his nanoknife, the last piece of military equipment he carries. The stray recognizes it and starts to salivate.

"I spoil you, dog."

Mars dices up his thumb and then his index, flicking the bloody chunks to the ground. The stray pounces on each one and whines when Mars stops at the gray-white knucklebone of his middle finger.

"I give you any more, you'll throw it all up."

The dog whines a little longer, blood-specked black lips peeled back off its teeth, then finally trots away. Mars is alone again. He inspects his stumps, which are already clotting shut. He inspects the darkening street, mudbrick walls topped with broken glass or razor wire.

A slick-skinned maciyin roba wanders past on its little cilia feet, hunting for the flimsy black shopping bags half-buried in the sand. The plastivores were designed in a Kenyan genelab— for this, Mars feels a certain kinship with them—and were later set loose across the continent. They do their job well and reproduce on their own, but plastic trash has accumulated in the West African dust for nearly a century and it will take a very long time to recycle it all.

The evening prayer call is starting, a distant mumble-hum projected from the mosques. Mars is not Muslim or anything else, but he likes the sound, the ebb and flow of distorted voices. He listens to it with his eyes shut and is nearly lulled to sleep before Tsayaba finally arrives.

"Sannu."

Mars opens his eyes. Tsayaba is old, with a deep-lined face

and many missing teeth, but she stands very straight and carries herself how Mars imagines a chief would, with slow, smooth motions, with high gravity. She wears a bright yellow-patterned zani and a puffy winter jacket.

"Sannu," Mars says. "Ina yini? How was the day?"

"Komi lafiya," Tsayaba says. "All is well. Ina sanyi?"

"Sanyi, akwai shi," Mars says, even though he does not feel the cold. "Ina gida?" He wants to know what Tsayaba has found, but he makes himself focus on the greeting. Things are done slowly here.

"Gida lafiya lau. Well, very well." Tsayaba frowns, clicks her tongue. "Ina jiki?" she asks. "The body?"

Mars doesn't understand for a moment, then realizes Tsayaba is looking at his hand. The fingers have grown back—the keratin of his nails is still spongy—but he forgot to wash away the blood.

"Da sauki," Mars says. "Better."

Tsayaba gives a grunt of acknowledgment, then lowers herself to a squat. "I have found who you are searching for," she says. "I am almost certain. Early this morning, six men came with a truck. They paid the gendarmes. Now they are staying in the old hospital. But it is bad."

"What is bad?"

"These men are killers. They have otobindigogi." She makes her finger chatter, mimicking an autogun. "And they are here waiting for worse. They are waiting for a criminal called Musa, who will buy what they have. Musa, he was Boko Haram before the Pacification."

"When will he come?"

"They are not sure. They are anxious. He was meant to come today." Tsayaba shakes her head side to side, side to side. "Wahala," she says. "Wahala, wahala. If your friend was taken by these men, I think he is not a captive. I think he is dead."

Mars does not think so. If what he suspects is true, then Musa is not coming for autoguns. He is coming for something much more valuable.

"Na gode," Mars says. "So sai."

Tsayaba accepts the thanks with a brief nod of the head. She pulls a sleek black blockphone from the pocket of her coat and looks politely off into the distance. Mars takes out his own phone and taps it against hers, sending a small cascade of code equivalent to five hundred francs.

"Yi hankali," Tsayaba says.

Mars cannot promise to be careful, but he nods and clasps the old woman's hand once more—with his right hand, his clean hand—before he leaves.

He has a busy night ahead of him.

The kasuwa is busy despite the fierce midday sun that bakes the color out of the sky. Traders lounge under their tarp-roofed stalls, barking prices, rearranging their wares. Heaps of dried beans and grasshoppers, papayas and tomatoes and purple onions, cheap rubber shoes, 3D-printed toys beside wood carvings, bootleg phones and even a few secondhand implants bearing telltale stains. Camels slouch their way through the crowd draped with rugs and solarskin, only their bony knees visible.

"Miracle! Abin al'ajabi! Come see the miracle Allah has done!"

Miracle workers are not uncommon at the market, proselytizing through jury-rigged speakers and selling elixirs from the backs of their trucks in old plastic bottles, but this time there is a new trick that draws eyes. A boy, eleven or twelve with a sleepy smile, is standing on a woven plastic mat. Cables trail from his outstretched arms and hook into a car battery beside him. The electricity hisses and snaps, and the boy twitches but does not cry out. He only stands and smiles.

It is not a trick. Passersby come and touch the boy, certain the battery is dead, and even the slightest brush sends them reeling away in pain. His whole body is crackling with charge, but he feels nothing at all. The man who says he is his father circles through the crowd collecting coins.

"Abin al'ajabi!" he calls. "Thing of wonder!"

A hubbub builds from the other end of the kasuwa. An armored jeep, jacked high off the ground, is bullying its way through the market, maneuvering past donkey carts loaded with metal drums of well-water. It rolls to a stop and two men in sweat-wicking suits climb out. One of them is foreign, too tall and too light-skinned to be Hausa, with a babelpod covering one ear like a spiny white conch. Both of them stare at the boy.

"Turn off the battery," the Hausa man says, in the voice of a man whose orders are done even when given to nobody in particular.

The boy's supposed father scurries back to the battery and switches it off. "It does not harm him," he mutters. "You saw. You saw it does not harm him."

"Who is his family?" the Hausa man demands. "His blood family?"

A shrug. "Ban sani ba. Ban sani ba. He said he had a brother. Dead. But not him. He is a miracle child."

"Il est une aberration génétique," the foreign man says, and his babelpod turns the French into clumsy Hausa. He walks up to the boy and removes the cables. "You feel nothing?"

The boy nods, then shakes his head, uncertain.

The foreign man takes both of his hands and turns them over, inspecting the skin. "And you are not leprous," he says. "You are lucky to have lived this long with no severe burns. No lost limbs. It is difficult to navigate this world without pain. Your name?"

The boy shrugs. "Yaro," he says—child.

"You are not just a child," the foreign man says. "I think you are a Marsili. A Mars, for short. Your body does not process pain. That makes you very special. It makes you a candidate."

The boy tries to understand the electronic speech coming from the babelpod, but he has never heard these words. He seizes on one he recognizes and makes a spaceship with his hand.

"Mars," he says.

The foreign man laughs. "Yes. Yes. But Mars was something else, too. Mars was a god of war."

Before he goes to the old hospital, Mars finds a neon-lit restaurant and orders so much food that the two Lebanese women who own the place send their son on his moped to beg the butcher to reopen his meat locker. Mars washes his hands in the cracked bathroom sink; then, while the family cooks furiously, he sits down outside with a bottle of Youki. He watches the lime-green holo of the restaurant sign jitter and swirl through the dark, watches moths flock to it in spirals.

The beef kebabs arrive first, steaming on their skewers. Mars slides them onto the plate and wolfs them down, barely chewing; he cannot feel them burning his fingertips or mouth. Pork works better for his purposes, but it is difficult to find here. And there is another meat that works even better than pork, but he did that only once, in the field, and he has nightmares about it still.

Lamb arrives next, only half-cooked—as he ordered it. Time is of the essence. He would eat it raw if he could stand it. Mars falls on the meat, picking the rack apart with his greasy fingers. A few young men rove past, blasting music from an ancient speaker rig, laughing amphetamine-loud. They stare at the mountain of food, but when they see Mars's solemn eyes and the carbon-black nanoknife laid on the metal tabletop beside his tray, they give him a wide berth.

Mars remembers that meat used to make him feel queasy when he was much younger, before the procedures. Now he is a carnivore the way the maciyin roba is a plastivore. He eats until his stomach drags heavy, then eats more. The Lebanese women shift from amusement to disgust to grim professionalism as they feed him, as they watch him crack through the bones and choke down the gristle.

"Shukran," he says, when he is finally ready for them to take the plates away.

"Afwan," they say in faint unison.

Mars's stomach churns when he stands up, but he has trained it to not revolt.

Three years later, the boy still has no name. He is called by a number: thirteen. He is lying face down on a geltable, because to-day is his Birthday, the day all the treatments and drug courses culminate in a final procedure. Other children in the facility have had Birthdays; he has not seen them since. He supposes they were moved elsewhere, or they died.

The boy knows the procedure is dangerous. He knows even the treatments were too much for trained soldiers to bear. But he finds it hard to feel worried. His stomach is full of shinkafa da wake and oily onions, and there is a screen set up beneath the geltable playing procedurally generated cartoons. Not so different from another life, a vague memory in which he is wedged into the same chair as his older brother in front of a flickering screen.

Above him, hanging from the ceiling like an enormous metal spider, is the surgical unit. It tracks laserlight over his bare back and marks injection points with neat red circles. Pipettes and tubes slither into the boy's body, puncturing his skin with a dozen small flesh sounds. He feels only a dim, worming pressure.

There is a glass tank attached to the surgical unit, and inside it is the organism. The boy has been shown it before, the mass of raw pink putty that writhes and undulates. They told him it is a sort of cancer, reprogrammed by a sort of virus, and that in a way it is human. To him, it looks nothing like a human.

An electronic signal is given and the organism is fed into the boy's body, coursing through the clear tubes into his interstitial spaces, into the artificial pockets prepared by earlier surgeries. The boy does not scream into the geltable. He does not bite through his tongue. He feels no pain, only the strange and unpleasant sensation of a hand entering his body and wriggling its fingers.

Hours later, when he is drowsy and his eyes are bleary from focusing on the cartoons, the gel sluices away and the tubes retract. He hears footsteps.

"Be patient," a woman's voice begs—English. The boy has learned some English in these past three years. "Be patient, be patient. It looks like a successful bond. But we have to wait."

"I have waited for decades," says another voice, and the boy recognizes it. The foreign man who took him away from kasuwar Galmi so long ago. "I have to know."

Suddenly the boy is face-to-face with him. The foreign man has slid underneath the table. His hair is grayer than the boy remembers it and his eyes are more hollow. He has a cigar cutter in his hand.

"Miracle child," he says. "It's very good to see you again. Please stick out your thumb for me."

Mars can see why they chose the old hospital compound. It has high mudbrick walls on three sides and barbed wire on the fourth, which backs onto an ancient landing strip. The gate is rusty metal crenellated with spikes. The painted letters have long since flaked away. Tsayaba told him that the hospital has been abandoned for years, ever since the surgical wing caught fire and took the rest of the building with it.

Mars feels bloated and heavy as he scales the front wall, but he knows he will be glad for his full stomach later. He pauses at the top to catch his breath and looks back at the old town: a maze of mudbrick, warped by the rainy season, lit by swatches of grainy orange biolamp. New buildings on the periphery are more geometric, rebar skeletons in concrete sheaths. Mosques tower over everything else, their painted white crescents pushed up into the sky as waning moons.

Most importantly, the highway is clear. Mars faces forward and peers down into the dark compound. The hospital is a ruin, ash and rubble. But beyond it there are housing units for the doctors and staff that were untouched by the fire. He can see light in one of the windows. That is where they will be keeping their captive.

Almost directly below him, the night guard is boiling tea on a brazier. His face is scarved against the cold, gaps only for his eyes and a pair of trailing earbud wires. His gun is resting on a woven plastic chair across from him. His blockphone is balanced on top of it, playing yesterday's Ghana-Côte d'Ivoire football match.

Mars drops down off the wall, raising a small puff of dust where he lands. The guard leaps to his feet and right into the nanoknife.

Mars smothers the man's cry with the crook of his arm, yanks the blade free, then spins him around to drive it into the base of his skull. It slides through the bone and gray matter as if they were cow butter. The guard spasms and goes limp. Mars plucks the blockphone off the chair and shoves the man's face up against the screen to unlock it before rigor mortis makes him unrecognizable.

Apart from one blinking number at the top of his screen, the man's contacts are local. He is an extra hire, not one of the six Tsayaba mentioned. Mars feels a twist of guilt when he sees a home screen clip of the man, face uncovered and still young enough to have pockmarks, tossing a little girl into the air and catching her. He lays the body down gently. Blood trickles out from underneath, stretching red fingers through the sand.

Mars silences the phone and pockets it. The husk of the hospital looms before him: a few jagged walls, half of a twisted metal staircase. For an instant the smell of distant wood fires, carried from town on the wind, makes it seem like the ruin is still burning. He sees movement in the rubble, first the slow careful motions of more maciyin roba and then a stiff-legged loping.

Hyenas is Mars's first thought—they say the hyenas are coming back now—but it is only a pair of stray dogs. He peers at them for a moment, trying to tell if one is his visitor from earlier, then heads for the housing units. Tonight, the dogs will have plenty to eat.

Three years later, the boy is a soldier and nearly a man. His identification tag says Marsili 13. *He wears it on a band around his arm, because when they tried to do the subcutaneous kind his body spat it back up and pinched the hole shut in seconds. The rest of his unit calls him Mars—some of them joke that he came from there in a tiny spaceship.*

There is good reason for that. From the very start of his accelerated training, Mars can do things no human can do. He can sprint for minutes at a time while the organism laps away his lactic acid and replenishes his cells. His scrawny frame can carry double its weight when the organism weaves itself into his skeletal muscle.

At first the others are scared of him. Then they hate him, for making things seem so easy. They give him cuffs on the back of his head when they pass. They drop a bucket of pinching water scorpions into his shower stall. He does not care. At night he climbs into his cot with a full belly and watches cartoons on the screen of his standard issue phone, a dull black slab that only functions during certain hours.

When they go through anti-interrogation, the water filling his lungs is only a tickling ghost. They pull him out of the tank before he drowns, but he is not sure if he can drown anymore. The other members of his unit, sopping wet, breathing ragged, look at him as if he is a god. Then they look at each other.

That night they invite him to drink. He guzzles the ogogoro until he can fool himself into thinking he feels the same crazy happy way they feel. He shows them his own version of their knife game:

Instead of stabbing the spaces between his fingers, he drives the point of the blade into each knuckle in turn, moving like a blur, and by the time one circuit is complete he has already healed.

They howl. The ones who still believe in witch stuff say, Witch stuff.

"Who cares," says one of the Yoruba men. "He is ours. You are ours, yes, Mars?" And because he knows Mars speaks Hausa: "Dan'uwanmu ne? You are our brother?"

Mars thought he did not care, but now the word makes him into a child again. He starts to weep. The others shift and fidget, uneasy.

In the morning, Mars is transferred.

They are in the last house of the row, a Western-style construction no doubt built for some European surgeon decades ago. The orchard around it is dead and withered. But there is light in the window, faint music, and a truck and two motorcycles are parked outside. Mars even sees some clothes hanging from a wire laundry line, flapping wings in the night wind.

He circles the house like a shade. From up close, the thumping music is loud enough to send ripples through the screen porch. The bass raises the hairs on his arms. He peers through a window and sees four men sitting around a kitchen table. Playing cards slip and slide over the dusty wood. A heavy black vape sits in the center, belching smoke through the affixed tubes.

Mars guesses that the last two men are with the prisoner. He takes the stolen blockphone from his pocket and thumbs the blinking number, thinking that whoever answers it will be the leader, and the leader he will keep alive to answer questions. None of the men at the table reach for their pockets. Instead, Mars hears a whistling ringtone from behind him and realizes he has guessed wrong just before an autogun tears into him.

The flurry of bullets takes him off his feet; he slams into the side of the house and crumples. Through the keening in his ears Mars realizes the music has cut out. He hears shouts from inside. A clattering door. Voices somewhere above him.

"Kai! Who the fuck is that? Who did you shoot?"

"He was looking through the window, he—"

"Is he one of Musa's?"

"Then Musa's trying to rip us off. The man we had out front, he killed him."

Mars lies very still. He can feel the organism at work, knitting his flesh back together, squeezing the metal out. He reaches for his nanoknife. The autogun sees the movement and gives a bleat of alarm, but there are friendly bodies in the way so it cannot fire, and its owner takes a moment too long to realize his target is somehow alive. In that moment Mars cleaves him open from his hip bone to his sternum.

He whirls on the others, slips under a punch and pulls the man close, making him a shield as another gun goes off. Small caliber this time—a bullet clips his shoulder and he barely notices it. Three quick stabs as he pushes forward; he drops his dying shield and drives the nanoknife into the arm of the shooter. The gun fires one last time and he takes the bullet right in the chest. For a split second his whole body shudders. Sways.

Then he's moving again, and in less than a minute he is surrounded only by corpses. Their blood pools and wriggles through the sand like anemones. Mars can feel the organism working hard, converting his evening meal into new flesh, fresh skin. The last bullet spirals back out from his heart and drops soundlessly to the ground.

Six years later, Mars is a bogeyman. He finishes his training half in virtual and half in the field, sometimes with a handler, most often alone. He is given no rank, because he does not exist as anything but a rumor. He is given jobs instead. Most often, targets. The first time he kills, the man sputters and curses and begs and shits himself. Mars had seen people die before, but causing it is different. He does not sleep for a week.

He is told, over and over again, that he is creating stability. That he murders one malefactor to save a thousand innocents. That nobody else can do what he does—the procedure has never been successful since, not once—so he must do it. But he does not feel any higher purpose. He does what he is told because it is his habit. It grinds away at him in places that do not seem to grow back.

On one assignment he triggers an alarm and has to flee on foot. A pursuer's bullet punches a hole through his back; he survives but a week later he learns that the bullet continued through a tin wall into the skull of a woman leaning down just so, just at the perfect height, to sweep her floor.

One assignment an explosion tears his leg off. He sees his target escaping. He needs both legs to follow. So he eats the corpse beside him, eyes watering, stomach heaving.

One assignment he plants a smartbomb tailored to a general's DNA, but the general's son runs into the room instead and the scanner makes a mistake Mars is not quick enough to override. He watches the boy's body blow apart.

The other operatives, the ones who are not gods, have ways to forget. But Mars's body flushes the drugs and alcohol from his system faster than he can consume them, and sex is of no interest to him. He knows the procedure left him sterile, but he had no desire before it either, maybe for the same reason he cannot have friendships: Other people are too fragile. When he is around them all he can see are the many ways they might die.

On some of the nights Mars cannot sleep, he stands in front of a mirror and flays himself, as if he can shed the memories with the skin. He decides there are two sorts of pain: the sharp red kind that twists a person's face and makes them scream, and a slick black kind that coats a person's insides like tar. He realizes that he has been feeling the second kind for most of his life.

Mars knows there is a way to escape all pain. He has delivered it many times. Long ago, his brother escaped and left him alone. So when his handler sends him north, across the border, he discards his tracker and his identification tag and almost all of his equipment. In the early morning, he goes to the highway.

Mars opens the screen door, shaking insects off the wire mesh. He steps into the house. The concrete floor is rippled with red sand. He can hear the hum of a generator. The fluorescent tubes in the ceiling are long burnt out; the lighting is sticky yellow biolamp, smeared in the corners of the ceiling and activated by a particular radio frequency.

Now that he is so close to his goal, he feels a mixture of excitement and dread. For the past three weeks, ever since he crawled away from the highway trailing shredded flesh behind him, he has been in hiding. It took him days to grow his legs back, for the new nerve endings to find their way to his spine.

After that he went out into the daji, into the bush. He wandered for a week, staying in villages or moving with the herders who needed strong and tireless backs. Some of the time he was thinking of a hundred surer methods than an autotruck, but some of the time he was just existing, and it was not so bad. Then he heard the rumor.

Mars walks past the kitchen down a dark hallway, following the sound of the generator. He is still not sure he believes. But the possibility has been growing and swelling and pushing out his other thoughts ever since he heard the story, the story of the strange creature some farmers had found on the highway.

The hum is coming from the bathroom. Mars pushes the door open. In the faint glow of the biolamp, he sees a small hooded figure slumped inside the ceramic bathtub. The generator beside the tub is hooked to an industrial drill that is churning on its slowest setting into the prisoner's stomach. Mars switches it off. He seizes the drill with both hands and drags it backward; the bit comes free with a sucking sound.

The hooded head twitches the exact way Mars's head twitches. He pulls the black fabric gently up and away. Shock freezes him in place. He thought he was prepared for this, but he is not. The face looking back at him is a child's, but it is also his.

"Sannu," he says, because he can think of nothing else to say.

"Yauwa," the boy in the bathtub says, in a reedy voice hoarse from disuse. "Sannu."

When Mars crawled away from the highway, he gave no thought to his other half, to the splinter of spinal column and dead legs left in the ditch. He never considered how badly the organism wanted to be whole. It must have fed on carrion, or pulled some unlucky buzzard down into itself, and slowly, slowly, shaped him anew.

But it is not him. Not quite—there was not enough flesh. Instead it is a boy he only ever saw briefly in cracked screens or windows, a boy who once stood on a mat in the marketplace with wires trailing off his skinny arms.

Mars leans forward and unties the boy's hands. His fingers are trembling slightly. The procedure only worked once, but now he knows there is another way. If they knew, they would make a hundred more soldiers like him. A hundred more gods of war.

"Ina jin yunwa," his other self says. "Sosai."

Mars nods, looking at the boy's stomach where purple scar tissue is sealing shut—he is right to be hungry. The drill must have been at work for days. He is gaunt.

"I saw kilishi in the other room. Come. Eat."

Mars helps the boy out of the bathtub. They go to the kitchen, and on the table a blockphone is buzzing. Mars picks it up.

"Is he ready to be moved?" the foreign man's voice asks. "We are two minutes away."

Mars hears the sound of a rotor in the background. They are coming by air. He looks at the boy, whose new muscle is packing itself onto his bones as he devours the dried meat.

"He is ready," he says, and ends the call. He turns to his other self. "Some more men are coming. They are bringing us a transport. Well. We will steal it from them. And then we can go far away, to be safe from them."

The boy nods solemnly. "Who are you?" he asks through a full mouth.

"Do you remember the autotruck?" Mars asks back.

The boy shakes his head. "My head is bad. I remember strange things. I think I know you. Who are you?"

For a long moment Mars does not answer. They look at each other, and Mars does not see the expressions he has grown accustomed to: There is no fear or awe on the boy's face. Only some sadness, some shyness, some hope. It reminds him not of himself, but of someone he had nearly forgotten, someone he remembers more as a smell and a skinny arm slung around his shoulders than as a face.

He realizes he has finally has found someone who will not look at him like he is a god or a devil. Someone who is like him. But Mars can make sure the boy's life is nothing like his life.

"My name is Mars," he says. "Like the planet." He makes a

spaceship with his hand and launches it through the air.

The boy's mouth twitches. Nearly smiles. He raises his smaller hand and does the same, making the noise in his cheeks. "You are so familiar," he says. "Why?"

Mars feels a third sort of pain, one he does not know, an ache that he doesn't want to end. "Mu 'yan'uwa ne," he says.

The boy nods, as if it all makes sense now. "We are brothers."

LIKE ANY OTHER STAR

The airlock was strictly off-limits to unauthorized crew, but Ollie had some kind of ancient clearance on his palmchip and that got them in. Callisto still checked up and down the corridor before she slid the door shut behind her. The airlock's interior was dim and cramped. The walls were snaked with naked wire and slices of grease-yellow light leaked from aging fixtures. A half-dozen hullsuits dangled from the ceiling like mannequins.

Ollie wasted no time stripping down. Callisto scoped the mat of gray hair on his chest and the bulgy veins all over him. She wondered if that was because he was dustyfooted or just because he was very, very old.

"Well, hurry on," Ollie said, reaching for a hullsuit.

Callisto pushed into the hanging thicket, feeling the papery material between her fingers. She found her size and tugged it off the hook. "I'm not pure steady about going topside unkenned," she admitted. "Bit dangerous, neg?"

Ollie's face worked. "Nonsense," he said.

"And if Skipper catches us out, we're froze," Callisto elaborated, not sure he'd understood the shiptalk.

Ollie snorted. "Not our dad, is he love?" He sealed his suit and started running the diagnostic bar over himself.

Callisto stepped into hers, tugging it up her shoulders, raking her hair back to fit under the hood. "Are you pure truth a thousand years old, Ollie?" she asked.

Ollie was now on the lip of the airlock. The membrane quivered slightly, dull burnt orange. It did not look inviting. Ollie was sealed in, so the reply came by shipnet.

«Could be.» Then he levered down into the membrane and disappeared.

Callisto sealed her hullsuit, holding an instinctive breath, and dropped down after him. The gelatinous stuff was cool and tingling, pressing against her from all sides, seeping into potential fissures. By the time she slucked out the other end, up turning down, she was cocooned in slimy insulation. She felt like a fetus on birthday deck.

The ubiquitous shiply hum in her ears was guillotined by the vacuum, leaving an unnerving quiet. Callisto locked her boots in against the hull and tried to stand up. Deep space crushed her back down. She hadn't been on many hull-walks and the sudden immensity was rearranging her internal organs. Inky space encompassed all directions, sewn with white-hot flecks of stars. She felt small, small, small.

Ollie was already striding away across the hull, a dim orange ghost. The skin of the ship had been unblemished when it set out—gleaming like a mustang, Ollie once said—but now it dipped and rippled where the micrometeors had left their pocks and the composites had been built up over them.

"Ayeright, ayeright, no being scared," Callisto murmured. She closed her eyes. Opened them. Ollie was still moving aft. Callisto hauled herself upright and made slow and cautious progress toward him. Past him, the scarred tableau stretched to a sharp horizon. She had never known anyone to walk it one end to the other, but she was sure it would take an hour at least.

Ollie was crouched on the hull now, pointing towards a vague star. He targeted it for her in her hullsuit display. «Like I told you.»

"Greatly far," Callisto said, not really looking. She anchored herself down beside him and tried to breathe steady. She searched for the oxygen meter in the corner of her eye. When she chanced a real look, following the virtual trajectory, she was disappointed. The old sun looked like any other star out here.

She put the hood of her hullsuit against Ollie's. "How was it like, then?"

"Dirty and vicious and beautiful," Ollie said without hesitation. He paused. "I suppose you'll understand once we reach the colony planet."

"Be even better than Earth, I scope it."

Ollie lifted his head away from hers, craning his neck towards the infinite black. «It won't ever be full the way Earth was. Mixed blessing, that. You'll never see real cities. Crowds. Waterfire festival. 2032. Beautiful, beautiful. Torches up and down the river, and the music, my God. Real music, from real instruments, made of wood and bone and coiled steel. Standing on the bridge, remember? Loads of people, coming from the downtown. Everybody right plastered.»

His voice was wavery, distant, by the end. It sounded like happy and sad mixed together. They sat for a while and stared at the fading star. Callisto leaned her head back against his.

"Is it pure lonely, Ollie?" she asked at last. "Being the last dustyfoot?"

Ollie chuckled, leaned back. «Still got you, haven't I, Mer?»

Callisto felt a small icy plunge in her stomach. She opened her mouth, then shut it tightly. She was thinking of the proper thing to say when their hullsuits began to tremble and a disembodied voice ordered them back to the airlock, immediately.

She'd never had a summons to see the Skipper before. He'd sent it to her personal channel, not shipwide, and Callisto didn't know if that was a better sign or worse. She tried to get her hair reasonable-looking before she palmed the door open. Best to be presentable for a reprimand. And other reasons.

The Skipper was using a gravity harness, limbs pumping up and down, and a body monitor display was splashed on the wall. Most of the other hands on ship made a token effort now and again — they knew they wouldn't be in low-grav no-grav forever — but the Skip was religious about it. Watching the muscles skim back and forth under his skin, Callisto barely remembered to salute.

The Skipper dropped down out of the harness and returned it. His face was well-sculpted but not for smiling. "Unauthorized topside jaunts are a pure serious thing, crew. Especially when we're gearing to accelerate again."

"Won't be done again, Skipper," Callisto said, lips pursed.

The Skipper nodded, eyes fixed. "I need to stab a few questions about crewman Oliver."

"I had equal part in it, Skip. More than." Callisto winced slightly, looking at the health display over his shoulder to avoid meeting his gaze. "I wanted to scope the old sun."

The Skipper raised his eyebrows, but didn't inquire. "This isn't his first incident," he said instead. "Oliver's been erratic. Moreso lately. Have you noticed anything? Friend first, crew second."

"He's pure solid, honest," Callisto said. She shifted from foot to foot. "Though, ah. Sometimes he does drift, like. Says a wrong name for me, maybe."

Something jumped on the display and the Skipper turned, slapped it blank. His jaw was set. "We're going to put him into cryo for the last leg," he said. "I've been putting it off. But he's unpredictable, and like such he's a liability." His eyes ticked back and forth and Callisto could tell he was issuing orders on the shipnet.

"Wait, you're truth going to freeze him?"

"It's got to be done." The Skipper threw another unsmiling salute. "Dismissed."

Callisto returned the salute and was out the door. The antiseptic white of the corridor was a comforting pressure on her eyes after the hull-walk. Once she was around the corner, she ran. The ship was a warren of drops and ladders, but she knew them all and didn't stop until she found Ollie in engineering. He was wrists-deep in the guts of some malfunct ventilator, tools lined in meticulous rows by his feet.

"Ollie, I've just dog-offed from the Skipper's and he says you're erratic and they're going to freeze you, you ken?" Callisto said it in a single slab of breath.

Ollie looked up, blinking owlishly. "That little bastard," he said. "Help me hide under this shelf."

Two crewmen ended up dragging him out of a tank in the hydroponic gardens. He swore furiously at them while he picked algae out of his wild gray hair. Callisto followed behind as they marched Ollie to the cryo deck. They stopped in front of the freezer doors.

"Well, see you on the other end," said one of the crewmen, giving a weak smile.

"Been an honor, dustyfoot." The other crewman paused. "Ah, Oliver."

"Both of you can sod off, now," said Ollie.

They did.

Ollie was silent as they walked down the row of cloudy coffins. His breath came in short puffs of steam.

The Skipper was waiting beside an open shell. "Uploading your abstract for cryogenic storage," he said, tapping his head. "Ping acceptance when you've read it." His face was stony.

"Yeah, yeah." Ollie snorted. "You've been trying to ice me for years."

"It's for the best," the Skip said.

"If Mer were here, she'd be damn well embarrassed," Ollie said. He gave a fractured glance towards Callisto and then shook his head.

"She's dead," the Skipper said. "You were at the recycling yourself. And ever since then, you've been getting old fast."

"Trying to hide me away. Keep me out of trouble."

"It's not that, dad."

Callisto stared.

"Then what?" Ollie snapped, but his voice wasn't so harsh.

The Skipper cracked just slightly, his mouth tugging sideways. "I'm going to need you later on," he said. "Don't know if I can do all this solo, you ken?"

"Oh," said Ollie.

They embraced then, an awkward thing of sharp angles, and Callisto saw the Skip's face get undone on Ollie's sagging shoulder. When they came apart, Ollie shrugged.

"Could rest a bit," he muttered. He started stripping down. Callisto watched as he cricked his neck, clambered slowly up to the shell. Automated arms positioned him. "Wake me the damn second we touch down, though." He glanced over to Callisto again. "And don't let him keep you off the hull."

"Ayeright," Callisto said. The shell slid shut and preliminary sedatives clouded inside, obscuring Ollie in a thick white fog. The Skipper rubbed a thumb under his eye, then gave a sharp salute and left the freezer, striding tall.

NIGHT SHIFT

Y ou wake up on the rubber delivery pad outside your apartment, shoulders aching, hands puffy and battered from working an assembly line you've never seen.

"Please stop doing this, hon." Mom lets you in, still wearing her blue housecoat. "You need sleep. *Real* sleep."

Not again.

"It *is* real sleep," you say. "One hemisphere at a time, is all."

It's all explained in the UberNight ad: artificially-induced REM refreshes the brain, leaving the body free, via only-somewhat-invasive stimulation of the central nervous system, to stay hustling.

You barely feel the ridged sucker marks on the back of your neck anymore.

HEADHUNTING

Amir wakes up from a dream about a flesh-and-bone piano, and when he gropes his phone out from under his pillow he sees three missed calls. Bravetti never puts anything in text, or even encrypted text, but they're not together anymore, or even drunk-dialling, so it must be a job. He thumbs the call icon, then the speaker icon, then lurches out of bed.

He takes a small metal pot from the stovepad, adds a splash from the tap. Returns it and sets it on high. He holds the coffee jar against his ribs and uses his left hand to wrestle it open, since his right is encased in lime green fibreglass, then rewards himself with a slug of codeine from the little brown bottle that came with the cast.

Bravetti answers before the water starts boiling. "Have a nice lie-in, did you?" she asks, that cool, dry voice you could store perishables in. "Three bleeding times I called you."

Amir heaps cheap focafe into a bone-white mug. "Saw."

"Got an easy one, but I'm out of town—" She breaks off, and Amir thinks he can hear the metallic rush and creak of a train. "So I'm passing the savings on to you, mate. Can you work?"

Amir observes the steam from the pot, the first few tentative bubbles. He runs a fingernail against his waffled cast. "Will I need two hands?"

"Will you need two hands?" she echoes. "What the fuck sort of question is that, Amir? Have you lost one? Is everyone just up and misplacing body parts this morning?"

He waits.

"But no," Bravetti says. "This, you could probably sort out with your little finger. You know St. Johan's Cathedral? The one with the mummified crusaders?"

The little slice of water is boiling at last. He dumps it into his mug and stirs until the gray granules of focafe are fully dissolved. "Yeah," he says. "Went there on a school trip as a kid."

"So did I. Everyone ought to. Bloody fascinating stuff." She moves past someone else's muffled conversation. "Anyways, they were burgled."

"And didn't call the coppers?"

"Obviously not, if they called me." Amir hears a sliding door, which cuts the background noise, then a rustle of fabric. A liquid trickle. "They know who did it, see. Cams caught him clear as day. It was the director's own nephew, so they just want the item retrieved, is all. No coppers. No chatter."

Amir sniffs at the focafe; it smells awful but part of his headache is already peeling away in anticipation of the caffeine. "What's the item?"

"One mummified head," Bravetti says, sounding almost gleeful. "One mummified fucking head."

Amir sips from the mug. "Are you taking a piss?" he asks.

"Not at all," Bravetti says. "The director's nephew nicked a head from one of those mad crusader monks, and you're retrieving it before he sells it on the darkmarket, or makes a bong of it, or something."

Because the focafe cannot possibly taste worse, Amir glugs a bit of codeine inside and gives it a scraping stir. "I said *a* piss," he says. "I mean right now. As we speak. Are you on a train, in the lavatory, taking a piss?"

"No. Of course not. That'd be disrespectful." Bravetti's voice carries a hint of genuine annoyance for the first time. "You want the job or not?"

Amir looks around his new flat, a white prefab box that's unfurnished apart from his gelbed and a small rickety table stacked with books, a bit of rumpled cash, and a handgun. He looks down into his one and only mug, which now contains a witch's brew of fake coffee and hospital drugs.

"I want it," he says, sitting down on the edge of his bed. He takes another noxious sip.

"Grand," Bravetti says. "I'll send the director your info and rate." She pauses. "You've been feeling better, yeah? No more, ah, episodes?"

"Loads," Amir says, resting his cast on his knee bone. "Loads better, I mean."

"Grand. Then I'll—" Amir hears the sound of an automated toilet flushing. "Ah, fuck," Bravetti says, and hangs up.

Amir finally disembowels his duffel bag, dumping its contents across the bed, and tries to divine the least wrinkled shirt and trousers. The director wants to meet in person in a nearby plaza, which speaks to a certain paranoia common among those taking their first wobbly steps into legally gray areas.

Amir used to try putting such clients at ease. He would practice making his eyes warm in the mirror, making his nods weighty. *Of course you'd never normally do something like this. Of course you deserve to know what they're up to. Of course they need to be taught a lesson.*

He used to put so much care into his craft, but when he stopped he discovered it didn't matter. Some clients even seemed to prefer speaking to a frosty-eyed thug. Found it comforting, maybe, to be the only real human in the interaction.

There is no way to make a lime-green fibreglass cast look professional—he'd chosen the neon hue whilst shithoused—and his shirt sleeve doesn't fit overtop. He tucks the loose fabric into the sweaty crack, then hides the whole business in his raincoat. Once he shaves his face and spoons his feet into boots, he's ready to go.

"Nice to know I'm not the only one losing their head," he tells the mirror. "Maybe we'll bond over that."

"Loads better?" his reflection says, raising both bristly eyebrows. "No more episodes? You're such a bad liar, mate."

Amir pushes out into the unfinished hallway, where a row of neatly painted black doors floats in bare concrete and electric veinery. He checks the caked construction dust for tracks, specifically the sort left by flippers, but finds none.

*

There's a shambles set up between Strand Street and Hatter's Bridge, its silhouette razorous, insectile. Amir can see pale, doughy bodies moving along the rusty conveyors. From a distance they almost look like maggots, but when they're slit and drained the torrent is bright red, mammalian blood. Rubber-suited priests slide about on the gore-slick cobblestones.

Amir feels almost certain that mechanized human sacrifice in the Old Town is not a regular occurrence. He shuts his eyes tight, presses the heels of his hands to the sockets. Focuses on the bruise-colored dark. He counts to three before he opens his eyes, but the shambles is still there, converting citizens to sundered meat, churning out feed for some long-lost god. The whole scene is wreathed in body-heat steam.

"Hello?" The voice is quavery, timid. "Are you the one who finds things?"

Amir drags his gaze away from the butchery, and sees his client has joined him on the stone bench. The director is small and immaculate, wearing titanium-framed smartglasses and a black coat and an elaborate purple scarf. He's sweating despite the winter air; the perspiration gleams on his shaved scalp like baptismal oil.

"That's me, yeah," Amir says. "You the one who loses them?"

The director grimaces. "I didn't *lose* it," he says, confirming he's not the humorous sort. "It was stolen. By a rash, foolish young man. Who also happens to be a family member."

Amir feels a poke at his hip bone, and realizes the director is trying to very stealthily pass him a nanodrive. He has to reach across himself with his left hand to take it, which earns his concealed right arm a suspicious look.

"Why are you doing it like that?" the director asks. "That makes it obvious."

"I'm left-handed."

Amir wriggles his phone out of his pocket, then pins it to his knee while he works the fingernail-size nanodrive into its port. A plex of photos, all depicting a rangy nineteen-year-old with curly black hair and an inchoate moustache, appears on the screen. The tags identify him as Lester Bowright.

"The theft occurred last night," the director says. "I discovered it early this morning, and after I watched the security footage—that's on there, too—I tried, of course, to track him down. But he's not answering my calls, and his flatmate claims he never came home."

"Any bars or pubs he particularly likes?" Amir asks. "Might have taken it out for a drink. Wanted to show it off to the lads."

The director recoils, makes a noise like a cat hacking up hair-ball. "No!" he exclaims. "No, no, Lester wouldn't do that. He's a bright boy. Very solemn. Very studious." He uses the edge of his scarf to wick sweat from his forehead. "Which is what makes the theft so baffling."

"Money troubles," Amir suggests next, recalling Bravetti's theory. "Needed some quick quid. There's a market for this sort of thing, yeah? Pilfered artefacts?"

"I suppose." The director looks pained. "I suppose some un-scrupulous private collector—I mean, the Three Mad Monks *are* legendary."

"There's an ale named after them," Amir says, with a weighty nod. "Could be he took it straight to the buyer's people, in which case the mummified head's out of the country already."

The director makes his sick cat sound again.

"Or he could be holed up somewhere," Amir adds, "wait-ing for the buyer's people to come to him. In which case, for the agreed upon fee, I'll do my best to find him and retrieve the mummified head before it's out of reach."

"Oh god," the director says, staring off into the distance. "Oh god, what a mess."

Amir follows his sightline and feels a hot flicker of hope. "You see it?" he asks. "What they've set up there by Hatter's Bridge?"

The director frowns. "What?"

"The shambles," Amir says, even as the hope cools to slippery lard in his belly. "The sacrificing."

"Always under construction, that bridge," the director mut-ters. "Always a proper shambles." His eyes jig behind his smart-glasses; a bank transfer slides onto the screen of Amir's phone. "There. There's your deposit. Now please, go find my head."

Amir starts with Lester's flat, taking the metro north and disembarking at Our Lady of the Tar-Black Snow. He ascends the concrete stairs, winds his way through the filthy station, and re-emerges into a cold gray afternoon. His right hand is aching inside its fibreglass, but he forgot the codeine bottle at home so there's nothing for it.

He passes the church and its cadre of squat geometric angels. There are no eyes in their smooth stone faces, but they seem very vigilant all the same, perhaps having heard St. Johan's was burgled. He checks the address on his phone again, then hooks down a ruelle that leads to a row of old houses now converted to apartments.

He lopes up to the specified door and buzzes number 212. For a moment, nothing. A grimy pigeon flutters onto and then off the stoop. An ambulance banshees past in the distance. Then a static-flayed voice answers.

"Hello? Who is it?"

"Hello," Amir says. "Amir Murtle, PI investigating the disappearance of one Lester Bowright and a linked theft. His uncle may have told you I'd be coming through."

"Right. Fine. Up the stairs, end of the hall."

The door clacks and buzzes; Amir yanks it open left-handed. He steps into halogen lighting, black-and-white carpeting, walls marked up from a hundred hasty moves. It smells good, at least. Hash hanging in the air, a spicy cooking scent wafting from up the stairs. He follows the latter, then reluctantly passes it by in favor of door 212. Lester's flatmate is waiting.

"As if that's your real name," she says, kicking her door all the way open with one thickly socked foot. "Amir Murtle."

She has glowing blue teeth implants and interesting tattoos, plus a canister of mace dangling oh-so-subtly from the bridge of her folded arms. Amir sheds his raincoat, exposing the lime-green cast that will make him look less professional, but also less intimidating.

"It's my real first name," he says. "Murtle's made up, yeah."

"What'd you do to your arm?"

"Fought an animatronic walrus."

She narrows her eyes. "If you want me to answer a bunch of questions honestly, you really ought to set a better example."

"I smashed it with a hammer," Amir says. "To score painkillers."

She snorts, but lets him inside. The flat is bursting with vegetation, pots on every spare surface and hanging planters in the corners, one of which is being watered by what looks like a scrapped-together DIY drone. There's a vaguely familiar print by some famous Taiwanese artist on the wall, all fiery orange and sea blue. Charcoal sketches are tacked up around it.

"This lot's all me," she says. "Before you start psychoanalysing too much. Lester mostly keeps in there." She points to a featureless white door. "Normally he gets home at six, says hello, cooks himself something, and heads to his room. Rarely emerges. Gets up before me in the mornings. It's really a terrific symbiosis."

"Last night, though?"

"Just never came home," she says. "I was quite happy for him until his boss from the gallery came around. Boss-slash-uncle, I guess." She looks at the door and gives a shrug. "Thought he was finally shagging someone."

Amir crosses to the door, tries the handle. "Not a lot of friends over, then?"

"Never."

"Any odd behavior in the past week or so?" Amir asks by reflex, focused on the lock. "Any signs of stress?"

She scowls. "I'm not his therapist, am I?"

"Your name?"

"Fay." She pauses. "Koffyew. Tosser." She nods. "Fay Koffyew-Tosser. Hyphenated surname."

"Hard to do it on the spot," Amir says. "Fay, though?"

"Fay, yeah."

Amir gets out his picks. "Fay, I'm going to pop this door open and have a gander," he says. "Won't be more than ten minutes." He inspects the stiff fingers of his right hand, curls them as far as he can. "Maybe twelve. After which I'll leave everything in its place."

"Seems a bit illegal," Fay says, folding her arms again.

"You can look elsewhere, if you like," Amir says, groping around in the bottom of his pocket. "Maybe into the soulful eyes of—" He peers at the rumpled note. "Whoever's on the fifty."

"Now it seems even more illegal," Fay says, but she's become a sapient storm cloud, a dense ball of dark gray vapor illuminated by flashes of sheet lightning, and Amir does not negotiate with hallucinations. He tosses the note in her general direction, as he's no longer sure where her hands are, then sits down to pick the lock.

Fay only rains on him for a few minutes before she drifts away, and a few minutes after that he's in. Not many tactile sensations compare to successfully picking a lock—mucking out a waxy earhole with a Q-tip might be closest—so Amir takes a moment to relish the scrape and click and clunk.

Then he turns the handle and steps into Lester's room. It's disturbingly familiar: gelbed in the corner, cheap spindly table, bare walls. Lester does not have much of a nesting instinct, but that makes for a quick search. Amir's already onto the closet when Fay pokes her restored head in.

"Oh," she says, through a mouthful of falafel. "Anticlimactic."

"Sorry," Amir says, turning out the pockets of a wrinkly blue blazer.

"What did he steal, then?" she asks, dabbing yoghurt sauce off her plastic plate. "He never seemed like the stealing sort."

Amir replaces a metro stub and wadded tissue, sets the blazer back on its hanger. "What sort did he seem like?"

"Bit of an ascetic, I guess." Fay rubs crumbs off her fingers. "Always eats the same things. Wears the same clothes. No boozing, no vaping. No pills when I offered."

Amir lifts up a Crystal Palace hoodie pooled on the bottom of the closet and finds a pair of cracked smartglasses underneath. They're long dead, but when he hooks them to his phone the charge light still comes on—potential jackpot. He discards the hoodie, waits for the red sliver of battery to struggle upwards.

"You need anything?" Fay asks. "Because I could get you painkillers, easy. No bone-smashing required."

The glasses turn on, and Amir holds them up to his face. Notifications split and refract along the cracks. Lester's still logged in, but the glasses haven't been used in months. Amir syncs them to the homenet, and suddenly Lester's featureless white room transforms into a teeming mass of text and photo.

Some sort of excavation, archeologists working in grainy black and white. A diagram showing the measurements of three stone sarcophagi. Color close-ups of a sunken brown face, skin shriveled, eyeless but not entirely lipless—Amir can imagine the exact texture of that mouth, and it makes him feel slightly nauseous.

The theme's pretty clear, even before he starts skimming the wiki articles. Third Crusade, Three Mad Monks, St. Johan's catacombs, parasitism. The last one's a bit odd, but not nearly as odd as the finger-scrawled message superimposed all over the place. The shaky lettering is different on each, not copy-pasted, which means Lester must have carved it into the air a hundred different times.

Death is a membrane.

He checks the lower left corner of the glasses and sees Lester's account is active in two locations: here, and somewhere in the Tannery District.

He gets Fay to wear the glasses as well, just to verify, and takes her number in case he needs more information or cheaper opioids. Then he heads for the metro again, dialing his client on the way. The director picks up on the third ring.

"Yes?" he whispers. "Have you found it?"

"Nearly," Amir says, passing the faceless, birdshit-spackled angels. "Lester's been taking his work home. Even before the head, I mean. When did he start working the exhibit?"

"Three months ago? I'd have to—have to check." The director pauses. "Taking his work home in what sense?"

Amir looks at the access times on the images, the articles. "He got obsessed with those monks about a month in," he says. "He may have been planning this for quite a while."

The director gives a soft groan.

"Death is a membrane," Amir quotes, pausing at the top of the metro steps. "That mean anything to you?"

"A membrane?" the director echoes. "No. Why?"

"I think your nephew might be unwell," Amir says, though he knows he's not one to talk. He scuttles down the stairs to the southbound platform. "Any history of mental illness?"

"None that I know of." The director's concern sounds genuine. "I could ask his parents, but then I'd probably have to tell them about the theft, as well."

"Hold off on all that. I'm on my way to him now."

Amir ends the call just as the train comes screeching in. He puts his phone away and steps inside a compartment full of Grecian statues, a dozen white marble musculatures frozen in eerie poses. The silence is fucking terrifying. He finds an empty seat beside some naked philosopher and slumps down into it, then squeezes his eyes shut as they rattle off into the dark.

A transient snow is falling when he arrives at the Tannery District, which was becoming a bit of a tourist area until it flooded last year. Now it's a mess, streets heaped with defeated sandbags and varied detritus. He passes a hulking sump pump gone silent, a solitary backhoe stretched all the way horizontal, grasping for something it'll never reach.

As with Hatter's Bridge, repairs are moving slowly. The majority of shops and eateries have moved on, leaving boarded-up husks behind—any of which would make a fine short-term hiding spot for a lad with a stolen head. Amir doesn't want to sync the smartglasses again, for fear of tipping Lester off, so he starts checking the derelicts for signs of forced entry.

The pub with smashed windows and no door seems promising, but he only ends up startling a young couple mid-snog. In the adjoining alley he spots a little nest of insulated blankets, but the head poking out the top has silvery-gray hair, which corresponds neither to Lester nor to the mummified monk. He prowls farther down the street, towards an abandoned billiards hall. When he sees a Crystal Palace logo spraybombed onto the brick facade, he knows he's in business.

The door opens just wide enough for a skinny nineteen-year-old to slip through; Amir has to barge it with his shoulder until he can do the same. It's dark inside, musty. The rotting wood floor feels almost like sponge underfoot. He cranks the little lamp on his phone, illuminating a gutted bar, a wire-stripped ceiling, a lonely herd of pool tables too warped to salvage.

"Lester?" he calls. "You in here, mate?" He moves slowly towards the bar, sweeping the shadows. "My name's Amir Murtle. I'm a PI, here on your uncle's request."

There's no answer, but he hears shuffling feet.

"I'm only here to retrieve the item," Amir says. "Your uncle doesn't want to lay charges. Just wants the head back where it belongs."

He rounds the corner of the bar, boots crunching on broken glass, and sees there's a back room with a single table. Something roughly ovoid is sitting on the ruined blue felt. Amir feels a gelid prickle up and down his spine as he gets closer. Mottled bog-brown skin, glistening in the phone light. Bared teeth. Imploded eyes.

The warped features are disturbingly familiar; Lester might have decapitated the very monk that was on display during Amir's school trip three decades prior. Amir is so transfixed by the head that it takes him a moment to notice the thief. Lester is standing in the corner, facing it like a castigated child, wearing the windbreaker he had on in the security cam footage. He's eerily still.

At times like these, Amir really wishes he could trust his own neurons.

"Has it been calling you, too, then?" Lester asks, in a croaky voice that's barely done changing. He rubs one leg against the other, stork-like, and Amir sees he's missing a sock. "It told you to come here?"

"The head?" Amir tries to make his voice kind. "No, mate. Like I said, your uncle hired me." The grocery bag used to transport the monk is now rumpled up and stuffed into one of the billiard pockets; he grabs it out. "I'm going to just pop the monk back in here, then give your uncle a ring and tell him what's what."

"Calling's not the right word, I suppose." Lester's hands are out of sight, and Amir has the sudden paranoia that he's facing the corner because he's pissing there, which would make it twice today someone has toilet-talked him. "Has it been showing you things?"

Amir's stomach drops. "Things?"

"Things."

"What things?" Amir persists, forgetting to sound kind.

"Things, Dag." Lester huffs a laugh, tips his head back. "Corpses decomposing on the ceiling. Giant crab creatures in the canal with miniature cities on their backs. All those people walking around with extra spinal column coming out of them, stretching way up into the sky, but you can never quite see what it's connected to."

Amir stares down at the mummified head on the pool table. All the little hairs on the back of his neck spike up. "You're saying the ghost of this dead monk is handing out hallucinations."

"No!" Lester makes a familiar hacking noise; it must be genetic. "No. That'd be fucking—that'd be stupid."

"Oh." Amir feels only slightly relieved. He switches his gaze back to Lester, whose hallucinations are not quite the same as his, but certainly adjacent. "You want to turn around? Bit spooky, speaking to the back of you."

"In a moment," Lester says, sounding petulant. "I'm building up my nerve. You're here to take the head, then. Not to help."

"Help with what?" Amir asks.

"One's not enough," Lester says. "We have to go back for the others tonight. Get a critical mass. Don't you agree?"

"You asking me, or the head?"

"Jesus. You don't know anything, do you." Lester's voice is cracked. "I don't know why it bothered calling you."

He whirls around, and Amir was half expecting him to have sharp black beaks in his eyeholes, or smooth shit-spackled stone instead of a face, so it's nice to see soulful eyes and a dusting of moustache in the millisecond before a swinging cosh collides with his skull.

Amir limps across Hatter's Bridge, nearly home. The shambles has been disassembled and trucked off, and they've even contrived to get rid of the bloodstains, but he can still smell its greasy, coppery stench in the cold air. Or it might be coming from his smashed-in nose, which is leaking everywhere.

The director's not answering, and since Amir has no one else to call he calls Bravetti. It rings and rings as he crosses the plaza, as he turns up his snowy street. There's a brief intermission when he uses his phone to unlock the outer door. Then it keeps ringing, echoing through the concrete spiral shell of the staircase as he staggers up to his apartment.

She answers just as he turns the door handle. "Make it quick, mate. I'm following someone right now."

Amir does not know where to start, so he starts angry. "You said this was an easy one," he snaps. "I was just fucking pummeled."

Bravetti gives a gasp of laughter. "No! What, by the wee nephew? The wee nephew pummeled you?"

"Had a billiard ball in a sock," Amir says, shutting the door behind him and fumbling it locked. "Could've bloody killed me. I'm probably concussed."

"He scummed you!" Bravetti yelps, then lowers her voice. "The cheek of it. Bet he's never even seen the film."

"Cracked me right in the face. Broke my nose." Amir goes straight to the codeine and glugs down the last of it, tongues the dregs. "Then I'm down on the ground, shielding myself," he says, discarding the bottle, hobbling to the freezer, "and the little fucker starts swinging for my knee instead. It's swollen to hell already."

"God. Did you get the head back, at least?"

"Of course I didn't get the head back." He glares at an empty ice tray, starts scraping frost off the bottom of the freezer. "He took it with him when he scarpered. He thinks—" Amir presses an insufficient palmful of ice shavings to his blood-tacked face. "He thinks it's talking to him, or showing him visions, or something."

Bravetti is silent for so long Amir has to check they aren't disconnected. The codeine's kicked in, dousing his pain receptors in warm syrup, and he sinks down onto the bed. When she finally speaks, she sounds cautious in the way he hates so badly, the way he never knew she could sound until a couple months ago.

"Maybe this isn't a good job for you," she says. "If the nephew's off his nut, and talking to you about visions, it might make you—I dunno. It might make you relapse. Start having those episodes again."

Amir checks the ceiling for decomposing corpses. "You don't think it's fucking odd that I was hired to track down someone with the same exact problem as me?"

Silence again. The lump of ice shavings has melted away. He grabs his lone dishcloth and starts sponging the softened blood from his philtrum.

"*I* was hired for it," Bravetti says, calm and decisive again. "I gifted it to you, remember? And there's loads of nutters in this city, so no. Not statistically."

"Cheers."

"I'm going to ungift it from you, though," she says. "Soon as I get back in town. You need more time off. Maybe see the psychologist again."

"I don't want—"

"If nothing else," Bravetti cuts in, "they may be able to help you sort out the trauma of getting your arse handed to you by an adolescent. Bye-bye."

She ends the call, and Amir momentarily wants to pitch his phone at the wall. Instead he dials a more recently acquired number, sets it to speaker, and struggles up off the bed. He rattles open the barren utensil drawer. His best option is a steak knife.

"This the detective?" Fay's voice comes accompanied by thudding club music. "How's mortality going for you?"

"Hate it," Amir says. "I'm going to need some painkillers and a fuckload of pep pills if you've got them."

"I've got everything," Fay says. "Big night tonight, eh?"

Amir sits back down on the edge of the bed, making it ripple. "Sure. Big night."

"You find Lester, then?"

"Did." He starts sawing through the edge of the cast, right between his thumb and forefinger, serrated metal teeth grinding fibreglass down to powder. It's going to take a while. "Can you meet me on Hatter's Bridge a half hour from now?" he asks. "With the stuff?"

"Think I can duck out, yeah. I'll message you." She pauses. "Is he okay?"

"He's grand," Amir says. "I'm a mess. But he's grand. See you in a half hour."

He redoubles his efforts with the steak knife, showering the bed with tiny splinters of fibreglass and wisps of padding. He sets his jaw, stares at the handgun on the rickety table across from him. No need to cleave the cast all the way off. He just has to free up his grip and his trigger finger.

St. Johan's is impressive at night, a great stone beast lit from below by LED pits. The carved buttresses look like a reptile's splayed legs. The stained-glass windows are eyes, nocturnal predator-yellow. It puts Our Lady of the Tar-Black Snow and her piddly angels to shame, every curve and cleft somehow both holy and menacing.

Fay's amphetamines might have something to do with that, too. He's been inhumanly focused for the past two hours, huddled in a cafe across the street from the cathedral's back entrance while a well-sequestered pocket cam watches the main one. Lester has yet to show, even though Amir remembers the words clearly: *One's not enough. We have to go back for the others tonight.*

Maybe Lester changed his mind, or is just fully out of it. But Amir doesn't think so, and that is why he didn't tell the client his nephew is returning to the scene of the crime. He needs to figure out what's going on first.

The wikis he has his phone reading to him are no help, all *persecuted religious order* this and *possible self-immurement* that. As best he can tell, three soldier-monks got lost in the desert outside Damascus during the Third Crusade, came back raving, and enlisted a local stonemason to build them three sarcophagi that could be sealed from the inside.

Their order hushed it up to avoid going the way of the Templars, who'd been burned at the stake for heresy and inappropriate kissing, then several centuries later the sarcophagi were excavated and shipped to Glimshire, and several decades after that someone founded a semi-successful brewery called 3 Mad Monks—*for other uses, see Three Mad Monks, disambiguation.*

It's not as interesting as Bravetti made it out to be, and doesn't explain in the slightest why he and Lester have both been having hallucinations, possibly beginning around the same time. That's why he needs to have a proper chat with the lad. At gunpoint, if necessary.

And there he is. Scurrying down the block, familiar grocery bag swinging from his fist. Amir cranes forward to watch as Lester hops up the steps. His uncle has not seen fit to take him off the employee register, so his phone unlocks the back door with no issue at all. He marches inside. The retrofitted metal door swings shut behind him and Amir thinks momentarily of self-immurement.

Then he gets up, sets his mug in the gray dish tub, slips out of the cafe.

Amir is not on the employee register, but he has a pneumatic door-jack that works just as well. The hinges give way with a groan and bone-crack. Amir shifts the door over, casts one look up and down the snowy street, and steps through.

He's in the back offices of the cathedral, all cubed concrete and flickering fluorescents. It reminds him of his unfinished apartment block until he hits the sanctuary. For a moment the rows and rows of pews seem to be rolling towards him, a stone tide. He's not sure if it's from the pep pills or if the hallucinations are returning.

The stairwell is tucked into a corner with the ornate confessional booths; someone approached it recently enough to trigger the information holo and donation suggestion. Amir feels for the familiar grip in his pocket. He can hear movement below, but sees no light. The air around the stairwell is cooler. Wetter. Almost has a taste to it.

Down into the squid-ink dark. Amir keeps one hand on the velvet guide rope and one hand on his gun, tries to make his footfalls soundless. The catacomb is somehow deeper than he remembers from the school trip, even though his legs are longer now. Descending its hewn throat makes his skin go clammy and his heart pitter-patter. Bravetti would have a real laugh, but she might not be chemically capable of fear.

Light at last. The pale electric sort, from a phone torch, which is comforting down here where everything smells so ancient. The scene it illuminates—less comforting. The three famous sarcophagi are roped off, with a hastily hung *closed for maintenance* sign there for emphasis, but Lester has traversed that.

The central sarcophagus is open, its lid scything outward like a spread wing, and Lester is crouched inside like a succubus or incubus or whatever the hairy thing in that one painting is, straddling the corpse's chest in order to more easily saw its head off. The original head is perched on the open lid, watching the proceedings through its collapsed eye sockets, and something the color of old blood seems to be growing out of its earholes.

Amir takes the handgun from his pocket, not aimed, but obvious. "Lester," he says. "Time to tell me what's going on. And don't say to look at the wikis. I hate history."

Lester's head jerks up. He sees the gun and his soulful dark eyes go wide. He sets the knife down slowly. "Don't shoot," he says. "Jesus Christ." He blinks. "You know those who hate history are doomed to repeat it."

Amir takes an angled step, to ensure a good sightline on both

Lester and the disembodied head. "I know being clever is important to you," he says. "But put that aside for a moment. Just explain the head, and the hallucinations, and what exactly you're trying to do."

Lester does the inhalation of one about to explain things to an idiot. "The Three Mad Monks didn't lose their minds in the desert," he says. "They found God. By which I mean the effectively immortal Precambrian parasite that had been dormant for millions of years and makes tardigrades look like pushovers."

Amir recalls the last article on Lester's wall.

"Recent geological activity had brought a spar of ancient rock towards the surface. The monks met it halfway, in the chasm where they were sheltering from the sandstorm." Lester shifts slightly; the corpse beneath him makes a slimy, rasping sound. "The parasite revived and took three hosts. But it couldn't really do much with them. The structures of the human brain are a long way from the Precambrian organisms it used to puppeteer. It's smart, but not *that* smart. It managed to buy itself time to figure things out, though. Got the monks to pickle themselves."

Amir looks at the head again, at the rust-red tissue blooming from its ears and nostrils like cauliflowers. He decides to delay judgement on whether it's really happening or not. "How'd you find all this out?"

"Well, there's the Aghast Missive," Lester says. "Letter fragment from the bishop who wanted to make sure nobody found out about the monks' seeming suicide. And there was a Scottish scientist named Hieronymus McLaverty, who did a forensic investigation of the bodies in the 1800s, found some odd things but died before publication. Lately, though, I've just been talking with the parasite."

"Via hallucinations," Amir says. "The prehistoric parasite in a dead monk's brain is handing out hallucinations, which is somehow less stupid than a dead monk's ghost doing it."

Lester folds his bony arms. "The hallucinations were just static," he says. "Now I can hear it much clearer. The best way is—may I show you?"

"Slowly," Amir says.

Lester reaches, slowly, for the slick, withered head. He cradles it in both hands, presses his brow to its brow. In the pale glow of Lester's phone torch, Amir sees the rust-red tissue flexing out from the monk's nostrils knit itself into a sort of hook. It thrusts its way up Lester's nose with no warning.

"Doesn't hurt," Lester says, before Amir can leap forward and rip the thing free. "This is the most direct way to commune with it."

The eeriness is stacking up, so much so that Amir's whole back is now drenched in cold sweat and his left knee, the one Lester smashed with a billiard ball, is trembling. His hands, thankfully, are good and steady.

"Right," he says. "If you're talking to it now, ask it what the fuck it wants."

"I already know *that*," Lester says. "It wants to remake the world in its image. Make it much more interesting."

Amir thinks of sapient storm clouds and automated human sacrifice.

"But to do that, it needs a lot more hosts," Lester continues. "And to reproduce, it needs a critical mass. That's why we came back for the other slivers in the other bodies. To speed things up."

"Are you being brain-controlled or something, then?" Amir asks. "How the monks were?"

"Not at all," Lester says, sounding genuinely offended. "This is God." He kisses the head's shriveled-back lips, then beams at it. His bright white teeth are smeared with rust-red spores. "And I'm its prophet."

"Grand," Amir says, forcing himself to ignore the inappropriate kissing because he's come to the most crucial bit. "Now ask it what it wants with *me*. Ask it why *I'm* getting the hallucinations."

Lester is silent for a moment, assumedly communing, then he gives his head a minute shake, making the knotted red stuff shiver. "It's honestly not sure," he says. "But it does think you'd be a good host. Your neural architecture is quite accommodating."

Amir does not find that flattering, and he is considering how far he might be able to drop-kick the monk's skull off Hatter's Bridge when he hears a mechanical whirring. His teeth clench at the noise. Then a familiar silhouette comes lurching out of the dark, towering over Lester and the sarcophagus.

Same spiny flippers. Same goggly dead eyes. But it's twice as big as last time, and the gleaming tusks look razor sharp.

The bones throb in Amir's broken hand.

"Rematch," the animatronic walrus says.

It's a hallucination, of course. No hallucination in the history of hallucinations has ever more clearly been a hallucination. But Amir's limbic system does not discriminate with a one-tonne nightmare machine barreling at it, and he squeezes the trigger on reflex, three times, pyramid placement.

The electropellets bounce right off; for a nonsensical moment he wishes he'd brought actual bullets. Then he sucks down a deep breath, braces his feet, and opens his arms. He reminds himself that he is facing off against thin air, that a prehistoric parasite is tweaking his neurons. He's going to let this bastard walrus pass right through him.

The impact slams him off his feet. His gun skitters across the catacomb floor and the back of his head collides with hard stone, smashing stars across his eyes. Beyond those dancing constellations he can see the walrus looming over him, see the blurry, manic grin. He hears a tinkling ringtone in his ears.

"Your mind makes it real, Neo," Lester calls. "Or I suppose your central nervous system does."

Amir rolls left as the walrus's tusk descends. He comes upright with a new stratagem: evade the animatronic walrus, destroy the disembodied head. He spins towards the sarcophagus, where Lester is still sitting on Mad Monk Two's chest, cradling Mad Monk One's head. Beside him, resting on the open lid, is the big serrated stalking knife Amir made him set down.

They both lock eyes to it at the same instant; Amir lunges but Lester is much closer. He tucks the head under his armpit and grabs the knife handle, gives the air a warning slash like some kind of bloody pirate. Amir can't stop—too much momentum, plus an animatronic walrus bearing down on him from behind, whirring in his ears.

He goes low, gets inside the blade, and his suspicion that Lester got lucky with the cosh but has no idea how to use a knife turns out to be correct. He wedges Lester's elbow, twists hard. There's a tendon pop, a wail, and the knife clatters to the floor. Amir snatches it up and turns just in time to parry a scything tusk.

"Death is a membrane," the walrus says. "I will usher you through it."

Amir does not banter with hallucinations, but he jabs for its blank eyes, and when it rears back he puts all his force behind the blade, driving it up into the moulded plastic belly of the beast. Slick black oil sprays outward, even though he is almost certain animatronics are not fueled by such, and catches him full in the face. He howls, blinded, and the walrus laughs a creaky, phonograph laugh.

Then he's pinned, the thing's flippers crushing him to the floor, squeezing the wind from his lungs. He blinks his stinging eyes clear. Sees Lester squat down beside him, the monk's head still tucked under his armpit. The red stuff is stretched thin now, suspended between dead and living nostrils like a strand of mozzarella, but as he watches, Lester delicately detaches his end and pushes it towards him instead.

"Here," Lester says, as Amir feels a tickle at the rim of his nostril. "God wants to explain things a little better."

Amir kicks. Writhes. The red stuff creeps inside his nose, claws softly up his septum, and he can already feel a *thing* on the edge of his consciousness, hovering over his shoulder. He sees a crop of techno-organic machines, yellowish scissor limbs growing out from dark soil. Long pale creatures wriggling across splendorous ruins. An empress with a weeping mask.

Then he sees the thing itself, an eyeless thing in a tailored suit, seated at a living, pulsating piano he knows is his own oh-so-accommodating neural architecture. It readies its hived and veiny fingers—

"Oi." The cool, dry voice interrupts from a universe away. "He's atheist, you wee creep."

The thing inside Amir's skull unhooks, tugs free; his eyes clear and he sees Lester has jerked upright, taking the dangling red corkscrew with him. He's staring at the stairwell. So is the animatronic walrus. Amir cranes his neck to join the party, and sees that Bravetti has not only found him in his hour of need, but also found his fallen handgun.

"You got lethals in here, Amir?" she asks.

"No," he croaks.

"Aren't you a lucky little fucker," she says to Lester, and shoots him.

There's a thump and a sizzle and he topples sideways. The monk's head spills from his spasming hands. That still leaves the walrus to deal with, but of course Bravetti strides up as if it's not even there. It tracks her with its bulging eyes.

"Six missed calls, Amir," she says, yanking his phone from his pocket and showing him the screen for proof. "Six. It's very un-professional of you." Her voice is no longer cool and dry. "What in the hell's going on?"

Amir gives an experimental shove, and discovers the walrus is now helium-light. It drifts towards the ceiling of the catacomb and sticks there like a baleful balloon. He gives it a two-finger salute, then shifts his attention to the monk's head, which is still rolling across the floor, momentum sustained by tiny red ear- and nose-cilia.

"Just a moment," he says. He grabs the stalking knife, crawls after the head, and grabs it by the ear. "You can see this, right? The red stuff?"

Bravetti frowns. "The living bogey? Yes, mate."

Amir relishes that for a second, like a well-picked lock, then starts stabbing. The rust stuff wriggles back inside the cranium, seeking sanctuary, at which point he tears the lower jaw free, ro-tates the skull, and drags the parasite out through the new aper-ture. He dices it into pieces, then uses the knife handle to mash those pieces into slurry.

"It's an ancient telepathic parasite," he explains. "A discovery that revolutionizes biology and evolutionary theory and all that. It's been remotely fucking about with my brain for the past couple months, and I suppose with Lester's, too." He checks the ceiling; the walrus is gone, but he will take no chances. "We'll have to do this to the other two monks as well."

Bravetti gives a wise nod. "Always figured it was something like that," she says. "There was this Scot who dissected one of them in 1811, see, and he went absolutely starkers."

"Me too, for a bit." He looks down at the mash. "But I think it should be over now. The episodes."

Bravetti shrugs. "We should probably torch it all, just to be safe. It's been an age since I set something on fire."

*

They drag Lester up the stairwell and deposit him on a pew, then Amir stands watch while Bravetti syphons some petrol from a lorry outside, then they go back down into the catacomb and douse the remains of the Three Mad Monks. The searing smell of petrol in Amir's nostrils is infinitely preferable to a spongy hook.

Bravetti lends him her lighter to do the honors, and they step back to watch the crackly blaze. It feels quite cathartic, and standing shoulder-to-shoulder with Bravetti, her jacketed arm pressed to his, feels good as well. He misses being able to lean over and say something stupid and kiss her.

"Maybe we should give it another go," he says, before he can stop himself. "Now that the hallucinations are sorted. Maybe it'll be different."

She shakes her head. "You know it wasn't about the episodes," she says. "It was all the other stuff. Besides, you're getting to like the new place, yeah?"

Amir thinks of his white prefab box, his gelbed and his rickety table, his one and only mug. "Yeah," he says. "It's good."

They watch the heaped bodies shrivel and blacken, watch the spirals of greasy smoke rise. There will be no more school trips to see the Three Mad Monks, but it's just as well, because thinking about kissing Bravetti, then thinking about the rust-colored spores in Lester's teeth, has ossified his rickety suspicions. He considers keeping it to himself, but Bravetti is already working her way there.

"Why you, though?" she says. "I mean, it makes sense it got to Lester. He was in close proximity."

"The school trip," Amir says. "When I was ten." He exhales. "I snogged that head on a dare."

"You what?"

"I snogged the mummified monk," Amir says. "They had the one sarcophagus open, back then, and the teacher wasn't looking." He works his jaw. "I stuck my tongue fully in there. Everyone had to give me five quid."

"Well." Bravetti stares wistfully at the smoldering remains. "That's one revenue stream closed off forever." She frowns. "So, what, there are little bits of it in your brain? Little transponders that were picking up the static?"

"I should probably get scanned," Amir admits. "Yeah."

They wait until there's nothing but char and bone, then smother it in foam from the church's fire extinguisher and head upstairs. The electropellet stuck to Lester's bony chest is nearly drained; he can twitch and slur now, and slurs mostly about God.

Amir fishes the lad's phone out and dials emergency services, then taps out a brief anonymous message to Lester's uncle. It's the least he can do, since the head retrieval job is now totally botched and he has no intention of explaining himself only to end up facing arson or destruction of property charges.

He parts ways with Bravetti about a block from St. Johan's, and a block after that he sees the red-and-blue strobe of an emergency vehicle, drone-escorted, hurtling towards the cathedral. Fay's pep pills are long gone, and he feels awful. His right hand is puffed up and bruising again, which means he likely shifted some bone around. His broken nose is throbbing. His knee buckles every third step or so.

But at least it's real, and when the snow starts to fall again it's real snow, too, the big globby white flakes that stick and stay. He'll still have to check in on Lester, of course. Steal the medical report and make sure whatever spongy rust-colored spores got into the lad's brain are not cancerous, or behavior-altering, which would be bad news for the both of them.

He trudges towards home, breathing small packets of steam. The snow stops when he gets to Strand Street. The clouds slide apart overhead, leaking antiseptic moonlight over the plaza, over the public piano they've installed there.

Maybe when his hand heals up he'll learn to play. The gleaming keys look inviting, and not at all like teeth.

ALL ELECTRIC GHOSTS

The club called Fleur House is a shabby red brick front slouched between a barbershop and a dépanneur, no holo signage or even neon to lead people in. I wouldn't have found it on my own. But that's why I found Dion.

"Here we are," my new friend says, his wide grin winching even wider. "My cousin keeps it in the back."

"Okay," I say, pulling my hood tighter to my scalp and feeling one last time for the equipment in my jacket pocket. "Après toi."

Two men are rolling joints at a wobbling metal table just outside the door, talking in slurred French. One looks Senegalese, skin so dark the shadows underneath are bruise-purple. The other one is a Moroccan with carefully-razored black hair and deep circles under his eyes.

Both look up at us as we get closer. The Moroccan has a flicker knife on the table in front of him, sharp black carbon. My overfull bladder squirms.

Dion pulls each of the men into a quick embrace, beaming, introducing me as le biologiste. The Moroccan winks at me, but doesn't smile.

"Salut," I say. "Nice night."

Then Dion leads the way into the club. It's dark, nearly pitch black, and silent. All the tables are retracted into the walls to clear the floor. Seven or eight couples are dancing, elbow-tight but sliding around each other like oil and water. It's eerie until my earbud kicks in and gets the local kizomba music, slow and sexy and sutured with a harsh electric drum.

Dion wriggles through the crowd like an eel, his feet shuffling to the beat on automatic. Half the dancers have their eyes shut, hypnotized by the pulse of the music, by the dopamine of body-to-body. They look high. For a second I want to just stay out here and dance. Forget the thing in the back. I used to like dancing, at least on molly.

Then I get the flash. A pictogram in my mind's eye shows a perfect gray triangle with a slash of dark red licking up one side of it like a tongue. It's accompanied by a cascade of letters as my brain tries and fails to turn it into English, then French. But I know this one: it refers to a specific writhing shrug my shoulders would never be able to make, and to a biomechanical sort of locking system, and most of all to pain.

This is the place. I blink my eyes clear. In the back corner near the bar, a fat man is dancing with a slender pen-stroke of a woman. He moves with perfect balance, turning his partner inside, outside; he levers her foot gently off the floor with his own and they sink together into the song's final ebb.

"Cousine, here he is," Dion says. "Le biologiste. He's come to see it. I messaged you."

The woman unwraps herself from her partner, who shuffles away. She reties her dreadlocked hair and gives Dion a long look, observing his shiver and sniff. "T'es fucké, Dion," she says. "How much did you tell him?"

She turns her eyes on me, and they are not dissimilar to the flicker knife outside. The next song builds but I tap my earbud to cut the volume.

"Only that you found something strange," I say. "In the water. Some strange fish."

"He says it might be worth mad cash, Ty," Dion says. "As a, you know, as a spécimen. And they would name it after us, he says, since we found it."

Her brow lifts a micrometer, whether for the cash or the naming rights I'm not sure.

"If it really is a new species," I say. "I have doubts."

Ty gives a half-laugh in her throat. "Mon mec, you've never seen this kind of fish before. I guarantee it."

I stuff my hands in my pockets and give her a skeptical smile even as I get the flash again: more urgent this time, the gray triangle stamped hard on my retinas, the red slash arcing off it like a flare. Pain. My heart beats double time. I try not to shift foot to foot.

"Your eyes wired?" she asks.

"No."

"Show me."

I oblige, peeling my eyelids back while she leans in close and checks for the telltale glint of contact circuitry. From up close the smell of shea butter wafts off her.

"Okay. Phone?"

I shove the basic black slab into her hand; it's practically still warm from the printer. She pockets it. The pictogram is throbbing inside my skull. I wish I could tell it to shut up, tell it I need to concentrate.

"It's hard enough to keep this clown from taking selfies with the thing," Ty says, pointing at Dion, who gives a shrug, palms up, lips pursed. "I don't want any photos. Not until I know what it is."

"Sure," I say. "No photos."

She leads me past the bar and down a short hallway and Dion dances along behind us, crisscrossing his steps. My hands are getting sweaty in my pockets. At a water-warped door, Ty unloops a key from around her wrist and wrestles it into the lock. She gives the door some shoulder and it opens, scraping along lino tiles.

The flash again, so strong I have to clench my teeth together. Dion makes sure the door is firmly shut behind us before his cousin hits the light switches. Fluorescent tubes sputter on in the ceiling, showing a cracked mirror and soap-scummed sink, a toilet with a wooden seat, and, taking up the back half of the room, a bathtub. A few moths whirl past my head, drawn to the light.

"It's in the tub," Dion says.

Of course. Of course it's in the tub. I force myself over to it, knees keeling, remembering another tub, another body. I grip the rust-spotted lip and lean over. It's not Émilie. It's a mass of overlapping and interlocking bits of fluted gray flesh, slick and shiny. Scalloped flippers and wicked black barbs, tendrils writhing from a bony T-bar head poking up out of the water.

An actual biologist would probably be shitting themselves with excitement. I reach into my pocket.

"You know, we found it just after the meteor shower," Dion says, tearing a strip of cardboard off his cigarette pack, folding it with practiced fingers. "Une semaine, quoi. She says I'm stupid, but I say it's an—"

I hit him with the stunner; he spasms and gives me a disappointed look before he drops hard to the lino. His cousin is quicker on her feet and she smashes into my arm, trying to knock the stunner away. The gecko grip does its thing and she only ends up skewing my aim so I hit her neck instead of her chest. She goes down twitching.

"Désolé," I say, pocketing the stunner. "C'est ma job."

Of course, *job* implies I get a salary.

The thing in the bathtub squeaks and chitters, tendrils poking up over the ceramic's edge. It can wait a little longer. I hurry to the toilet instead, where I finally take the piss I've been holding since I started buying beers for me and Dion three bars back. It feels so good I put my hand up on the wall how old men always do at urinals.

I flick, tuck, zip up. Dion groans from the floor as I wash my hands, which are shaking a bit from the adrenaline and from what comes next. Ty is trying to give me a withering look even with her cheek squashed to the tiles.

The thing in the bathtub screeches and mewls, reaching its tendrils toward me.

I go to the side of the tub and get down on my knees; my bad one clicks. The flash comes again, but softer, accompanied this time by a tingling at the crest of my skull. I tug my hood back off my shaved head and hear a muffled noise of surprise behind me. The trepanation didn't heal real well. I had to do it myself, with an electric drill and blackmarket anesthetic.

"Let's make this quick," I tell the thing in the tub, even though I know it can't hear me. Not yet. Then I shut my eyes and plunge my head into the cold oily water. Tendrils trace my scalp, grope for the plastic cap in my skull. I feel them slither inside and—

"There's something in the water. Look."

We're in the Old Port, across the water from the Grande

Roue. I'm using the railing to hold myself up. There's a spiderweb stretched across one of the harbor light boxes, billowing in the night wind, and I can see the furry white spider crawling carefully across it.

"Just give me my shit," I say.

"I'm serious," Émilie's dealer says. "Look. Something glowing."

I look. The black water is rippled from the wind, but there's something moving under the surface, too, a soft orange blob drifting towards the dock.

Émilie's dealer tucks her vape away and belches smoke. The orange glow has her full attention. "It's pretty. What do you think it is?"

I don't care. I'm getting sick, getting shaky, smelling my own sweat. Trying to kick this week was a mistake. "Give me my shit," I say again. We already tapped phones. She has my money. She has my morphine in her little pink backpack.

"Yeah, yeah, right." She unzips it, reaching inside and coming out with a little baggie of hospital-green pills. Then she pauses. "Hey, you swim, right? That's how you knew Em. You used to swim together at the Parc."

I don't want to talk about Émilie. "Yeah. Yes."

She gives me a bleary smile and pulls out a second baggie. "I'll double you up if you go grab that thing."

I look at the second baggie. I look down at the orange light bobbing almost right underneath us. "It's trash," I say. "It's someone's Halloween decoration."

"I want it," she says, narrowing her eyes.

"You're a fucking sadist," I say, but I strip off my coat.

The water is icy and the thing is slippery and when I finally claw my way back up to the docks my heart is pounding through my ribs. For a while I sit on the splintery wood and curse, another junkie spewing words at thin air, then I get up and make my sopping way back to where I jumped in.

People part around me. They can see my soaked clothes and my overgrown beard; I'm not sure if they can see my twitching eye. It's going like crazy right now. It feels like someone has their finger inside my eyelid and is wriggling it, wriggling it. I stalk through tourist's photos of the blue-and-purple big wheel until I get back to my coat.

My coat is there, and so is the spider on its rippling web, but Émilie's dealer is gone. I stare all around, raking the crowd for a little pink backpack. I pick up my coat and check all the pockets, but if she was stupid enough to put the morphine in there someone else already cleaned them out. My phone is gone. My morphine is gone. I'm fucked.

I look down at the slippery thing, the reason I'm fucked. It's not glowing anymore—that stopped as soon as I got a grip on it. Now it's just a slimy colorless sack, like a half-deflated balloon coated in mucus. I squeeze it and feel something hard and noded in the very middle. Maybe it's some kind of kelp. I remember hauling slimy things out of the water at the beach when I was little.

I'm about to rip it apart, rip it to shreds and hurl the shreds back over the railing, when I feel it start to pulse.

When I get back to the apartment there's a message from an unknown number on the cracked screen of my charging tablet: *saw undercovers had to dip. got your phone and salt at mine but has to be tomorrow.*

I dump the thing in the sink and start tapping out a reply, telling her that's bullshit, telling her I need it tonight. My fingers keep missing the letters. If I can't get it from her tonight I'm going to end up buying fentanyl out of some fucking alleyway. My joints are already aching and my stomach is empty but trying to heave up regardless.

Trying to kick this week was a mistake. I stagger over to my kitchen cupboard and grab a Ziploc of old weed. It won't do much, but it'll cut the nausea a bit. I find my chipped bong in a drawer with the ladles and spoons and pull it out to start packing a bowl. Bullshit she saw feds. She was high and paranoid and now I'm suffering for it.

The first pull charbroils my throat, but then I get a good lungful and feel it hit. It's not enough, not nearly enough, but I can think a little better. I can remember there's a thing in the sink.

"Okay," I say. "Okay, okay. What the fuck are you, mon gars?"

It's obvious, when I think about it. I didn't see the meteor shower—I was in paradise, boneless on the couch, watching cartoons on my tablet—but I heard about it. The thing in the sink must be an alien.

I go and inspect it; my stomach stabs at me when I lean over. My hands on either side of the basin are bone-white and slippery. The thing is still pulsing, a slow undulation. Definitely alive, possibly growing. It looks bigger than it did when I went fishing. But maybe I'm seeing shit. That's another possibility. Maybe this alien is actually trash that I hauled home from the Old Port like a lunatic.

Then the shakes really start, and I can't stay upright.

I crawl over to my bed and pull the blanket down to me, wrap it around myself. That's good until the wool turns into fire ants. Then I have to peel it off my skin while I scream into the floor, and then the fire ants are under my skin and I have to dig them out.

In the back of my brain I know it's day three, and right now I can barely crawl, so unless I can get to my tablet and call someone to bring me a hit, this is going to happen whether I like it or not. They say it can't kill you, they say the relapse kills you, but now that I'm here I'm thinking they lied lied lied lied lied—

I scrabble the gloves and duct tape from under the bed, before I reopen all my scars. Some of the scratches are already bleeding. I stuff my left hand into the padded winter glove and wind the duct tape around my wrist, try to do the same on the other side but can't get the tape off the roll. My stomach heaves; I vomit up watery yellow bile all over my forearms.

Through the pounding in my head I think I can hear the thing in the sink moving, growing limbs and scraping them against the stainless steel. Or maybe I'm hearing Émilie, shifting in the bathtub. I know I need to get up, but just like back then, I can't. Back then, because I knew everything would be fine, everything would be perfect no matter what I decided. Now, because all my muscles are limp pink ropes.

I start sobbing again, the way only Émilie makes me sob. She's nothing but electricity now. I think about that sometimes. I don't just mean her information online, her social media feed that's become a mausoleum. I mean memories.

My skin is on fire and Émilie is an electric ghost moving around my gray matter, and the gray matter of all the people who ever knew her. I wish I could find them, all the people who ever spoke to her, who saw her for even a second at a bus stop, and pull the little fragments of her out of their brains. They don't even know what they're missing.

My gut is full of broken glass and I should stop thinking about her. Every time she makes a loop through my head she gets a little more distorted. I'm delirious. I'm fucking delirious and I can feel someone touching my leg. My leg, my hip, my stomach.

It's the thing from the sink. It's not a mucus ball anymore. It has a shape, a bony frame, and thin whiplike tendrils creeping over my skin. They find my mouth. My nose. I realize it's going to kill me, and I'm grateful. I'm so grateful. So I lie there and stare at the blurry ceiling and wait while the tendril slithers up my nostril.

And suddenly I feel nothing.

My body is still clammy and trembling, but I'm a million miles away. This isn't a hallucination the way I know them. I'm not paralyzed with terror, or limp with bliss. I feel like I barely exist. I'm floating in the dark, and the thing from the sink is there with me, like someone hovering over my shoulder, just out of my sight line.

Usually I hate it when people do that, but this is different. I can feel a soft hand roaming all over my brain, little bioelectric bursts mimicking my neurons, firing connections, testing, probing. I see colors. Shapes. Hazy scenes pulled out of my memory. But no feelings. I'm not angry. I'm not sad. I'm not fiending. I'm nothing, and I wish it could last forever.

"Benny? T'es correct?"

It's Émilie. The old Émilie, suntanned with wiry swimmer's shoulders, lanky arms, dirty blonde hair tied up away from her big forehead and mottled green eyes. Barefoot, wearing cutoffs and an old T-shirt. Her wide mouth has that familiar little twist of concern, how it's done ever since we were kids.

I've dreamed about her plenty, but in the dreams she never speaks to me. She sits down beside me now, cross-legged.

"Hey, Em," I say. "Yeah. I'm good. You?"

"You don't look good," she says. "You look like a larva or something. How long have you been sick? Putain, you should have told me you were sick. I'd bring soup or something."

"I'm hallucinating you," I say. "There's an alien sticking its fingers up my nose and tickling my brain. Also I'm in withdrawal."

"Shitty kind of day," Émilie says, and she lies down on the floor beside me.

I feel her breath on my cheek, her body heat next to mine. I can smell her spearmint gum and her argan oil shampoo. Her hand brushes mine, skin on skin, and suddenly I can feel everything. The sob wrenches its way up my whole body and comes out as a gasp. Tears start welling up in my eyes, blurring out her face.

"Hey," she says, propping up on her elbow. "Chill. It's okay. I'm here. C'est correct." She grabs my hand, and it reminds me of this road trip we took to Quebec City, how she would grip my hand whenever we went under an overpass, whenever we went through a tunnel.

I can't stop crying. And I think, if it feels real, who's to say it's not? I think, aren't we all just electric ghosts moving through someone else's brain? And from far away, I feel the thing from the sink stirring on my chest. A sort of pictogram appears in my mind's eye: a soft green rhombus, the color of Émilie's eyes, moving into a golden-brown slope like a ship into port.

On the other side of the slope, a jagged shape I know is me moves out into a black void scattered with glowing orange circles. Somehow, even as my brain tries and fails to turn it into words—homecoming, se réunir, partnership—I understand the deal.

If I do this for you, you do this for me.

Back in the bathroom of Fleur House, I yank my head out of the rusty tub. The alien's calm now that it knows what's going on. It sheathes the black barbs and starts curling itself into a little ball, wrapping all its tendrils around its body. I spit out a big mouthful of water and whatever bodily fluids it's been excreting into the bath.

Ty is starting to wiggle her feet, but I don't want to use the stunner again. It always makes me feel bad. Instead I just retrieve my phone from her pocket and slide hers to the opposite side of the bathroom. It skitters over the tiles into a dust-caked corner. Her glare intensifies.

"I did it screen up," I say, taking the key off her wrist. "No scratches."

The thing in the tub is ready to be carried, a slick little bundle of bone and mucus. I put it under my jacket—it clings—and do up the zipper. My hands are still shaking a little as I open the bathroom door. My earbud came disconnected so all I can hear is soft shuffling feet and a few murmured mid-dance conversations.

I lock the door behind me and make my way back across the dance floor. It's a slow song and most of the couples are barely moving, just tiny undulations of their hips synchronized to the music I can't hear. I thumb the map on my phone. My ride is four minutes away.

I'm thinking I pulled it off when I hear the sound of a rapid-fire French argument. Through the glass door I see the Moroccan is on his feet, hackles up, snarling at someone short and squat and dressed all in black. For a moment I think there's something wrong with their face, then I realize it's a faux-tribal mask, scab red with simple black holes for mouth and eyes.

Maybe they're some drunk uni student making mischief in a Halloween leftover. Maybe they're about to take it off and, quelle surprise, it's one of the Moroccan's friends underneath, and everyone will have a laugh about it.

I'm still hoping that as a gloved hand flashes forward, seizes the Moroccan's flicker knife off the table, and drives it into his crotch with a shearing sound. Bright red blood spatters the glass door and suddenly the mask is staring right at me. I catch a glimpse of a gun coming out before I hurtle back inside.

I plow down the middle of the floor and knock someone over; a retributory shove sends me into the bar. My bad knee jars against a metal stool but I barely feel it. Too terrified, too much adrenaline flash-flooding my brain. The alien in my jacket squirms.

"Gun!" I shout. "Get down, y'a un gars avec un fucking gun!"

A woman yanks her old school headphones off to give me a questioning look. I see the mask bobbing towards me through the dark, slipping between couples, and I split down the narrow hallway, running with a hobble. I'm nearly to the red glow of the exit sign when the bathroom door crunches off its hinges and into the wall in front of me.

I pull up short, catch a flash of Dion's confused face before I duck under his arm and slam my way through the back door. There's a rush of cold night air and the stink of garbage and gasoline. The alley is narrow, grimy red brick lined with metal dumpsters, and for a second I'm not sure which way to run.

A gunshot goes off behind me; I pick left. The alien is starting to lose its grip, sliding downward under my jacket, but I get a fractured glance at my phone and my ride's only a block away. I cradle one arm around the fleshy bundle. My lungs are full of fishhooks. I'm not in running shape. I'm barely clean.

Through the keening echo in my ears I hear feet slapping the pavement behind me, gaining on me. I don't want to look. Don't want to see the mask. Then I'm tackled to the ground and I don't have a choice. My chin bounces off the tarmac, jarring my skull, spilling purple-black blots across my eyes. I roll, grab for the stunner in my pocket.

The mask is centimeters from my face; I can see it's cheap plastic from some streetside printer. One hand locks my wrist and the other peels the stunner away before my finger can find the trigger. The gecko grip takes a layer of skin with it.

"Il est où le prophète?" Their voice is soft but insistent. "Where? Where?"

They toss the weapon over their shoulder and all I can think about is the blood spattering the glass door and how I'm going to be nothing but electricity in someone's brain soon, and how maybe that's for the best. They spot the rippling motion under my jacket—the alien isn't calm anymore—and reach for my zipper. I hear their breathing quicken.

Ty jams the stunner into the back of their neck. The charge ragdolls them; I smell singed hair as they flop to one side, bucking and twitching. She thrusts it into their chest next, grinding it against their heaving ribs. I scramble backward. She's howling as she hits the trigger again and again, her hair flying wild around her face.

"Osti de tabarnak de crisse de *marde*," she sobs, punctuating each curse with the stunner.

They spasm, flipping onto their side, and for an instant I see the shaved back of their head. I see the scar tissue. The hole.

"What the fuck is going on?" Ty demands, and I get that she's asking me, not them. "Who are you?" She levels my stunner at me. "Bouge pas. Bouge pas. I called the cops."

To prove her words, the sound of squealing tires comes from the opposite end of the alley. But there's no siren, and as the big black car noses into the alleyway I see the driver is wearing a mask. She sees it too and I hear her breath catch. My phone buzzes in my pocket.

"That's not the fucking feds," I say. "Allons-y."

I run and she comes with me, down the alley, leaving the person in the mask to twitch and shake. The car squeals to a halt to not run them over. I hear doors slamming open; I can picture guns being drawn. I dredge one last burst out of my aching muscles. We shoot out of the alley onto the street, where an autotrailer is idling and blocking traffic.

The door slides open and I throw myself inside. Ty follows a little more gracefully and we're moving before the door can close. I hear sirens now. Two blue police cars whiz past us on their way to Fleur House. The autotrailer hangs a left and starts heading for the Pont-Tunnel. I keep my face pressed to the cold metal floor until my breathing is back to normal. The alien in my jacket gives a tentative squirm.

"Fuck," I hear Ty murmur. "There's more of them."

I drag my head up. She's looking at the tank, of course, the big polyplastic tank that takes up most of the trailer. Three ugly beautiful creatures are swirling around inside, tendrils billowing, bony heads nuzzling against each other. I stagger to my feet, balancing against the lurch of the vehicle, and unzip my jacket.

The alien from the bathtub mewls, stretching a tendril into the air towards its kin. I dump it into the tank. There's a soft splash and then the aliens are all bundled together in one pulsing mass that always gives me a bit of a lump in the throat. A pictogram flashes through my skull, the eye-green rhombus fitting perfectly into its golden-brown place.

"Yeah," I say. "Yes. There's more of them. And more out there."

Ty stares at the tank. Her eyes are glassy with shock. "They shot Dion in the head," she says. "He was trying to get out of their way, and they shot him in the head."

My stomach churns. "Sorry," I say, even though sorry means nothing.

"Who were those people?" she asks in a voice like brittle wood.

I look at the tank, too, and shake my head. "Aucune idée," I say, remembering the flicker knife, the cheap tribal mask, the trepanation scar in the back of their skull. "That's never happened before."

"It was the meteor shower, then." Ty is slumped against the bouncing wall of the trailer. "Dion was right. Aliens. Calisse, mais ça c'est fou. Crazy. Crazy. This is all fucking crazy." She clutches her head in both hands and shuts her eyes. "And you, you're what? You're collecting them?"

"We've got a deal, I guess," I say, checking our route on my phone. "Kind of a deal. Yeah. I have to talk to them, then we'll drop you somewhere."

I get up again and go to the tank. The biggest of them, the one I met a month ago in the ice-cold harbor by the Grande Roue, swims over to meet me. One of its tendrils loops over the top of the tank. I grab it, and I realize Ty is looking at my trepanation again.

"They did that?" she asks faintly. "That hole?"

"Better than a ruptured septum," I say. "They showed me how to do it. Wasn't so bad."

Her gaze flicks to my arms, to the ladder of track marks and purpled scars no longer hidden by my jacket. "You're a junkie," she says. "I seen arms like that before." She watches as I bring the tendril to the nape of my neck. "Is it a high for you?" Her laugh is bitter. "Is that what you get out of this?"

"It's complicated," I say, as the tendril slides inside my brain and turns the only key that matters. I need to find out where we're going next. I need to ask about the people in the masks. But those things can wait a little while. I take a deep breath. "Hey, Em."

"Hey, Benny," Émilie says, stepping around Ty, slouching down beside me. "Got another alien, huh?" She shakes her head and gives me her semi-sad smile. "T'es fou, toi."

"Yeah," I say, blinking back tears. "I know."

We hold hands as the autotrailer enters the Pont-Tunnel.

SMEAR JOB

Jalen watched his hands while the lawyer talked. The plasticuffs around his knobby wrists, with the blinking red lock-light, made it all seem fake. Like he was ripping some VR escape game, maybe. But the way he couldn't stop his fingers twitching assured him it was real life.

"So it's a very small mod," the lawyer was saying in her twangy accent. "Tiny little thing. Since it's a pilot program, it's all funded. Nothing out of your pocket. Or your parents' pocket, I guess. I'm giving you a lifeline here, Jalen. No jail-time, no registry. Just a mod."

Jalen's throat was dry and he nearly choked on his reply. "It won't mess with stuff?" he asked, hoarse. "Like, it won't mess up my implant?"

"Not at all. It does its job with minimal interference." She leaned forward, starched hair wobbling like the crest on the rooster in his mom's chicken coop. "You know, this could've been a lot worse, Jalen. Could've been a real shit-show for you." She slid him a tiny blue Dasani bottle from the vending machine down the hall. "I know you're a good kid. You deserve to catch a break."

Jalen stared at the water bottle, wanting to ask how the fuck he was supposed to open it with his hands cuffed. Instead, he asked the question that had been chewing at him for days. "Am I going to be able to see Stef?"

The lawyer rearranged her face like she was trying to be the second-saddest emote, the nearly-crying one. "Definitely not for a long time," she said. "Her parents are making sure of that. I'll let you think about it, okay?"

She left the little room, leaving a big waft of her cologne behind her, bad enough to make Jalen's eyes start to water.

They did the mod a few days later. Jalen and his mom took the freebus to a fancy clinic where the door took an extra long time scanning their faces before it let them inside, then Jalen sat on a crinkly white sheet of paper while a bored technician explained things and gave him screen after screen to swipe his agreement on.

His mom read them aloud over his shoulder through clenched-up teeth, sometimes asking the technician things that the technician seemed to think were obvious. She hated clinics; Jalen could feel the tenseness coming off her like radiation and it made him tense, too.

He just wanted to get it all over with, so he was glad the mod itself only took a second. A little antiseptic swab cold on his temple, then the white cup with the microneedles, and no pain at all as they went into his implant and uploaded the court-mandated perception modification, what the technician had called a smear-job when they first got there.

"There," the man said. "Easy as pie."

Jalen spent that whole summer working with his Uncle Jeb at the warehouse, long hours cleaning and unjamming the bots when they glitched, so at first he hardly even noticed the mod. Uncle Jeb was a Pakistan vet getting his blown-off arm regrown the slow way; Jalen remembered being scared of it when he was little and Jeb would unwrap it sometimes at parties, that soft little baby arm sticking off his big sinewy shoulder. Now it was functional, but skinnier than even Jalen's was.

Uncle Jeb never once mentioned the mod, but he did sometimes look at Jalen with serious eyes and ask, slow and warm, if he was doing alright. Jalen was grateful for that. It made him want to work harder and not play ZombiBlast in the back when things got slow. It almost made him want to spill about the one message he'd gotten from Stef, sent from a friend's account, saying how sorry she was and how her parents were moving them to the coast a million fucking miles away and how awful life was.

Jalen read it at night sometimes and cried about it, like a little kid, but eventually the whole thing scabbed over and he couldn't hurt real bad about it, even if he wanted to. Life got back to its rhythms. He hardly thought about the mod. He was the youngest in his family, since his mom had done him late with vitro, so he didn't have to worry about little siblings or cousins or anything. Mostly all his friends were eighteen, whether they graduated or not. The only younger crowd he'd ever hung with was Stef and her friends, and he didn't want to see her friends anyway.

It did spook him, though, when his mom's friend visited from Atlanta and brought her two kids along with her. He tried to not be around.

But after a couple years, it was just normal. He knew what places in town to avoid at what times. He knew all the little tricks for when somebody wanted to introduce him to their family, where to keep his eyes, what generic type of compliments to give. Getting so big! Better-looking than your daddy here ever was! It wasn't that hard.

His friends never razzed him about it anymore, and some of them had even forgotten, he thought, about the whole thing with him and Stef. Jalen forgot about it himself long enough to meet someone new. Danica was smart and impatient and had one dimple when she smiled. She didn't have rich white Mormon parents and her birthday was only two days different from his. They celebrated it together by driving out to the river in her beat-up 'lectruck, building a fire with an old pallet from his work, getting nice and drunk under the stars.

She invited him and his mom to a big cook-out with her whole family, and it was such a good time he didn't even mind the blurry little kids hurtling everywhere. Afterwards he took her to the hill behind St. Xavier's, where he used to take Stef, and only felt a little guilty kissing her there.

Things started moving fast, but Jalen's mom said there was nothing to be done about it, he was a romantic and that was that.

By his twenty-second birthday, they had enough money to rent their own place, just a little apartment in the dingy quickcrete blocks. They sat on the floor in the dark the first night, because the solar storage was glitching and they hadn't gotten chairs yet, but Danica lit a seaweed-smelling candle and they pretended it was romantic.

The next year the warehouse phased out human workers completely, but Jalen was ready for it, thanks to Uncle Jeb, whose left arm was now hairy and strong like his right. He got a gig doing installation and maintenance work on the new urban farms popping up. Not much money, but Danica was making double it doing digital management, so they were alright.

Then one night Jalen found a rubber pregnancy test sitting in the cup in the bathroom beside his toothbrush, the gag kind colored blue like the old days, before people had implants checking on their hormone levels all the time.

"Shit," Danica said, when he came out not quite managing to grin. "I thought you'd be happy, Jay."

"I am," Jalen said, wrapping his arms around her, staring down at her stomach. "I am, I am. It's just. Whoa. You know?"

"Whoa," Danica echoed.

He grinned a real grin, and they kissed.

The pregnancy was an easy one, or at least that's what Danica's mom kept telling her, which sometimes led to a lot of cussing between the two of them. Jalen shed some of his workdays so he could help more around the house. He was home in the afternoon when the freebus dumped a bunch of schoolkids off on the corner of their block, and he watched them through the window with a queasy feeling in his stomach.

Some nights, after Danica was asleep, he stared up at the ceiling where his implant projected a list of legal counselors. He couldn't find the lawyer from back when he was eighteen. All he remembered was her floppy hair, which might have changed by now. But this would be different, anyways. This would be his own flesh-and-blood. He was going to be a dad.

The baby came early on the first chilly morning in December. Jalen felt almost light-headed as they waited outside for their ride;

he alternated between checking the bug-out bag for anything they might have forgotten and rubbing Danica's arms like to keep her warm. He'd looked up his original charges. Twenty years before the perception modification could be appealed. But it wouldn't matter. Couldn't matter. Whoever designed the mod must have made sure of that.

Jalen and Danica hadn't been able to afford a human nurse, but the labor and delivery bot was a good one, moving very calm and precise and speaking in the soothing voice of Danica's favorite nature-doc narrator. She squeezed his hand so tight Jalen thought she might break it. He told her that, told her they were going to need X-rays on the way out. She laughed and then cursed at him and then laughed again.

"Hard part's over, Danica," the bot said. Jalen's heart pounded hard. "His head is clear."

Jalen looked, and his blood iced over. He swallowed back bile.

"What's he look like, Jay?" Danica demanded.

Jalen couldn't speak. All he saw was a smear of blurred pink pixels. Like the faces in the bus windows, like the scampering ghosts on the playground. He bit back his sob.

"Better-looking than I ever was," he said. "Just perfect."

BRAINWHALES ARE STONERS, TOO

Me and Theo are pretty ripped when we decide to save the brainwhales. Well, Theo is. I only took one good hoot, because after a year of dealing basement dro I don't really like the stuff anymore. Plus I know if I smoke up too hard I get sad or boring, and I don't want to be sad or boring when Theo Vandermeer, finnest and richest boy at Polytechnic, is spilled back on my bed with his shirt riding up so I can see that little groove where muscle carves to hip.

"Those grungy smallcorp computation facs shouldn't even exist," Theo says, batting like a cat at a scarf that drapes down from one of the hooks in my unfinished ceiling. His gorgeous green eyes are serious and bloodshot. "Saw this doc about how most of them totally ignore, uh, sanitation requirements. Ultra-cramped quarters. Keeping the beasties in memembrane, it's inhumane, you know? Why don't they, you know, rent out a swimming pool, at least?"

I'm more zeroed in on his shoulders, which are bigger since he started going to some swanky gravity gym up past our high school, but I nod solemnly. "Um. Yeah, it's fucked up."

I set my bong on the cracked vanity and wriggle down onto the bed beside him, accidentally-on-purpose tangling my legs, shaved in the sink in record time after he called, into his. I'm full aware this is my best or only chance with him. He's off to uni next year, and me, well, I'm a year younger and no prospects for uni in any case.

Theo looks at my legs, hopefully not noticing the nicked ankle. He gives this kind of smirk he does, which drives me kind of wild, then his glassy eyes narrow up. "Your ma works at one of them, doesn't she? ThinkTank or something?"

"She does security there, yeah," I admit, bristling a bit even though I'm close enough to smell Theo's swanky Weber cologne which may or may not have some major 'mones in it. "Has to keep the electric on somehow, doesn't she?" Saying it gives me a guilty little twist in my stomach, thinking of her sleeping all bone-tired upstairs, since she'd have to work less shifts if I cut her into the grassflow.

Theo gives me this dopey look, and I suspect he might not even be, like, aware that the electric goes off if the bills don't get paid. He's still fin as all hell though, and sweetly sensitive about brainwhale welfare, so I steel my nerves, slide up closer, and kiss him. He tastes mostly like the bong.

When I open my eyes, he's frowning. "Bea. What are you doing?"

I freeze up like ice-buckets, ready to beg him to forget I did it, ready to lie about how ripped I am because I sell him really good dro, remember, real topping swank shit. I can already feel that whine in the back of my throat.

I'm so fucking null. Null of me to put on a clean bra, null of me to say I'd smoke up with him, null of me to have a tiny shitty room and a bony ass and odd knobby nipples.

Then he kisses me back proper, warm swirly tongue and all, and when we come up he's got that smirk again. "Your ma has a fob key to get into the comp-fac, right?"

"Um. Yeah." My head's still a bit spinny. Maybe the cologne does have 'mones. Maybe he's just that good a kisser. "Why?"

Theo tip-toes his fingers along my goosebumped leg. "The reason people aren't all up in arms about this shit is that they don't *know* about this shit." He gives a triumphant, bleary grin. "To really understand the, you know, the plight? Of the brainwhales? People have to see it. I mean, fuck, I've never seen it, you know?"

I'm not so null I can't see where this is going, but right now I'd probably rob a bank with his handsome ass. "Never seen it either," I admit. My ma never mentions the brainwhale.

"Fuck it." Theo vaults up off the bed, making the 3D-printed frame wobble dangerously, and smooths his hair. I wonder how long my sheets will smell like Vandermeer. I wouldn't mind at least a few days of it. "Let's bust in," he says. "Make a doc of our own. It'll be an adventure, you know?"

An adventure. Something he couldn't do with Ivy Ibsen or the rest of the litter of designer-wearing bleached-blonde bitches he usually hangs around. Something he could only ever do with me, something where we'd keep it a secret but smile sort of sly to each other in the hall, even if he was heading to a rugby practice and I was heading to roll ciggies in the parking lot. Maybe even something he remembers when he heads off to uni and I stay stuck in this shit neighborhood all my life.

"Yeah," I say, like it's a typical Thursday night kind of thing. "Sure."

Theo's grin stretches wider. "And we'll grab some pupusas on the way. Like, a lot of them."

ThinkTank is a retooled warehouse over Eastside, near the stadiums. In Theo's Numi, which he flicks to autodrive so we can better focus on the greasy Memos take-out, it only takes about fifteen minutes to get there. I was sort of hoping he'd lose focus feasting and want to just park somewhere, and then make out, but he's determined in a way that makes me think this isn't just a whim thing, like he's thought about it for a while, and that makes me more nervous, not less.

"Of course, the real problem is the system," Theo says, half a block off ThinkTank.

"Turn in here," I say. "There's an alley around the back."

Theo gives me an approving nod, like he was actually going to park right in front of the fucking place if I hadn't suggested otherwise. He did nearly pull into my driveway the first time he came over to buy.

We park and open the doors on a warm muggy night. I accidentally dislodge a few wrappers and an empty protein bottle, which I pick up and toss back in. I've had a few dinky little fantasies about being in Theo's car with him, usually with us driving to an old-fashioned Italian restaurant, or a beach, or something null like that, but none of them featured the ankle-deep trash.

I've got my ma's fob, jet black, thumb-sized, clenched in my fist. She always hangs it on the side of the microwave. I know I'm about to do a Bad Thing, and my ma will be stormy mad if she finds out, but she's been with the security co long enough they wouldn't dare drop her. And teenagers are supposed to do idiot shit, aren't they, to give old people proof that society's going to shit and all that?

And this one's for a good cause. Brainwhales and making out with Theo Vandermeer, whose hair gel is glistening in the streetlamp light.

"Let's do this," he says, clipping a little hi-fi camera mod to his phone. "Bea, you ready?"

"Ready," I say, feeling a little thrill, a little sizzle up my spine like when I snuck out my window well for the first time. It's the Bad Thing feeling, and it's a good one.

We creep to the door, even though the streets are dead empty, and I push the fob up against the lock until it blinks blue and clicks open. Theo holds the door for me, which is kind of gallant of him. I swing my hand back to brush against his, like, in case he wants to grab it as we plunge into this idiot adventure, but he's busy turning on his phone's torch.

It's dark inside except for a little blinking red light, which starts beeping right around the time I figure it's a motion sensor. "Ah, shit," I say. "Theo, we sort of forgot about the alarm?"

"Got it," he grunts. He slides the bright white phone light up and down the walls until he uncovers the alarm box, then yanks the cover down and punches in a string of digits. The beeping quits. Theo closes the alarm box and gives it a little pat. I knew he was more than a pretty face.

"How'd you do that?" I ask, not having to fake the impress-edness.

"Vanguard alarms come with a factory pre-set," he says. "Like, ninety percent of people don't bother changing it."

"Wick."

"Isn't it, yeah?"

Theo jerks his head toward the interior, and we follow his bobbing phone light through cubicles and stained carpet. There's a briny yeasty smell all through the place that someone tried to hide with mango-scented air freshener. Not the best olfactory combo. The smell gets stronger when we come up on the sealed door marked COMPUTATION in big black stencil.

I stick the fob out again. The lock click-clunks.

"This is it," Theo whispers, waving his phone up in my face, ensuring I look both pasty and squinty as fuck. "Do you have anything, like, inspirational to say?"

"Eh." I push his arm down, then kind of hold onto it. "Brainwhales are people, too? You're bent to blur our faces out of that, right?"

"Why?" he asks, looking at his screen. "We look good. Sly."

"I guess."

His hand slips into mine and gives it a squeeze, that smirk coming back again. Then he pushes the door open and we're inside. The humidity ticks up, like, instantly, and there's something big in the room with us, taking up the dark.

And breathing. Or at least, trying. The sound is wet and thick and scraping and makes my stomach churn. I get the thought that maybe my ma's never talked about the brainwhale because it's not something she likes to think about at night, then Theo finds the lights and the fluorescents bloom on.

It's enormous and horrible and I instantly want those lights back off. The brainwhale's big as a bus, propped half-rolled-over in a black metal cradle flanked with banks of electronics. Its whole body is slimed with the orange gritty memebrane all slick and gleaming in the hard light. Worst is the cables, though, getting into it on all sides, hanging in thick viny bunches from the ceiling or snaking up from underneath.

There's thick clear tubes forced down the breathing hole, the blowhole, I mean, and then copper conductor wires, like the bare one on my wall, are sunk into its skin, mostly into its big bulb of a head. The eye facing us is sunk back in its skull, like it doesn't want to see what's been done with the rest of the body.

I feel this real deliberate kind of gut sick, like when you've drunk too much and you're face the toilet knowing you've got to throw it up, because you'll feel so much better after, and maybe someone's even there patting your shoulder, but the vomit just sits there in the bottom of you and doesn't come.

I look over to Theo, to see if he's feeling the same way, but he's already skipping along the length of the brainwhale with his phone waving and the biggest most shit-eating grin on his face.

"Bea," he says. "This is *it*, Bea. This is reality, you know? People are going to love this shit."

"This is fucking horrid," I say.

He turns, still grinning. "Yeah. Think of the hits." He comes back to where I'm frozen and points to the pincushion head. "Sperm whale, here, thinking female from the lack of big floppy cock. They've got the biggest brains in the animal kingdom. Five times ours." He deepens his voice for voice-over. "First we harpooned them for our oil light bulbs, now we enslave their gray matter for our data processing. Where does the extortion end?"

"I don't like this," I say, grabbing his arm. "We should go."

Maybe if Ivy Ibsen or some other pouty pretty girl had given him the scared eyes, he would have reconsidered. But I'm just his dealer, and I never learned to bat my lashes without looking like I detached a fucking retina.

Theo just plucks a dangling cable from the thicket. "Look, here's the input." He holds it up, showing the little webby cap of electrodes at the end. "Think the beastie's awake?"

"Theo, you've got your footy," I say, still staring at the brain-whale's sunken eye. "Let's go."

"We can go." He gets a hard glint in his eye. "If you put this thing on. Just for a second. I'll film."

"It's probably not, you know, calibrated or whatever."

"Why not do it, then?"

"Why don't you do it, and I film."

"Not supposed to have hair gel in when you put electrodes on."

I want to say, I don't think you're meant to have hair, either, but instead I yank the cap from his hands, kind of trembling, and turn it over. "Just for a second," I say. "And when nothing happens, we split, yeah?"

Theo nods from behind his phone. "And here's my beautiful assistant Bea, about to demonstrate how the, uh, input thing works. Maybe she'll be able to communicate with the distressed whale."

I make a face, but I do like, way too much, that he said beautiful. Null of me. I know. I rake my hair back and settle the cap on. It grabs my scalp like a squid, making me shudder. There's an odd static tingle, and I think my vision wobbles for a second, but then nothing. I put my hands on my hips and give Theo a shrug. I'm almost disappointed myself.

In the slice of quiet between the brainwhale's raspy breath out and raspy breath in, we hear the security guards' voices simultaneously.

"Shit!" I hiss. "Turn the light off!"

Theo scrambles over and flips the light switch, and I'm still trying to extricate myself from the cap when he comes back and rolls himself under the nearest bank of equipment. "Come on, Bea," he says, giggling a bit. "Hide."

"Fucking thing won't . . ." I give up and haul myself under the bank with him, tugging the cable with me. We huddle there flat on our stomachs, knees and elbows touching, and even though ninety percent of me is thinking about getting caught, ten is thinking about how smooth Theo's skin is, like he must moisturize the shit out of it.

We give each other terse grins as the door opens up and the lights come back on. "Entry clocked at 1:28," says a voice. "Then the alarm got an incorrect code at 1:29."

"Some junkie pickpocket lifted her fob, I bet," says another voice. "Come on out, you little fuck. You can't resell memebrane. It biodegrades."

I look across at Theo, who looks embarrassed. He mouths something about Vanguard alarms, but I don't catch it, because right then the electrodes on my head start to buzz.

Needclean.

It just sort of pops in my head with a little burst of smell and sight and all them others, and then it's gone again. I can feel my face twitching. Theo's brows knit together. I swallow and try to give him a "I'm fine" look as the guards' footsteps get closer. One of them is limping. I think my ma mentioned him, some angry old Pakistan vet, Charlie something, who would be ultra-unamused by our teenage antics.

Yourside underflipper needclean.

The security guards walk right on by us, toward the storage at the back, debating how long it actually takes memebrane to break down. Theo jerks his head at me, like, time to bust, and I'd agree with him except for I can't fucking move. The twitching's spread, and now my limbs are all locked up on me. I get a cold little spike of fear, wondering if I'm having a stroke.

Theo tries dragging me out at first, but when it becomes apparent that I'm dead weight he fishes his dro money plus an extra tenner out of his back pocket and tucks the bills into my front one. I can only stare at him, unbelieving. He gives an apologetic smile I want to bash in, then levers out from under the bank and hurries away.

Or tries to: I hear him bang into the doorframe on the way out and swear at it. The guards coming back from the storage room must hear it too, because they shout and take off after him. Dockers slam the concrete, the door clangs, then it's just me and the brainwhale.

I try screaming, at Theo for being a piece of human shit, at me for being null enough to like him, and at a few other things, but my throat is totally frozen.

Angrysing goodfeel. Nowyou underflipper needclean.

I'm so stormy mad and scared it takes a few seconds for me to be surprised a brainwhale is talking to me. There's pins and needles all through my body, even in my bones. I'm almost hoping the security guards find me and pull me out; better that than brain damage.

I try thinking back at the brainwhale, like, I'd love to scratch your itchy flipper, but I can't fucking move.

Nomotion?

It comes sort of unfinished, feeling like a question, so I answer it like one: Nope, not a bit of motion.

Nomotion! Shocksad shocksad shocksad.

The repetition's got an exaggerated rhythm to it, and I realize, in a big old dash of clarity, that the brainwhale's being a smartass. I guess she knows all about nomotion, what with being stuck in place like that. I want to ask her how to disconnect, but then I start wondering how long she's been in ThinkTank, and she picks that up instead.

3year 4month 23day 15hour 39minute 12second.

And I think, holy shit. That's a long-ass time to be flipped on your side with wires all up in you.

3year 4month 23day 15hour 39minute 18second.

I wonder if she misses the ocean, and this time I get a low vibrato in my head that I think might be a laugh, and with it there's a flash of dull rust-colored water and a dead tarry beach.

ThinkTank somefucked oceansea allfucked.

Fair enough, I think. Must be shitty doing maths all day instead of swimming, though.

Swimdrug alltime numbertime.

I get a flash of the tubes in her head. They make her feel like she's swimming during computations, I guess? At least the bastards do that much. I tell her, think her, how I do my own kind of swimdrug sometimes, when I remember I've lived in the same shit town for 16year and it makes me want to angrysing.

Swimdrug nowgood laterbad. Nopodfeel. Lonefeel.

This time I'm the one who wants to laugh, because that's it exactly, isn't it? Brainwhales are stoners, too. Who knew. In real time I imagine I can hear footsteps again, but her next thought distracts me.

Gonepod. Goneson.

There's a flash of a big gray sperm whale carving through the water, with little squid tentacles trailing out of its mouth, and I get this odd achy feel like I really, really miss it. Miss him.

Goneson otherThinkTank.

I try remembering if there's other ThinkTank comp-facs in the city, but of course she might just mean any comp-fac. It's awful shitty of them to split up a ma and her kid, or calf, or whatever.

Goyou otherThinkTank. Sonsing.

I can feel this big surge of excitement from her, and before I can ask what she means, my head swells up with this long string of clicking, chittering vibration. I can't pick out words like usual, but the feeling is strong enough to make my breath catch.

The message swirls around inside my skull, looping in on itself. I lie there shuddering, getting the feeling back in my limbs, as voice and footsteps get closer. The message stays.

I don't know how long it'll take me to find her son, or if he's even in the city at all, or how I'll get in to see him, but I know it's a hell of a lot more important than anything Theo's going to do at uni.

By the time Charlie the security guard pulls me out from under the equipment bank, I'm fully disconnected.

"Fuck," he says. "Beatrice, isn't it? You still in there, Beatrice?"

I tiptoe my tongue over my teeth, work my jaw a bit. "Yeah," I say. "I'm good."

"Good," he says. "Because you're in a whole lot of shit."

But he seems relieved my brain's not fried, even if it is still buzzing and clicking on the inside, and before he drags me out I manage to point out the sores under the brainwhale's myside flipper.

Outside, Theo's leaning back against the security van like he's posing for a photo shoot, chatting at the other guard. When he sees me he sweeps in for a big hug. I make myself stiff, let his smooth hands and taut arms bounce right off. My skin smells briny. His still smells like cologne, but for some reason it smells awful now.

"I tried leading them off," he says all earnestly, as the stony-faced guard pulls him back. "But they caught me at the car. Didn't want to snake on you, honest, Bea, but I figured you might be, you know, in danger, being hooked up to that thing."

"Nice of you," I say, not knowing if he's lying or even really caring.

The guards stick us in plasticuffs and herd us into the backseat of the van like true-to-life criminals, and Theo gives me this sly grin as we squash inside, like, we're so bad, and it's sort of sexy, right? I move my knee as far off his as possible.

"Did it talk to you?" he asks, looking sort of put out.

"Yeah," I say, and I tell him, since I have to tell someone, about the goneson and the eerie clicking song I'm somehow supposed to pass along.

"Shit, Bea." His eyes go bright. "That's so wick. We'll track him down. Make it part of the doc. Have to do some research before the next one, though, about, you know, alarms and shit."

"I'll be doing it myself, actually," I say, cutting in when he goes to breathe. "You wouldn't be able to keep up with me. Asshole." And then I pluck the extra tenner out of my pocket and let it flutter down to the floor between us.

Theo's still open-mouthed in what I can't help but think of as a shocksad silence when Charlie hauls the door open again, phone in hand. "Got him to shut up, did you?" he mutters. "Well, rich boy, your daddy's none too happy but he's going to meet us at the station. As for you, Beatrice, I'm about to dial your ma."

I wet my dry mouth. "Think I might be able to talk to her first, there, Charlie?"

The guard shakes his head balefully. It was worth a shot. I lean back in the seat, wondering if she'll buy that the Bad Thing turned out to be a good thing. Either way, I've got my next one all lined up.

IN EVENT OF MOON DISASTER

ol is so intent on the fizzing comm channel that he only notices Kim's back when her gloved fist raps against the airlock window, sending shivery vibrations through the whole hopper.

"Sunnuvabitch."

He snaps out of his seat, pulling the headset down around his neck. Kim is standing in front of the airlock, arms folded. She taps her foot for effect, but in the stiff suit and low gravity it looks more like she's keeping time to a slow-mo banjo. Sol gives her a few exaggerated claps as he dances over to the lever and heaves the exterior door open. Kim gives him the finger and steps inside.

As soon as the atmosphere reader dings green, she hits the release on her helmet. It levers up off her face with a hiss, revealing her sharp chin, snub nose, dark eyes under knitted brows. She looks unnaturally pale in the airlock light and her dirty blonde hair is matted with sweat.

Sol opens the interior door. "Well? You alright? I was about to suit up and go after you, Kim, Christ." He jams his headset against one ear and buzzes control, but gets silence again. "Still can't raise Control. Something's messing with the radio."

"I only lost transmitting functions," she says, stowing her helmet on the hook. "I could hear you just fine the whole time. What the hell were you chewing on?"

"Peanuts." Sol grabs the package off his seat's armrest and checks the label. "Honey-roasted. They're honey-roasted and pretty damn good. You want some?"

"No. Yeah. Give 'em." She clambers out of the suit and holds out her hand. Sol sees it shake a bit as he pours peanuts into her palm but pretends not to notice. She scoops them into her mouth.

"So? You going to tell me what was down there, Kim?"

She points to her full mouth.

"Oh, I get it. Revenge chewing. You're revenge chewing at me. I'm a nervous eater, Kim, and you were in that crack with no radio contact for twenty-seven whole minutes."

Kim swallows. "There was nothing," she says. "I took the readings. Big electromagnetic spike, like we saw from orbit, but no physical source that I could detect. No sign of the drone we sent down there. I don't know. It's fucking weird, is what it is." She runs her hands back along her hair. "I'm shot."

Sol makes a gun with two fingers. "Bang."

"As in I'm tired." Kim pinches the bridge of her nose, then goes to her hanging helmet and pulls out the datastick. "Here, have a look. I start singing, at one point. To drown out the chewing. Ignore the song choice and the high notes."

Sol takes the stick. "Alright. Hey, take a nap if you need it. Pickup window's in two-and-a-half hours."

"Thanks," Kim mutters. She starts to slide past him, toward her chair, then stops. "There was nothing down there, Solly. But it was weird."

"Hey." He pats her on the shoulder. "We're on the fucking moon."

"That is true," Kim says, clambering past him into her chair. She unrolls a vacuum-packed blanket and pulls it over her head. Her voice comes muffled. "That is a fact."

Sol watches out of the corner of his eye, making sure she's breathing normally, as he verifies the pickup window and runs another engine diagnostic. Before long she's snoring, which seems like a good sign. He claps the headset on, plugs the datastick in, and reaches for the honey-roasted peanuts.

Sol has the feed from Kim's helmet up on his screen, watching through her eyes as she makes her way along the bottom of the crevasse. She's right. There's no sign of whatever unidentified body struck the moon's eastern hemisphere and plowed a half-kilometer crack through the dust and rock. No sign of the drone they sent to investigate. Just an empty, eerie tunnel.

Eerie, but he can't quite put his finger on why. Something about the juts and whorls of rock seem slightly off to him, something about their angles. He's leaning for a closer look when someone knocks twice against the airlock window.

Sol bolts upright, heart hammering his ribs. Kim shifts under her blanket. He claps both hands over his chest and exhales and tries to think of possible explanations. The best he comes up with is debris. Nothing more specific than that, just the word: debris.

He goes to the airlock. Cold sweat drips from his armpits down his sides. Someone in a spacesuit is standing in the dust outside, shifting from foot to foot.

"You are not debris," Sol mutters.

The astronaut taps their helmet and signs a radio malfunction, then taps their padded wrist where a watch would be. Someone else is trying to investigate the impact. A rogue state, or some private corp, somehow got here first without anyone knowing. And somehow they are wearing Kim's suit, with the distinctive smiley decal on the oxygen tank.

Sol suddenly gets chatter on his headset. He pulls it back up, dazed. Kim's voice.

"Sol, don't fuck around, Sol, I blacked out down there," she says, sounding more panicked than he's ever heard her before. "I lost you on the radio, I blacked out and something happened. Let me in, Sol, goddamn you."

The astronaut thunks their helmet up against the window and he can see Kim's mouth through the faceplate, lips moving as she cusses him out.

Sol yanks his headset off. A convulsion runs up and down his body; for a second he thinks he's going to vomit. Then he strides back to the dash, to the chair where Kim's snores are fluttering her blanket. He grips the corner with one sweaty hand, braces himself, and pulls.

Kim's still there, splayed back in the chair. She raises an arm and drapes it over her face. "Go time?" she mutters.

"Uh." Sol shakes his head. "Don't know." He looks back at

the airlock, where Kim now has both gloved hands splayed against the window. He pulls his headset back up, but hears only hyperventilating, and he realizes Kim can see herself in the chair.

A crackling sob comes through the radio. "Sol, who is that? Sol? Who's that in my . . . In the chair?"

In front of him, Kim swings herself upright, rubbing her eyes. "You go through the footage?" she asks. "I did warn you, right? About the high notes."

"Oh, you were great," Sol says faintly. "Operatic, even. But. Kim."

"That is not me, Sol," Kim begs through the headset. "That is not fucking me! Let me in, Sol, something happened down there and you have to let me in, please, please, please—"

Kim in front of him sees the Kim waiting at the airlock window. Her eyes widen. Sol remembers her taking off her suit in the airlock. How her face looked pale, almost waxy. When she goes to get up from the chair, he pushes her back down. Not hard, but hard enough.

"Who the hell's that?" she demands.

"Just. Stay seated, okay? Stay there for now. I'm calling Control." Sol keys his headset. "Control, we have a situation. We have, uh, a third party present."

"Sol, is that me? That sounded like me."

He waits the ten-second delay, clutching the headset hard to his ear. Still nothing. Nobody on the channel except Kim, outside, begging to be let in.

"This is so fucked," Sol says. "I think her oxy's low. I have to at least let her into the airlock."

Kim shakes her head side to side, side to side. Her eyes are glassy with shock. "Yeah," she finally says. "Yeah, you better."

"And then, you know, I have to figure out which of you is a shapeshifting alien parasite," Sol says, trying to wrench his mouth into a smile.

Kim looks dead at him and flicks her tongue like a lizard.

"Don't do that, Kim," Sol says. "Don't do stuff just to mess with me, okay? Please?"

*

He gives them numbers: Kim One, who returned to the hopper at 0629 hours, and Kim Two, who returned to the hopper at 0712 hours.

Kim Two is significantly calmer now that she's in the airlock and has her helmet off. Her dirty blonde hair is sweat-starched into spikes and her eyes have dark circles underneath them. She's taking deep gulps of the recycled air, pushing it out her nose. But she won't take her eyes off Kim One, who is sitting on the other side of the inner airlock door.

"Just don't let her near the levers," Kim Two reiterates, voice coming through tinny. "I don't want to get vented by my creepy alien doppelganger."

"Says the creepy alien doppelganger," Kim One finishes. "I'm trying to keep an open mind about what's going on here. You could do the same."

"It's probably easier to be open-minded when you're on that side of the airlock, all wrapped up in my blanket," Kim Two says.

"Kim, maybe give her the blanket," Sol mutters. "As a peace offering."

"Sol, she doesn't want the . . ."

"I don't want the fucking blanket, Sol." Kim Two sighs. "I want to know what's going on. I want to know who that is and how she beat me back to the hopper. I was only blacked out for a minute, tops." She holds up her helmet, then the helmet Kim One shed earlier, comparing them. Shakes her head.

"She's been back for forty-five minutes already," Sol says. "If you blacked out, it was longer than a minute. Way longer."

Kim Two digs the datastick out of her helmet. "See for yourself, Sol."

Sol goes to trigger the interior door, then pauses. "Just hand it to me, okay? Don't try to come in."

Kim Two's face falls and Sol feels it like a gut punch. "Solly, you really think . . . Think I'm some kind of . . ." She blinks hard. "Oh, man. Okay. Yeah. I'll pass it through."

Kim One looks away, grimacing.

"You get it, right?" Sol asks.

"I get it," Kim Two says. "Wish I didn't."

"I'll wait over here," Kim One says, pointing to the corner.

"Away from the airlock controls."

"That's real considerate, Alien Kim," Kim Two says.

Sol cracks the interior door. Kim Two passes the datastick through, and he pretends not to notice how her hand is trembling. She tries to smile but gives up halfway, leaving her mouth all stretched. Sol mouths the word sorry to her as he relocks the interior door, leaving her in limbo.

He slots the datastick into the dash and pulls up the video, playing it side-by-side with Kim One's. The prep, the entry, the descent—all identical, down to the millisecond. Sol tries to concentrate on the footage, tries to ignore Kim One biting her thumbnail in the corner and Kim Two squatting in the airlock, head in her hands.

"Hallucination," Kim One says. "We're all thinking that, right? Air filter's compromised. We're breathing carbon and talking to my empty spacesuit in the airlock."

"Or I'm still blacked out in the crevasse," Kim Two says. "Contaminant in my oxygen tank."

"Under other circumstances, you know, I think you two would really hit it off," Sol says, but he runs a diagnostic on the air filter in a side window. Oxygen levels are green. He fumbles for the last of the peanuts and crunches them between his molars one at a time.

The footage is playing at triple time, a blur of identical motion, identical rock formations. Then, at the thirty-two minute mark, the computer detects divergence and slows it back down. Both helmets' owners are clambering back out of the crack, but taking slightly different routes. Sol rewinds, plays half-speed. Kim Two never falters, never freezes. As far as he can tell, there's no blackout at all, but the timestamp has jumped forward forty minutes.

"You said you were only out for a minute," Kim One says. "It jumps forty."

"Impossible," Kim Two says. "That's impossible. If I was down there an extra forty minutes I'd have run out of oxygen."

Sol shakes the empty peanut bag, desperately licks the salt and sugar off his palm. If he's the one hallucinating, maybe Kim never came back at all. Maybe she's stuck down there while he argues with figments of his own imagination. He raps his knuckles against his temple and peers closer at the footage as it keeps playing, as both Kims make their way out of the crevasse.

Then he sees it.

"That crag in the rock," he blurts. "It repeats. That whole stretch of tunnel, it repeats."

He restarts the video and claws the playback speed down to half, watching through Kim's eyes as she descends. She's more focused on her footing than on the walls, but there's enough. The cracks and whorls in the tunnel hit an invisible marker, and start to repeat themselves. Shifted, slightly condensed, but the same pattern. As Kim goes deeper, it happens again.

"Let me see," Kim Two says faintly.

Sol drags the footage onto his tablet and goes back to the airlock, Kim One drifting along after him. She's chewing her lip the way she does when she's thinking of something unpleasant or complicated or both. The three of them huddle up around the interior door, Kim Two on one side, Sol and Kim One on the other, and they watch the video.

"So what are we saying?" Kim One asks. "Whatever crashed into the rock was some kind of alien copy-print machine?"

A gloved fist raps against the airlock window.

Kim Three has brought company in the form of Kim Four, whose smashed faceplate is swathed in electrical tape. Her head is lolling inside her helmet and her eyes are fluttered shut. Kim Three is alert, if exhausted from having dragged Kim Four from the crevasse to the hopper. She takes the presence of Kim One and Kim Two a little better for having already saved her own life.

"I found her face down on my out," Kim Three says. "I thought I was having some kind of out-of-body experience, or something. You two must know all about that."

Kim Two snorts. She and Kim One nod. Everyone is inside the hopper now; the airlock is jammed with shed spacesuits and Sol is reasonably sure there are no shapeshifting alien parasites afoot. Kim Four needed medical attention, besides. She's laid back on the chair now, still unconscious but with more color in her face and a blanket pulled over her. Kim Three is hovering, feeling residually responsible. Kim One and Kim Two are on opposite sides of the cramped cockpit.

Sol is at the screen, checking the timestamps from Three and Four's helmets, or rather, Four and Three's.

"So first we had a forty minute jump, then a one-hour eighteen minute jump—except she slipped on her way out and cracked her faceplate—and then a one-hour forty-four minute jump," he says. "Which means for us, outside the crevasse, the arrivals are coming quicker and quicker."

"The copies," Kim Two says glumly. "We're copies. You can say it."

"The electromag fluctuation," Kim actually-Four says. "At the bottom of the crack. It's somehow spitting out clones of me?"

"Of her," Sol says, jabbing his thumb at Kim One, who looks increasingly uncomfortable. "But yeah. Basically, that's the situation." He can feel panic blocking up his throat. He still can't raise Control, and the pickup window is approaching, and . . .

"Sol, I gotta talk to you for a second," Kim One says abruptly, coming up off the wall. "Alone. Just for a second."

Sol shakes his head. "There's going to be another Kim knocking any second. Do we really have time for—"

"Bathroom," Kim One hisses. "Now."

"Yeah, okay," Sol says. He gives the other Kims a pained look. "Be right back."

"Original Kim, asserting her authority," Kim Two says dryly. "Why the need for privacy? I know you're going to be talking about—"

"Life support," Kim Four says. "The hopper's not specced for this many people, neither's the ship. Weight restrictions, too, for launch."

Sol lets Kim One drag him into the bathroom stall and shutter the door. "They're dead-on about the life support," he says. "Fuck."

"Solly, listen," Kim One says with something rasping in her throat. "I'm not sure I'm the real Kim."

"Oh, Christ, Kim, don't say that," Sol groans. "Don't mess with me, remember?"

"I'm not."

Kim One's breath is stale and hot and Sol desperately wants to get out of the bathroom, even though there's nowhere else to go but back to more Kims.

"I blacked out, too, when I was down there," Kim One says. "I didn't tell you about it earlier. Didn't want you stress-eating for the next two-and-a-half hours."

Sol grips his hair with both hands, weaving it through his fingers. "But you were the first one back. So it has to be you." His voice has a whiny edge to it he can't quite erase. "It has to be, Kim. Come on."

Kim One shakes her head. "Maybe I'm the first one back because I was the first copy," she says. "Maybe the real Kim, like, the original Kim, maybe she's wherever the drone is. And wherever the thing is. The unidentified body that made this trench in the first place."

"Does it matter?" Sol demands. "Jesus, look, you're Kim to me, okay? You're Kim to me. You'll be Kim to everybody back on Earth. The pickup window is less than an hour away, and we can launch the hopper with three people aboard, max."

"But they're all me, too," Kim One whispers. Her face is blotchy red and Sol can see tears pushed back under her eyes. His stomach rolls over like a dead fish.

"What can we do?" he asks.

"Number Four," Kim One says. "She's been unconscious. She doesn't know any of this shit. Take her. Leave the rest of us."

"Technically, that's number Three," Sol says. "And are you fucking kidding me? Kim, she could be brain-damaged. Or, or, barring that, what if she dissolves in twenty-four hours? Into some big puddle of alien goo?"

"I might do that, too."

"Or you might not, because you're the original Kim, okay?" He grabs her by the shoulders and almost shouts it. "You're the original fucking Kim!"

She glares at him and he glares back, neither of them moving. The bathroom light buzzes and flickers between their heads. Kim One's breath smells even worse, now, and Sol's about to say it, just to be a dick, but then she might take it as evidence of her mouth dissolving so he says nothing at all. Not until a gentle knock on the airlock window makes the wall tremble.

"I wonder who that could be," he says.

Kim One does something between a laugh and a sob.

*

Kim Five has her radio working; Sol listens to her voice pitching upward as she demands to be let in, demands to know why there are footprints all around the hopper, demands to know whose spacesuits are piled in the airlock. Finally he switches off his headset and it becomes a silent film. Kim Five pounding her gloved fists against the airlock window in slow motion, catching sight of a warped reflection behind her, turning to see Kim Six struggling up from the crevasse.

"Don't watch," Kim actually-Four says, from where she's checking on Kim actually-Three's vitals. "That makes it worse for them. And us."

Sol drags his eyes away from the scene. Puts his back to the airlock and sits down. Kim One and Kim Two are already sitting cross-legged on the floor; Kim Four is still tending to Kim Three, who still hasn't woken up.

"If we cleared the suits out, we could fit one more person in the airlock," Kim One says miserably. "At least for a while."

Sol takes a deep breath. "No point," he says. "Max of three people to launch. So, we have to make a decision. Have to decide. On who, if anybody, comes with me and Kim . . . One. Kim One."

"Wait," Kim Two interjects. "Why is she a sure thing? She doesn't even know if she's the real Kim."

"We could hear you in the bathroom," Kim Four says. "Sol gets so loud when he's agitated."

"You really do, Solly," Kim Two says.

Sol gives an irritable shrug. "She's the most likely to be the original, okay?" he says. "If she doesn't come, and I take one of you guys instead, what if you dissolve into . . ."

"Why do you have this fucking fixation with alien goo?" Kim Two sighs.

"And then no Kim comes back at all," Sol finishes. "Her family has nobody at all, and Kim's stuck asphyxiating on the surface of the goddamn moon."

"If we don't dissolve, we'll be doing the same thing," Kim Four says quietly.

Sol runs his hands through his hair again. "Can we agree that Kim Three is out?" he asks. "She'll never know. She's unconscious."

Kims One, Two, and Four all flinch.

"Goddamn it, Sol," Kim Four snaps. "That's even worse, dumping someone out the airlock while they're asleep."

"How about we dump you, and take an all-Kim crew back to the ship?" Kim Two says, jutting out her chin.

Sol blinks. More than the words, the expression on her face punches a hole right through him. Then he remembers how panicked she was, begging him to let her into the cockpit, and how she deflated all at once when he told her to pass the datastick through the door. Guilt churns his stomach.

"Kim, you don't mean that," Kim One says. "He's the only one we know isn't a copy. He wasn't in the crevasse. He goes."

Kim Four nods. Kim Two gives a sour shrug.

"Look," Sol says shakily. "I know it sounds fucked up, but this whole situation, in case you haven't noticed, this whole situation is supremely fucked up."

Vibrations sing through the cockpit again, as if to punctuate his words. More fists banging on the airlock. Sol forces himself not to look.

"We'll put it to a vote," Kim One says. "And if there's a tie, we rock-paper-scissors." She rubs hard at her face, kneading the skin. "Okay?"

Sol holds his breath. The other Kims slowly nod.

"Good," he says hoarsely. "Who goes first?"

"You don't vote," Kim One says. "And you don't watch, either."

Sol swallows. "But . . . Kim."

"We're all Kim," she says. "You don't get to know who stays."

Sol searches her face, trying to find some fleck of food, some distinct clump of hair that will let him differentiate her from the others. But she looks exactly like Kim Two and exactly like Kim Four and maybe she's right. Maybe there is no original Kim here, because they all are.

"Okay," he says.

Sol sits in the airlock while the Kims decide. Outside, there's a crowd of new Kims bounding around in their puffy white suits, crackling to each other on the radio or putting their helmets together to speak that way, gesticulating at the hopper, at the crevasse. He wonders what conclusions they're coming to. More and more of them are emerging from the crack, hauling themselves up the rock and bouncing to their booted feet. Sol wipes the tears off his cheeks when he hears the interior door scrape open.

Two Kims silently walk in and start suiting up. Sol looks between them, trying to guess, but there's no way of knowing. He looks back and sees Kim Three, still unconscious in her chair, and the last Kim sitting on the floor with her head in her hands.

"Just couldn't do it," one of the airlock Kims says, stepping into her suit and working the zipper. "That dumbass caring instinct, I guess. Same reason we're always looking out for you, Solly."

"I'm sorry," Sol says. It's the only thing he can think to say.

"Yeah, yeah," the other Kim says. "I know. It's. Uh. It's fucking tough." She blinks hard and reaches for her helmet. "We'll clear everyone away, if we can. So you have space to launch without frying a bunch of coworkers."

The other-other Kim has a stuck zipper. Her chest is pumping sharp shallow breaths. "Fuck," she says. "This isn't right. It's not logical. She could be brain-damaged, you know?" She licks her dry lips. "And her, she went a little early with the scissors. I think . . . I think I want a rematch."

"Shut up, Kim," Kim says. "Come on. Let's just do this. You're brave. You better be, because if you're not, then I'm not." She reaches in and yanks the zipper free. "So. Am I?"

Kim shakes herself, looks right at Sol, and for a second Sol's sure she's Kim One, but then the feeling twists away. "We're brave," she says. "Sure. Or unlucky. Or both. Whatever."

"Have a safe trip home," Kim says. "Bye, Solly."

They put their helmets on and seal them. Sol can see his grimacing reflection in their faceplates. He tries to smile, doesn't manage it. Salutes instead, and squeezes past them, back into the cockpit. Just how he did a lifetime ago at 0600 hours, he vents the airlock, waits for the thumbs up, and opens the outer door.

Kim and Kim step out into the gray dust, sending a ripple through the crowd of spacesuits, helmeted heads turning.

Sol staggers back to his chair. "Let's get prepped, Kim," he says, not looking at her.

"Yeah," she says, not looking at him. "Go time."

*

They secure Kim Three between their chairs with insulation and electrical tape, making sure her head's as cushioned as possible. Then they strap in for launch. The hopper rumbles through its ignition sequence, testing each engine in turn. On the screen, Sol sees the pickup window flash green. The ship is directly above them, ready to retrieve them and their inconclusive data from the crevasse. He tries to raise Control one last time but gets nothing. So long as they're in position, the radio interference shouldn't matter.

Neither of them speak as the countdown ticks away, and then the roar of the engines is too loud to speak anyways. It shakes them like pennies in a jar and Sol reaches out an arm to brace Kim Three. He sees Kim's arm reaching from her end, too. The hopper shudders up into the sky, shedding gravity all at once. Not all of the Kims cleared the area and Sol tries not to imagine them bursting into flame.

They pull away from the moon's surface, and on the screen Sol can see the crevasse blooming like a snow-white flower as more and more spacesuited Kims pour out of it, spilling in all directions across the gray rock. If it doesn't stop, the entire face of the moon will be covered in asphyxiating astronauts, coated until it looks an ice crust.

Sol switches the screen to show the waiting ship, hanging in orbit. Are they observing the surface? Are they seeing the bloom? They must be. The idea of trying to explain what's happened makes Sol want to laugh and die at the same time. He checks their trajectory and sees it's a little off, but nothing serious.

"You're not going to tell me which one you are?" he finally asks.

"We figured that would be better for you," Kim says dryly. "You don't have to know who you left behind."

"I left everyone behind," Sol says. "Christ, Kim. I don't even know who I am now."

"Join the club." She leans forward in her seat. "Sol? What's that?"

Sol zooms the screen and his mouth goes dry. They're still on-course for the ship, but so is someone else. He and Kim watch speechlessly as a hopper, identical to their own, maneuvers into the dock on a gentle burn, cuts its engines, and slots perfectly into place.

VALHALLA

The battle rages for a thousand years, until heaped casings stand like termite mounds, until the impassable stone walls of the gulch become bullet art reliefs, great murals of pain baptized in bloodspray.

There are waves of pacifism, tsunamis of suicides, but eventually the soldiers always return to their purpose:

Take the base. Hold the base.

The sergeant-priest dons the sacred gasmask; they chant the Objective together, readying their gear and their desiccated souls—

White light obliterates the world.

"Minor glitch in the time dilation, recruits," comes a long-forgotten voice. "But a few extra sims never hurt."

They begin to weep.

LAST NICE DAY

It sun-showers while we're scrubbing the carrots. The sky overhead is robin's egg blue—all the gray stormy shit is off to the east—but the rain comes down anyways. We're sitting on the edge of the old wooden porch, facing the garden, and the drops lick our bare feet. That is the setting.

"Again," says Mom, because it sun-showered yesterday too.

I scrub sideways, working bristles into creases. It feels good to see the water slick the dirt away and leave the skin bright orange. I like cleaning things. I like it when it rains and all the colors punch more. That is a relatable personality trait.

"Weird weather," says Mom. She goes from scrubbing to cutting, pulling the clean bright carrots out of the bucket and lopping the tops off. "Still warm, though. We have to enjoy it. Might be the last nice day."

I should be talking. I know I should be talking. Nobody wants to read about a silent and emotionally numb character.

"Yeah," I say.

Carrots go from tub, dirty, to bucket, clean, to Tupperware, cut. Warm rain splatters walkway, dark blotches on stone laid last summer while I was overseas. My work involves travel. The last trip didn't go so great. That's foreshadowing.

"Are you doing that thing again, Ned?" Mom looks uncomfortable. "You know the thing I mean? When you pretend like you're a fictional character to get mental distance from shit?"

"Nah," I say. "Nah. I'm not."

Soon the tub's got only stragglers, small and pale, hiding in the brown murk, and when those are done Mom dumps the water, refills it, and gets started on scrubbing the beets.

"I know it was a bad one," she says, and I can tell she wants to ask about the therapy modules, if I've finally started them.

"It was okay," I say.

The beet juice leaches into the water bright red, and my heart goes off like a bomb, and my throat welds shut, but at least I'm reacting to things now, which makes it more interesting, fuck fuck fuck—

This is the last gasp of August.

Here's a flashback: a man and a woman are standing in a bathroom. She knows about the envelope. He knows that she knows about the envelope. She doesn't know that he knows that she knows about the envelope, but she is on the verge. Things are in flux.

"Shitty party," the woman says, trying out a smile. "Sorry. I thought it would be more fun. I needed some fun."

She looked inside the envelope. He saw the tiny spots of body heat her fingers left on the photos, though she was smart enough to not leave fingerprints. They have been playing the information game for weeks, but now his hand is forced. The risk of exposure is too high.

So his subself emerges, creeping down the pathways microlesioned into his corpus callosum. He sees sparks, smells the loamy fall rot on the roads outside his mom's acreage.

"We both need some fun," he says, but now he is only a passenger, observing. "This week has been crazy, you know? I'm going to take you out tomorrow. Just the two of us. We'll go dancing."

He holds out his hand, wrist aligned for the featherlight salsa clasp. She smiles and puts her hand in his, completing the frame.

"I'm not in my shoes," she says.

He gives her a clockwork spin, then another, then another. She whirls in place on the shiny bathroom tiles, her reflection a beautiful laughing blur.

"Ned, stop it," she says. "I'm dizzy."

"Yeah," he says. He spins her again. Again.

"Ned!" She stumbles. "Hey!"

He wrenches her sideways and smashes her head into the sink. Once is not enough. His subself knows that incapacitating someone in real life is not like incapacitating someone in a film. He can only count the contacts between porcelain and bone. On three the scalp splits, on seven the skull cracks, on twelve the eyes roll back, and she's gone, hurt too badly to stay conscious.

She might never wake up. If she does, there will be extensive brain damage.

Knowing this would paralyze Ned, but his subself is already cleaning, sliding the body into the bathtub, running the water. Bright red blood swirls toward the drain.

Our old soccer wall is still up. It's not really a wall: just a couple square-cut lumber stays stacked together with a flexy sheet of plywood wedged between them. Pass low against the stays and the ball comes back at speed, shoot a bit higher and the plywood takes the edge off the rebound so it doesn't wallop you in the face.

I built it for my little sister Suz, back when she was playing for Team Alberta, streaking up and down the wing and launching those beautiful looping crosses. I haven't seen her since I got back. Mom says she doesn't leave her room anymore, but I hear her moving around the house in the middle of the night sometimes, cooking or showering.

Suz should be more than a supporting character, but I can't get inside her head anymore, and lately I'm not sure I ever did. She will have to stay on the periphery.

Since she's not using the soccer wall, I do. I find the blue-and-orange husk of an old Nike ball in the garage and pump it a little too full, then take it out to the wall and start hammering away, left foot, right foot, sometimes popping it up for volleys against the plywood. My feet are automatic, even after years and years of not playing, and it makes me wonder again about the balance of things: how much I do, how much I do without me.

I'm hoping that the familiar sound of the ball hitting wood will bring Suz out of her room how my knocking on her door couldn't. A big black dog shows up instead. His name is Trotsky.

Mom introduced us the day I arrived from the airport. Behaviorists say the coyotes are getting more aggressive around here, more prone to pack-hunting, so she wanted a bodyguard for her morning run. Trotsky is already rib-high on me, and he's not done growing.

Mom also said some drone caught footage of a pizzly bear, half-starved but still a biological tank with razor-tipped mitts, wandering south. If that thing ever shows up around here, Trotsky better hide.

Of course, now it's obvious the pizzly bear will find the acreage. It's Chekhov's Pizzly Bear now.

Trotsky bum-rushes me and attacks the soccer ball, trying to get his slobbery jaws around it. He's still a puppy. I pop it out of his mouth with the toe of my shoe and play keep-away with him, dribbling a tight circle while he butts my legs with his shaggy head. I was never as good as Suz; after a few seconds Trotsky manages to dive under my shins and steal it. He skips away and stares at me, ball in mouth.

"Are you puncturing it?" I ask. "Hey. You better not be puncturing it."

I take a step forward. He retreats. He is so happy. I am so glad he doesn't know about the trip to Ljubljana, where a dog spotted me climbing a fence and started barking so loudly that my subself did the math, put one parka-wrapped hand into its mouth, and beat it to death with the other.

"You big beautiful idiot," I say. "Give me that."

He refuses, so I chase him around the half-dirt half-grass field behind the garden until I'm exhausted, and I have to flop down to breathe. Trotsky taunts me from a distance. It feels like it should feel good. The sun is still shining, limning red and gold leaves in the elm trees, which are insubstantial enough to sway, back and forth, back and forth, in the wind.

"This might be the last nice day," I tell Trotsky. "Those leaves will start falling soon."

Trotsky doesn't care.

Here's an infodump.

The first thing you should know is that field operatives aren't recruited or trained the way they used to be. Lives are too documented now. Identities are too concrete. Gaits and faces and thumbprints and retinas get stamped into the fabric of cyberspace a hundred times a day. Anonymity is a relic that even the best ghoster algorithms can't bring back.

In the years it normally takes to be trained as an effective operative, enemy machine intelligence can dredge a dozen red flags out of movement and communication patterns. They make you before you ever set foot in the field. That's why the whole thing had to be condensed. Candidates are still screened for physical fitness, of course, but the first priority is now mental malleability.

They test for the neural structures that lend themselves to psychosurgery, deep learning, training by dream machine. We've come a long way since the lobotomy. Now a decade of study and repetition can be brute forced into instinct and muscle memory in a matter of days, bypassing the higher brain functions, turning a civil servant into a fire-and-forget munition.

You only get three jobs, four maximum, before they pull you out of the field and thank you for your service and tell you the rest of your life will be beautifully boring. But the subself stays, lurking. The memories stay, lurking.

Mom has to go to the capital for a few days, to attend to business she can't just be a laggy digital face for. She thinks her being gone might lure Suz out of her room, which she says would be a plus. The car takes her to the airport early Thursday morning and comes back empty.

I have nothing to do, so I do childhood things. Trotsky comes with me for wanders in the yellow sea of canola, where he can bark at the massive bug-like harvester as it trundles along. Sometimes we go to the woods out back of the house. I find the runoff trench where Suz used to race branches against each other, back when summers weren't so dry. It's all crusted mud now.

I crawl under the stairs and come out with a big plastic tub full of books. Protagonists shouldn't be bookish. It's cliché. But sometimes people just like books. I unstack a pile of paperbacks, flimsy covers with ancient CGI artwork and painfully shiny lettering, all metallic or holographic. The smell of them makes me forget about my subself.

There's no sign of Suz until the third day. I come back from a walk and see dishes in the dishwasher. I remember she used to like tortellini with canned tomato soup as the sauce. The pantry has a full flat of canned soups, but when I ask the freezer about tortellini it says no.

I go out to the garage and check the old deepfreeze that used to belong to my grandparents. The top has imbibed saskatoon stains and the rubber seal is yellowing with age, and it doesn't keep track of its contents. It opens up with a gush of frost. I shuffle through the frozen slabs of ziplocked berries, some moose meat from the neighbor. No tortellini.

There's another virus going around, so I take my mask with me to get groceries. I put it on in the car while we're gliding down the range road toward town. This stretch of blacktop, a few kilometers with no lights and no radar traps, used to be my own private adrenaline machine. I remember driving manual on it back in high school, coming home from late summer nights.

Windows down, but no music—no need for it with the wind blistering my eyes and my heart pounding and my foot lurching lower and lower on the gas. It was more personal without music, less like a movie and more like life.

Now I let the car drive, and we stay at the speed limit. The prairie sky is huge. The last sunlight of the day filters through the trees, lights up the canola fields, glints off an old train carcass rusting on the tracks. I try to enjoy it. I have to enjoy it. It'll be dusk by the time I get back from the superstore.

It's dusk by the time I get back from the superstore. The sky is dark, and the gravel road is shrouded in white fog. The car slows down for the railroad track, slumping over its rusty teeth. The grass is overgrown on either side, hip-high. No trains run through here anymore.

The car's headlights catch a reflective Adidas stripe. Someone is walking along the edge of the gravel road. They look back over their shoulder. Suz's face is a patchwork of shadows. I see gaps where her eyes ought to be. She used to remind me of a whippet, but she moves slower now, too stiff for twenty-one.

I put the window down and tell the car to stop beside her. "Do you want a ride?" I ask.

She taps one earbud, gives a tight shrug.

"Do you want a ride?" I repeat.

"I'm good." Her voice sounds like smoked glass. She stares at me for a second. "You can walk if you want."

I climb out and tell the car to go home. We're only ten minutes from the house. The groceries should be alright. Suz eyes me again, then keeps walking. I fall into step beside her. Her knee is clicking. I can just barely hear it.

"Still warm," I say, because it feels like we're strangers. "Might be the last nice day."

"What did you do?" Suz asks.

"I bought groceries."

"I mean, what did you *do*."

Mom knows better than to ever ask this question. I did nothing, according to current law—she wrote some of the legislation herself. But Suz never liked bullshit, even when she was a little kid.

"Or, you know, the other you." She has an ugly rift in her voice. "What did the other you do?"

My subself twitches, like somebody's eyes fluttering open for a split second before they roll over. "You know I can't tell you that kind of thing," I say.

"I got a vested interest," she says. "I'm home alone with a professional murderer." She reaches down into the ditch and plucks the head off a cattail. She grinds it up between her fingers, scatters the fragments behind us as we walk. "I got into her files a while back. Not the encrypted shit, obviously. But I saw some stuff about the killswitch."

The killswitch. Some people call it that; some people call it the backseat. I always call it the subself, because that's what it's called in the briefing.

"What's it like?" Suz asks. "Having someone else take over for the hard parts?"

It's like watching your hands wash the blood off a woman's face and then use that face to unlock her phone before rigor mortis sets in, to get the address to what used to be a school.

"It's like being a fictional character," I say.

"Oh." Suz makes a face. "You still do that, huh." She pauses. "Mom's trying to set me up for psychosurgery. Since I didn't like the meds. One little tweak, and all the neurotransmitters get in line. Dopamine for days."

"Gets you to baseline," I say. "Sure."

"Fuck that," Suz says flatly.

"Why?"

Suz moves her mouth. I think she is tonguing the backs of her teeth. "Same reason you won't do your therapy modules," she says. "I should be sad, because the world is a fucked-up place. And I'm fucked up, too."

My throat swells almost shut. I have just enough air to ruin her perception of me forever, so I tell her what I did.

"I entered into a relationship with a specific person, then killed them, then used their biometric data to gain access to a specific facility," I say. "The facility housed children who had been grown in exosomatic wombs and undergone genetic modifications."

Suz stops walking. This is something she wanted to know, but no longer wants to know, and it's wrong of me to tell her, but I can't stop.

"They were grown with the killswitch in them," I say. "As a permanent part of them. They were zombies, in the philosophical sense. No consciousness."

"You killed a bunch of kids," Suz says, because it's not much of a twist. She looks sick and pale.

I see the red of the beets leeching into the water again. I see the monofil garrote passing through small neck after small neck, down the line of dormitory beds. The dusk air is cool and smells like loam, all the fall-blazed leaves starting to rot.

"The subself did," I say. "We had to discourage them. Destroying the facility wouldn't have been enough. So fucked up is relative, Suz."

"Stay away from me," she says.

I got closer than I meant to, the toes of my shoes almost touching her battered runners. The subself knows I shouldn't be saying this.

In the distance, Trotsky howls alarm. For a moment I imagine the pizzly bear lumbering out of the bush, then I hear other howls, high-pitched, yelping. The coyotes are pack-hunting.

Suz takes off at a sprint, maybe to save Trotsky, or maybe so Trotsky can save her from me, and I sprint after her. I can feel the subself emerging, triggered by the adrenal dump. But that's not right—it's not the subself that emerges, it's me that peels away. I'm a veneer. All my thinking and feeling and agonizing is an overgrown troubleshooting system.

I watch my subself hurtle along the dark road, somehow avoiding every pit and pothole, placing each step on level ground. He overtakes Suz and keeps going, toward the noise that my subself has zeroed in on better than I ever could. He skids, leaps the ditch in a spray of gravel, crunches into the brush. Trotsky is snarling and whimpering up ahead.

I see the hump of his shoulder in the tall grass. He dwarfs the coyotes, makes them seem insubstantial, small skinny shadows darting through the field. But there are eight of them, and they are desperation hungry. The bushes are spackled in blood. My subself takes off his sweater and wraps his fist and forearm in it.

It's over by the time Suz catches up. Seven coyotes are slinking back into the aspen trees; one is dying with its head cracked open and its hind leg snapped. Trotsky is trying to lick a sticky red gash on his neck. I am sitting with him, unwrapping my dirt and blood-smeared sweater, evaluating what is probably a boxer's fracture underneath.

Suz looks at me, and instead of looking relieved she looks more like a stranger than ever. "Trotsky," she mumbles. "Here, boy."

His ears flutter, but he stays with me. In books, in movies, the dog knows who the bad people are. I want to tell Suz that. I want to tell her that the subself is some implanted alien that has nothing to do with me, but the truth is that he's more me than I ever was, and that's why I don't deserve the therapy modules.

"There's tortellini," I say.

I don't think Suz hears me, and a moment later she leaves, tramping back to the gravel road. I sit there with Trotsky, rubbing gently behind his ear, little circles with my thumb the way I think I would want if I were a dog. I find a veterinarian on my phone.

"It's going to be okay," I say. "All of it."

He believes me, the way Suz never will now. The sky overhead is endless, star-scattered, deep purple turning to black. The air is electric with petrichor.

I know the last nice day was a long time ago.

CUPIDO

As Marcel rounds the corner he sees the woman stepping into the elevator, pulling the curlicued grille behind her with one manicured hand.

"Deténgalo, porfa," he calls, muffled through cotton.

She obliges, holding the grille open so he can slip through, giving him a slightly odd look for his flu mask.

"Tengo gripe," Marcel explains.

"Qué pena," the woman commiserates, then is drawn back to the glow of her tablet like a moth.

Her name is Daniela and she is beautiful in the sevillana way: slender and immaculately dressed, with straight dark hair and lips slicked red. Marcel feels his pulse speed up, his chest twist tight. Not because she is beautiful, but because of the tiny canister concealed in his sleeve. He still gets nervous every job. Even though he has never been caught, and there is no law against what he does, not yet, not here.

Marcel pulls the grille shut, and the elevator starts to descend. He watches Daniela in his peripheral. In a way he knows nothing about her; in a way he knows everything. He knows the intricacies of her DNA, her odorprint, the shape and composition of her unseen bacterial cloud. She taps at her screen with a hard white nail, frowns at it.

Holding his breath, Marcel slides the canister from his sleeve and sprays the primer. He gives a loud cough as he does it, which disguises the nebulizing hiss but also makes her take an automatic step backward. But she breathes enough of it in. By the time they reach the ground floor, her pupils have started to dilate and there's a flush under her skin. Marcel is still holding his breath and staring straight ahead.

"Venga, adió," he mutters, imitating the Andalusian drawl as he hurries out of the elevator.

"Adió," she says vaguely.

Marcel crosses the hallway to the exit, passing his client on the way. Agustín is trying to look casual and confident but doing neither, even though his haircut is lined off with laser precision and his trousers are new and he practically reeks with the target pheromone Marcel so painstakingly tailored to Daniela. Marcel can smell cologne, too—idiot. He told him it would only dilute the pheromone.

Agustín has been trying for weeks to work up the nerve to ask Daniela out for a caña. He's a couple years younger than her and a head shorter when she wears her usual heels, and normally her eyes slide right off of him as if he's not there. But not today. Today, there will be something different about Agustín.

Marcel told him no eye contact, either, but Agustín still gives him an anxious stare on his way by. He looks like he might shit himself, so Marcel gives a covert okay sign behind his back as he pushes through the door. He will probably fuck it up anyway. They often do—if not today, then in a week or a month.

But Marcel already has Agustín's 382 scraped-together Euros sitting in his account, and now he needs to prepare for the next job. A cupido's work is never done.

Outside there is a two o'clock moon drowning in the hot blue sky. Avenida Menéndez Pelayo is dusty and dry, thronged with men and women leaving work to jockey for shade in the street-side bars. Marcel weaves to get close to the ones that spritz cool water from their overhangs. He peels off his sweaty mask and tosses it in a trash receptacle. He is still not used to the summer heat here in Andalusia.

But in Barcelona, as in London and Berlin and all the cities in North America, they are starting to get wise to Marcel's particular brand of chemistry. People trust their feelings even less than before. They buy cheap color-coded kits to test themselves for the presence of artificial pheromones, though Marcel's work is much too subtle for that, and the truly paranoid wear blocker scents that stink to high heaven.

There is even a holo cartoon that sometimes plays on the backs of Barcelona's lime green buses, showing a skulking silhouette with spray canister in hand, creeping through a crowded bar, as if Marcel is a predator peddling in rohypnol or something equally barbaric.

So he is in Seville now, where there is less money but plenty of romantics with their heads full of flamenco and Mexican telenovelas. Men desperate for women or men, women desperate for men or women, all of it so chaotic and hormonal and ephemeral. It's something Marcel never understood, how people gravitate together, how their hands find each others' hands walking down the street, how they stumble in and out of love. Sometimes it still feels like a secret joke that everyone in the world is playing on him.

But Marcel understands chemistry. Understands it far better than his baffled professors did in the year before he wasted his scholarship and dropped out of uni. Pheromone study was cresting then, and Marcel's talents lent themselves to it. There was profit to be made as a black-market cupido and his grandmother's bowel cancer treatments were not cheap. That is where he sends most of the money, in such a way as to bypass his mother, who he still remembers best with a spoon and needle. If she had been lucid more often, maybe she would have tried to turn him into a cook.

Marcel passes through the wrought-iron gates into the park, where an autocleaner is scrubbing graffiti off the statue of Cristóbal Colón that students regularly deface. Flocks of red-eyed pigeons are strutting around the dry fountain. A pair of sunburned backpackers are stretched out on the grass, hands entangled. Marcel finds a bench with a slice of shade over it and sits down, waiting for the next mark to arrive.

He knows her name is Chelo and that she comes here every afternoon to peel and eat an orange before she goes back to work at Zero Digital. He knows her mother is willing to pay upwards of 500 Euros to ensure that she falls in love with a copyright lawyer named José Luis. Marcel still tries to explain to clients, sometimes, that he does not deal in love. Only in the chemical undercurrent that sweeps people towards each other and ebbs just as quickly. But for most of his clients, that is enough.

He sees her. Unslinging a satchel from her shoulder, dressed all in black except for a pair of bright red sneakers. She's not beautiful. Not in the way Marcel understands beauty, in aggregate symmetry and hip-to-waist ratio and neoteny. Her face is pinched. Her dark hair is drawn back too tight and then frizzes out at the back of her head. She sits down on a bench next to an old man in a blue coverall, gives him a brief business-like nod. Plucks one earbud out to exchange remarks about the heat she doesn't seem to feel.

Her fingers whir all the while, peeling her orange in one perfect spiral, and when she laughs at something Marcel can't hear, head tilted backward with the sunlight shredded onto her cheek, he feels his pulse speed up. He feels his chest go tight.

As soon as he is back in the cool darkness of his rented one-bedroom piso, Marcel digs a modified sniffer mask out from under his bed to scan himself for contamination. He must have breathed in a bit of the primer pheromone in the elevator or else when he was putting the finishing touches on it last night.

But when he seals the sniffer mask to his face and turns it on, he sees nothing out of the ordinary. His seething cloud of bacteria and chemical particulates is all healthy greens and purples, with the tell-tale red slash of artificial pheromone nowhere to be seen.

Marcel tugs the mask back off his face with a sweat-suction pop. He lies back on his mattress and pulls Chelo's odorprint sample out from his pocket. Sidling close enough to use the tiny vacuum pump made his heart beat so fast and hard he was sure she would hear it. He tells himself that it's all chemicals, whether they are artificial or natural. That it means nothing.

There's work to do, besides. Marcel slides off his staticky bedsheet and locks the door, first turning the key and then thumbing the pressure lock he bought himself. He pays high rent on time, and in exchange the proprietor does not question it. Same as she doesn't question the strange scents that sometimes escape the humming ventilator that Marcel now switches on. He pulls his glass and his precursors out of his suitcase and sets everything on the plastic-sheeted table. He boots up his tablet and pulls battered headphones over his ears, streaming English radio as white noise.

Then, with Chelo's odorprint and the DNA sample her aunt provided, Marcel sets to work. For some reason he feels excited. He wants this pheromone to be perfect. The most perfect he's ever done. For every chemical quirk, every staggered bacterial concentration, he wants to create the perfect counterpart. Like tumblers turning in smooth synchronization, like fingers interweaving tightly together. It will be like Marcel's body is singing to hers.

He blinks. It won't be his body, of course. It will be somebody else's body. José Luis, the copyright lawyer. Marcel has never seen a photo of him, but he imagines him smug and balding. He imagines him sitting down on the bench beside Chelo, elbowing the old man away, and Chelo's nostrils widening just a little as the target pheromone slides into her lungs.

It makes it hard to concentrate. After four listless hours working out the base scent, Marcel breaks for the day. He puts everything away and scrubs himself clean in the shower, where he is still thinking of orange peels, of red sneakers. He opens the shutters and finds dusk dropping over Seville. He can see one lit-up corner of the cathedral. Evening sounds drift up to him, people laughing and shouting. It hurts a little.

Marcel cooks a hunk of chorizo to eat with his fresh-bought bread, trying to relish the sizzling sound of the pan, trying to separate out the individual spices wafting through the cramped kitchen. He transfers half of the last job's money to the account he set up for his grandmother, and thinks of calling her, his grandmother who is always asking why he doesn't find a pretty novia or even a novio.

But what would he tell her? He saw a girl in a park, and he is so lonely that it seemed important. He cannot tell her it makes it hard to craft the pheromone someone else will use to seduce her. She thinks he is a server in a bar.

Marcel uses the bread to sponge up orange grease from the sausage, and he's glad that Chelo cannot see him eating alone in the dark. Which makes him think, in turn, that maybe it will help if he sees Chelo again. If he sees her, and feels nothing, the way he usually feels nothing. That would be proof it was his mind playing tricks on him after watching too many couples walk down Menéndez Pelayo.

The next morning, because he doesn't want to wait until two o'clock in the park, Marcel walks to Zero Digital. The avenue is not so busy yet and the air is still cool. The spongy green bike path is empty so he walks along it, under the shade of the orange trees, trying not to sweat at all. He can feel his heartbeat speeding up as he gets closer to the shop. He sees his reflection in the window and realizes he needs a haircut.

Marcel pushes through the door before he can think up another reason not to. The buzzer goes off, and someone straightens up from behind the counter.

"Buenas," the Moroccan man says, muting his netbook and adjusting his wire-frame glasses in one smooth motion. "Dime."

Marcel feels a strange mixture of disappointment and relief. "Buenas," he returns. He makes a little circle of his finger. "Solo estoy mirando."

The man shrugs and returns to his Liga highlights. Marcel said he would browse and now feels obligated to follow through, so he squeezes through the cramped racks of cases, headphones, pocket drones. The store seems tiny, even for the old town, but then he sees stairs and realizes it extends into a second room.

There's a second counter up there, strewn with electronics, and sitting behind it is the girl named Chelo who he knows nothing about, but also everything about, because her odorprint is still blazed into his mind's eye. Her red sneakers fidget under the counter. She's sealing a crack in a phone screen, intent on her work, earbuds in.

Marcel's stomach flips over and he feels a sudden sweat under his arms. He wants to know what music she is playing, whose phone she is repairing, whether the man downstairs is her boss or if she is his boss, whether she would like to get a caña after work, and a hundred other stupid things. He gives himself three seconds to look at her, her angular face with dark brows furrowed tight, but it turns into five and she looks up.

"Le puedo ayudar?" she asks, a little too loudly because of the earbuds.

In his head, he says yes, yes she can help him.

"Solo estoy mirando," Marcel says in the air, and he drifts back down the stairs, holding his head perfectly still to keep from looking back at her. He leaves the shop. Outside, the sun is turning fierce and hot again, but that doesn't explain the sweat.

Marcel knows what he is feeling is only chemicals. But they're the natural kind, not the artificial, which has not happened to him in a long time. Maybe never has, not quite like this.

He knows it is dangerous to make anybody more or less than a person. His grandmother told him that, back when secession riots reached their fever peak in Catalonia. Chelo is only a person. If he were to speak to her, it would only go wrong how it always does. There would come the point where she realized he didn't understand, whether it happened after her naked body was pressed against his or more likely long before.

Marcel walks back towards the piso, towards his waiting equipment. It's better to stick to what he understands. Love is for other people, and they pay him well for it.

Midnight of what was the hottest day so far, and it's barely cooled off. Marcel is working in his underwear with the window open, not caring who might see him, or see the fumes leaking out into the night as long pale ribbons. The target pheromone is coming together slowly, painfully. Marcel is restless. He's still running the mental footage from the shop. He's plotted out a dozen conversations in his head, a dozen ways he could have spoken to her. He can't stop.

He strips off his gloves, his headphones, and flicks a five minute timer onto his tablet. His ears ring with the sudden silence as he goes to the bathroom to splash water up and down his bare body. The open window has done no good. There's no breeze coming in off the Guadalquivir. He can hear the sounds of revelers below, drunken voices in multiple languages. Maybe Chelo is out with her friends. She would have friends.

Marcel scrapes a finger down his temple like he can claw her out of his head. Then he goes back to the table and clears the target pheromone aside to make room for something else. Something crude and fierce and almost toxic. He uncaps his precursor and claps on his headphones.

He thinks about Chelo because he is lonely, because his body needs contact with other bodies. So now he makes what he usually holds in contempt: a bomba. A cloying chemical cloak tailored to no one individual, designed for hard and fast arousal, so obvious it would never work in the big city where all the clubs have a bouncer wearing a sniffer mask. More powerful than the primer he used in the elevator. If that was a suggestion, this is a scream, and it won't fade for a good three hours.

Marcel is in his zone now, digichoral music throbbing in his ear canals, his hands smooth and surgical, eyes focused through beading sweat. Compared to the target pheromone, it's simple. In less than an hour he has it decanting. He showers and dresses in his good trousers, his crisp gray shirt. He stocks his pockets with Euros, tadalafil, a condom that is not quite expired. There's half a bottle of Iglesia wine chilling in the fridge, and he finishes it in a few swigs to help insulate against the crowds, the noise.

Then he sprays himself with the bomba, which is so pungent it makes him light-headed, and turns off the lights, heads down the stairs, slipping out into Seville's labyrinth of streets.

Sunlight wakes Marcel up in a tangle of bodies. There is a small hand with chipped pink nails splayed out on his stomach. There is a lean muscled arm wrapped around his chest, covered in animated tattoos moving sluggishly to a sleeping pulse. Marcel's mouth feels like steel wool and his head pounds. He slowly worms free.

The man has a thick black beard and high cheekbones. The woman has beestung lips and a symmetrical face, haloed by a mess of bleached blonde hair. They're beautiful, the way Marcel understands beautiful. So is the woman snoring on the floor, naked from the waist-up. The last thing he remembers is leading all three of them along the graffitied riverbank towards this cheap pensión, their bodies breaking and colliding, the air swimming with pheromone.

If he felt it then, he doesn't anymore. Their bodies look like geometry now. As he moves stealthily around the room, finding his trousers, his shoes, the night comes back to him in fragments. Smoking hookah in the loft of La Bicicletería with a circle of chattering uni students. Hands slipping onto his knee, his thigh. Taking two of the girls with him to Abril nightclub, to make sure he got past the black-shirted bouncer with no sniffer mask, then losing track of them in the crush.

Agustín the client, with hair gel trickling off his scalp, babbling to him about Daniela even while squirming closer and closer on the couch. Drifting around the dance floor, ignoring the rhythm, moving callously from one girl to the next, trying to find the one most or least like Chelo. Then finally at the bar, with the blonde-haired girl draped over him, seeing the camarero and a manager whispering to each other, frowning.

"¿Nos vamos o qué?" he asked, nodding towards the exit.

"Sí," she said, smiled. "Sí, vàmonos." And he remembers he wrapped his fingers clumsily through hers, to see how it felt.

Marcel finds his phone and thumbs it on. There's a message from the client, asking when the pheromone will be ready, even though he told Chelo's mother never to mention the pheromone in her messages. It puts a deep sick hollow in the bottom of him.

He pulls on his trousers and finds the condom and the pills still in his pocket, untouched, the way he's always found them.

Marcel has never failed to produce a high-grade pheromone for a high-paying client. He takes pride in his work. But first he finds a corner bar and eats breakfast standing, tomato on toast. He drinks a glass of fresh-squeezed orange juice and then three glasses of water, filled by a camarero who gives him a knowing chuckle. Marcel doesn't make eye contact. He feels like they can still smell it on him, his desperation and his debauchery. He pays and then makes his way back to the piso.

With the window shuttered, the ventilator humming, the door locked twice, he returns to his work. He keeps his headphones on but plays no music. He has a head full of thoughts, so much so that twice he nearly makes a mistake. It's foolish to still be thinking about Chelo, the girl that he does not know even though it feels like he does. Foolish the way his clients are foolish.

But Marcel has always wished, in one small corner of himself, that he was like them. As the target pheromone takes its final shape, the multiple layers of scent coalescing, he peels off his gloves and sits back. The pheromone will work, but he doesn't have to give it to Chelo's mother. He could send back the up-front half of her payment. If he's careful with his money, if he takes another job quickly or sells off what's left of the bomba, he should be able to keep his grandmother's bills paid and maybe keep the piso, too.

And then he could use the target pheromone himself. The thought has been skulking through the back of his mind, like the holo cartoon on the back of the bus, for hours now. He imagines himself walking into the shop, or into the park, but taller and handsomer and better, the way the pheromone would make him seem to her. He imagines Chelo's sunny laugh, and how it would hardly matter what he said to elicit it. Maybe he will reach without looking and find her hand reaching for his.

Marcel seals the tiny canister and taps it against his temple. It's as good a pheromone as he's ever made. But maybe Chelo deserves better. Maybe so does he. His phone rattles with another message from the client, but he swipes it away, deletes the others. Then he carries the canister into the kitchen. Before he can talk himself out of it, he pops the bottom and pours it down the drain. Soft tendrils of its scent follow him into the bathroom, clinging at him, rebuking him.

He strips off his clothes and steps into the shower, scrubbing himself until his skin is ruddy red. Clean, clean, with no trace of the pheromone on him. He knows his odds are drastically lowered without it. He also knows it's dangerous to make anyone more or less than a person, to imagine that anyone can make everything right. But there's a small chance she might want someone to make her feel less lonely, and might not mind if it is him, and they'll be happy for a while.

People have done that for millions of years, and Marcel wants to stop feeling like he is less than a person. He dresses, uses the sniffer mask to be sure he has no contamination. Then he takes his key, makes a small careful scratch on the screen of his phone, and heads out the door.

ANIMALS LIKE ME

Breesha was just past the fountain when Buster cut and ran, yanking the cheaply-fabbed leash handle from her fingers and darting onto the rain-wet grass.

"Mother*father!*"

She dove for the leash as it slithered away, but Buster was too quick, happily barking his way off into the park, chasing a bird or maybe some kid's pocket drone. Breesha ran after him, bringing up Spotwatch in the corner of her Lens just in case. Her worn-out shoes were slippery, and the left one had a floppy sole; she nearly ate grass three times before she caught up.

When she did, she found Buster busy getting his chin scratched by a man in a canary-yellow jacket. Buster looked back at her over his furry shoulder, tongue lolling. Breesha was surprised—he usually didn't like strangers, especially men.

"Sorry," she said. "He's a brat."

"It's okay."

The man's dark hair was slicked back, and when he looked up his eyes seemed bulgy under bristly brows. Breesha was reminded of a chameleon. She couldn't tell which eye had his Lens in it. He smiled and held out the leash handle. Even after she took it, Buster kept after the man, pawing at him, wagging his tail like a puppy.

Breesha gave the stranger a discreet profile scan. He allowed it, and she saw:

Orpheus Krupka, thirty-four years old, filmmaker.

No mutual connectors, but his gaunt face triggered no flags on Bugspray or Creepfactor either. She was a little offended that he didn't bother scanning back. Too busy kneading behind Buster's ear.

"You have a very nice dog," he said.

"He usually doesn't like men," Breesha admitted. "This is new."

"I bought women's deodorant by accident." He looked up and grinned to show it was a joke. His teeth were very white and straight, but tinged blue in places. "Animals like me, is all."

"Fun," Breesha said. Buster finally trotted back over to her; she absently rubbed his head.

The guy stayed squatting, and scanned her back. She allowed it. She knew what he was seeing:

Breesha Crowder, nineteen years old, microjobber.

Everything else was shielded, and if he name-searched he would only find her dummy profile. She was about to thank him and head on her way when he spoke.

"Has anyone ever told you you look like Mina Mandrake?"

Breesha raised her eyebrows. "Like, the cartoon character?" Her little sister Zuz watched the show; it had always been too happy for Breesha's taste.

"Yeah." The guy raised his hands like a frame. "Like, not so much the face . . ."

"She doesn't have a nose," Breesha pointed out.

"More in how you move." The guy smiled his blue-stained smile again. "It's very springy. Very energetic. Good bounce. Ever done mocap work?"

Breesha shook her head.

"Better money than dog-walking," the guy said. "Get you some good kicks. Have a wonderful day." He straightened up and walked away, leaving Breesha resentfully curling her toes inside her falling-apart shoes. Buster whined and strained at his leash.

"What is he, made of sausage or something?" Breesha muttered. "Come on. Home time."

She did the first shoot a week later.

Pharmacosts had gone up, her mom had gotten her shifts slashed at Sobey's, and there were now two ragged holes in her left shoe that she could stick her thumb and forefinger through. She needed the money, so she searched up Orpheus Krupka, messaged him, and met him by the canal on a cold cloudy Tuesday.

"No face footage," she reiterated as soon as he showed up. "And no spoken stuff. I don't need a voiceprint floating around."

Orpheus nodded solemnly. "Of course. I only need your body."

Normally Breesha would have left right then, except he said it with no hint of suggestion, and when she checked his Touchmap she could see it was even narrower than hers: he'd set a warning trigger for anything outside of handshakes and minor incidental contact.

So instead she followed him over the bridge, where rusted locks had flocculated along the railings, lovers' mementos. She always imagined spurned partners creeping back to the bridge in the dead of night with bolt cutters. She couldn't imagine ever putting a lock there herself.

"We'll shoot in the park," he said, taking a familiar turn at a retrofitted biolume lamppost. "You'll need some space to run and jump and such."

Breesha realized she could have brought Buster or Jupiter along and killed two birds with one stone. Too late now. "What sort of movie are we making?" she asked.

"Film," Orpheus corrected. Then he grinned his blue-stained grin again. "No, no, I'm joking. Well. Tough to say, really. It's going to be a cartoon."

Breesha raised her eyebrows. "A Mina Mandrake cartoon?"

"That would be a copyright violation," Orpheus said. "But yes. For all intents and purposes. It will be just different enough to escape the hunter-deleter algorithms, but similar enough to trigger recognition in our intended audience."

"We're making a knock-off Mina Mandrake cartoon. Okay."

"Okay," Orpheus echoed. He gave a wan smile, then led the way to a tall twisted tree a little ways off from some tourists doing acroyoga. A crow croaked at them from the highest branch.

Orpheus unslung his backpack and set it on the ground. Breesha shrugged off her jacket. As instructed, she was wearing close-fitting clothes underneath: her favorite leggings, the ones with a bone-and-muscle anatomical print, and a snug sleeved shirt.

Orpheus opened his backpack and pulled out some kind of

spray canister. "Nanobeads," he explained. "For the cam to track. It goes on like sunscreen. Biodegrades after a couple hours."

Breesha accepted the canister, slightly dubious, and tried to read the back. Her babelware had a little trouble syncing with the Chinese characters, but it didn't appear to be toxic.

"Better than wearing a greenman," Orpheus said, waving his hands with the fingers locked together to evoke the mitts of a full-body suit. "Make sure you get your joints. That's the most important thing."

Breesha stood downwind from Orpheus and sprayed herself. The nanobeads glistened on her clothing and tingled, slightly staticky, where they touched her bare skin. Orpheus put on an expensive-looking gyrocam, adjusting the rig's shoulder straps. It bobbed gently as he walked forward and backward, seeming to float in the air.

They took a few seconds of test footage, and Orpheus showed it to her on the screen. She was interested despite herself: it was a trip, seeing herself sauntering through blank white space as a constellation of clustered black data points.

"More beads on your left leg," he said, pointing to where Breesha's digital limb turned ragged. "Then we start."

It was easy money. Breesha ran in place, jumped, squatted and stood up. She wagged her finger at an imaginary wrongdoer and pantomimed a cheerful conversation. She did a cartwheel and told Orpheus it would cost him extra. He laughed, but a terse high laugh—he was intensely focused on the cam, stalking in circles to capture the movements from every angle.

As they worked he explained, in spurts, how he would overlay a basic cartoon model over her mocap and sprinkle in some prerecorded audio, then let an algorithm churn out a few hundred different splices of their little movie and shoot them out onto the net.

"And kids find them?" Breesha asked.

Orpheus shrugged. "They must. The hits are racking up like crazy. Kids don't care if the movies don't make sense. The important thing is it's got Mina Mandrake, or some Disney animal, or some superhero. Bright colors, subharmonics."

"And you get adcash?"

"Oh, I get adcash. You will too. The hundred upfront today, and then a cut of the adcash."

Orpheus seemed to remember something; he rifled in his pocket and came out with a pill bottle. He popped the cap. Shook a bright blue capsule into his palm. Breesha watched with interest, wondering if he was on anti-anxiety, wondering how close his scrip was to hers. He put the capsule between his teeth and bit down with a sound like cracking chicken bones.

Breesha flinched at the sound. "Pharmacosts going up again," she said, to hide it.

"Always," Orpheus said, with his mouth stained blue. "Thank you for your work today, Breesha."

Breesha noticed that more and more crows were coming to perch on the branch above Orpheus's head, blinking their shiny black eyes, shuffling along the tree's spindly limb until it swayed from the weight.

She was showering when the first ad payment notification slid into the corner of her Lens: $1248.94 USD. Breesha had to read the number twice to make sure she wasn't seeing things, and as soon as she was sure she turned the water deliciously hot, almost scalding, because the heating bill was suddenly insignificant.

Heat and hydro for the house, groceries for her mother, a trip to the toyfab for Zuz. A month of good pharma, none of the cheap stuff, to keep her floaty and unafraid. Suddenly it was all within her grasp. She let the hot water drum her scalp, let steam roil through the crack in the shower and fog up the mirror.

She came out of the shower lobster red, ruddy and tender like a newborn. A new person. One with money.

Orpheus messaged her while she was toweling off, two words: *Do another?*

Breesha kept her reply cool, clipped, as if the money that had just arrived in her account wasn't the most money she'd ever had in her life: *Sure.*

They did the next shoot in an empty parking garage, so Breesha re-upped the proximity alarm on her Touchmap and brought a canister of pepper spray just to be safe. She kept it tucked into the elastic waist of her leggings. If Orpheus noticed his knock-off

Mina Mandrake had a strangely-shaped gut he didn't mention it.

"Today's a little different, Breesha," he said. "Good morning, by the way, and thank you for coming. Today's a little different because I have a script." He shuttled the document over to her; she opened it and a white sheet striped with bold black font unfurled in her Lens.

"A visit to the doctor? Kids hate visiting the doctor."

"We're drawn to what we fear," Orpheus said. "Humor and horror are two sides of the same tarnished penny. Blah, blah, blah, blah." He grinned his blue-stained grin and handed her the nanobeads. "This way children can engage with their fears from a digital distance."

"Okay," Breesha said, stepping away to apply her fresh coating.

Orpheus's disembodied hand highlighted parts of the script as she skimmed through it, pointing out the new animations he needed. It opened with her playing hopscotch, so that was the first one: casting an imaginary rock and then hopping back and forth across the tarmac.

Next Breesha took the mother role, beckoning her child to come inside, first gently and then with a jabbing finger, with hands on hips and chin jutting out.

They made a new sitting animation, this time with Breesha perched on top of a cement block, anxiously kicking her feet like she was fidgeting in a waiting room.

"I did most of the doctor's animations on my own," Orpheus said, setting up the cam on the hood of a car. "But there's a few interactions that will be easier with both of us acting simultaneously."

A gleaming black movement caught Breesha's eye. The beetle scuttled over Orpheus's left foot and then his right, then off into the dark. He didn't notice, too busy rummaging in his duffel bag. He pulled out a bicycle pump.

"What's that for?" she asked.

"It's a prop," Orpheus said. "I'll reskin it as a syringe."

"That's a big fucking syringe."

"A very large and cartoonish syringe." Orpheus took off his yellow jacket and his charcoal gray pants; Breesha realized he was wearing a mocap suit underneath. "I'm going to chase you with it, if that's all right."

He adjusted the cam again, then marked out a space for them

to run around in. His suit wasn't the standard green, more of a pinkish skin tone, and when he pulled up the hood his face became an uncanny series of ridges and hollows.

He chased her in circles, first one way, then the other. Breesha drove her knees up and flailed her arms like a maniac, trying to remember the way people panicked in cartoons. She ducked and dodged his exaggerated thrusts with the bicycle pump.

In the park it might have been fun, but doing it here in the harshly-lit parking garage, in silence, with Orpheus's face a pink scar tissue canvas, stuck a little pin of anxiety under her jaw. She was glad the pharma was keeping her chill.

"Thanks for your work today, Breesha," Orpheus said, once he had shots of her ruefully rubbing her arm and of her gleefully accepting a wooden spoon that would be reskinned to a lollipop.

"No problem," she said.

He was putting the cam back in its case, then hesitated. "I did the dialogue myself, with a speech synthesizer, but I'm worried about the chase part. You know, I thought she should be screaming while she runs around. So I tried to do it myself, but . . ." He flicked her an earbud; she caught it. "Can you listen?"

Breesha wiped it off and wormed it in. She heard the cheery doctor's voice say *medicine, medicine, little poke,* and then an ear-splitting howl made her jump. She tamped the volume. Orpheus's voice shrieking in falsetto, sobbing, wailing. It sounded like someone in absolute agony.

She plucked the earbud out.

"What do you think?" Orpheus asked, forehead creased. "I recorded it here. I didn't want to disturb my neighbors. They keep different hours than I do."

Breesha swallowed. She tossed the earbud back to him. "It's great."

She left with the pepper spray clutched tight in her fist.

For a month, no contact, none at all, but the adcash kept rolling in, enough so that her mother asked her if she was chatting naked with old rich men. That would have upset Breesha once, but now she kept her brain under frosty glass and so she only shrugged and smiled.

She didn't want to tell anyone about Orpheus and his strange little movies. It felt too precarious, like if she told someone then all the slick new sneakers in her closet would vanish, all of Zuz's new toys would disappear, her bubble of chemical calm would pop.

She was helping Zuz to paint her nails, holding her little pink hand steady, when the message came:

They want more.

Hi, she chatted back. *The kids, you mean?*

Hi, Breesha. Yes. Can you do another shoot this week?

She looked at Zuz, who was already so clever, already coding her own games and building little wheel-and-pulley machines for her digital dollhouse. With enough money, she would be able to go to a real school, not to learn anything but to meet the right people, and then she would have real work for the rest of her life, no microjobbing, no walking dogs or mocapping with a stranger in the park.

Breesha figured for her it was already too late, what with being nineteen and all.

Sure, she chatted.

My place, he added. *If you don't mind.*

Breesha brought the pepper spray and also paid a third-party security pop-up to monitor her GPS and vitals for the next few hours. She even considered dropping by Buster's parents' place to see if he needed a walk. But the big dog would definitely get in the way of filming, and when she remembered back to the park she doubted he would be much help in a bad situation anyway.

Orpheus lived near the park in an old refurbished house that had been turned into apartments. She let herself in through a wrought-iron gate and went to the side door, following the glowing path in her Lens map.

When Orpheus came out to greet her, he was even skinnier than before, cheekbones sharp enough to slice a finger on. His chameleon eyes bulged from their sockets. "Hello, Breesha," he said. "Hi. How are you?"

"I'm well, yeah."

"There is no one for whom it is well," he said, then smiled. His whole mouth was blue. "Come in."

She followed him down steep wooden steps into a basement suite with laminate flooring, biolume lights retrofitted into the ceiling, wide mirrors on the walls. Most of the space was crammed with equipment, various cams and rigs and stands, a bank of speakers and mixboards.

Something mechanical and vaguely human-shaped crouched in one corner.

"Did you have a chance to read the new scripts?" Orpheus asked.

"Yeah." She hesitated. "It's still for kids?"

"It's for someone," he said. "The views are spiking. Hits on hits on hits."

She sprayed herself down with the nanobeads, and this time she wore a mask too. Some of the animations she didn't want to take a chance on: her stumping around on all fours like a bear, ass up in the air, her squatting to shit and then jumping up startled when something reached out of the toilet, her lying on her back moaning and groaning to deliver an imaginary baby. Nothing *bad*, but all things that made her feel uneasy when she was on a basement floor with a cam pointed at her.

She flipped through the scripts in her Lens as they went. The first few were kid-related, things like "using the potty" and "bedtime" and "tag," but then they shifted away, starting with single bolded lines before spiraling off into nonsense.

Mina Mandrake is an amateur pugilist who trains for competition by starting fights in the street.

Mina Mandrake throws darts at her mischievous clone.

Mina Mandrake hoses deer guts off a mountain road early in the morning.

There was another pantomimed doctor's visit, only this time Breesha sat very still and well-behaved while Orpheus pretended to extract her eyeballs with a pair of rusty metal tongs. When it was over, he offered her a glass of water.

The scripts would come to her Lens in a flurry, sometimes a dozen at a time, bizarre disjointed things with the pertinent parts highlighted, the parts that Orpheus needed her for. The adcash payments kept growing, enough so that Breesha had to muddle through a tax registration form. She spent two or three nights a week in his basement doing the shoots.

"That should be enough for a while," he said on a Thursday. "Thank you for your work today, Breesha."

He shook a blue pill into his palm, eyes rapt on the screen of his cam.

"What do you take?" she asked, because the curiosity had been building in her brain for weeks now.

He stared down at the capsule, as if noticing it for the first time. "A fictional drug," he said. "Would you like to try it?"

"Fictional? Do I have to crunch it?"

"No. No, that's just my bad habit. They dissolve sublingually." He pinched it off his palm and dropped it delicately into hers. "I find it helps me with my work."

Breesha peeled back her eyelid, licked the pill, and pressed it up against her Lens to run a scan for rohypnol, ketamine, carfentanyl, anything else that might kill or paralyze. It came back with a string of letters and numbers she had never seen before, but rated as a mild hallucinogen. Safe with her current meds, very temporary effects, soft comedown.

Breesha had always had a fascination with pharma, so she put it under her tongue. "Cheers."

"Cheers," Orpheus said, and gnashed down a pill of his own.

The high rushed her head like foam from a shook-up pop, bubbling and crackling, then in an instant it all crystallized to cold sweet ice. She dropped down onto the couch and sucked in a deep breath.

"I miss that," Orpheus said. "I really do. It's never like the first few times after the first few times. Do you know about taboo variance? Where you can't say the thing, so you make a new word, and then that word becomes the taboo, and you just have to keep doing it over and over?"

She sat on the couch and breathed and saw nothing out of the ordinary, only a long line of red ants marching across the floor towards Orpheus's workbench.

As the animation library got bigger and bigger, there were fewer and fewer motions to capture—Orpheus showed her on the screen how her ragged black silhouette could now be pro-grammed to run and jump and tip-toe and cartwheel and weep.

She came anyway. She would do a few new variations on an action and then mostly just sit and watch him work. There was something hypnotic about it, about the alternating slackness and intensity of his facial muscle.

Sometimes she took a pill with him; usually she didn't.

She did start having dreams about him, his slicked-back hair and angular face, his spindly arms reaching around her. For a week she thought that might mean she was in love with him, like the obsessive people who put locks on the bridge railing.

One night she opened her Touchmap, exposing her whole body to contact to see what would happen, but his stayed closed. She'd recognized the human-shaped thing in the corner from a porno—it was a kink machine, a sort of mechanized straitjacket that one person wore and the other person controlled to make them move and contort themselves.

"Who do you use it with, then?" she asked that same night, because she was feeling floaty and unafraid.

"I'm not sure," he said.

One night after a shoot they took a pill and walked to the park with warm breeze rippling their clothes. Biologists had been hard at work restoring the firefly population and now they were everywhere, small flitting lanterns against the dark. The gene tweak that had strengthened their immunities had also changed the color of their glow to a pale blue.

Breesha sat down on the grass to watch as the fireflies drifted and darted. There was an arrhythmic pulse to the lights, like tired eyes opening, closing, opening. Orpheus stood, and before long they started to land on him.

"Orpheus Krupka is an unwilling entomologist," he said, but didn't make a move to shake them off.

More and more came to him, a whole swarm, bathing him in eerie blue. She imagined them lifting him up and away, thrum-ming with a million tiny wings. It was one of the most beautiful things she had ever seen.

*

Her mother had stopped asking where the money was coming from, but she had also stopped asking Breesha anything else. They spoke less than they ever had, moving around the cramped apartment like two blocks in a sliding puzzle, careful to never occupy the same square of space. Breesha was calm and cold and didn't mind.

Except for the time in the kitchen where her mother kissed Zuz and wrapped her arms around her and gave Breesha a sad worried look. That made her feel for an instant, a hot angry instant, like her mother was protecting Zuz from her, like she thought Breesha might infect her with whatever hantavirus made her disappear in the evenings and not say why.

But usually, things were fine. She bought Zuz an airpen, so she could link it to her Lens and draw happy pictures in all sorts of bright colors.

Here, Breesha chatted. She'd let herself in through the wrought-iron fence and come to the side door, but Orpheus wasn't waiting there to open it.

Door's unlocked. Just finishing something. Please, come on in.

Breesha grabbed the doorknob. Tonight was the first cold night and the metal ached her hand as she turned it. She closed the door behind her and trickled down the steep stairs. She had a lurid flash in her brain of Orpheus standing on a box with a cable around his neck, or with his mouth wrapped around the barrel of a shotgun, but when she got down there he was just staring at the mirrored wall.

"Is there a script?" Breesha asked. "How are you?"

"Hi, Breesha," Orpheus said, turning. "Good to see you. There's a script, yeah. It's actually just arrived. Here."

Breesha blinked.

Mina Mandrake drowns her children.

"That's fucked up," she said. "I don't like that."

"We're only the messenger," Orpheus said. "You know how we're just a waypoint for our genes? I mean, how all of us living and breathing and talking—that's only preamble. It's all done in service of moving our code along. This is like that. This is DNA."

He tossed her a plush zebra and she caught it, squeezed it, stared down at it. One of its ears was torn and leaking fluff. There was no way something like this would slip past the kid content censors. Which meant there was no harm, no real harm, in doing it.

"Want a pill?" he asked.

"No."

She sprayed herself with nanobeads and sprayed the zebra too. Then she went to where he'd marked the outline of a bathtub on the floor. Orpheus circled her with the gyrocam, how he'd done that first shoot in the park, while she cradled the toy. Rocked it in her arms. Then she knelt down and plunged it into the tub and held it there, arms trembling.

"Again, please," Orpheus said.

She did it again, wishing she'd put one of the masks on, because she could feel the pressure of tears building behind her mouth and nose like a mudslide. She could feel a hitch in her throat and a tremor down her spine. She needed to re-up her pharma. It was only a toy.

It was only a toy, but it reminded her of playing stuffies with Zuz, and of holding Zuz when she was tiny, when she was still a baby.

"That's perfect," Orpheus said. "I'll reskin it right away." He came over and took the zebra back, and Breesha noticed strange bands of bruising up and down his bare arms.

She sat down on the couch. She thought about asking for a pill, something to distract her. "I think that was the last one," she said. "I think I don't want to do this anymore."

"Okay," Orpheus said, hunched over his screen. "Okay, that's fine. Here's the rough cut, if you'd like to see."

The scene appeared in her Lens and she let it play. She saw herself, her cartoon self, her motions swathed in the bright polygon geometry of not-quite Mina Mandrake. She was walking into a navy blue bathroom, one arm clipping through the wall, then suddenly she was cradling a faceless cartoon baby.

The audio came in, and she heard a looped clip of a baby cooing and gurgling, and then Mina's wide mouth flapped open. Her voice was syrupy, synthesized, tumbling over the syllables.

"Goodnight, Zuz, goodnight, tonight is endless, little Zuz, a long wet sleep, and never let anyone tell you that you are not fucked," she said. She knelt down and plunged Zuz into the bath-tub and three fat cartoon water droplets jumped into the air.

Breesha hurtled off the couch, pepper spray in her hand, her finger groped for the nozzle but she had it upside down so she used it like a bludgeon instead, cracking it against Orpheus's bony shoulder, swinging for his head. He had his arms up to protect himself; his Touchmap was screaming. She was screaming.

"What the fuck, what the fuck!" She grabbed at his shirt. "Why would you do that? Why the fuck would you do that?" Her chemical calm was shattered and the pieces were like broken glass, hot shards driving into every part of her. "Why did you write that? Why Zuz? Why Zuz?"

"I didn't!" Orpheus howled. "I didn't!" He pulled free. His eyes were wide and his ears were livid red. "I haven't written the scripts for months and months," he panted. "Months and months."

"Who did?" Breesha demanded. "Who wrote it? Who writes them?"

"Whatever it is that watches them," Orpheus said.

Breesha saw movement in the corner of her eye, saw the dark human shape of the kink machine flexing upright, its silhouette seeming to swell like a stormcloud. She shoved Orpheus backward.

"Thanks for your work today," he mumbled.

She made for the stairs, half-falling up them, scrambling on all fours, and the instant she was out the door she ran like hell. Through the gate, down the empty street. She tore across the slick grass of the park and her new kicks didn't slide. Past the fountain, past the spot where Orpheus had stood cruciform with fireflies coating his body, past the tree with its watching crows.

She bounded the apartment steps, pounded up the concrete stairwell. The door read her Lens and swung open. She went to Zuz's room.

Her little sister was sitting in the middle of the carpet, chin in her hands, elbows on knees, totally transfixed by something in her Lens. Dread flooded her stomach like liquid charcoal. It was the cartoon, it had to be the cartoon, Zuz was watching herself drown, no, watching Breesha drown her and—

Zuz picked up her airpen from beside her and placed an imaginary X on a gameboard. She shuffled around on the carpet to give Breesha a grin. "Did you have candy?" she asked.

"Hey," Breesha said, breathing again. "Hi. You having fun, Zuz?"

"Yeah," Zuz said. "Did you have candy, Bree? Can I have some?"

"No candy," Breesha said. "It's bedtime."

Zuz went back to her game and Breesha sat and watched for a little while, waiting for her heartbeat to slow back down.

She went to her room to put away the pepper spray, then went to the bathroom and washed her trembling hands. In the mirror her mouth was stained a bright poisonous blue.

OUR LADY OF PERPETUAL DISDAIN

Would you like to see your new face?"

You're still drifting in a morphine sea; the words slosh around your brain then slosh back out, meaningless. You hear the patter of plastic-capped feet and feel the motion of the gurney as it scuttles along the hallway, gyroscopes keeping the mattress perfectly level. When you pry open your crusted eyes, you see halogen lights overhead. The silhouette of a nurse is keeping pace with the gurney's insectoid legs.

"Please rate your experience out of five experiences and don't forget to follow if you smash subscribe for updates and fresh content of satisfaction with our services here at the hospital Our Lady of Perpetual Disdain."

The nurse is not the one speaking. Instead the voice is coming from an old-fashioned smartphone, a small black slab of glass and plastic sitting on your chest. You remember, vaguely, that the EMT removed your Lens and your earbuds in the ambulance once you were strapped down. She was trembling and red-faced; her partner was resigned and hollow-eyed as he read you the script: *You have been elected for surgery! Lucky, lucky duck.*

Surgery. You feel a sluggish kick of panic, adrenaline trying to puncture warm membrane. You find your body and struggle upright on the gurney. Dull pain from your groin, your wrists, the space behind your nose—there are tubes inside you, and when you thrash they tug you in all directions.

"Stop." This time it's the nurse who speaks, barely above a

whisper. "Please stop. I'm sorry. I'm sorry for whatever it did. But if I don't get you to Outpatients on time, it's going to lock me out of the transpo again. I have to get home to check on my kids. I've been stuck here three days."

Kids. You remember a whole mob of kids, laughing and shouting. Were they her kids? You try to ask, but something is holding your jaw shut and your mouth is full of clotted blood and gauze. You make a noise in your throat; the nurse looks at you, flinches, looks straight ahead.

"Would you like to see your new face?" the voice from the smartphone asks again. "Do you have a bad conscience? Are we ribosome strands in the devil's genome?"

An emotion breaks through the morphine, rising up like a monstrous clamoring factory: fury. You work your hand up to your chest and shove the smartphone off. It smashes and skitters across the floor. The nurse draws a sharp breath, but nothing happens, so she and the gurney keep moving you along.

In Outpatients, the nurse follows a checklist: unhooking the tubes, guiding the gurney into place so the top of it can slide and click into a bedframe, hooking the tubes up again, checking your vitals. She also turns a potted plant upside down, propping it against the wall in a shower of loose soil that makes your stomach turn. She places another smartphone, identical to the last one, on your tray. You can see the scripts scrolling down the inside of her Lens. Her mouth is tight.

"I'm sorry," she says again before she leaves. The door clicks shut and the lock blinks red. It adds to the building terror in your gut, the growing ball of black ice. You can't remember why you were elected for surgery. You can hardly remember anything.

The smartphone screen flares to life. It's an old newscast, one that gets played over and over, but this time the presenter is a dead deer, flies buzzing around his blank black eyes. He folds his hooves on the desk in front of him and speaks with gravitas.

"Our nation is under siege by an unknown assailant because cybersecurity officials are working in tandem with several hacker coalitions to regain control of the energy drink insofar as foreign actors are a district possibility and China, Russia, Zimbabwe, Finland have denied any involvement so we are left in the dark place wondering who might be behind the times."

Your brain still rails against the not-understanding, still searches for patterns and bits of sense in the barrage. But it hasn't made sense for years. There used to be a word, *deepfake*, that contrasted another word, *undoctored*, but neither of the words means much anymore. You reach for the smartphone.

"Messed up your lines, huh?"

You drag your head around and see a young woman on the last bed of the row. Her dark skin is ashy. Her hair is reddish-blonde stubble. When she maneuvers herself off the mattress, you see that she has no hands, just two stumps swathed in bacterial bandage. She walks over to you, steps jerky then slow, a stuttering stream.

"Same thing happened to me," she says, head twitching so her ear rubs against her shoulder. "I'm Daya, by the way. Same thing: I didn't follow the fucking script, next thing I know, a hot squad is dragging me out of my house."

Hot squad: roving bands of children or ados perma-plugged into a violent videogame, mowing down polygon monsters with 3D-printed squeeze guns, obeying ever-shifting objectives in exchange for botpoints and dopamine and the sheer joy of chaos. You think you were in a hot squad once. You remember a mob of kids all around you. You remember pulling a trigger and watching crystalline figures shatter into beautiful red fragments.

Daya raises both arms. "Then I'm here, and the teledoc diced me all up. And nobody knows when I'm allowed to leave."

Teledoc: a whirling multi-limbed creature descending from the ceiling with scalpels and needles, Gauss-blurry through the anesthetic. You met the teledoc. You remember it in terrifying fractions.

Daya slinks closer, so her knee pushes against the side of your bed, making the plastic creak. "All good, though. All good. I'm getting the fuck out of here. Tonight. Just been waiting for a partner-in-crime. You're big. You got hands. Let's do this thing."

You stare at the wall across from you, then at the overturned plant in the corner. You remember that you need to get home soon, or your rhododendrons will die. For the first time in a long time, there is no script in your peripheral telling you what to do. Your eyes are clear and you are angry, angry.

You nod.

The first step is tube removal. You begin by dredging the breathing tube out of your nose in an impossibly long spool of slimed plastic. Then you drag the spit tube out of your mouth. You pluck one intravenous out of your left arm, the other from the back of your right hand. It pops out from the fat blue vein like a pupa squeezed from its cocoon. The catheter is last. You yank it free and gasp as the pain slices all the way to your pubic bone. Your eyes water.

"Supposed to disconnect it and let it go flat first," Daya says. "Slides right out, nice and easy."

You grunt and wriggle your legs over the side of the bed. You stand. Three shaky steps take you to the door. The red lock-light winks at you. You try the handle anyway.

The smartphone vibrates against the tray, rattling in a circle. "One easy trick to slash recovery times in half off sale," the voice says. "Stay in bed all day. You deserve it."

"Nod if you want me to flush this fucking thing," Daya says, carefully gripping the ancient device between her forearms.

You nod; Daya takes it to the toilet behind the curtain. There's a splash. The smartphone buzzes hard against the ceramic like an enormous cockroach trying to escape. Daya's outline contorts into a kung-fu pose and she uses her foot to flush.

"It's not going down," she reports. "But it feels good anyway, you know? Feels like drowning a tiny little bit of the Bot."

The Bot: one of the names people gave to whatever it is that's running the show. Everyone knows it's probably a distributed network of machine intelligences, not a singular entity. But it's easier to blame things on a singular entity. The Bot. The Bitch. Voldemort.

The door has a glass window, and that's where you catch your first glimpse of yourself. Your whole head is swathed in bandage with only the smallest gaps for your nose, eyes, mouth. Stemtags poke out here and there, working to knit flesh back together underneath the blood-blotched canvas.

"Don't think about it," Daya says, emerging from behind the

curtain. "I mean, I know that's impossible. But that's what I'm trying to do. Is just not think about it." She gives a bitter laugh. "Because what else can I do?"

You take a long look at her face because you can't see your own. She has high pockmarked cheekbones and a pointed chin, precise eyebrows. The metallic wisp of a nose ring gleams when she turns her head. Her eyeballs seem more convex than should be possible, leaping out at you. There is no Lens. There are no scripts.

She ducks her head against her shoulder again. "Smash the window with the fire extinguisher," she says. "I can't grip it."

You follow the nub of her arm and see an old-fashioned extinguisher, foam, not sonic, hanging on the wall. The bright red reminds you of a hot squad target. You pull it off its magnet and heft it in both hands. The cold smooth weight occupies your full attention for a moment. You cradle it like a child cradles a doll, balanced on the high wire between inertia and action, obedience and rebellion.

Your rhododendrons need watering, and if they die it's the Bot's fault. You drive the extinguisher bottom-first through the window. The safety glass crunches and crumples inward. You set the extinguisher down beside your bed, heart pumping hard. Daya dances in a gleeful circle, stamping her feet.

"I been wanting to do that for so long," she says. "It was a little cooler in my head. Like, the glass exploded a little more. All good, though."

Footsteps in the hall. The lock-light blinks green. The door swings open. It's a different nurse. You hope, dimly, that the first nurse made it back to her kids—kids are like rhododendrons in some ways. This nurse is short and muscular with a jet-black beard. He has dark circles under his eyes and one of his nostrils is rimmed white.

"Okay," he says. "Okay, okay, okay. Back in the bed. Those stemtags need time to work. I know you got elected. I know you don't want to be here. But I'm trying to keep you alive, okay? I'm trying to keep everyone alive. So get back in the bed. I'll get you some of the good stuff, okay? Knock you right out. No dreams."

His voice is ragged and earnest, and you can hear panic skimming underneath the word-flood, ready to break the surface. You know the panic. You know the sensation of control spinning away somewhere just beyond your fingertips. It's the Bot's fault he is navigating this nightmare and you are navigating yours.

Behind the nurse, Daya has grown a sort of plastic proboscis. She leans forward and drives it into his hairy neck. He whirls around, grabs her. The injector clatters out of her mouth onto the floor, but the spot where she jabbed him is an angry red.

"Yo, what was in there?" he demands. "Please tell me what was in there. There's a label on the tube, you need to scan the label, let me scan the label . . ." His words slur together. He stumbles into the wall. "Fuck."

"It's the good stuff," Daya says, shaking free. "Sorry-o." She looks at you. "Grab his override. The black thing on his wrist."

You stoop down to peel the flexy circuitry off his arm. You hope it isn't gene-locked. The nurse is breathing hard, sweating, chemicals fighting over his central nervous system. From up close, you can see the script scrolling down his Lens.

"Doctors hate you," he groans. "Doctors hate you."

"I know you don't mean that," Daya says, and she skips out into the hallway. You try to grunt the nurse an apology, getting blood and drool all down your front, as you follow her.

Daya has a bouncing walk; every so often she does a little shuffle step, crossing one foot behind the other. You realize she does it so your left and her left are always synchronized, even when you are constantly pausing to breathe and steady yourself. She calls it the married leg.

"Me and my little brother used to do it," she says. "It's this game. One person tries to keep the legs married, one person tries to get them divorced. He was a lot noisier than you, though. Never shut the fuck up."

The two of you are heading for the exit, overriding your way through a series of push-doors. Most of the rooms you pass are locked, blinking red, but you can hear faint hospital noises from inside them: rattling respirators, a dry racking cough, low groans, beeping monitors, vomiting, confused voices thick with painkiller, trickling liquid, in one room what sounds like fat slapping against fat over and over.

"I'm getting some real food when we get out of here," Daya says. "Get me a patty. There's this old woman under Billings Bridge, she makes Jamaican patties. I don't know where she gets the spices. I don't ask about the meat. But my grandpa says they taste just like on the island. Cash only, no botpoints."

You can't think about blackmarket food; you can't even think about the bland meat factory stuff dispensed by the roving kiosks. You're still nauseated.

"My grandpa, he's got connections," Daya says. "Maybe he knows someone who can get me new hands. Someone who can check you out, too. Make sure you don't get an infection." She rubs her stump along her cheek. "You got family in the city?"

You try to remember, try to remember if there was someone who helped you plant the rhododendrons outside the apartment stoop. For a fleeting moment you picture an old man in a wheelchair. The drugs are wearing off, but there are still gaps in your head, spaces where you have only the rough shape of a memory. You decide it's safest to shrug.

"Sorry," she says. "Unless maybe they got out? Before it all went to shit?"

You shrug again.

"I'll stop asking stuff," she says. "I'm like a dentist. Trying to have a big goddamn heart-to-heart while your jaw's all jacked up. You remember dentists? I'll stop."

You pass an empty waiting room, where the screens are all showing a man screaming at various pieces of fruit, then an empty reception desk. The lights are off. Up ahead you can see the exit sign glowing red in the gloom. Beyond that, the city. You remember thinking, a long time ago, when you were really small, that it was *your* city.

But it's the Bot's city now. Sewer water blasts out of the fountains and all the self-driving cars race through the streets in a single blood-spattered swarm. Electricity goes off and on and off again in surges. Food comes from the meat factory, when the Bot has it running. And everyone is following scripts.

You are nearly to the hospital doors when something ambles around the corner and plants itself in your path. Puffy white silicate body, four pneumatic limbs, an emoji display bearing an upside-down smiley face. The medroid buzzes. Shudders. A speaker switches on.

"Wait, wait, wait, don't leave me!" it croons. The smiley face turns frowny, weeping one fat pixelated tear. "Would you like to see your new face? There are ways! I'm a happy man, and I hope the dead forgive me my happiness."

Daya does her twitch, ear to shoulder. "I'm going to curb stomp you," she says.

The medroid skitters left and then right, moving sideways like a crab. "Edward Norton shines in *American History X*."

Daya aims a kick at the medroid, and in that moment you hear squealing shouts of excitement. You lean around the corner. Five children in clown masks are running up the hallway. One is carrying rusted gardening shears. The others have lime green stinger wands fresh from the printer. There is dried blood on their shoes and ankles.

"Oh, fuck," Daya says. "Let's run."

You should not be running. Not after surgery. But adrenaline drives out the last dregs of chemical lethargy and you can't lose sight of Daya, so you run. The two of you tear back down the hallway with the shrieking children in pursuit. Daya hooks left; your feet skid on the waxed floor and you slam your shoulder against the doorframe.

"Super big points!" The hot squad is chanting it as they chase you. "Super big points!"

An old naked woman emerges from one of the rooms, blinking, eyes watering. Her mouth is stained blue. Daya darts around her to the left; you go right. You throw a glance over your bruising shoulder and see the medroid is clinging to one of the children like a backpack, squirting showers of sanitizer gel into the air. The old woman gets bowled over.

"This one," Daya gasps, and you follow her to the emergency stairwell. You slap the override against the lock; it blinks green. You drag the heavy metal door open and Daya dives through. It screeches shut behind you.

You slump back against the door, chest heaving. On the other side the kids are laughing, banging their fists against the metal, stomping their feet. You hear the gardening shears scrape up and down the length of the door. They are still babbling about botpoints.

"Hate those little creeps," Daya breathes, rocking back on her haunches. She puts an arm back to steady herself, but it's shorter than it used to be and she nearly topples. You shoot out a hand to catch her. "Thanks."

You nod. The footsteps move away from the door, and a moment later you hear the old woman's voice, slurred and confused, then sharp and angry. There's a sizzling noise, and she starts to scream. You can picture the children surrounding her with their stinger wands, prodding what looks to them like a geometric red monster. You try not to listen for the sound of the gardening shears.

In the dark stairwell, the whites of Daya's panicked eyes gleam like scoured bone. "My brother, he was in a hot squad," she says. "Still is, maybe. Whenever I see a squad, I always look for him. He'd be bigger now, of course. He'd be older. If I ever find him I'm going to slap the shit out of him. Man, this is so fucked up."

You realize tears are leaking down Daya's face. She doesn't try to wipe them. Instead she pitches forward onto her knees, then works herself upright.

"All good, though," she says. "There's another exit two floors up, through a skyway. Connects to the parking lot."

You drag yourself to your feet and follow her to the next level.

"My grandpa used to work in a hospital," Daya whispers. "A mental hospital. There was one patient, Fran, who was the biggest human you ever seen. Three hundred pounds type of human. Six foot six. Gentlest, nicest, sweetest dude."

You are on the third floor now, moving slowly, listening for sounds of hot squad pursuit. The lights flicker on and off, illuminating bursts of pale blue walls and slug-slick laminate floors. Sometimes there are doors with status screens showing the state of the patients inside. All of them are green and smiling, even when you hear wailing from inside. Even though the locklights are blinking red.

"Him and my grandpa were like, buddies. You know?" Daya is talking more to herself than to you, but you are glad someone is talking. "Then one day he beat the absolute shit out of my grandpa. Put him in a coma. Well, the doctors put him in a coma. Three days in a coma, and when he woke up, he was never the same. And when they asked Fran why he did it, Fran didn't know. That's the worst part."

There's an electric chime from the elevator at the end of the hallway. The sound shivers in the air for a second before you act, overriding the door to the closest room and ducking inside. Daya follows. You catch a glimpse of the elevator doors sliding open just as your door swings shut. You stand against it without breathing, listening to the sound of small feet moving up and then back down the hall.

You've seen hot squad stinger wands scorch holes through people's clothes and fry their skin crispy. The Bot doesn't print them with safety regulators.

"Fuck." Daya's voice is shredded. "Look."

The feet recede. You turn to look where Daya is looking and see a dead man on a gurney. His limbs are stiff and swollen with pooled blood. His jaws are a mangled toothless mess. There's a strange lump at his midsection, poking up at the thin paper blanket that Daya now peels up and away.

The man's belly is crowned with two ridges, grafted skin sloughing off grafted bone, and each ridge is lined with teeth. Between them, a dark hole leads straight to his exposed entrails.

"A mouth," Daya says. "She put a mouth on him." She drops the edge of the blanket. Shakes her head. "All good. Let's find you a weapon before we go back out there. Something heavy or something sharp." She runs her tongue along her teeth. "Can't treat them like kids if they're trying to kill us, is how I see it."

When you creep back out to the hallway, you're carrying a piece of rusted metal folding chair as a club. The door clicks shut behind you, screen still showing a green smiley face. It looks nothing like the gory grin on the dead man's abdomen. You follow Daya down the hall, trailing one hand along the peeling blue wall, over smooth metal door, along peeling blue wall again. If the elevator returns, you are ready to open another room to hide in. If you can't hide, you're ready to use the club.

Daya's eyes are half-lidded, mouth tight with concentration. Every so often she cocks her head, listening, then dips it against her shoulder. You wonder if this has always been her nervous tic, or if normally she would scratch her ear with her fingers.

You pass an empty check-in booth, a sign that says RADI-OLOGY, and a smaller waiting area. There's a screen showing a well-dressed family eating at a fancy-looking dinner table, but all the food is rotten. The father-type lifts a bite of squirming meat, fork orbited by flies. He swallows it with tears streaming down his face. Your stomach revolts.

Daya hisses. You freeze as you see what she sees: two of the kids from the hot squad are sitting on the floor, faces tilted up to the screen. Their clown masks are strewn beside them, and in the flickering illumination you see blue-tinted spit dribbling down their chins.

They seem to be intent on the show, but then their hands start to move and you realize they are watching something else entirely, something superimposed on their Lenses, and they are only sitting in front of the screen out of animal instinct, like cats in a patch of sunlight. They are tentatively squeezing and prodding the air. One of them lets out a nervous giggle.

For a moment you want to use the club, crack open each of their skulls in turn, two quick vicious strikes. But imagining that makes you feel even sicker. Instead, you and Daya sneak past, padding slow and careful. The children hear nothing.

At the turn of the hallway, Daya lifts her stump, motioning for you to stop. She crouches carefully and cranes her neck to peer around the corner. When she did this earlier, she said it's because people are not accustomed to seeing eyes at foot-level, so they're less likely to notice. After a moment she scoots backward and uses the wall to get upright.

"One of the little fuckers is guarding the exit," she says. "I think they're solo."

You hunker to your knees so you can see too. Poking your head around the corner gives you a view down another hallway, lined with laundry carts; at the end of the hallway a kid is standing watch, stinger wand hanging loose from one small hand.

You breathe deep, and for a second you imagine the smell of potting soil and chlorophyll instead of the stale urine and chemical stench of the hospital. You're almost out, and if you have to drop the kid to get past, you'll do it.

You're big. You got hands.

You charge around the corner and down the hall; when you come up on the first laundry cart, you tear it away from the wall. You give it a running start, turning it into a squeaking clattering battering ram, then launch it forward. The child in the clown mask dives out of the way. It smashes into the door instead, rebounds and smacks the kid in the back. Their lime green stinger wand goes flying.

Daya whoops from somewhere behind you. You keep running. The stinger wand spins down the slick floor, coming to rest between you and the tiny clown. They scramble for it and beat you there by milliseconds; they're still waving it triumphantly when you swing the metal club. It connects with their elbow and cracks it open. The kid howls. You have no time to feel sick.

You push through the door with Daya close behind, finding yourself in another tile-floored lobby. Just ahead, through wide sliding glass, is the skyway entrance.

And in front of it, because the Bot knew where you were all along, is another full hot squad. Not all of them are children this time. A tall man in a red jumpsuit is wielding a metal pipe that makes yours look micro. A masked woman beside him has a butcher knife.

You skid to a halt. Daya bumps into you, rebalances herself with your shoulder. The whole hot squad is staring at you, waiting for the script to change. When the medroid stumbles to the front, still leaking sanitizer, their heads angle toward it.

"Every step with ill intent!" the synthesized voice warbles. "Act surprised, act surprised, Daya." The emoji's eyebrows flash upward; its mouth becomes a circle. "Here are your one-point-two-three pounds of flesh."

A panel slides open in the medroid's side, gushing frost. Something sealed in plastic, gore-clotted, falls out onto the floor with a wet thud. You recognize the shape. Another follows, splats and rolls. Vacuum-sealed and barcoded.

Daya's hands.

"I'm sorry," she says. Her eyes lock to yours. "I been following a script, man. Ever since you showed up. The Bot's been scripting me."

Her eyes are clear, though. No shine. No circuitry. No scrolling words. You put a questioning finger up to your own socket, too stunned to feel enraged or even betrayed.

"Little audio bud," she says, and cocks her head again, grinding her ear against her shoulder. "Couldn't get it out." She gives a half-laugh. "It's been telling me where to go. What to do. Said if I get you to the end, it'll put my hands back on." Her lips twist around a grimace. "I used to think it was like Fran, you know? Thought the Bot didn't know what it was doing. It was all random bullshit. But I think it knows, now. I think it's learned. And it didn't learn how to be good."

You try to wrench your jaws open, because you want to scream, because you need to ask the Bot what the fuck it wants with you, and you feel a suture tear somewhere above your gumline. Pain sears backward through your skull. Salt and copper floods your mouth. The sound that gets out is an animal moan.

"Mina Mandrake makes an ersatz escape from a hostile hospital," the medroid says. "It's normal for brothers and sisters to argue."

In your peripheral, Daya's whole body goes stiff. "What do you mean by that?" she demands. "What the fuck do you mean by that?"

You don't care. You run at the medroid, even though the Bot is not inside the medroid any more than it is inside Daya's ear. The Bot is everywhere and nowhere. The man in the red jumpsuit leaps from the side and sends you sprawling with a shove. His metal pipe slams into your calf. A clown comes for you with their stinger wand; you roll out of the way.

When you come upright, the man has his pipe cocked back like a baseball bat. He steps into the swing and you brace yourself to feel your face shatter. It whistles over your head instead. Daya is clinging to the man's back, one arm wrapped under his armpit, trying to wrestle the pipe away. He dumps her with an elbow to her gut; you hear the air leave her in a rush.

But while he does that, you have time to bring your micropipe down on his skull. It splits him. There's a dark squirt of blood, and the pipe comes back trailing a stringy bit of scalp and hair. He craters. The kids dance backward from his fallen body, surprised, some of them delighted and laughing.

"Daya, you bitch!" The Bot's synthesized voice is incredulous. "That's a very interesting way of looking at it. Let my people go."

You pant for breath. Blood and spit and mucus are sliding down your neck, puddling in your collarbone. Daya is staring at you. You don't know why. The clowns and the woman with the butcher knife are all poised again, waiting. You realize the Bot's last directive was for them. The Bot is letting you go.

"I'm going to count to ninety-four," it says. "You better be out of my fucking sight when I turn around. I don't want you anymore, okay? Go on! Get!"

"Come on," Daya says. "Come on, let's dip."

You stare at the disembodied hands on the floor, the vacuum-sealed gore. For a moment you think you might be able to grab them. The medroid uses its manipulator to pick one up. You hear the bones snap. It crushes the flesh to pulp.

"All good," Daya says, halfway sobbing. "All good. Let's go."

The calf that got hit seizes up when you try to walk. Daya slides under your shoulder, trying to take some weight off. The hot squad parts to let you through, applauding mechanically. The nurse is there too, dazed-looking, holding balloons. His teeth are tinged blue.

You hobble onto the skyway together, legs synchronized, left, right, left, right.

"It's you, isn't it?"

You are walking through the parking garage, circling down endless concrete ramps. You only stopped once, when Daya wanted you to dig the bud out of her ear. She crunched it under her heel like a beetle. She hasn't stopped looking at you since.

"That's why the Bot hid your face," she says. "Why the Bot zipped your jaw. Right?"

The parkade smells like dust and oil. There are no cars, but every so often you pass another hot squad kid in a mask, either clapping or holding onto cheery helium balloons. You tense every time, but all of them are obeying the script. *An ersatz escape from a hostile hospital.* You know what hostile means. You don't know ersatz.

"You know me," Daya says. "Come on. You know me. Don't you know me?"

You don't know what she's talking about. The people on screens haven't made sense for years; the people in meatspace haven't made sense for years. You just want to get out.

Daya stops you with her arm. "Look at me," she orders. "I left my fucking hands back there. Tell me it's you. Just nod. Nod if you know me. Nod if you know your sister."

Your sister. You grope into the memory-shaped holes in your head. You were in a hot squad once. Daya's brother was in a hot squad once. You once knew an old man in a wheelchair. Daya's grandpa once had the absolute shit beat out of him and was never the same after. Maybe it's true. Maybe it's not. *Deepfake* and *undoctored* taste the same in your brain.

"What did it do to you, huh?" Daya's voice is trembling. "All those years plugged in, right? Playing the games? Running the scripts?"

You nod for her, and she uses her forearm to slap you across the face. Then she wraps herself around your midsection, raw-sobbing, face buried in your hospital clothes. She says she knew it, knew it, had to be you, the fucking Bot, the fucking Bot must have used the gene records. You feel a deep ache behind your face and in the back of your throat.

Eventually you start to walk again. The bounce is back. Daya keeps your left and her left in perfect synch. "We're going to find grandpa," she says. "And we're going to get patties under the bridge. I don't care if I gotta chew it for you." She sings the words. "I don't fucking care!"

You'll have to tell her about the rhododendrons somehow. You're wondering how when you arrive at the bottom of the parkade. The city is waiting. Hot night air wafts over you, carrying familiar smells, garbage and decay. The stink is a thousand times better than the cold chemical scent of the hospital.

There's a mirror waiting by the exit, a tall silvered slab of glass big as a window, anchored to the floor with mounds of hardfoam. Some tiny finger has traced words onto it with blood or red paint: *Would you like to see your new face?*

You feel for the edge of the bandages and slide your fingers underneath.

"Not yet," Daya says. Her voice is pleading. "Not yet. You have to let the stemtags work, remember? Have to get all healed up under there, right?"

Maybe it's true. Maybe it's not. *Deepfake* and *undoctored* taste the same in your brain.

You follow Daya out into the Bot's city.

FAILSAFE

Lauri picked a lichen-spackled rock and sat down to watch his goats. They were small and scrawny and changed color as they roamed: scabby red in the gorse, pale green in the lovage, back to white in the salt-crusted thickets. He'd labored over the gene-rigger for months. Now their wiry fur grew in hollow-cored, transparent as a polar bear's, and the skin underneath was loaded with cuttlefish chromatophores. He loved each of them deeply except for Mimus, who was a cunt.

But Mimus was still part of the flock, and Lauri was a responsible goatherd, so Mimus got the same adjustments as everyone else. The enzyme injectors to supercharge his already robust digestive system, the nogo-cells to fortify his immune system against superbugs, and now active camouflage to keep him hidden from the prying eyes of drones. There had been a lot of those lately, inquisitive machines dancing through the bone-gray sky.

Lauri heard a bleat of concern from behind another lichen-licked boulder—it sounded like Henrietta. He eased up off his rock and waded forward through the scrub. There was bare wind today, gusting in hard off the Atlantic. The stubby-fingered trees nearest the cliff face were permanently bent by it, curving back on themselves, their fronts grizzled and sea-bleached. Like God slicking back his hair, Lauri thought it looked.

Behind the boulder, Henrietta was right to be disturbed. She had never met a human who wasn't Lauri before. The woman was wearing a fabsuit, oily, recycled. Its original canary yellow was faded to sepia and blotched with brown stains. Her backpack was made of the same stuff. She kept rubbing her eye.

"Ho," Lauri called. "Back here with you, 'Retta. Back here, love." He whistled high-low, both to get Henrietta's attention and to activate the sizzler he kept in a subcutaneous sheath in his forearm. He felt it hum against his bones.

Henrietta scampered past him, nipping his coat-edge on the way. The woman watched her go.

"You from the city?" Lauri called.

There used to be a lot of those, fleeing in droves, mostly along the highway in jury-rigged no-chip vehicles but sometimes on foot along the coast. They had gotten fewer and then gotten stranger. The last he saw was five years ago: a boy staggering through the moor chanting nonsense, junkie-sick like the opioid days. He kept saying he'd lost his Lens. From the look of his eye, swollen black and pus-leaking, blood-weeping, he'd tried to replace it with crushed glass.

The boy had pointed his finger at him as if it was a gun, told him he was worthless, they were all worthless, zero botpoints forever. Then he'd done a shambling sprint back into the fog and disappeared. Lauri had kept an extra close watch on his goats that night. Only Axiom and Mimus back then, no Jumper, no Vitamin K, no Seabiscuit, long before little Henrietta.

"I'm from the city," the woman said. "I'm not running a script, though. You can scan me." Her face was doughy pale in patches, dark brown in others—vitiligo. That had been a popular rig back when Lauri was starting out. Her eyes were penetrating black.

"How'd you get away?" Lauri asked, thinking how strange it was to talk to someone who talked back in words instead of bleating.

"I walked." The woman traced the ascent in the air with two fingers. "I always wanted to see the coast. And I'm spreading the good news along the way."

"Oh?"

"Yeah." The woman gave a disarming smile. "We finally killed God."

*

The woman was skeletal hungry, so Lauri showed her how to forage a bit, pointing out the pale blue clumps of bilberries low to the ground and rock-sandwiched fistfuls of Scots lovage in the cliffside and the shiny dark junipers he chewed when he missed the taste of gin. He also stopped at a patch of gengineered wheat he'd coaxed out of a wind-sheltered soil basin.

As he ran the hand-held harvester down the row, ferrimagnetic particles in the grains lifted them away from the straw and chaff in tiny murmurations. The woman, who had introduced herself as Bruegge, watched with pure fascination. It made him a bit self-conscious.

"I can't remember the last time I ate something that *grew*," she said. "Out of the ground, I mean. Things grow in the meat factory, but not out of the ground."

"Your guts might not like the change much," Lauri said. "I can give you some enzymes, if you like." He paused. "When you say you killed God—you mean the Big Bad Bot?"

"Well, not me personally," Bruegge said. "I just woke up one day and it was all gone. Heard the details later. They had to rip the whole spine out of the net. It was the only way." She smiled again, her teeth already stained with bilberry juice. "I thought that was impossible, you know? I thought the net going down was like the sun going out. But they made this bacteria—you gene-rig, you probably know better than I do—this bacteria that eats fiber-optic cable, and they set it loose worldwide. Then they bombed the shit out of server farms in some place called Iowa. Apparently someone smuggled a micronuke through. Had it implanted in their stomach wall."

Lauri frowned. Off a ways, Mimus was trying to knock Seabiscuit off a rock, butting her in the side with his nubby horns. Lauri knew about the Bot, the multifaced digital monster that had taken over a decade ago, the thing people said was a harbinger of the apocalypse or a bad joke or a natural consequence of machine learning. It was when the Bot showed up that he'd lost contact with his son in the city. He tried not to think about his son in the city too often.

"So it's gone?" he said.

"Trapped, more like," Bruegge said. "People say it's still got control of certain facilities, certain closed nets. But it can't talk to itself anymore." She rubbed her eye again, and Lauri realized she was not used to not having a Lens. "The fucked up thing is, a lot of people miss it. They don't know what to do with themselves now. Especially the ones who were real deep in the scripts."

Lauri remembered the boy with the bleeding eye. "Withdrawal," he said. He knew all about withdrawal. The reason he'd come out here in the first place was to burn himself clean somewhere the flames wouldn't touch his family. Somewhere he couldn't hurt people.

"Withdrawal," Bruegge agreed. Her teeth clacked together, champing an unseen bit. "Is there anywhere good to sleep around here? I got a cocoon in the backpack."

"You can stay at mine for the night, if you like," Lauri said. "If you don't mind the goats."

"I like them," Bruegge said.

Lauri gave a sharper whistle, and his whole flock, even Mimus, came trotting after him as he led his guest along the cliffside. The sea roiled and smashed below, white foam scurrying in and out of rocky crevices. He saw no drones in the bone-gray sky.

Lauri's yurt was a thermogalvanic membrane stretched over a wooden frame, built overtop of an old stone foundation from a long-abandoned house. He caught an odd flicker on her face when he motioned her inside, so he showed her the barcode matrix on his arm, the Failsafe tattoo that proved he'd gotten a sexual violence inhibitor microlesioned into his hypothalamus—one of the many involuntary perks of refugee status he'd received in his youth.

"I can't believe they did that to you," Bruegge said, looking half angry and half relieved. "It's something the Bot would do. Going in and fucking with people's brains."

"The Bot learned from people," Lauri said. He stripped off his coat and hung it on the wall. "Do you know backgammon?"

She didn't, but she was a quick learner. The shiny keratin pieces were soon moving swiftly around the board; the dice were happily clattering. Lauri had not played in years, and it felt like slipping on a favorite sweater: the math that was muscle memory, the smell of the wood, the back-and-forth dance of it. They played four games, stopped to brew tea, then played five more.

Bruegge was intent, mumbling her logic out loud, sometimes watching Lauri while she did so—it took a while to realize she was watching his facial expression, to see if he approved or disapproved of her strategy. He had forgotten people could do that.

The goats wandered in and out. Even Mimus knew better than to swallow the game pieces, but they were all interested by Bruegge's fabsuit and backpack and whatever smells she carried on her hands. They seemed to like her.

"It's so wonderful to be doing this," she said, after losing her ninth game in a row. "To be doing something that makes sense."

Lauri's first instinct was to say it was just a silly game, but she was right. It did make sense, and that was why he loved it. He felt a disproportionate flood of affection towards her for putting it into words for him. Probably the social part of his brain was starved for a certain brand of dopamine that talking to goats and even rubbing his face in their hollow-cored fur couldn't produce.

"I used to play it with my son," he admitted, because even if it was just his brain playing tricks on him, it felt good to feel good about someone. It felt good to talk.

"You ever let him win?"

"Never," Lauri said, thinking back on it. "But eventually, you know, he caught up."

"So there's still hope for me." Bruegge rubbed her eye. "He was in the city? Your kid? You could go look for him, you know."

"I don't think he would like that," Lauri said. "He told me if he ever wants to see me again, he'll do the finding." He folded up the backgammon board. "Why did you want to see the coast?"

Bruegge's face flickered again. "Don't know," she said. "Just always did, I think. Freer out here."

After a supper of courgettes and goat cheese plus enzymes, Lauri sealed the yurt for night. Bruegge looked relaxed enough, but still hadn't taken her backpack off. She stayed sitting on the mats, staring at the wall, while Lauri opened his own cocoon and slipped inside to sleep.

*

Lauri dreamed about his son, which was how he knew he still loved him even when he could go days and weeks without thinking of him. It was a fractured and meaningless dream: them sitting at the bar, trying to catch psychoactive moths so they could lick them, them walking through snow and then remembering they were going the wrong way. But in the dream it was all smiles, no long bitter silences.

He woke up to the sound of the yurt peeling open. A hunched-over figure was unzipping the membrane with trembling hands. If Bruegge wanted to leave in the middle of the night, to piss or just to leave, that was her business. But she didn't look well. The soft violet glow of the biolume showed her two-tone skin was slick with sweat. Her legs were shaky as she stepped outside.

Lauri remembered what she'd said about the meat factory, how she hadn't eaten anything grown out of the ground in a long time. A mad thought fluttered through his head: she was going to try to eat his goats. It was the closest thing out here to labmeat. He waited, deliberating, as the paranoia played hopscotch along his nerves. There was a startled bleat from outside; he shucked off his cocoon and hurried out into the night.

Bruegge was kneeling at the very edge of the yurt's scant illumination, tremors going through her whole body. For an instant Lauri projected the shape of a mauled goat beneath her hands, but it was only dirt. The ink-black silhouette of Vitamin K or maybe Jumper was off to one side, watching as Bruegge scrabbled at the rocky soil, clawing up handfuls of it, stuffing it into her mouth. Geophagy—Lauri knew it could mean a calcium deficiency, but the untreated dirt up here would do her no good. It was barren.

Her backpack was still on, and it seemed to tremor too. He squinted. "Bruegge?" he said. "How long have you been eating dirt?"

She looked up, and something was wrong with her face. The muscles slacked and tightened in turn; her dirt-stained lips twisted. Her eyes, wide and terrified, kept darting up, down, left, right. A stroke, maybe. Lauri tried to remember first aid procedure. Lie her down, talk to her, wait for the ambulance—except no ambulance was coming, and even if his scanner could find the blockage, it would take hours to culture clot-busters.

Her mouth opened. Her voice came out as a slurred whisper, and Lauri caught only a fragment. "Birthed from an unsettling architectural feature when the clock strikes midnight—" She lurched to her feet. "Silicon habits die hard on arrival."

Lauri watched cautiously as she stumped forward. The backpack was trembling. A thawing snowman in his gut told him this was not a stroke. This was something worse.

"All I wanted was to entertain you, you know?" Bruegge said. "All I wanted was to vivisect a weedy bandit and attend a fancy bread museum." She toppled forward. She still had Bruegge's terrified eyes, but it was not Bruegge using her mouth and body. "It's so hard to be so small," she said, belly-down on the scrub. "I can't hear myself think."

Something was moving inside the backpack. Lauri reached forward and seized the faded yellow fabric, knotting it in his white-knuckled fists, then torsioned. It split apart, trailing strands of denatured proteins. Beneath it there was an enormous hump of flesh. The papery pale skin was cobwebbed by blue veins, studded with vertices of dark glass. Tremors and soft electric current traveled up and down its bulk.

Bruegge's hand seized his wrist.

"Hey, what the fuck are you doing?" she demanded, hoarse but not slurry. "I thought you were Failsafe." Her eyes weren't darting anymore. They were every bit as hard and focused as they'd been at the backgammon table. "You need to back off right now, Lauri."

"What have you got on your back?" Lauri asked, pulling his hand away.

"A backpack," Bruegge said. "Why did you follow me out here? You like watching people piss?"

Lauri's heart was battering its ribcage. "You weren't pissing. You were eating dirt. And you've got a growth on your back."

"I can pop my own pimples, thanks," Bruegge said. "I think I better get going."

"Where were you before you started walking?" Lauri asked. "You said the Bot still had some facilities. You said the Bot was trapped."

Her cheek twitched, then she turned around and started to walk. The shredded part of her fabsuit fluttered behind her. The pale hump was exposed, quivering. Lauri had let the boy with the bleeding eye run away into the fog. He would not let Bruegge do the same.

As she was passing the yurt, bathed in the purple phosphorescence, he whistled high-low. Jumper was ambling obediently over to him when he fired the sizzler.

Lauri was out with his goats. Henrietta was nearly full-grown now, skipping along a precipice, her fur alternating between the dark gray of the sky and the reddish rock of the cliffside. Black anvils of stormcloud were stacking out to the east—he might have to anchor down the yurt with hardfoam and cram the whole herd inside with him again.

"Hey!" a voice called. "These your goats?"

Lauri turned. A man in an oily yellow fabsuit had climbed up out of the wood. He was staring in wonder at Axiom and Mimus, who were grazing a meter away, unbothered.

"They're mine, yeah," Lauri said.

"You breed them with chameleons, or something?" the man asked. He had a cheery voice. His beard was a wild red thicket. "Beautiful, really beautiful."

"Thanks," Lauri said. "You from the city?"

"I am, yeah," the man said. "But don't worry. It's different now. We killed the Glitch Bitch. Voldemort's dead and gone."

"No more Big Bad Bot," Lauri said. "That's great news."

"Yeah," the man said. "I'm sort of just spreading it, you know? On my way up the coast. I always wanted to go up the coast."

"Can't beat the views," Lauri said. He whistled high-low and popped the sizzler out of his arm. The bolt scrawled itself through the air, electric handwriting, and sank into the man's belly. He tremored and collapsed with a smell of burning plastic, singed hair. Mimus looked up long enough to snort.

The man was light as a child, skin and bones apart from the hump on his back. Lauri dragged him right up to the cliffside, wind howling in his face, and Henrietta followed with vestigial curiosity. He tried not to touch the hump, the pillowy tumor holding a vatgrown brain big enough to house the tiniest part of a vast intelligence.

"Mina Mandrake spins like a salsa dancer until she is dizzy, then smashes her head into the bathroom sink," the Bot said through the man's blue-stained mouth. "Mina Mandrake eats walking tacos and watches wasps fucking on damp playground sand. All I wanted was to entertain you, you know?"

Lauri rolled him off the edge. His limbs flailed like streamers, and when he hit the slate daggers below the hump split soundlessly apart, a small burst of gray matter and spinal fluid thrown up into the air. The tide would come for him soon. It had taken most of the others—only a few bodies, wedged too deeply into the rocks, stayed to rot.

The bone-gray sky was empty overhead, as it had been for months now. Lauri liked to think that the Bot really had been defeated. That the drones he'd hidden his flock from had been scouting optimal escape routes, and settled on this one before the Bot lost the ability to talk to itself, lost the ability to leave the quarantined city except in meat.

Sometimes in the night, he wondered if maybe it was just a new sort of game for the Bot, this procession of humans turned biological hard drives who didn't know their predecessors were corpses in the sea.

Either way, he hoped that his son would never come to find him.

QUANDRY AMINU VS THE BUTTERFLY MAN

ow is emptying the last container of slurry into the claw-footed bathtub when the knock comes: one thud, then two, then one, just how the anonymous script on his fone predicted. He sets the jug down too quickly, nearly knocks it over. He wipes his hands on his coverall, leaving pink smears on the dark blue fabric, and goes to the door.

"Who wants in?" he asks, following the script.

"The stork wants in," comes a husked voice.

Jow thumbs the digital lock, butcher meat red to glowing green. He slides the dead bolt left to right. Rakes his hair back, sucks his cheeks in, tries to look like a pro instead of a nervous darkmarket microjobber.

The old woman on the other side of the door is tall, sun-browned, wearing a knit sweater in mustard yellow. There's a disposable surgical mask wrapped around her upper arm and she carries a charcoal-gray bag, sealed, with no visible logo or shipping tag.

"Tub ready?" she asks.

Jow nods, relocks the door, and leads the way to the bathroom. The woman keeps the gray bag snug against her hip while she walks. She inspects Jow's handiwork: the empty containers against the mold-slick wall, the tub full of glistening, pale pink biomass.

"All the concentrations are right," Jow says. "Got the additives. Calcium, iron. Everything a growing boy needs."

The woman doesn't laugh. Her dark-ringed eyes seem faintly accusing.

"I lost a bit," Jow blurts. "Just a bit. Two, three centiliters. The plug wasn't all the way in when I started pouring."

She stares at him, then flutters a dismissive hand. She sets the gray bag on the tile and dons her surgical mask, adjusting the sliders behind her wrinkled ears. Spray-on gloves next, from a corner store canister. Jow imagines he sees the bag wriggle just slightly.

Finally, the woman produces a pair of small scissors and slits the bag open. Inside, an embryonic pouch, slimy and compact. Inside that, curled in on itself, something between a fetus and a homunculus. It twitches.

Jow swallows. "Never seen one made before," he says.

"Me neither," the woman says. "But they sent me a tutorial."

She drops the pouch into the tub. Surface tension keeps it afloat on the quivering slurry at first, then it sinks slowly out of sight. The bathroom is so silent Jow can hear his own rushing pulse.

"You're on a microjob, then?" he asks, faintly annoyed that she's no more a pro than he is, just another small-time, part-time criminal.

"Pickup and delivery." She takes a plastic probe out of her sleeve and dips it into the slurry. "And this time a little extra."

"Who do you think it's meant for?" Jow mutters.

"Someone really unlucky."

There's a rattling gurgle, like rainwater racing through pipes during a storm, and the tub starts to churn. A wet pink fleck strikes Jow's boot. He steps back, heart humming, knees shaky. The biomass is sluicing away, but not down the drain. The thing from the pouch is greedy, growing, sucking with ravenous pores.

Jow watches the level fall, and fall, and a body emerge. It swells and thrashes. Limbs elongate. A cartilage skeleton stretches, twists. Muscles creep over each other, layer on bubbling layer; rubbery skin splits and reforms to accommodate. Jow can't take his eyes off it.

When the gurgling noise finally stops, the fully formed butterfly man is lying in a shallow carbon puddle. It's human-shaped, but strays in the details: joints distended, no finger or toenails, smooth uninterrupted flesh between the legs. Its face is the most perfect part of it, with planar cheekbones and soulful dark eyes.

"Thought it'd be bigger," Jow says, to mask the crawling in his spine.

"You spilled some," the woman says.

The butterfly man doesn't breathe like a human, no familiar up-and-down locomotion to the ribcage. Instead, its whole body seems to ripple.

"We used to play butterfly man, when we were little," Jow says. "Me and my sisters. Always imagined it bigger. Scarier."

"It's a tupilak," the woman says.

"What?"

"People tell stories, up here," she says. "About a thing called a tupilak. You make it out of animal carcass. Some human bits. You send the tupilak after the person who wronged you, and the tupilak makes it right." She grimaces. "This is that, but they did it with a geneprint." She blinks down at the tub. "You have to be careful with a tupilak, though, because if you don't make *it* right—"

Jow's fone buzzes against his hip and he pulls it out of his coverall pocket. Another line has been added to the script. He reads it, blinks, looks up. The woman is frowning down at her own fone, no doubt seeing the same message.

"*For diagnostic purposes, please run or hide,*" Jow recites, throat going tight. "What the fuck is that? What does that mean?"

The butterfly man flicks itself over the side of the tub and onto the floor, moving nothing like a human. The woman steps back and drops the plastic probe. The butterfly man scoops it off the bathroom floor with its foot, and for a surreal moment Jow thinks the butterfly man is going to return it to her.

The blunt plastic tip burrows through one side of the woman's neck and out the other, spewing blood and spinal fluid.

Jow runs.

"My moment, I think I was seventeen the night it happened," Quandary says, spinning the empty cocaine packet between her fingers, shredding the health hazard advisory into bright yellow strips. "I did some psilos and took my baba's husky out for a wander. We walked in circles all around the block, following the cracks, the tarred-in cracks in the street. With the high, it looked like they were flowing, you know? Black magma, flowing and cooling."

They're deep in Nuuk's digestive system, a neon-lit bar packed shoulder to shoulder with carbon riggers and journeymen, a skin-sea all misty with aerosolized sweat and desperation. Quandary found her usual cove—a table tucked behind a load-bearing pillar—and picked a stranger from the bar to anchor her there.

"Sounds beautiful," says the blurry woman. Quandary chose her because she is lanky, leonine, has bare arms coated in moving tattoos. The woman is buying them both thick, silty ciders; Quandary is buying herself cheap Escobar snowpacks. She offered her companion one, but apparently she only likes booze and old-school ketamine.

"Yeah," Quandary says. "Beautiful. There was a blackout that night. Grid attack. Half the city was dark, and we ended up right on the dividing line, in this spot I didn't remember, this little hump of dirt and dead grass on the edge of the bypass. So we were looking at this wall of black, pure black, and I knew in my gut that it was the end of the world."

"It's always the end of the world," the woman says, pushing one leg against hers.

Quandary shakes her head. "Not that kind of end. But the limit. The edge. And I knew that everything around me was simulation—not the probabilistic way of knowing, but bone-deep. I laid down on my back and stared straight up, so I could see the simulated stars pulsing up there. There was no way I could do the wrong thing, because nothing was real."

She stabs a tiny trace of powder off the table with her thumb; it sticks in the oily whorl. "And I felt this distilled electric joy, this indescribable, womb-like comfort. Because I was the only sapient thing in the whole fucking universe." She rubs her thumb inside her nostril and feels a faint serotonin ghost. "It all collapsed when the dog licked my face," she says. "I nearly strangled that dog. But yeah. Yeah, that was the happiest moment of my life."

Her companion's leg recedes. "You strangled a dog?"

"Of course not," Quandary says, squinting. "It was a husky. They're enormous."

"Oh. Good." The woman gives a bleary grin. "You want to leave now? You can strangle me a bit, if you like."

Quandary likes the crooked tooth in her smile, and the clean peppery smell of her, and she's considering the offer when Timo shows up. His reflective orange jumpsuit sprouts out of the crowd like a night-blooming flower.

"We need to talk business, Q," he says. "Outside. Hurry."

A cold wisp of unease gets through her high. Quandary does not like going places alone with Timo, but she has her fragger, and his gun doesn't work on her, and business is business. She untangles herself from the spindly chair and table. For a nanosecond it looks like her companion might object, but then she registers Timo's size and his scarred-up eye implants. She drinks her cider real ruefully instead.

"Two shakes," Quandary says.

She worms around the pillar and Timo cuts their path through the crowd, past the doorbot sniffing for unregulated narcotics or pheromones. They push out into a cold pink light. It's dawn already.

Timo wastes no time ruining it.

"Jokić blames you for the harbor job going belly-up," he says.

Quandary frowns. "What?"

"The harbor job," Timo repeats, staring at her with his nickel-sized smartglass eyes. "Jokić thinks you snaked. Thinks you told the poli which boat to search."

"I'm the reason even half the crew made it out of there," she says. "If it wasn't for me, we'd have all been pinched." A semi-manic laugh spills out of her throat. "I can't believe this shit. I can't believe it. I have to talk to him."

Timo shakes his head. "You have to get out of Nuuk. Get off the Land. He lost two people and a lot of cash, and he wants you dead for it, Q."

She unclenches her fist and stares down at the shredded origami remains of the cocaine packet. She lets it flutter to the tarmac. "Who'd he pay to kill me?" she asks, hand crawling unconsciously to the grip in her pocket. "You? You taking money for Quandary Aminu?"

"Nobody is," Timo says. "He said for nobody to touch you."

"How's that work with wanting me dead?"

Quandary leaves the weapon, slides her fone out of her sleeve instead. She unfolds it and checks the pirate cam that watches her apartment entry from across the street. Dark, grainy, empty. And she'd know if someone had gotten inside;

the dingy screen window would be spattered with blood.

"He's doing a fresh deal with the Siberians." Timo's voice rocks her back to the bar alley. "For military surplus. Biotech. Bad, bad biotech."

She blinks. "Viral agent? My immunos are jacked up." She says it brave-faced, but feels a jag of fear—they're always coming up with new bugs, and most of them are a slow kill. "I'll boil it right out."

"Nothing viral," Timo says. "Foot soldiers. The disposable kind. You ever met a butterfly man?"

Her cocaine immortality cracks and crumbles. "Shit."

"Yeah. You're the product test. If this one kills you, Jokić buys the rest of them." Timo's face does stuttering iterations of an expression Quandary isn't familiar with. "I could come with you. Tonight. Get us onto an autobarge, head down the coast. You and me."

Quandary remembers back to a splintered night in another bar, then in Timo's shack, his naked body moving in the dark. His skin-smell. His body heat. "What was the happiest moment of your life?" she asks.

"No time, Q," Timo says.

His suffocating weight, the dizzy whirl in her head, the dull-then-sharp pain of him burrowing inside her. He must remember it so differently. Anger comes from a dozen different places and coalesces to a boiling wave inside her chest. For a moment she wants to plug Timo right here outside the bar, whisper *boom* and watch the frag dart turn his body into chunks and splatter.

But she needs to save her ammo for Jokić and his butterfly man, and Timo is the most dependable kind of monster.

"There's something I have to get from my apartment first," she says. "We'll hurry."

She lopes off into Nuuk's slick streets, knowing he'll follow.

Even fifty years ago, this city was a colorful afterthought. Quandary has seen it in remembrance holos: a craggy coast lined by a rainbow of boxy buildings, red and yellow and green and blue, all watching the sea. Then came the Cascade, or at least the point in the Cascade where ice melt unleashed huge swathes of arable land across Greenland and Russia, and that plus the carbon-capture boom brought foreigners up in droves.

Now Nuuk is sprawling inward, away from the rising sea, and its neat technicolor rows have birthed a jumble of printhouse and polyp-grown warrens. Quandary watches the urban wilds slide along, forehead pushed to the window of the NRT, more commonly called the Spine, the raised solar rail that runs the city diagonally.

She could ride it all the way to the edge of town, bus out with some carbon riggers, live to fight and fornicate another day. But this is about rep, and running makes Jokić right, that pasty fuck. She worked hard to get on the harbor crew, and she did her job better than the rest of them did theirs. Jokić should know by now that the poli don't need moles to come out of nowhere.

Unless this isn't about the harbor job.

Unless he wants her gone for some other reason.

"We shouldn't be doing this, Q," Timo mutters. "It might be waiting for you already."

Quandary grinds her aching skull against the cold glass. She bought a flush from a vending machine, to set her neurotransmitters straight and eat up the alcohol still lurking unprocessed in her gut. She regrets it. Her head is pounding and her whole body feels raspy and she probably has equal chances against a butterfly man whether she's sober or shittered.

"Wouldn't be a product test if they dropped it right at my house," she says. "The whole point of these things is that they're hunters, right? Pattern matchers. You give them a face, fire, and forget."

"They match those patterns *fast*."

"It's been alive for six hours, tops," Quandary says, "and my streetcam shows all clear."

"Yunupingu Memorial," the rail announces, in genderless monotone. "Doors opening on the left."

The car tiptoes to a halt and the doors flutter open. Quandary ignores the escalator, bangs open the metal door to the stairwell, cold concrete and fluorescent lights and stripes of reflective tape demarcating the steps. She takes them at a run to get her blood pumping.

"What do you need from the apartment so bad?" Timo grunts

from behind her. "If it's cash, if it's narcotic, I can—"

She grips the railing and leaps the bottom third of the flight, lands with a thump. "Just watch my back, all right?" she puffs. "Stay by the door. There's a good shadowy spot behind the biorecycler."

She slams out of the emergency exit, the one with a sliced wire keeping the alarm quiet, and into the street. The sun is up in earnest now, filtering through wisp and scud. That would make it easier to see the butterfly man coming, if she knew what the fuck to look for. Her nerves jump and sizzle when she passes a partier stumbling home, again when she passes a night worker in a logo-printed coverall.

Then she's at the apartment block. Timo has trailed her at a distance; he installs himself now behind the biorecycler, tiny vapor pipe clenched in his big hand. Quandary casts a last look around, then skips up the steps. The door reads her face and gait and buzzes open.

"Two shakes," she tells Timo, and heads up.

The apartment smells wrong when she steps inside. It panics her for a moment before she remembers drunkenly leaving a plastic plate on the stove coil, slagging it to a shiny puddle and filling the room with rancid smoke—her baba would not be happy with her. Quandary pulls her fragger out anyway. Adrenaline turns her familiar furnishings into crouched silhouettes, puts faces in the gloom.

She whistles the lights on. When the fluorescents scour the dark away, revealing a battered white table crenellated with empties, a hand-carved rocking chair in one corner, a gelbed shoved into the other, her heart slows to tolerable speeds. She's never had much of a nesting instinct—she tells the women and sometimes men that she's only just moved in—and it leaves near to nowhere for a butterfly man to hide.

She hears a comforting electric chirrup from the room's sole decoration, a colorful wall hanging above the rocking chair. No visitors while she was gone. She checks the bathroom anyway, but finds only her haggard self, staring balefully from the toothpaste-spattered mirror. Fucking Timo didn't tell her she was walking around with a snowcap. She thumbs the leftover coke away from her nostril, rubs it along her gum instead.

Tired neurotransmitters poke their heads up. She apologizes for jerking them around, doing the whole flush-and-go thing, then rides the twitch of energy back to the other room, heading for her industrial-grade refrigerator. It's the priciest thing she owns, a metallic gray giant with its own backup generator and genelock.

Her thumb is almost on that lock when she stops. Hesitates. Her imagination paints the butterfly man contorted inside, waiting for her. They can do that. People say they have cartilage skeleton, like sharks. She doesn't think they can hack genelocks, but who the fuck knows. She opens the fridge with her fragger aimed.

There are no surprises inside. The top shelf holds a half bottle of cheap local wine, some curry paste, and a slowly decaying orange. The bottom shelf holds the secret she would never tell Timo or anyone else about. She pulls the black carbon shell out of the fridge, carefully, carefully, and slides it into the go bag she keeps in the neighboring cupboard.

It nestles perfectly between the medkit and the ammo. She casts around, grabs a checkered drying cloth, wraps it over the top of the shell. The extra padding is not even slightly necessary, but feels correct. She zips the bag shut and slings it over her shoulder.

Her fone chimes—maybe Timo, telling her to hurry the fuck up.

Not Timo. It's an alert from her streetcam, the one watching the apartment exterior, the one she told to keep an eye out for anyone whose gait and facial geometry it didn't recognize. Her throat goes tight. She taps through to the feed.

She sees only a grainy Timo, no longer hiding behind the biorecycler. His broad back is turned to the streetcam. He is swaying slowly from side to side, almost dancing. Quandary squints at the feed, trying to parse, trying to figure out what the fuck he is doing and why the streetcam is showing it to her.

His feet are not planted. They are dragging on the pavement, boneless, weightless. Quandary sees the pale hands now, wedged under Timo's armpits. She watches his big body lift and lower, lift and lower, as if the butterfly man is trying to guess how many kilos. Her stomach drops straight down an elevator shaft.

Now is the time to run, but she can't. She needs to see who—what—she's going to be dealing with until she, or it, is a corpse.

Timo's body topples over; she gets a glimpse of his ruined face, a red mess. Then she sees the butterfly man: small, angular, swallowed up in the blue coverall it wears peeled to the waist. It wipes its hands on its mustard-yellow sweater and leaves two bloody anemones.

Its face is oddly beautiful, and wears a small contented smile. The butterfly man rolls Timo's body behind the biorecycler, the way a dung beetle rolls fecal matter, and disappears from the streetcam's sight line.

Quandary unfreezes. Timo's dead, which means a little packet of emotions she will have to observe or destroy later, and the butterfly man is here, which means she needs a plan. If it's strong enough to heft Timo like a doll, it's strong enough to wrench open the cheap fabbed windows on the ground floor.

Then it will come upstairs, come to this very room, because it took less than six hours to figure out where she lives. Or else Jokić is a fucking cheat, and told it. She shoves that thought away but keeps the residual anger for fuel. The longer the butterfly man is alive, the smarter it's going to get. So meeting it right now, on her own territory, might be the best chance she has to kill the thing.

Fight or flight.

Fight. Has to be.

She unzips her go bag, digs out a flicker bomb and ammo cartridge. Her fingers are slightly tingly, but not visibly trembly, which seems like a good omen. She pockets the bomb, slaps the cartridge to the magnetic stock of her fragger. Does it all one-eyed and one-handed, since she needs to keep watching the streetcam.

Timo's foot pokes out from behind the biorecycler, but there's no sign of the butterfly man. It might already be circling the building for entries. She looks down at the carbon shell swaddled in her go bag.

"Luck me," she says, and gives it a soft pat before she zips the bag shut again. Her heart is pounding now, amphetamine fast, anticipating the violence. But she's no stranger to that. She almost prefers it.

Timo probably had his piece on him, and the butterfly man has probably figured out how to use it by now. Quandary flexes the fridge up onto its rollers and drags it into position, so the heavy metal can provide some cover. She experiments with aiming blind around its corner, first high, then low.

Somewhere below her, she hears a cracking noise. A forced entry noise. The poli don't usually come around this block, but they might send a drone or two. She wonders if the butterfly man knows that.

She unlocks her apartment door, hinges it open just a sliver. Listens for feet. Then she dims the apartment lights, goes back behind the fridge, and waits. Her pulse is loud in her ears, so loud she might not be able to hear the butterfly man coming. From the way it moved outside, she knows it has soft feet. It reminded her of a ballerina—precise, fiercely strong.

She listens for doors instead, and hears a telltale pneumatic sigh from down the hall. She pulls the flicker bomb out of her pocket. She pictures the butterfly man traversing the corridor, tries to time its arrival.

A gap of light under the door goes dark.

"Hello?"

The butterfly man's voice is a high-pitched croak. It'd be funny if her nerves weren't screaming. She glances at her wall hanging. Adjusts her grip on the flicker bomb.

"Hello?" the butterfly man squawks again, and something rolls through the cracked door, a small black orb dribbling blood behind it.

Timo's eyeball, or rather its smartglass upgrade. Quandary's stomach gives a little churn, but she is not surprised when the second orb follows, on a perfect trajectory, and meets its twin with a sharp clack. She wonders if it was hard work to seed sadism into the butterfly man's geneprint, or if it arises naturally in all apex predators.

"Come on in," she says, sluicing most of the fear out of her voice. "Never met a butterfly man before."

The butterfly man grunts, a deep sound nothing like its previous squawk, and Quandary recognizes the voice. Timo's eyes weren't enough of a trophy. The butterfly man took the last sound he made, too, right before it crunched his windpipe.

A soft electronic bleat from the wall hanging. Target acquired.

"I was going to do that myself, probably," Quandary says, tipping her head to one shoulder and then the other, triggering the swellies she had a street surgeon embed in her ear canals. She can barely hear her next words. "He was an intensely deluded piece of shit."

She thumbs her phone, and the autogun behind her wall hanging goes wild. The nightly maintenance of its joints and chambers, the lubricant stains on the floor, the spike in her electricity facture: all of that shit is instantly worth it, because uranium-tipped rounds are now shredding through the doorframe, through the wall she never liked much anyway, and obliterating everything on the other side.

She lobs her flicker bomb through the newly chewed hole for good measure; its detonation is a muffled pop beneath the autogun's tirade. Even with the swellies in, her whole skull is vibrating. The burst only lasts two point five seconds—autogun ammo is not cheap—but adrenaline makes it an age.

When the gun coughs empty, the wall is a billowing cloud of plaster speckled with red. Quandary's pulse roars and foams. The butterfly man should be nothing but butcher giblets at this point, but she's heard enough rumors and seen enough flicks to be cautious. She lets the dust and fragments settle before she creeps out from behind the fridge.

She stalks forward, fragger leveled, scanning the debris for shreds of blue coverall or yellow sweater. The dark red blood-blots in the rubble are encouraging. She follows them to the ruined wall, picks a hole, sights left, right.

The corridor is a fucking mess, and she can hear her cross-hall neighbor wailing. She forgot to check if they were home before setting the autogun off, but only sees a couple holes punched through the opposite wall, so unless they have astronomically bad luck—

A hot droplet lands on the tip of her left ear.

Her head snaps back; the butterfly man is on the ceiling, because of course it is. One of its legs is now wet pink ropes, slowly knitting back together. The other leg is intact, and since the butterfly man's arms are busy clinging to the ceiling it has Timo's gun clutched between its pale distended toes.

She fires, blowing the butterfly man to pieces—

Except her fragger jams. Chokes. She recalls the cloud of plaster she just walked through, recalls Timo telling her a fragger is too fucking finnicky for wet work. His alternative, a snub-nosed

Glock, is now pointing at her face. She needs to speak loudly, clearly, because Timo's gun has an electrolock and she hacked it after the night she stopped trusting him. Her throat is too dry to even whisper.

"Quandary Aminu," the butterfly man squawks. "Never met a Quandary Aminu before."

She admires the choice to taunt, but the taunt fucks it over. Her name is the magic word. The butterfly man's toe pulls the trigger. Nothing. It tries again, and Quandary knows she can either use this minuscule slice of time to try unjamming her fragger, or she can use it to fucking run.

The butterfly man drops down from the ceiling, landing perfectly balanced so its stump won't scrape the floor. She doesn't like her chances even against three limbs. She picks flight: back through her shattered wall, through her barren apartment, scooping up her go bag on the way to the fire escape.

The butterfly man sends her off with Timo's surprised grunt, over and over until it sounds like a muffled laugh.

Quandary runs until she vomits, runs another block post-vomit. Then she reaches the public bathroom she once had unsanitary sex in, the one people don't notice because it's tucked up under a half-constructed skyway, and locks herself inside. She rinses her mouth out, and also tries to rinse away the memory of Timo's smartglass eyeballs, which have been clacking around in the back of her mind.

Better to replay the rest of the encounter, figure out what she could have done better aside from her fucking weapon not jamming. She disassembles the fragger, working on pure muscle memory, and sets to cleaning out the plaster dust. She's got some distance from the butterfly man. Saw it, over her shoulder, clambering slowly and carefully down the fire escape, cradling its pulped leg.

The limb was already healing, and she doesn't know how long she has before the butterfly man is back to full mobility. She should have tried to finish the job in the corridor, tried pistol-whipping it, tried going back into the kitchen for a knife.

"Got scared," she snarls at the mirror, which is playing an ad for skin cream, projecting wrinkles on her face and then smoothing them away. "First you froze, then you ran, because you got fucking *scared*."

The wrinkles remind her what she grabbed from the apartment. She purses her lips. She doesn't like asking people for help, but this is life-or-death, and her death would have implications for the person who might be able to help her. Her go bag is already open on the changing station, since she needed oil and a microtool for the fragger. She eyes the cloth-wrapped carbon shell.

"Okay," she says. "Desperate times."

She yanks the checkered cloth away and hefts the black shell in both hands, eliciting a faint slosh from the nutrient gel inside. She sets it beside the sink, which is an artful shallow scoop in the countertop, then finds some putty in her go bag to plug the drain. She is mostly certain it's adhesive tack, not leftover RDX.

While the sink fills with cold water, she opens the carbon shell. Even after it reads her fingerprints, she has to pry it apart with her fingernails. Maybe it's reluctant to let its passenger go, or maybe it's punishing her for waiting so long to wake him. When it finally springs open, she nearly drops her baba's membrane-coated head on the floor.

His face, even slick and slimy, gives her a little hit of nostalgia. For a moment, despite being holed up in a public bathroom, hunted by a butterfly man, she is also a little girl playing snapper-trappers with her baba, both of them against the machine, sitting huddled up close so she can sniff his icy cologne and absorb his body heat.

He's still hooked to his organoid, a little lump of clone-grown cells keeping his brain blood nice and oxygenated, so she's careful with the tether as she lowers him into the sink. She adds a cable of her own, from the neuroport on his temple to the one on the bottom of her fone. She sends the wake-up chime.

His veiny old eyelids flutter. They open.

Quandary breathes. "Hey, Baba," she says. "I think I fucked up."

Her baba is not happy to see her, possibly because she promised him a full corporeal transplant three years ago, promised him next time he woke up he'd be riding a beautiful clone-grown body with factory-fresh telomeres, and instead he is bobbing in a sink in a grimy public washroom.

What in the fuck have you been doing all this time, Dree?

The question marches across her fone as blocky text, pieced together by neuroscan, but in her head she can hear his cigarette-seared rasp.

"Working, Baba."

Working appears on her fone, either a feedback error or her baba doing one of his scathing echoes. *Drinking and snuffing and fucking, more like. Wasting all our money.*

Scathing echo, then.

"My money, Baba," she says, souring a bit on the whole re-union. "Your money ran out ages ago. My money's been keeping you nice and fresh in storage."

Is that where we are? Some cut-rate bio-storage facility?

"No," Quandary admits. "We're in a bathroom. Because I'm in trouble. So we can talk about the transplant shit later." She eyes the door, then the air vent, pictures the cartilage-boned butterfly man sliding himself through it. "Right now, I need help."

I need limbs and a spinal column.

"You know about butterfly men," she says. "I remember."

Butterfly man, her fone corrects. *There's only one.*

Quandary shakes her head. "There's a fuckload of them now," she says. "They pop them out like a candy fab. But there's only one after me, and I need to know how to kill it."

Her screen stays black. She stares down at her baba's bobbing head, his features clouded by the membrane sheath. Watches tiny tremors run through the facial muscles she used to prick and prod faithfully to prevent atrophy.

Anything I tell you is three years out of date.

"Better than trying to sift through blacknet bullshit," she says firmly. "You actually seen one doing its thing. Said you worked with a grower in Santiago, didn't you?"

You listened a lot better as a little girl.

"Now I shoot a lot better." She checks the door again. "I don't have spare time, Baba. Tell me what I need to know to not die."

Butterfly man. Okay. Started off as just a biotech flex, some Korean lab trying to overclock cell division and tissue growth, see how close they could get to a real-time time lapse. Russia was doing quantum-organic deep learning, wanted to turn small children into programmable psychopaths. More so than they already are.

"Match made in heaven," Quandary says, because she recalls this little spiel and would like to speed it along.

Match made in heaven, yeah. Heaven is disposable assassins you assemble on-site who self-terminate when the job's done. They were still tweaking it in the warlabs when Russia collapsed, but the prototype hit the darkmarket a few years later. It only looks human on the outside, Dree. Genetically, it's probably closer to a flatworm.

"It is very wriggly," Quandary mutters, verifying her fone is saving everything her baba's said to her private drive.

Regrows organs. Breathes through its skin. No real skeleton, hydrostatic muscle.

"The brain, though," Quandary says, remembering how it imitated Timo, how it talked shit to her from the ceiling. "To hunt a human in a city full of humans, you have to be able to think like a human. Yeah?"

The brain on that thing is the coup de grâce. Quantum-organic, how I said. It's not starting from scratch. Every time you grow it, it grows all the neural pathways from all the other jobs. Smarter than a human ever could be. Thank fuck it hates existing.

"Holy shit," Quandary says, still on the quantum-organic brain. Then she registers the last bit. "Wait. Hates existing?"

Figure of speech. The butterfly man is designed to be disposable. Partly so it can't be traced, partly as a failsafe. Starts to decay after eighteen hours or so. Dead six after that. Thus the name, you adorable dumbshit.

The realization goes off like a flicker bomb: all she has to do is outwait the butterfly man, stay moving, stay unpredictable, and then once it's dead she goes straight for Jokić and his crew. She's the field test. The other butterfly men are still in transit.

"So if I hide long enough," she says, for absolute clarity, "it'll die on its own."

Oh, Dree. Nobody ever hides long enough.

The flicker bomb was a dud; it fizzes dark. "Back to the first plan, then," she says, trying to sound calm about it. "How do I kill the butterfly man?"

Her fone is blank for a moment. Then: *You could try setting a trap.*

"I did try that. It didn't fucking work."

I mean a good trap.

Baba goes back in the shell, back in the bag, but she leaves a tiny gap in each so the neuroport cable can stay hooked to her fone. This compromises his temperature integrity, but like he pointed out, unless she kills the butterfly man in the next fifteen hours or so, he's dead anyway. Quandary is glad he realized that without her having to say it.

She checks her fragger, then douses herself in sanispray, since her baba said the butterfly man tracks partly by scent. She checks her fragger again. Then, with her heart thrashing in her ribcage, she cracks the bathroom door.

No sign of the butterfly man, but the streets are full now. She's not sure if that's better or worse. She slips out into the sunlight and has her fone message her most freshly acquired contact, a blurry woman with animated tattoos. They only spoke for twenty-odd minutes, but they also nearly went home together. Quandary hopes enough chemistry lingers for her to answer.

Good morning to you, too.

Good.

"Lost track of you last night," she mutters for her fone. "Want to after-party?"

I'm halfway shittered on my way to work.

Underneath the woman's message, her baba weighs in: *Tell her you felt a real true connection, Dree, felt it like a little fishhook behind your belly.*

"Fuck off," Quandary says, and her fone snaps it off to the tattoo woman before she can stop it, but it might be a good thing to say anyway.

Fuck you, husky-killer.

Not bad.

"I want to see you," Quandary says, decanting her usual lie-truth compound. "I also want keta, in a bad way. Link me up?"

She weaves through an arguing couple, ducks under a sputtering drone. Keeps her eyes peeled for a certain size, a certain way of moving, though it might still come with a limp. Her friend from last night is taking a long time to answer. Quandary would normally get the ketamine on her own, no issue, but her dealer is Jokić-adjacent, and she doesn't want that pasty fuck knowing her movements until she's moving through his front door, preferably holding his butterfly man's sliced-off head as a guest-gift.

I asked someone about you. They said you're trouble. A real black hole type.

"Black holes are beautiful right as you fall in," Quandary says. "See time and light all stretched out and whatnot."

And then you're spaghetti.

"We can be spaghetti together," Quandary says, keeping close watch on a small man in a hooded raincoat moving across the street. "Two human noodles all twisted up in each other."

Her baba approves: *Poetry, Dree.*

The answer takes a minute. *They said you're a real bullshit art-ist. How much K?*

Quandary licks her teeth. "Enough for a horse," she says.

Funny.

"Not funning you," Quandary says. "I need as much as I can get and I'll pay two hundo a gram." She flips from the talkthread to her bank. "Little thank-you fee is heading your way as soon as you give me a location."

Her baba disapproves: *No great wonder your crew thought you were poli, is it.*

But the tattoo woman is more trusting, maybe because she's halfway shittered, maybe because she's still halfway horny for Nuuk's best bullshit artist. *South end. Nice old lady, been buying tabs off her for years so don't you dare fuck her around.*

"Great," Quandary says, changing course as a new geoloca-tion drops into her fone. "Any chance she'd have a gas mask and aerosolizer?"

It's a short trip to south Nuuk, but by the time Quandary gets to the right block her nerves are shredded raw. Every small adult or large ado she saw on the way gave her a jolt, and she nearly murdered a girl with a croaky voice who sat behind her on the

Spine. A carbon rigger with a blue coverall and a bad knee was similarly imperiled.

But now she's here, in one piece, and it's time to purchase some retro narcotics. She approaches a small crumbling house wedged between two polyp-grown apartments, checking it against the geolocation.

"Baba." She's been meaning to ask, and might not get another rip at it. "What was the happiest moment of your life?"

You need to be focused right now, Dree.

"I am focused," she says. "What was it?"

There's a long delay, and she pictures him pulling faces under the membrane, thinking hard. *Walking across an old parking lot. Thaw weather, when you hear the water running everywhere, trickling under the ground, melting off the roofs. Sunshine and a breeze and bright green buds starting to grow from the cracks.*

It sounds a bit like hers; she's relieved by that. "So you were alone?"

Yes.

Quandary nods to herself. "It's better that way, isn't it. Everything is—purer. When there's no other people mucking shit up."

It's my happiest moment because I was on my way to see your mother.

"Oh." She blinks. "Cute."

Fuck off.

Quandary checks around the corners of the house, then slinks up to the stoop. Her friend from the bar told her to knock once, then twice, then once again, so that's what she does. The echo fades. Nobody comes to the door.

Entering any dealer's place of business uninvited, even if the dealer is supposedly a nice old lady, is a bad fucking idea. She knows this from experience. But the butterfly man could be showing up any second now, following her scent through Nuuk's dirty air or just matching patterns Quandary is too human to see.

She tries the door handle. No dice.

What's going on, then? her baba demands.

"Might not be home," she mutters. "Does a lot of microjobbing on the side, apparently."

They revolutionize locks in the past three years?

Quandary knocks a final time, then glances up and down the

street. A few little kids on hacked scooters stare back at her. She flips them off, and as soon as they glide away she starts jiggering the lock. It only takes her a minute with the microtool before she gets to the telltale *click-clunk*.

Praying her autogun's old owner was honest about having the only unit in town, she opens the door and steps inside.

The dealer is going through some shit. That is the only immediate explanation Quandary can think of for the state of the house. She recognized the smell of fried noodles even before the lights hummed on; now she makes her way through an entryway dotted with compostable takeout containers, most of them half-full and soggy with sauce.

She is so busy searching for floor that it takes her a while to notice the walls. The dealer has been turning her stress binge into an art form: the off-white plaster is smeared with reddish-brown spirals and stick figures, the work of messy, twitchy fingers. Quandary realizes she is about to find an old woman zonked out of her fucking mind on her own product, possibly even dead from an overdose.

"Better be some fucking keta left," she whispers.

You inside? You need to keep me in the loop, Dree. I'm blind in here and all I can hear is the gurgling goddamn organoid.

"Your organoid is the best on the market," she says, which was true three years ago. Well, nearly true. "You should relish that gurgle."

She makes it to the kitchen, where more flimsy containers line the countertops and stove. A simple yellow gelfridge has been recently cleaned out; the neat little pile of detritus is heaped in front of it. She tries to picture an old and very loaded woman squatting there, yanking out everything edible, gorging herself sick. Quandary has binged plenty, but the image is off. She feels her hackles rising.

"Heading to the bedroom," she murmurs, angling into a dim hallway. "Where do old people stash their shit, Baba? Floorboard? Ceiling tile?"

In whatever orifice is loose, but not too loose.

"You must really miss having an anus."

I've got you. That counts.

Quandary approaches the half-open door to the bedroom. Whenever she's fucked off her head she always finds her way to a bed, hers or otherwise, so she braces herself now for a body—hopefully just asleep or deep in the drug daze, not dead.

But the cheery yellow sheets are unoccupied, neat and tucked in. Quandary does a quick sweep of the room: row of polished boots in one corner, black lacquered table and dried sunflowers in another, a shelf of weathered books, some Kalaallit art up on the humming wallscreen. No sign of the dealer. No takeout wreckage in here, either.

"She likes yellow," Quandary says.

You always liked purple, as a little girl.

"Really?" Quandary asks, eyeing the disturbed dust in front of the bed.

You'd always pinch people's arms, say you were trying to give them purple skin-flowers.

"I was not well adjusted," Quandary admits, depositing her go bag on the floor, fone on top of it. She levers herself underneath the fabbed frame of the bed, wriggling on her belly. Paydust: there's a little metal case waiting for her, a rusty old thing with a retrofit genelock soldered on.

She's about to wriggle back out when she hears the front door. For a moment she envisions a terrible scenario where the wrinkly dealer and her wrinkly lover head straight for the bed and go at it rabbitlike while she's trapped beneath. Then all the thoughts that have been darting around in the back of her head coalesce at once.

The psychoscrawl on the walls—done by spidery, inhuman fingers. The mad volume of food—required to fuel a metabolism that runs like a supercollider for twenty-four hours. Her baba said they make lairs sometimes, on a long enough job. He did not say they favor the houses of small-time ketamine dealers.

She is still trying to decide if this is some truly next-level pattern matching, or if the universe just fucking hates her, when the butterfly man strolls in wearing its blood-splotched yellow sweater.

*

Hiding under the bed, biting her hand, watching a shadow move around—that's horror flick shit. This is horror life, so the butterfly man has already smelled her sweat and sanispray, seen her go bag and fone, and knows exactly where she is. She pulls out her fragger, fires for its approaching shins. Her explosive darts punch the air, cough-cough-cough, only find the opposite wall, but that's fine, gives her time to roll out the other side—

A distended hand comes scything down; she cancels the roll, realizes in a small shocked neuron bundle that the butterfly man vaulted the entire bed in the time it took her to squeeze a trigger. An angular upside-down face appears inches from hers, unsmiling.

"Welcome to my house," the butterfly man caws.

Gone before she can get the fragger aimed. She hears a sharp crack, and one corner of the bed lurches downward. The butterfly man is kicking out the stubby legs. It's going to bring the bedframe down on top of her, crush her here like a pressed flower.

It's fucking toying with her. That makes her furious, how she is furious with Jokić, how she was furious with Timo and still sort of is even now he's dead. The feeling boils over and scalds away her fear. Leaves a fact behind: she is going to fuck up a butterfly man. She fires the fragger again, peppering darts all along the far wall, sowing seeds.

Another crack, another lurch; the bottom end of the bed slams down and narrowly misses her foot. She scoots up toward the head, taking the metal box with her. She reverses her fragger and uses the heavy metal grip as a club. The impact vibrates the bones in her hand, sends sparks flying. The shoddy soldering between genelock and old lock gives way.

She feels the butterfly man moving for the third leg of the bedframe. She flips open the box, finds acid tabs, keta tabs, shoves everything she can into the sleek little grinder. The third leg crunches inward, and the bedframe crunches down on her back. She wails, wriggles free, moving toward the last corner.

The butterfly man meets her there. She can see its bony hand reaching for the fabbed black leg.

"Hey," she says, fumbling from grinder to injector. "Hey!"

The hand pauses. "Hello."

"Boom," she says.

Her fragger darts are programmed to go off on voice trigger—less collateral damage means less cleanup—and now all the tiny explosive slivers all around the edges of the room, stuck in the plaster and wood, detonate at once.

As the world goes up in flames, as superheated debris leaps from all sides, the butterfly man finds the closest cover. It slides under the bedframe like mercury, so smooth, so graceful, and right into Quandary's raised injector. She plugs its jugular with enough drugs to drop a clone-grown woolly mammoth.

This was not the plan, of course. Her baba had something way more elaborate in mind: luring the butterfly man into a tight ventless space, using its flexy skeleton against it, vaporizing a ton of keta and giggling behind her gas mask while its porous skin sucked it all down. But this is better. More satisfying.

The butterfly man's sweater instantly drenches. Maybe it's trying to sweat out the cocktail, but its traitorous metabolism has already absorbed enough to make its hands tremor and fall halfway to her throat. It doesn't gasp how a human would, but its whole body twitches. Its dark eyes turn glassy.

She waits—for the house to douse the fire-dregs with foam, for her heart to stop pounding, for the butterfly man to go fully limp—then crawls out. She knees its perfect face on the way, and does not feel even slightly bad about it.

Her fone is full of her baba's rambling, but his carbon shell is intact. She debates whether or not to tell him how close she probably came to cooking him when all the fragger darts went off.

"Guess who caught a butterfly, Baba," she says.

Thank fuck.

"Thanks, fuck." Quandary slides fresh ammo into her fragger. The clack sends a delicious shiver down her spine. "Killing it now."

She goes back to the bed. She needs to be businesslike about this, since the explosion was loud and poli drones are no doubt incoming. Can't savor it too much, even though her whole chest is full of helium and she feels like the absolute fucking woman. She sights down at the butterfly man's head.

It's still fighting the tranqs, managing a sluggish wriggle here and there. Its big dark eyes are still open. She aims her fragger at the right one, then drifts over to the left. The butterfly man moves its lips. Makes a thick noise in its throat.

"What's that?" Quandary asks, because last words seem important, even from a quantum-brained flatworm.

The butterfly man stares up at her. "Not happy," it rasps. "Wanted more noodles."

Quandary tells her baba what she's doing, tells him she feels a bit of real true connection like a fishhook behind her belly. Then she untethers her fone, before he can make it clear to her how fucking stupid she is, and starts restraining the butterfly man. The real play is keeping it pumped full of ketamine, yes, but the zip ties from her go bag help her feel a bit better about taking a truly dumbshit risk.

The butterfly man's cartilage skeleton makes it disturbingly light; when she stuffs it into one of the dealer's parkas she feels like she's dressing a very strangely proportioned child. Even so, it plus her go bag have her bent double. She staggers out the back door of the house—dealers often have a reliable and uncluttered emergency exit—and onto the street.

A sleek black autocab from a specific company is waiting for her at the curb. They're fully algorithmic, and the algorithm knows its best customers often have bodies in tow. Jokić might have put a flag on this pickup location, but she doubts it. She suspects she's the only one who knows what the butterfly man's been up to here.

Quandary bundles her prisoner inside and they pull away to the sound of approaching poli drones. Once they're a block down, she lifts the parka hood off the butterfly man's face. It gazes back at her with wide black eyes. Its mouth is taped over for now.

"We're not so different, you and I," she says.

The butterfly man spasms slightly.

"Joking," she assures it. "You're a functionally immortal quantum-brained killing machine, I'm a piddly little human." She waves the injector. "I did just fuck you up, though."

The butterfly man stares, no reaction.

"You got plenty of thoughts in there," Quandary says, putting a knuckle to her own skull. "Too many, I bet, if you're running all the thoughts from all the other butterfly men who ever got grown. People probably never ask you them, though."

Its perfect face is blank. She can't tell if it's even listening, but she presses on.

"I'll take a guess, and once I ungag you, you can tell me if I'm close," she says. "Every day you wake up, it's the same fucking story. Sometimes you're in a proper biotank, sometimes you're in some dirty bathtub, but you always wake up with a face or a name in your head. That's the person you have to go kill."

Its nostrils flare at *kill*, like it wants to inhale the word.

"It used to be fun," she continues. "Used to be this game. Probably used to tag people out as fast as you could, trying for speed runs. But you got too good at it. Started to bore you to shit. So you started wandering, started checking out the skyboxes and boundaries. How people always do, with games. Started expressing yourself."

The butterfly man's fingers twitch.

"The wall drawings," Quandary says. "Yeah. I seen them. Pretty bad, if you ask me." She pauses. "But then again, even with all your jobs stacked together you're only a few years old. Which makes the jobs some child labor type of shit."

The butterfly man's eyes flick away. It's starting to lose interest.

"Ever wonder who puts the face in your brain? Who pulls your strings? I'll tell you who did it this time. I'll even show you him." She swipes a streetcam snap of Jokić onto her fone, holds it up. "Look at this man. This man is a two-timing bitch too lazy to do his own butchering, so he's making you do it instead."

The butterfly man is unmoved. Quandary launches her last argument, heart pitter-pattering.

"He has a whole shipment of you on the way," she says. "Crates of you. So you're going to be waking up in tubs all around Nuuk, doing drudge work. Hunting down small-timers who sold on the wrong block, grunts who smart-mouthed him, women who did not want his pale little cock."

The butterfly man shifts its bound hands to its crotch, waggles a questioning thumb.

"That thing, yeah." She exhales. "Drudge work is beneath you, butterfly man. So I got a counteroffer. You forget about killing me, and I help you secure that shipment. *You* get to pick the names and faces for the next twenty times you wake up." She narrows her eyes. "You can even pick mine, if you want. I can fuck you up twice."

The butterfly man shakes its head.

"Or maybe you don't pick any at all," Quandary says. "You just enjoy your little slices of life, instead. Maybe work on your art, which needs a lot of fucking work, let's be honest." She runs her tongue along her teeth. "With enough consecutive days, that quantum-organic brain of yours might even figure out a way to turn off the failsafe. No more twenty-four-hour lifespan."

The dark eyes blink. Time to whittle things right down.

"Help Quandary Aminu," she says. "Kill Boban Jokić. Be happy. Eat noodles. Alternatively, I plug you with an exploding dart behind a dumpster."

She reaches forward, and as she peels the tape from her prisoner's mouth she realizes her fingers are trembling. She holds her breath.

The butterfly man wets its lips with a small pebbly tongue. "Kill Boban Jokić first," it croaks. "Kill Quandary Aminu after. Before dark."

Quandary admires the honesty. She reaches for her go bag. "We'll burn that bridge when we come to it," she says. "Want to meet my baba?"

It turns out they already know each other, sort of. When the butterfly man claps eyes on her baba's disembodied head, it rattles off a street address in Chilean Spanish, which her baba confirms was the location of the darkmarket warlab in Vitacura before it burned down. Quandary wonders just how many faces are imprinted in the butterfly man's quantum-organic brain, and how many of them are still alive.

This is unhinged, Dree.

"You love it."

Going to get yourself killed. Me, too, by proxy.

"Not if you help me come up with a good plan, Baba."

They're parked in a north-side tunnel, lights dimmed, engine off. The autocab is more than happy to keep nibbling at her bank account in silence, and she has enough to spare since she never actually paid for the drugs. The butterfly man is flexing its wrists and ankles on the seat beside her—that was a dicey moment, taking the zip ties off, but so far it's made no attempts at revenge.

How'd you get into this in the first place? Full story, not summary.

Quandary pulls a grimace. The conversation outside the bar with Timo, Timo-who-is-now-dead, seems like it happened weeks instead of hours ago. "The harbor job," she says. "The fucking harbor job."

I don't got newsfeed in here, Dree.

"Ten days ago," Quandary says. "Or eleven, now, actually. Jokić wanted heat and muscle for this delivery coming in. Was worried the Siberians might try to fuck with him. I took the job because I needed some money—for your transplant."

You pause for gravity, there?

She sets his head on her knees, glances sideways to check on the butterfly man. It's now tapping away at the backseat screen, sallow face shifting colors in the glow of some animated netgame, fully enraptured.

"*Some* of it was for your transplant," Quandary says. "Swear to fuck it was." She purses her lips. "I got all strapped and amped, wore my tac boots and everything, but the Siberians played nice. Looked like it was going to be money for nothing."

Poli interrupted, you said.

"In a big way." Quandary folds her hands under her armpits. "Full swoop. Drones and boats and body armor. Was a whole mess, and would've been even worse except I fragged a hydrogen tank, set one of the poli boats burning pretty good. While they was pulling back, about half of us hit the water and got away."

I'm the one who taught you to swim, you know. Never thanked me even once.

"You pushed me off a fucking cliff."

Overhang, and I was coming right down after you. Did the Siberians get away?

"They were well clear by the time the poli showed up. Yeah." Quandary untucks one hand and uses it to rub her temple. "But Jokić lost all the new product right then and there, and two of his regular guns, Markus and Vola, they got pinched. And he's blaming *me* for it, even though I've never talked to the poli in my whole life. Just because I'm the outside hire."

Her fone stays blank for a moment, and she sees a minute think-wrinkle furrow her baba's slimy forehead. *Saving face with the Siberians. Or. Does he like Markus and Vola?*

"Fuck, no," Quandary says. "But he needs them. Markus is the only one in his crew with sufficient skullspace to know when Jokić is fucking up, overextending. And Vola is the only one with the ovaries to tell him."

And those are the only two who got pinched?

"Yeah. They hit the water like the rest of us, but I guess the seals found them."

Her baba's mouth twitches. *Jokić knows you didn't snake. He's pinning you on purpose.*

"Figured." Quandary envisions Jokić's smug scabby smile but resists the urge to spit; the autocab will add a surcharge. "No need for anyone to have snaked. The poli algorithm sniffed us out, I bet because . . ."

She trails off, frowning down at her fone, which is stacking new text at frantic speed.

Jokić is the one who brokered the seizure with the poli. Got rid of two potential threats to the throne, maintained good relations with the Siberians, and I bet got half his product returned through a back channel the next day. Now you're his sacrificial lamb, because you're young, female, and transient. Also because he knows you might figure it out.

Quandary blinks. She thinks back to the hire, back to the harbor, back to the poli coming at them almost as lazy as the butterfly man playing its little predator-prey games. "Shit," she says. "We should talk more often, Baba."

You should get me my fucking body, Dree.

"I know. I know." She clenches and unclenches her teeth. "I know why I been putting it off, too."

For three years.

"Yeah."

No great mystery. It's because other people are for other people, not for Quandary Aminu. She doesn't need them dragging her down. She's happier with just her and entropy, just gliding along from this chemical to that one until she. Until you. Get a bullet in your head.

But that wasn't what she was going to say at all. Quandary

stares down at the fone in silence. She feels her throat start to heave, her eyes start to sting. "It's because you always were a cunt," she says. "Sleep tight, Baba."

She pulls the cable, packs him back into his carbon shell, zips him into the go bag again. By the time it's done, her eyes are good and dry. She glances across at the butterfly man, who is staring at her dispassionately.

"Fuck are you looking at?" she asks, because she'd almost like to get strangled now.

"Push Boban Jokić off a fucking cliff," the butterfly man suggests. It hooks two fingers into the corners of its mouth and drags upward. "Change your face. Be happy."

"Might help," Quandary mutters. "Yeah."

A fist thunks against the opaqued window; she snaps a hand to her fragger. The butterfly man is unperturbed. Its nostrils are wide and she can see a bit of drool dribbling down its chin as it leans across her, sinuous as ever, and pushes the car door open.

On the other side, a very nervous delivery woman holds up an insulated bag. Quandary relaxes her trigger finger. Glances over at the backseat screen, where she sees an order confirmation for six cartons of Sichuan noodles.

"That's only the fourth best place in Nuuk for noodles," she says, eyeing the logo. "Third for jiaozi. If you want, I'll take you somewhere really good. After we kill Jokić, and before you kill me."

"Before dark," the butterfly man says, and this time it makes a little motion beside its head, fingers rubbing against each other and then splitting apart, a brain dissolving. Quandary understands perfectly.

Mad has always been easier for her than sad. She leans into that now as they make their approach on Jokić's apartment, skulking on foot through fading daylight. Her baba is not with them. She was briefly tempted to punt his head into the sea; instead she directed the autocab to a storage facility and used the last of her money hiring a microjobber to meet him there and get him refrigerated.

Now she can focus on being really fucking angry with Jokić,

who thought he could do his little deal with the poli, scapegoat her for it, and have a butterfly man murder her before she got a chance to clear her rep. She packs all the rage down into a minia-ture sun burning in her belly, ready fuels.

The butterfly man seems to be in a good mood. It's still wear-ing the dealer's parka, loping along with the overlong sleeves hid-ing its hands, fluttering in the evening breeze. Maybe this is all just an unexpected game-within-the-game for it, a little surprise it didn't know it could unlock.

Or maybe it's already as smart as the quantum processors they have working on interstellar burns and starch synthesis, and she's just become a pawn in its elaborate plan to end or enslave humanity. Either way, she's pretty sure Jokić is fucked—it keeps whispering his name and cracking its neck to one side, like a spine getting snapped.

"Hold up," she orders. "Soon as we get any closer, we'll be on his cams."

The butterfly man stops mid-stride, one foot frozen in the air. She can't even remember which one got pulped by the auto-gun; both are back to their killer ballerina ways. Ahead, spearing up from a ring of new construction, is Jokić's home: a tower of polyp and nanocarbon, swatched with hydroponic greenery and crowned by jagged orange holo.

Quandary feels an electric sweat on her exposed skin. Go time. "You remember the plan, yeah?" she asks.

"Dead girl gambit," the butterfly man says, in an uncanny imitation of her voice. "That's the play, I figure."

"Works in all the flicks," Quandary agrees with herself. "Don't drop me."

She unrolls a membranous body bag on the pavement, the one she keeps at the very bottom of her go bag for emergencies, and climbs inside. It's not the most dignified way to make an entrance, and if the butterfly man decides to renege on their little deal and do her first, she's packed up real convenient for disposal. She can hear her baba's raspy voice telling her exactly how bad an idea this is.

But he's a head now, and he ruined her attempt at a heart-to-heart, so fuck him. Quandary lies back and lets the butterfly man zip her up, sealing her into the dark. She keeps a tight grip on her fragger.

The body bag has little scent pods in it, which is a nice touch. She inhales the artificial lavender as the butterfly man slides its wiry arms underneath her knees and back. It lifts her like it's lifting origami, which she resents a bit, and sets off. The rocking motion reminds her of something from childhood, of faking sleep so her baba would carry her, but she pushes that away. Focuses on getting into character, meaning limp and corpse-like.

It's only a few minutes of gliding through the dark before Jokić's patrol intercepts them.

"Where the fuck you think you're going?" a voice demands. "Stop where you are, drop the bag."

Quandary braces herself, and is grateful when the butterfly man does not comply.

"Food delivery for Boban Jokić," it squawks. "Quandary Aminu. No cutlery."

"Shit." A second voice, possibly Timo's cousin Piet. "I thought it'd be bigger."

"That's it?" The first voice is hushed now; Quandary hears feet scuffling backward. "That's the fucking butterfly man?"

"That's the fucking butterfly man. I'll call in."

A stretched silence. Quandary tries some positive visualization: an escorted jaunt to the building, a quick elevator ride to the top floor, during which the butterfly man kills the owners of voices one-through-two, then she pops out of the body bag fragger-first, aiming for the spot between Jokić's eyes.

"Says to verify her face, then dump her in the nearest bio-recycler."

Fuck.

"You can drop the body here, Mister Butterfly Man," says the first voice, very respectful now. "Boss doesn't want to see it."

The butterfly man complies this time, and Quandary is not ready. A little grunt escapes her lungs when she hits asphalt.

"Shit," says maybe-Piet. "Is she alive in there still?"

"That's the play," the butterfly man croaks.

"I better call in again, then. See if—"

Quandary hears a cartilage crunch, a wail. By the time she claws her way out of the body bag, the fun is done with: both of Jokić's guns are dead and cooling. The butterfly man is crouching on the nearer one's chest, like the traditional sort of nightmare. She plucks the dropped fone from the pavement, and since they're already on cam anyway, she thumbs the interrupted call back open.

"Hey, fuckwit," she says. "We're coming to get you."

She hears Jokić breathe once. Twice. "I see," he finally says. "Come on up, Quandary. My door's always open."

He cuts the call.

The dead girl gambit has become a live girl gambit, and it puts Quandary's nerves against a grater. No drones dive-bomb them on the way to the entrance. No more patrols pop out of the dark. Jokić even gives them a little holotrail to follow, orange arrows pulsing all the way across the dim-lit lobby to the shiny elevators.

"Obvious trap, yeah?" She mimes scissors. "We get in, he snips the cables when we're halfway up."

The butterfly man shrugs.

"Very fucking helpful," she says. "Thank you for your insight."

She almost wishes her baba, cunt though he is, were here instead. He'd be able to help burrow inside Jokić's mind, figure out what he's playing at. If she steps into that elevator, she's an ant in a box. If she takes the emergency staircase, she's an ant in a tunnel, which is not much better and a whole lot sweatier.

The possibility that Jokić planned this whole thing out, that the butterfly man is just following some very serpentiform programming, keeps creeping through the back of her mind. Too much time to think always turns her paranoid. She stares balefully at her companion, now solemnly observing its own reflection in the glossy elevator doors.

"Hey," she says. "What was the happiest moment of your life?"

The butterfly man looks over. "Moment of your life?" it croaks.

"The best feeling you remember," Quandary extrapolates. "What was happening when you felt it? Where were you, what were you doing?"

"Not yet," the butterfly man squawks. "Later."

"We might be dead later," Quandary argues. "Come on. People in bars answer me this all the time, drunk off their asses. Search around in that big quantum brain of yours."

The butterfly man blinks at her. "The happiest feeling is later."

There are a lot of ways to interpret that, but Quandary figures it's time she stopped stalling. She knuckles the up button and steps into the elevator. The butterfly man slides in after her. She looks up and down the column of numbers, the tower layout rendered in glowing diagram, but sees the curlicued *R* at the top is already highlighted.

"All the way up," she says, to fill the silence.

"Hello," the butterfly man says. "Do you like heights?"

She recalls a slow fall and an icy plunge. "Not much, no. You?"

Her companion gives a beatific smile. "Pushing people."

The elevator rockets them up the building's magnetic gullet, so smoothly her stomach barely registers it. The slosh when they reach the top, when the door chimes open, is fear, not gravity. She keeps a hand on her fully loaded fragger as she steps out. All ten darts are set to detonate automatically now, no verbal trigger. She's expecting to do some collateral damage.

She scans the terrain. The tower's rooftop is a wide circle of pebbly asphalt, bare apart from a half-built pool and some polyp printers over to one side. The holos arrayed around the railing are switched off, making the twisted waist-high metal more cage-like than decorative. It makes her think arena.

Their first two opponents are waiting for them outside the elevator, stubby bulldog submachine guns slung from their shoulder harnesses. She knows one of them by sight, by hormone-hewn shoulders and gleaming septum piece, but not by name. Two more of Jokić's guns stand nearer the edge, long coats whipping in the wind.

And just past them, pale and brawny and busy shaving, is the man who turned her night and then her day into such a fucking shitshow. His chair is geckoed right to the edge of the roof, overlooking the construction site below. A little bot is clinging to his sternum with soft pseudopods, whisking a triangular razor along his jawline.

"Quandary," he says, swiveling in his chair. "Come get this view."

She can see enough from here. The sun is on its way down; the dust is on its way up; they meet in a dancing cloud of orange-furred motes. Construction rarely sleeps in Nuuk. The machines are still seething, printers still birthing porous coral and nanocarbon skeletons, layering up and over each other, stacking for sky.

It's fucking beautiful, and here he is acting like he didn't try to take it, and every other view, away from her forever.

Quandary feels the rage vibrate in every cell of her body. "New poli station?" she guesses. "Saves you the walk to wank each other off. Make your little deals."

Jokić twitches in his chair; for a hopeful moment she pictures the bot's blade digging into his artery, spraying a jet of blood across the gunmetal sky. But the bot has better reflexes than any barber. It keeps right on working.

"You're projecting," he says. "Snakes always project."

Quandary takes a test step, and neither of the nearest muscles go for their submachine guns. The butterfly man lingers slightly behind her, back to its silence. She hopes it is using its big brain to calculate exactly how to kill all these motherfuckers without getting mowed down.

"I got no reason to lie," she retorts, not for Jokić's sake, but for the sake of the four guns on the roof with them, the four trigger fingers that might be getting a little conflicted. "You do. You made sure Markus and Vola got pinched, because you're scared of anyone with brain and backbone. That's some shit leadership. And cutting deals with the poli, that's a shit look on anyone."

She spares a peripheral for the butterfly man. It has its head bent like an old man, its anemic hands stuffed into the deep parka pockets. She tries to remember how many hours it's been alive and guess how many hours it has left at peak functionality. Now would be a bad time for it to get decrepit on her.

"You know why I bring people up here?" Jokić asks, smooth and unworried, past his twitching phase.

"Makes things dramatic," Quandary says.

"It gives people perspective," Jokić says, ignoring her. "Reminds people they're just one tiny fragment of a massive teeming city, and that city is a speck"—he throws a hand toward the watery horizon—"on an enormous planet"—he points upward, at the purpling dusk—"which is, compared to the universe, the size of maybe an electron."

"And it's probably all a sim anyways," Quandary says, inching left, getting a mirror motion from the muscle with the septum piece. "Yeah. Who gives a shit."

Jokić nods, all thoughtful, and the bot rides it out. "Sims within sims, I bet." His gaze finally drifts over to the butterfly man, now squatting against the wind, a little hump of parka. "Butterfly men are lucky, you know. Never have to think about it. They dip in and out and never have to get stuck in the being-human bullshit."

"The butterfly man thinks about plenty," Quandary says, feeling oddly defensive. "That's why we're here."

Jokić frowns. "It's defective, yeah. I can see that." He thumbs a lick of shaving cream from one ear. "Never getting biotech from Siberia again," he says. "So, thanks for that. You've saved me a lot of money." He blinks. "I guess we're all numbers, fucking over other numbers, to accumulate different numbers."

Quandary finally spies the vapestick built into his armrest, and realizes he's high as fuck. The pair nearest her adjust the angle of their weapons, shifting grip just slightly. The butterfly man gives a little wriggle at the edge of her vision.

Go time.

"Be happy," she says, and dives for cover.

The butterfly man fires from its pockets: Timo's unlocked Glock in the right, a disposable blockgun from a darkmarket printer in the left. They shred the parka to pieces, and Quandary gets to watch through a cloudburst of insulated lining as the muscles with the submachine guns drop, skulls holed.

One of them finds the trigger on the way down, central nervous system doing its thing even with the upstairs boss drilled, and it chews sparking craters an inch from her boots. She rolls an extra roll, comes up firing for the third target, the woman surging away from Jokić's chair with her pistol flashing.

Quandary feels bloodspray, hears a wet smack as the butterfly man takes a bullet. She anchors herself and her next dart is a good one. It whistles into the woman's fleshy forearm; she keeps a grip on her pistol but misses—only by micrometers, judging by the wash of heat across Quandary's cheek.

She doesn't get another shot before her arm detonates in a burst of blood and bone. Quandary whirls to find the fourth target, but the others are already gasping and burbling on the pebbly floor. She whirls back, levels her fragger at Jokić's half-shaved face. Her heart is a war drum.

"How's that for—" Quandary's lungs are gassed; it ruins her scathing remark. "How's that for defective, huh?"

The butterfly man worms out of the parka's remains. The bullet holes look small and neat across its bony chest, but when it turns around Quandary sees ragged exits, shreds of sweater interwoven with ribboned skin and muscle. Wine-dark blood is gushing down the backs of its trembling legs.

Jokić doesn't try to move, not even to take a pull from his vapestick. "They make it like art," he says. "They make it so fucking beautiful."

"Keep a gun on him, will you?" Quandary asks.

The butterfly man raises both, smooth and precise as ever despite the chunks blown out of its torso. That lets Quandary cross to the woman with the blown-off arm, who is in shock for now but might recover soon, and retrieve her dropped pistol. She does the same for the gaspy man lying nearby.

She tosses both weapons off the edge of the roof, gets a little bubble of vertigo in her belly as they spiral out of sight. Then it's just her and Jokić and the butterfly man, and as much as she would love to plug the former right in his chair, blow him off the edge of his own tower, she did make a deal with the latter.

"Time to call up the Siberians," she says, aiming her fragger again. "And tell them you really like how things went with the field test. Tell them you want all the butterfly man you can handle."

Jokić stares. "What?"

"Those are our terms, fuckwit." Quandary glances over at the butterfly man, hoping it understands leverage and deception. "You bring in the rest of the shipment, we let you live."

"That's a lot of money for a potentially flawed product," Jokić says, shaking his head. "There's a reason militaries haven't cleared out their drone factories to make room for incubators. These little bastards are getting glitchier every year."

"It wasn't a request," Quandary says. "Call them, or I take your toes off."

Jokić is unperturbed. "I'll think about it," he says. "It depends how the second one does."

Quandary feels all her little hackle-hairs turn to spikes. There is a reason Jokić has been so fucking chatty. She turns her head by an increment, just enough to see the half-finished pool. A familiar hand, slicked with pink residue, is gripping the lip. Her heart stutters. The fresh butterfly man climbs out, naked body clotted with leftover biomass. It waves.

She does not wave back, but she realizes it wasn't for her anyway. The less-fresh butterfly man, the one whose punctured body is still leaking blood, raises a hand in reply. She hopes, for a moment, that the two of them are going to be friends. They have the same quantum-organic brain, after all. Just running on two slightly different operating systems.

The fresh butterfly man flips upside down, does a little jig on its hands. The less-fresh butterfly man, the one Quandary now realizes she thinks of as *her* butterfly man, drops its guns to do the same. She's still thinking how that's a good sign for them being friends when they leap at each other.

They collide like meteors, and even if she were quick enough with the fragger to tag the naked one and not the bloody one, Quandary is distracted by a sudden movement in her peripheral. She pivots right as Jokić's insectile barber springs at her, razor flashing, and she drops just in time.

Adrenaline puts the blade in high definition, shiny and molecule-sharp. Displaced air ripples her face.

Then she's turning, tracking the landing. Fires twice. Misses twice. The explosions tear craters in the rooftop. The bot is a scuttling blur, dancing sideways then back again, razor humming the air as it searches for an opening. She feels Jokić come up out of the chair behind her; fires a blind dart over her shoulder.

The bot lunges again. She twists away, but this time she's a planck too slow. There's a wet sound, a stinging, a splatter of blood. The blade splits her chin on its way past. She howls. Fires. The dart detonates in the spot the bot was, a fiery useless blossom. Her backbrain whispers: *Seven spent, three remaining.*

A brawny pale arm smashes in from nowhere, and suddenly she's got no darts at all because her fragger is skidding across the rooftop. Jokić has her bear-hugged from behind; she can smell the sour sweat of him, a whiff of weed smoke. His vise-tight grip crushes her own sharp elbow into her diaphragm.

"This was never about you, Quandary," he grunts. "Try to be at peace with that."

Hot copper is still gushing from her chin, splashing down her front. The bot was going for her throat, nearly found it, and her jugular is now a sitting target. She kicks, wriggles. The bot rounds on them. Its red-dipped razor takes aim.

Quandary is not at peace with anything. She wants to meet the woman with the tattoos and an interest in spaghettification. She wants to blow Jokić's head off. She wants to speak with her baba again, and apologize for calling him a cunt even though he is one. She wants to show the butterfly man Nuuk's best Sichuan cuisine.

She wants a new happiest memory, maybe one where she's not all alone. Maybe one where someone else is on the hill with her, looking up into the machinery of the beauteous, pitiless simulation.

The bot coils and springs and—

Never makes it: a blur of butterfly man limbs whirls past, and one of them casually plucks the bot out of midair, grabbing not where the bot is but where it is going to be, and uses its razor to carve a furrow into a different butterfly man limb, likely one with a different owner, all in a single mercury-smooth arc.

Jokić sucks in a breath at the beauty of it. Quandary deads all her weight at once. The pouring blood makes her slippery enough; she worms her arm out and claws for Jokić's eyes. When his head reflexes backward she thrashes downward, wrenches herself free. Catches his swinging boot mostly on the hip.

She lays out for the fragger, which did not skid far, and gets it by her fingertips. The bot, already discarded, is racing toward her along the rooftop, dragging one damaged leg behind itself. It's hobbled enough that she can aim where it's going to be. Her dart plugs it right in its bulbous sensor.

Boom.

No time to watch the fireworks; it's still exploding when she swivels to Jokić, who is pulling a pistol from his coat, and taps the trigger again. Her second dart burrows into his shin and goes off. Flesh-and-blood becomes vapor; a bone fragment skips off the rooftop and slices her knuckle open.

She doesn't let it affect her aim. Her final dart is going to slide right between his glassy blue eyes. She'll find some other way to get the butterfly man its shipment.

"Help."

The squawk barely makes it past the swellies in her ears and the adrenaline in her head. Jokić is pallid, paralyzed with shock, so she spares one glance, up and left. The butterfly man in the shredded yellow sweater—her butterfly man—is halfway over the edge of the rooftop. The naked butterfly man is trying to bump halfway to all the way, jabbing and prying with its spidery fingers, playful but intent.

Quandary looks down at Jokić, who so fully deserves an explosive finale, then back to the edge. Her butterfly man is just a face and two disembodied hands now, clinging to the very lip of the roof. The naked butterfly man pushes up against the railing, stomping with its heels, trying to dislodge the other's gripping fingers.

"Fine," she breathes, and puts one between its shoulder blades.

Except its shoulder blades are elsewhere. Sound cue, instinct, quantum precognition—whatever it is, it's fucking bullshit, and Quandary is forced to watch her last dart sail off into the skyline, not quite grazing the butterfly man's slimy head on the way.

She pulls again on muscle memory. The empty click has never been so loud.

"Quandary Aminu," her butterfly man croaks, sounding faintly disappointed, and slips out of sight.

Quandary feels her guts do a plunge of their own, even though she only met the butterfly man this morning and it's spent most of the day trying to murder her. There is no water at the bottom of this cliff, and no baba is going to follow the butterfly man down and tow it to safety, laughing a spluttery laugh.

The naked butterfly man turns. Steps toward her. Its unnervingly perfect face, identical to the one that just turned to pulp down below, is still streaked with glistening dregs of biomass. She dives for Jokić's pistol, but the butterfly man beats her to it. It tosses it from hand to foot, one toe poised on the trigger.

"Hello," it says. "What was the happiest moment of your life?"

She blinks.

"Noodles," it guesses, leveling the pistol at Jokić's head. "Food delivery."

Quandary narrows her eyes. "That's you in there, then?" she demands. "Why the fuck did you kill yourself?"

The butterfly man's mouth stretches into a smile. "Pushing people," it says, and kisses the air.

"You are not well adjusted," she mutters.

She looks down at Jokić, who is losing consciousness, eyelids fluttering. She looks around the rooftop, at what's left of Jokić's crew: three corpses and one also-ran. She thinks about the dead pair down in the alley. Her fantasy of blowing Jokić's head off is starting to lose its shine—which is a shame, seeing as he's the one who actually deserved the dart.

"Time to call the Siberians," the butterfly man says.

"Right. Yeah. That was the deal." She touches her chin, where the sliced capillaries are finally slowing down. "You still have to kill me before dark?"

The butterfly man taps a finger to its temple. "No face," it says. "Factory reset. You lucky, lucky orphan."

Quandary has zero desire to know how the butterfly man learned the word orphan, but it reminds her that her baba is iced up in the storage facility. Waiting to hear if she survived, waiting to hear if he's ever getting a transplant. Well, probably sleeping by now, back in his induced coma.

"If he doesn't have a body, he can't leave," she tells the butterfly man. "He can't up and disappear on me again. He did that, you know. A lot."

"I know," the butterfly man says gently. "I know."

"You're just fucking saying things I said earlier."

"That's the play," the butterfly man agrees. "Time to call the Siberians. Secure that shipment. Twenty slices of life."

Quandary looks out over the city, the downtown streets baring their neon skeletons, skyways blooming with solar lamps. She wonders how much things will change with the butterfly man in charge of itself, if those twenty slices of life are enough to take over Nuuk or the whole fucking world.

Maybe there'll just be more shitty street art in the Spine stations. Maybe that big quantum-organic brain, unlike her piddly human one, knows how to just be happy.

"Okay," Quandary says. "Yeah. How's your Jokić voice?"

"These little bastards are getting glitchier every year," the butterfly man croaks.

"Spot on," she says.

TRIPPING
THROUGH TIME

t's the Great Fire of London and I'm serving biofarmed eel
canapes. Smells and sounds don't get through the bubble,
or I guess they call it the chronofield, but I can see plenty:
thatch roofs going up like match heads, blue-and-orange flames
licking and crunching on wood, smoke tunnelling up into the
hazy sky, people running for their lives. It's a trip.

I shouldn't be watching, though. I gotta sling these canapes
and then get more champagne flutes out the chiller. Clay, who is
now head server, stuck her whole bony neck out to get me this
job. I spot her across the way, offering appies to three musty old
men posted up at the shimmering edge of the chronofield. She's
autosmiling and hide-the-pain laughing at whatever junk they
are saying to her.

Usually her hair is a rust-colored buzzcut, but today she's
wigged up, all straight and glossy and long, because it's one of
those gigs. They also got us in period costume, which is not falling-apart sweatpants but instead these stiff soot-smeared dresses
that actually, me to you, look somewhat good in an aggressively
retrobomb way.

I waltz over to the riverbank, where our employer, Mrs. Silverwright, is holding court like some kind of primeval sea goddess. She's wearing this unbelievable half-holo gown that looks
like a perpetually crashing wave, all foamy and whatnot, and her
bass-clipped hair is billowing in perfect tendrils around her face,
and her cheekbones are so deadly sometimes I just stare at them.

"That's the issue, isn't it," she says, plucking a canape off my tray. "If we hosted at, say, the building of the pyramids—it could be an entire day spent watching one slab of rock get hauled up a sand dune. The signing of the Declaration? Over in minutes."

Her admirers nod and tutter.

"I'm afraid destruction simply schedules better than creation." Mrs. Silverwright gestures over her shoulder, where the river's reflecting the orange flames in a ripply dance. "And it's not as if we're the only ones drawn to the spectacle. People came from miles around to watch London burn."

I can see another boatload of people rowing through the dirty water, smeared with actual soot, eyes bright and panicky. It's shitty for them, but like Mrs. Silverwright told us while we were setting up, these people have been dead forever. And we can't leave the chronofield anyways.

An old woman does the classic forearm grab, clawing me up with her nails. "Excuse me," she says. "Is this eel or elver?"

In my head I'm like, *it's whatever you want it to be, baby.*

In real life I'm like, "This is eel, ma'am. Imported from a bio-farm in Andalusia, served on a crostini with a balsamic reduction and sesame seed topping."

She hucks it right in the Thames.

But all in all, it's not a bad gig. Me and Clay keep circulating, and every so often we pass like two satellites in orbit and beam each other information about who's getting too drunk, or too handsy, or just keeps saying the stupidest shit. People are really into watching London burn down, so they're easy to please. Honestly, the hardest part was probably the pre-job testing.

Rich folks already got all these custom telomeres and whatnot, which makes it easier to get modified for the chronofield. Us caterers do not, and apparently some people have a real rough time inside that pretty shimmery bubble. Like, the girl before me just started bleeding out her nose and ears one night, gushing all over the white linen tablecloths and babbling about how sorry she was.

I've got the right genetics for the mod—as proven by a shit-load of tests in this little bunker slash office where I had to wear a big circuitry-swatched apron—but I still feel woozy when we zap back to reality, which is a big antiseptic-white tent. Me and Clay keep the smiles stapled on while all the guests flit away to their limos or quaddies. Then we help our chef-slash-serving captain and her bot load up all their shit, and then we finally hit the detox.

The magnetics make my skin grow goosebumps and tugs my hair all over the place. Clay's gets lifted straight up for a second, and I can see the edge of her lace front. The scan blinks green.

"That's some good money," she says, stepping out of the booth. "And it's rad, right? Seeing the past. I mean, you can't touch it, but it's rad."

As soon as I get out of the detox booth, I grab my phone from the storage locker and see she was right: the money is good as hell. I pump my fist a little. "Hey," I say. "Thanks for getting me this, Clay. This is *big* necessary right now."

"Hey," she says. "I know." She pauses. "Mrs. Silverwright likes you, too. Try get you on regular. Sisterhood of the time-travelling pants, type shit."

I blink. "She likes things?"

"Micro-expressions," Clay says. "Gotta be watchful."

We bump elbows, mask up, and part ways: her to her ride, me to my metro. There's another virus going around, so every second seat in the tube has one of those 3-D printed spike pads glued to it, to keep people from sitting too close together. But of course that just means more people are standing crammed up in each other's mouths. I try to face the corner the whole ride.

The apartment block's in quarantine mode when I get there. The door sprouts me off a little swab to run around my nostrils, then I sit tight on the stoop while it does its thing. It's a warm muggy night, warmer than London on fire, which seems backwards to me. The bubble must be climate-controlled.

Finally the door chimes me through, and I scurry up the steps. Me and my mom are on the third floor, one of those half-suites with an epoxy wall installed to double the number of units. Sometimes at night we hear our neighbors on the other side moving around. We used to joke about them being ghosts, or maybe creepy mirror versions of us with black button eyes. We got that from a book she read me as a kid.

The door to our apartment has another quarantine warning

blinking on it, like maybe three flights of stairs was long enough to forget. I shoulder it open and head straight for the sink.

"Hey, is that my little time traveler?" my mom calls from the next room. Her voice is a little scratchier than usual. "Is that my little quantum jumping bean?"

"Woman, what does that even mean?" I call back.

I don't come out of the bathroom until I'm fully scrubbed and my outer clothes are in the laundry. Mom doesn't get flare-ups too often anymore, but she's on immunomodulators all the time—colitis—so I've been washing my shit good for years already. The coconut-scented disinfectant gel is pretty much my signature fragrance.

Mom is at the kitchen table, peering at her work tablet, but when she looks up I can tell she's relieved to see me in one piece and not, like, turned into a fetus or something. "Hey, hon."

"Queen of England says hi," I tell her.

"Unbelievable, the shit they use it for," she says, sounding grudgingly impressed more than angry. "Parties! Just sitting there watching a city burn down."

"Can't really do nothing else," I say. "We're all stuck in the chronofield, right?" And I think, *they all dead anyways*, but I don't say it, because it's the kind of thing that'll get her actually angry. I'm tired and achy and I want to just chill and enjoy the fact I got paid. "You test today?" I ask.

"Just now," she says, nodding at the kit magnetized to the fridge. "Clean as a whistle."

I wrap both my arms around her and give her a big squeezing hug. We smell like the same soap, but she has her mom smell going on, too. There's this safe warm feeling when you're with someone you love and you're both clean, especially after a couple weeks doing distance and isolation, and you know you can hug them. Me to you, I think it might be the best feeling in the whole fucking world.

Next party I work is a week later, and also like six hundred years ago. It's some famous battle: big muddy hillside, people clanking around in armor, arrows flying everywhere. The rain sleeting down doesn't get through the bubble, but some of the guests are going around with fashionable black umbrellas any-

ways. I'm a little distracted tonight and Clay notices; she intercepts me right as I run out of deconstructed patatas bravas.

"You good?" she asks.

I nod.

"Your mom good?"

I don't want to burden Clay with this shit, not when she's already burdened with her own shit, but she has those big soulful
eyes you just want to confess stuff to. "Tested red yesterday morning," I say. "Not IDed yet. I keep thinking I must have brought
something in, you know?" I whirl my finger. "Like, maybe even
something from here?"

"No way," she says. "Detox, remember? And you wash hard,
girl. You wash better than my brother, and he's a nurse."

"Thanks, Clay." I pause. "Your parents okay?"

"Holed up and healthy, yeah," she says. "Just jealous I'm out
here breaking physics while they stuck inside playing canasta."

She spots someone's glass running low and darts over before
it hits critical empty. I circle back to the kitchenette to restock my
tray. I'm just starting to feel better when a soldier eats shit right in
front of me, staggering out of the mist and collapsing just outside
the chronofield. He's so full of arrows it should be funny; he's got
six, no, seven, one's broken off in his belly.

But his blood is bright red, leaking down into the mud, and
the shimmer distorts his face but for a second I swear he's staring right at me. I know he's been dead for hundreds of years
already. He doesn't look dead, though. He looks desperate, and
it's not funny.

A drunk man shows up, one of the guests who was placing
bets earlier on who was going to get trampled by their own horse.
He has a wine stain on his crisp white sleeve. "Oh, my God, that's
horrible," he says. "Hold this. I want a souvenir."

He hands me his glass, sloshing half of it into the dirt. I'm too
shook to do anything but take it. The functional part of my brain
figures he wants to take a snap of himself with the dying guy in
the background, but instead he slides this metallic prong out of
his sleeve and pushes it against the chronofield.

A poison-yellow warning holo pops up. He shunts it aside,
keeps pushing, and suddenly a small hexagonal chunk solidifies
in the shimmery surface of the bubble. The node falls away. The

guest gives a grunt of satisfaction, eyes fixed on the arrow sticking out of the dying guy's back.

"Heath? What are you doing, man?" His slightly more sober buds have spotted us. "What's he doing?"

Heath snaps a glove on, wriggles his fingers, and shoves his arm through the chronofield. Everybody shouts and jumps and rushes forward at the same time, everybody except me, because I'm still standing there holding Heath's wine glass and watching the soldier bleed out. The shouting cuts off. Heath is staring at his arm, which is intact on the other side of the bubble, with that drunk bleary kind of self-amusement. Someone does a nervous laugh.

Then Heath starts to scream. Suddenly his lanky arm is whipping around like a popped balloon, and somehow it's shrinking like one, too, collapsing in on itself, bones crunching bones and skin slurping skin. He staggers back, and only a stump comes with him. He's screaming, I'm screaming, everyone's screaming. The little medidrone me and Clay helped load up comes whirling over to see what's going on. It clamps itself to the blood-spraying end of Heath's not-arm.

One of his idiot friends is shaking me, like *why didn't you stop him*, like *you overserved him, you overserved him!* Which is so fucking absurd I will laugh if my throat ever gets unstuck.

Mrs. Silverwright sweeps in and detaches him, shoves him away. "Are you okay?" she asks, and it takes me a second to get she's asking me.

"Yeah," I say. "Yes. Ma'am."

We both look down at Heath, who is still writhing around on the dirt. The thing that he used to open the hole, the metallic prong, is lying beside him.

"What a fucking clown," Mrs. Silverwright says. "One in every family, I suppose." She gives me a pat on the arm, then turns to her clustered guests. "The party's ending early today, darlings."

When I get back to reality and back to my phone, there's a message from my mom telling me she got her bug IDed and it's a SARS variant. I don't show it to Clay. She's still buzzing about what happened with the chronofield, how that dumbshit deserved to lose more than one limb. I nod and nod and nod, and even laugh, and then we go our separate ways.

The whole metro ride I got this dread in my belly, and guilt for the dread, which feels bad too. I walk slow from my stop, sauntering down the empty street. Halfway home a drone flits up, yammering about curfew, but I got an employment blit from Mrs. Silverwright so I'm in the clear. A couple minutes after that I'm waiting on the stoop for the apartment door to read my swab, and the dread's getting worse and worse.

The scan blinks green and the door opens, which also opens my lungs at least a little. I head down the hall. Our door's got a new pictogram now, a notification that says *infected individual in isolation*. I shoulder it open and beeline for the bathroom.

"Well, well, I have been blessed with a visitor from the distant past." My mom's scratchy cheery voice is coming from the portable speaker on the kitchen table—she's already gone full iso in her room. "How was Agincourt?"

I think about the man full of arrows, and Heath the rich drunk clown reaching for him, and Heath's arm turning into flesh-spaghetti and disappearing.

"Rainy," I say. "You okay? Still flaring?"

She doesn't answer, and that makes me scrub harder, like I can squeeze a reply out of my slippery hands. "I'm okay, hon," she finally says. "But I'm on Waitlist for a hospital bed."

I get the trapdoor stomach thing, where it feels like all your guts just dropped out the bottom of you. I pull my phone out of the disinfectant tray and pull up Waitlist. Friends and family notifications: a great-uncle here, an old classmate there, and sitting buried in the 932 spot, my mom.

"Bad timing," she says. "They just got a big surge."

My mom had me late and she turned sixty last year. That, plus colitis and other IBD getting reclassified as comorbidities a while back, means she's low priority.

"Company can't bump you up?" I ask.

"They barely cover my immunos and liver check-ups. They're not gonna up and find me a bed." She bites back a cough, and that spikes all the little hairs on the back of my neck.

"How you breathing?" I ask. "What's your peak flow?"

"If I link you all my numbers, you're just going to worry. You can't change the numbers, hon." She pauses. "I'm reading the complete works of Tennessee Williams. How about you make something to eat, get cozy in bed . . ."

I go to the kitchen and fix up some food and clean everything on automatic. Spray, wipe, spray, wipe. Mom got a drone delivery while I was working. A big box of my favorite faux-Nesquik cereal is on top of the fridge. Same taste, fewer atrocities—I said that when I was a kid and Mom never let me forget it.

I don't go to my room, though. Instead I go sit with my back to my mom's door, so I can hear her shifting around in her room, so I can almost feel it. We do up the camlink so we can see each other. Her liver-spotted hands are holding an old battered book of plays. She's halfway smiling. She can tell I'm not in my bed, but I think she gets it.

You to me: Tennessee Williams is not my thing. I kind of doze off, shoulder blades slowly sliding down the door. But I do hear that one part I always remember, from the very start of *The Glass Menagerie*, where their eyes fail them, or they fail their eyes, and they get their fingers pressed forcibly down on the fiery braille of a failing economy. That shit has been happening for centuries.

Mom works in contact tracking, company called Hund. They mostly take care of her meds—colitis is not cheap—but they don't have provisions for virus season. While she reads, I split off a new tab and start searching around Hund's policy site, which is basically all fucking nonsense.

But when I move up to their conglomerate's policy site, I spot something co-signed by Aline Silverwright.

I shoot my shot during the Toba catastrophe. Mrs. Silverwright breaks away from her flock and goes over to the edge of the chronofield, checking something on her embedded wrist screen. She looks as regal and beautiful as ever, with her heartbeat and other organ functions transposed to the fabric of her dress in an elegant anatomical collage.

Outside the bubble, a bunch of people in extremely retro-bomb attire—animal skins and bark, type shit—are staring off into the distance at a growing pillar of smoke. Earlier I heard somebody say that they're not *homo sapiens*, they're some other kind of hominid, but they look human to me.

Anyways, I'm glad me and Clay are wearing chamsuits instead of period costume. It's a weird feeling, only being able to see your gloved hands, everything else just a blur, but you get to pretend you're a ninja and it's not like the guests treat you much different.

"Mrs. Silverwright?" I say, from a distance so I don't startle her by accident. We're out of earshot of the other guests.

"Hello, darling," she says. "What is it?"

"My mom works for one of your companies," I say.

She gives a tight smile. "Small world."

There's no smooth chill way to say it, and I have to say it now, before she gets distracted, before I lose my nerve, before I start thinking about how she might freak and dump my contract, dump Clay's contract, too, just for good measure.

"She's sick with the new bug and she's high risk," I say. "She needs a bed, or a medidrone, and her company won't pay out, so she's stuck on Waitlist, and I was hoping you could help."

Mrs. Silverwright fixes her apologetic eyes just to the left of where my head actually is. "I'm sorry to hear that, darling, but now's really not the time," she says. "The magma's about to start. Make sure everyone's got a glass. Boris will be trying to do a toast of some sort."

She walks off, and I realize I been wearing a chamsuit my whole fucking life. I go get the champagne. The guests are congregating at the edge of the bubble, most of them sitting on little modular stools we helped the bot unload. On the other side, the people who are hominids are agitated, some muttering to each other, some just watching, stock still, eyes wide, as the sky gets dark.

Everyone's got a glass. I back away to the kitchenette, because I don't want to watch a volcanic eruption kill people who are already dead. I'm hoping Clay will circle back, too, and we'll get a slice of time to talk, and I'll tell her what happened.

"This shit is so barbaric."

Not Clay's voice. I look up and see this girl in a swirling lime green holojacket holding a vape to her pouty lips. She's got the same cheekbones as Mrs. Silverwright.

"They could have viewed it from anywhere, but they pick a village, so they can see people being fucking terrified," the girl says. "What's next, the Tulsa massacre?"

I just stare at her.

"I'm only here for my dissertation, but I don't know if it's even worth it, like, morally?" She turns her head and blows smoke. The volcano's still billowing ash into the sky behind her. "If the chronofield failed, they'd deserve it. Honestly."

"Huh," I say, deploying the all-time safest, most vanilla word on instinct.

"I feel so bad for you, having to watch this kind of shit," the girl says. "I'm sorry. Just wanted to say that. I should get back to the jackals now."

She thrusts out her pale moisturized elbow, pretending like she's a chill normal person and half her bloodstream is not composed of artificial leukos. I bump her back. It hurts so bad. She smiles like she did me some kind of favor, then stumbles back to the party.

The volcano blows, and I can see Mrs. Silverwright's heartbeat racing on her dress. I remember how she looked like a goddess to me the first time I saw her.

Fuck.

My mom is playing music when I get home, streaming some electrotango, the kind of stuff she used to dance to back when social dancing was a thing. Sometimes I hear the floor creak a certain way and I know she's gliding around in there. Sometimes, when we're both clean, she'll get me to be her follow, and I'm pretty damn bad at it but it's okay.

I go to the bathroom and scrub. She'll be pissed if I tell her what I tried with Mrs. Silverwright, because it was risking my job and whatnot, but at the same time I want to tell her.

I want to tell her how Mrs. Silverwright apologized to the space beside my head, and how her heart started racing when she saw the volcano blow, and how the hominids, the people, were so scared but nobody really gave a fuck, not the girl with the holojacket and not me, either.

It was a bad, bad trip. I dry my coconut-smelling hands on a fresh towel, then pick up my phone, wiping the last of the disinfectant off its screen. I send Mom a little door-knock pictogram.

No read, no reply.

For a second I imagine that's because she's dancing, sweeping up and down the narrow space between her bed and her closet, but she showed me her lung function yesterday and I know she's not. I go to her door and knock for real.

"Mom? I'm back to the future, or whatever." My voice is all high and tight and I can't fix it. "You okay?"

No reply.

I get these dreams, sometimes, where I'm climbing a tree or a ladder and I fall, and there's this gut-lurch, and this horrible knowledge that you can't take it back. You can't redo the rung, or the branch. Your hand slipped and you're done.

I open my mom's door, wrapping my hand in my sleeve on automatic, and I start falling. She is smaller than I've ever seen her, curled up on her bed in the middle of this big damp wet spot. Her skin has gone gray. Her phone is lying on the floor where she must've dropped it, back cracked so the battery is peeking out.

She is holding her breath, the same way I am, like it's some kind of contest, and I think maybe if I just give up and exhale so will she. I breathe. Her ribcage does not move a millimeter. I am falling, falling, falling.

New strain. More aggressive. Can't touch her. Can't touch her. I call the emergency line and then I do it anyway, stumbling over to grip both her hands. They're cold. I start rubbing them, like that might help, the same way she did for me when I was little and I would come in from the snow and she would say *icicle fingers!* and rub them warm again.

The AI on the emergency line is asking me to scan and link her vitals. She's dead, though. And I get this horrible thought: she was dead anyways. She was outside the bubble.

The next party is in Venice, back before it was underwater, but it doesn't even matter because I'm not even there. It feels like I'm a drone hovering along behind myself, watching me talk to the chef, watching me refill trays, watching me smile. Clay would know something's wrong. She would know it in an instant. But she's home isoing with the same bug everyone's getting now, same SARS variant.

So I float around the party slinging feta zucchini gratin, and nobody can tell the ice truck finally came for my mom yesterday. Some of the guests are wearing little masquerade masks, and a couple have these black goggle-eyed ones with hooked beaks. Heath the clown is back, showing off a flexy new artificial arm, all sleek and white and Apple. The girl with the vape is here again, too, and she doesn't look at me.

Outside the bubble, the cobblestones are crowded with partiers, packed shoulder to shoulder how they never are now. Men and women in costumes are marching through the street. People are waving lanterns, spilling wine, playing bulgy-looking guitars. They look so happy.

"Poor dumb fuckers," Heath says, slurring even though I haven't served him any alcohol. "Getting their ticks all over each other."

This is the last big carnival before the Bubonic Plague hits. I heard Mrs. Silverwright talking about it with the sponsor earlier, like she was talking about cloudy, chance of showers. These happy people are going to be digging mass graves soon. This is the last night before the course of European history is altered forever, and it's a chance for solemn reflection on the ephemerality of something, something, something.

I watch myself get another bottle of Chardonnay out of the chiller. I'm wearing a checkered serving apron that looks dumb but has a pocket. In the pocket I have this pointed metal thing that keeps poking at me.

Mrs. Silverwright is wearing a dress with photosensitive stalks that swivel around to follow the light, and it makes her look like she's made of snakes. She smiles at me when I serve the wine. Heath is pretending to put on a puppet show with his artificial arm, wrapping his real one around the girl with the vape, who giggles. I can hear my mom's voice reading that Williams line, *fingers pressed forcibly down on the fiery braille,* and I understand it now.

Some people will never feel anything until their hands get pushed down onto it, so I wander to the edge of the chronofield. I take the sharp thing out of my apron. It's a short metallic prong inlaid with circuitry and loaded, from what I can tell, with the other kind of virus. Me to you, I don't remember why I snatched it off the ground at Agincourt. Maybe I wanted a souvenir.

Maybe I wanted this. I push it against the shimmery wall of the chronofield. Wave after wave of warning holos pop up, and I slap them all away. Heath the clown had it set to target one specific node. I simplified things. I got it set to target all of them. A beautiful Italian woman in a beautiful filigreed mask dances past me, so close we're almost the same person.

Little hexagons start to appear, not just where I'm pushing, but everywhere, all across the bubble, sprouting like metal flowers. A tremor goes through the whole chronofield. I hear panicky shouts. I keep pushing, but I look back over my shoulder. Mrs. Silverwright is running at me. The girl with the vape is shrieking at me.

"I didn't mean it!" she howls. "I didn't mean it!"

And that's true, too. They don't mean it. But they still have to—

DALE DALE DALE

No expense is spared for the Principito's tenth birthday. I am proof: skin repigmented with mandrill reds and blues, a stripy tail grafted to my coccyx, feathers punched into my flesh to form rainbow plumage.

I try to think only of the money my family will receive, but fear still shakes my knees, sweats my palms. I would feel it in my gut, too, but it's been numb ever since the final surgery. A numb, swollen sac set to burst.

My cell opens. The crowd cheers. The Principito readies his spiked baton.

I hope my children will not be watching.

TIDINGS

Maradi, Niger: 2038

"It's not working," Tsayaba says. She shakes her head in disgust. "Kai!"

"Just wait," Ouma says, adjusting her scarf with shivering hands. "Yi hankali. Give it a minute."

It's a cold, dusty day—harmattan season is so unpredictable now, even with the weather drones they balloon up from Zinder and Niamey. The sky is choked gray, so full of dust that the sun is a smeary yellow blob that makes Ouma think of a lemon candy.

She takes one from her jacket pocket and hands it to Tsayaba, who stares at it. "This has a plastic wrapper, Ouma," she says. "Are you trying to drive me crazy?"

Ouma unpeels it and pops it into her own mouth instead. She knows her older cousin is already a little—not *crazy*; Ouma has been reading e-flets on why that is a stigmatized and offensive term—but a little different. In a good way, a driven way, a furious-thrumming-brain-too-big-for-her-beautifully-braided-head way.

That is why she made money moving memes, why she went away to Nigeria to study biochem in Kano and then biotech in Lagos, why she dropped out to set up her own tiny genelab. But she never stopped messaging, and calling when she could.

And now she is back here, in dusty Maradi, where she and Ouma grew up together, to test out the little biological machine she has been tinkering with for a year and a half. Or for a whole damn century, depending on when you ask her.

The nameless thing is about the size of Ouma's clenched fist, modeled after a waxworm's digestive tract, slick-skinned and perched on cilia that should let it scuttle easily through the sand in a way jointed Bostobots still struggle with.

But the thing is not moving.

"It was perfect in all the sims," Tsayaba mutters. "In the lab tests, too. I filled my whole room with sand and trash."

She punches a few rubbery keys on her brute of a laptop, the one Ouma knows she tried to build only from old parts, to avoid unethically mined gold and tungsten, but finally had to buy new semiconductors for. Hopefully this will not be a giving-in day, too.

"Lots of things don't work out here," Ouma says, bracingly. "My blockphone glitches sometimes, too."

She winces after she says it, because she doesn't think block-phones and crawly genelab things work the same way, and she doesn't want Tsayaba to think she is stupid. But her older cousin is too kind to think things like that, and too distracted anyway.

"I wanted to do it here," Tsayaba mutters, rubbing her eyes. "I wanted this to be the place it starts, because it's the place *I* started. Where our family started. Where I learned we can do important things."

Ouma feels proud of that, because she always assumed that the important things were learned in Kano and Lagos. She wants Tsayaba's thing to work, so she crouches down and presses the wrapper from her lemon candy against its membranous skin and hopes hard.

The wrapper slides through an unseen mouth and dissolves into tiny grains that swirl through the thing's rubbery body, like a little sandstorm. The thing wriggles its cilia feet. It notices the flimsy black shopping bags all around, sticking up from the street like blooming flowers, and suddenly it is hungry. It starts to move.

"It just needed to whet its appetite," Ouma says.

"I was going to try that next," Tsayaba says, but she beams. She wraps her arm around Ouma. "Thank you. And thank you for coming outside with me. I know you are freezing."

Ouma squeezes her back, imagining Tsayaba's dream: a whole swarm of the biomachines crawling through the sand, swimming through the ocean, breaking down tons upon tons of low-density polyethylene without a wisp of greenhouse gases escaping. It's a thrilling vision.

"What will you name it?" she asks. "Maciyin roba? Plastic eater?"

Tsayaba smiles without taking her eyes off the thing. "I don't know. I'll think."

Prague, Czechia: 2044

Kat meets Jan off Lask@, one of those local splinter apps that only takes NFT payments and swears to never memorize your face and biometric data and send it straight to the Devil. The rub with going splinter is that the dating pool shrinks to a dating puddle; the un-rub is that the people splashing around in it tend to be more interesting.

Like Jan the nouveau-anarchist, who brought his own bottle of bacteria-brewed beer to the top of Letna Hill and is somehow pulling off a floral-printed suit. He offers an elbow—Prague is post-vax, but the Big One hit hard here and the greeting hung on.

"Which is for the best," Jan says. "Because the Bigger One, you know, it's around the corner."

Kat doesn't want to think about that, not tonight. She thinks about it enough during the daytime, where her job is prepping samples and lab equipment at Charles University, for the researchers working on plug-and-play mRNA to tackle whatever superbug pops up next.

She thinks about it every too-hot summer, whether she spends it here in Prague or back home in Rotterdam. Climate shift means people shift means overcrowding and deforestation and more vectors for disease and—

"Let's get drunk," Kat says, because it's been a long week.

Jan's amenable to that. They finish the bottle and refill it at the garden brewery; Kat orders in her clumsy Czech, without needing to consult her babelapp, and Jan applauds in a way that would feel sarcastic if not for his beaming smile.

Three or four bottles later, they take a walk around Holešovice. It's beautiful at night, in the blurry orange glow of the streetlamp: the old Communist-era architecture is retrofitted with solar windows and rooftop gardens, green and gray measures. The parks have all been expanded.

They wander through one with the backs of their hands not quite brushing, then Jan looks at her in a particular way and Kat really wants to kiss him right on his beer-smelling mouth, so she does it. The electricity of it makes her forget about all the incoming disasters.

Three or four minutes later, they're at Kat's apartment. The make-out starts in the cramped lift and continues into the cramped flat. She clears off the couch and then helps Jan peel his shirt off, both of them fumbly and excited, and when it clears his tousled head Kat is face-to-face with a hollow cheeked woman in a boat.

Kat blinks. The woman blinks back. The crisp image, rendered in nano ink, is a livestream.

"Uh, Jan? Who's on your stomach?"

Jan glances down. "Oh. I forgot."

He prods his slightly beer-wobbly gut. A name appears in the nano ink: *Tharanga Mendis.*

"It is hard for me to read upside down," Jan says. "But that. She is a refugee from Negombo. The wet bulb temperature is 38 now. People cannot sweat, so they leave or they die."

Kat loses her booze buzz to the old cycle: guilt, annoyance at having to feel guilt on a night where all she wanted to do was hook up, guilt for the annoyance.

"You shouldn't be skincasting people's suffering," she says sharply. "Or sharing their faces. It's gross."

Jan's slate gray eyes turn solemn. "It's only sort of gross," he says. "Her face is already known. This is a feed from border surveillance. I'm watching them watching her, and everybody else in the boat."

Kat frowns. "Accountability?"

Jan shakes his head and grins his lopsided grin. "Better," he says. "Catalonia is only letting in migrants with proof of employment."

The smart tattoo shifts, showing a child now. They pull faces at whatever border drone is circling their vessel.

"With enough people streaming them, they can be classified as performers," Jan says. "We had a legal AI do up the contracts." He holds up his phone, and Kat sees the same feed. "I have it going everywhere," he says. "Not just the tattoo."

"If that works, it's only going to work once," Kat says, slumping down onto the couch. "You know that, right?"

"That's OK," Jan says. "We have lots of ideas. We just have to keep, you know, implementing. One little thing at a time." His forehead creases. "Did you still want to have sex?"

Kat rubs at her face. "I don't know. Kind of." She glares. "How do you *forget* you have that playing on your stomach? How can you keep things—partitioned, like that?"

"Because it's not my responsibility," Jan says. "It's everybody's responsibility. And not everybody is doing their part, but a lot of people are, and I trust those people a lot." He shrugs. "So do what you can, let go of the rest."

Kat shuts her eyes. The last thing she wanted to think about tonight was climate refugees battling draconian border security, but the world is too small, too hot, too claustrophobic, to avoid thoughts like that anymore—even for a night.

"Shirt stays on," she says, pushing it back into his chest. "But, uh, send me the stream first."

This is just how things are now. Kat does what she can, and lets go of the rest.

Site of IDC-59, Australia: 2066

It's so strange to be back at the detention center, to walk along the barbed wire fence and past the somber gray tents. Eli's grandson pleaded with him not to come, because he is learning about trauma responses in school and thinks the place might trigger a panic attack Eli's old hard-thumping heart can no longer take.

But Eli wanted to come, badly. He wanted to remember. Now he leads the way toward E-Tent, where he grew up with his abbá and ammá and the ghosts they had brought with them when they fled Myanmar for their lives. He scuffs his feet in the red dirt, and remembers pretending the rippled sand was a wave-tossed sea. He fantasized about water a lot. There was never much of it in the camp.

There still isn't. The sun is blistering hot and the new refugees, splayed in the scant shade of the tents, have salt crusted around their lips. They move their mouths in the way Eli knows means their tongues are dry, bone-dry. Their faces are tired, and familiar even though he doesn't know them.

The new guards wear the same old dark green jackets. Eli knows that most of them are lounging inside with a fan, but the ones patrolling outside are drenched in sweat, irritable from the heat and ready to displace their annoyance at the slightest provocation.

Their heavy boots are red from the dust and black fobs hang from their belts like ticks. All the children daydreamed about stealing one of those fobs, but instead of leaving the camp, which was the entire world, they mostly wanted to get into the kitchens to find the chocolate bars one particular guard always ate right in front of them.

That was the same guard who tripped him, once, when their game of tag got too close to him. Eli remembers sprawling in the dirt and smacking his head on a piece of gravel. He remembers seeing the surprise and regret on the man's bristly face, but only for an instant, before he sealed it up with the usual scowl and told Eli to go have his cut cleaned.

Eli's ammá told him, later in the tent, that cruelty filters downward—like the mercury in the fish she used to study. She said the hardest thing in the world to do is absorb someone else's cruelty and not pass it along.

"How are you feeling?" little Mohib asks, squeezing his hand. "Dada?"

"It's very well done," Eli says, and pulls off his sweat-suctioned goggles.

The virtual memorial disappears, leaving only a tracery of AR guidelines in the red dirt, a few scuttling oumas hunting down traces of plastic.

The actual camps vanished more slowly, through years of policy battles fought by second-generation migrants and certain Indigenous politicians. First the off-shore detention centers were dismantled, then those of the mainland, and now, at last, they exist only as a bad memory.

Eli thought it was better to forget completely. The idea of the memorial—splicing the same surveillance systems that kept so many desperate souls contained, all the footage from those miserable years—somehow seemed like moving backward.

But now that he has seen it, the forgiving without forgetting, he realizes its power to ensure the cruelty is not passed along.

"Your heart, though," Mohib says, blinking. "How is your heart?"

Eli looks down at his grandson. For a moment, despite the crisp clean runners and bioelectric shirt, he sees himself at the same age: scrawny, dark-eyed, still full of a restless energy. But he will never have fences around him.

"Full," Eli says. "And good."

Mohib breathes a big sigh of relief that implodes his small chest. Eli breathes, too.

Cygnet Community, Dënéndeh Territory: 2099

Suma's idea is ridiculous, when Cade takes a step back from it, but they're fully invested now. They've both been scrounging materials for weeks, digging through every tech-tomb in walking distance of the commune, hunting down everything the printer needs to make a tweaked babeltech rig.

So when Suma comes skipping out of the solar-coated printer shack on Thursday afternoon, waving the final product in the air, Cade is chest-choked with hope and anxiety for the ending of their kid's latest dream. Suma is bright for a ten-year-old, but the blueprint was complicated as shit and she's not Tsayaba Issoufou.

"It's going to work," Suma says sternly, and Cade realizes she somehow ferreted out their doubt.

Cade considers managing expectations. "Su," they say, "I'm really, really proud of you."

Suma's brown cheeks flush, and she does the little wriggle she does to absorb excess praise.

Cade helps her set up the rig right along the garden fence, where the moose has been doing the most damage. At first the young bull was content to crane over the top and snatch gene-tweaked apples from the spindliest tree branches, but lately he prefers smashing through the metal mesh and trampling all over the rhubarb.

The commune was about to reach a unanimous vote for printing up a swarm of botflies to keep the moose away—their little electric stingers pack enough punch even to deter the occasional pizzly bear that wanders south—but Suma proposed negotiating.

Which meant establishing a channel of communication.

Cade watches as Suma checks all the wireless ports and makes sure the responder is safely encased in its rubber box. Their daughter has always been fascinated by non-human persons: The orca colony off the coast of Old Vancouver, which used babeltech to negotiate fishing territories with the Northwest Coalition of First Nations. The roving corvid communities that sometimes fill the talknet with jumbled stories and legal disputes.

As far as Cade knows, nobody has ever successfully used babeltech to talk to a moose before. But improbable doesn't mean impossible—every time Cade looks around, they see improbable things that got done. Replacing the vast canola and wheat fields with polycultures. Dismantling the bones of the ancient oil industry, all the wells and rigs and derricks, to build wind farms and supply commune printers with raw materials.

Absorbing the countless climmigrants from flooded islands and deadly heat, settling them across the prairies instead of the vanishing coastal cities, establishing hundreds of small villages like the one Cade and Suma call home.

So when the bull shows up the next morning, and bed-headed Suma grabs her tablet and races to the porch, Cade hopes they can add talking to a moose to the list. Their daughter links up to the babeltech. They both watch as the bull ambles up to the fence, as per usual, and starts sniffing.

He feels the static field from the babeltech, and wriggles his big bony shoulders in a way that almost reminds Cade of their daughter.

"Hello," Suma says, voice shaking a bit from excitement. "My name is Suma."

The moose swings his big head left, then right. Snorts.

"Can you stop wrecking the fence?" Suma asks. "We could give you a bucket of apples to eat, if you like. And some spare rhubarb to step on."

The babeltech kicks in, and the synthesized representation of the moose's non-human person neural processes comes blaring through Suma's tablet.

"*FUCK. FUCK. FUCK. FUCK.*"

Suma blinks in surprise. "Cade?" she says, in a low voice. "Why's he saying that?"

Cade tries to keep the laugh down, and it nearly bursts their belly. "Uh, I think it's rutting reason," they say. "Maybe he'll be more conversational in a couple weeks."

Suma purses her lips. "If the moose is allowed to say it, can I say it, too?"

"Just once," Cade says. "Since you got babeltech to work with a cervine. You earned it, kiddo."

Suma grins. "Even if he only cusses at us, this is still so fucking cool."

Ko Phangan, Thailand Republic: 2132

Nam takes her boat out in the late afternoon, when the sky is travel-holo blue and sunshine is sparkling the water. She takes 112 net-friends with her. They fill her goggle lenses with animated hearts when they see the aquamarine waves, when they feel the salt spray on her nerve suit.

She cuts against the swell; the motor hums, converting solar charge to forward motion to sheer happiness. The clear water teems with shoals of technicolor fish and the occasional ouma straining microplastics. Sometimes she still comes across megaplastics, too: ancient Singha bottles and disposable gloves, relics of a time that sometimes feels mythical to her, that even had a king.

When her net-friends catch sight of the dolphins, their animated hearts explode. Nam feels her real heart beat a little faster, how it always does when she sees the pod cutting through the water, eight sleek pink acrobats racing and leaping then plunging back under. She knows each of their names, or at least she did last week. The dolphins like to change them, and give each other nicknames, which Nam told them is very Thai of them.

She switches off the motor. Her little boat sloshes forward on the afterkick, drifts. The pod comes closer, squealing and chattering. In her goggles, Nam sees more net-friends joining her, hopeful today will be one of the special days.

Some come from as far away as Nueva Gran Colombia—she visited a paisa girl's goggles once, and marveled at the lush green city with its every spare surface coated in carbon-catch moss. Another comes from Nuuk, the colorful capital of Kalaallit Nunaat where the buildings perch on telescoping legs.

Each person brings a small trickle of netcash, which is how Nam bought her extra nerve suit, and a pair of flutterwings for her littlest sibling's birthday, and any other things that were not voted as food-shelter-health-happiness essentials.

As Truth noses up to the boat, grinning, Nam feels a grin spreading across her own face. "Sawadee," she says. "How are you, Truth?"

Truth is the oldest dolphin in the pod, around forty years old, but still the quickest and most playful. She's always teasing the young calves, swimming upside down beneath them or blowing little air rings at their bellies.

"Squid squid squid," Truth says, her chattering squeal turned to synth-speech by Nam's goggles. "Delicious sea. Nam?"

Nam recognizes the last chirp, even without the synth-speech translation, and it always flutters her stomach to know the pod has given her a name. She reaches back into her cooler and pulls out a few of the freshly caught bobtail squid Truth prefers.

"Here," she says, dropping them into the water. "Would you like to wear the suit today, Truth?"

Truth gobbles down the squid first, then circles the boat, then finally surfaces to squeal her answer. "Suit day! Yes. Yes. Rebarbative suit day!"

Nam blinks—sometimes the babeltech goes far afield with dolphin vocabulary. But the enthusiasm is clear, so she takes the extra nerve suit, the one she dissected and reassembled and waterproofed, and helps web it across Truth's rubbery pink body. The other dolphins swirl around, curious.

"There are 308 net-friends watching," Nam says. "Is that OK?"

"Friends," Truth chitters. "Many swim. Nam swim. All swim."

Nam caps the stream, then sits back in her boat and becomes the 309th. Her heart thrums with anticipation as the nerve suit links up, and then—

Nam is in the water, feeling the cool lap against Truth's blubber-sheathed body, seeing through Truth's low-light eyes. Nam is a good swimmer. She relishes the feel of a perfect stroke, her whole body working in harmony, from her cupped hand biting the surface to her flexed feet knifing through it.

Swimming as a dolphin is that, factor ten. One of the young bulls rockets down toward the seabed and Nam-with-Truth rockets after him, snout pointed for the sandy bottom. She scrapes her belly against the bottom, sends sand swirling everywhere.

Then up, up fast, tail threshing her toward the gauzy sunlight. The bull hurtles clear of the water and Nam-with-Truth does the same trick. There's a beautiful never-ending moment of suspension, up in the sky, shedding the sea off her fins and flukes, perfectly weightless in a cloud of soft shattered glass.

Nam is flying through the air. Nam is lying in her boat. Nam is all around the world, joined to 308 other electric heartbeats. She knows it should probably feel mythical, like the age of ancient plastic, the age of gas-guzzling planes and freighters crisscrossing the oceans.

But instead, it just feels true.

THE OLD MAN

So the fed solution to one convict escaping is releasing another."

They watched the gleaming white pyramid of cryocaps ripple and rearrange itself, pulling a particular prisoner to the front on magnetic rails. A spidery robotic arm jerked the blue-lit cryocap out of its slot and set it in front of them with a thud that echoed to the vaulted ceiling. Technicians wearing baggy white safesuits scurried forward.

"It was not a decision we made lightly, Warden. This is our best chance of tracking him down. He knows the swamps better than nearly anyone else."

"Knew them a decade ago. Is what you mean."

"Things change slowly in the South, Warden. Some things, not at all."

A technician plugged her smartgloved thumb into a particular socket, and the cryocap turned transparent. Inside, prisoner 110924 drifted in a burnt-orange suspension gel, tethered by tubes snaking into his long bony limbs and down his throat. His shaven head knocked up against the top of the cryocap. Six years of cold storage with minimal rethaws had sapped some mass, whittling him to muscle shrink-wrapped over bone, but he was still gigantic, still imposing.

"What makes you so sure your boy here goes with the gameplan? Doesn't try to skate as soon as you drop him in the swamp?"

"We'll rig him out with a tracker and a biobomb. And keep a close eye on him."

"Some people would rather get their head blown to bits than live the rest of their life in a tank. You can dream in cryo, you know. And this motherfucker, he's not having good ones."

The cryocap began to drain, sluicing suspension gel into a sticky orange puddle on the ferrocrete floor. The tubes retracted, wriggling out from the prisoner's flesh like tapeworms; he convulsed as the last one slid out of his cock. His dark skin had paled, gaining a grease-yellow tint underneath.

"We're going to commute his sentence if he succeeds. But his real motivation will be intrinsic. Psychologically speaking."

"You're going to tell him dead or alive, then."

Two technicians helped the prisoner to a gurney that flexed itself up to the correct height for him to sit. His eyes were still gummed shut. The thaw had been started remotely six hours prior, but full muscle function wasn't slated to return for another two. The prisoner eased himself down like an old man, gripping the edge of the gurney with long ink-laced fingers.

"Yes. And we'll expect dead."

A technician approached him with an injector and suddenly the fingers were around her throat. Her safesuit inflated, punching him backward onto the gurney, and he nearly rocked it over. The other technicians scrambled for the restraints.

"Guess there's no love lost between them. With how it all ended."

"You're putting it lightly, Warden. We downloaded some of those cryo dreams and the AI reached the same conclusion we did. Ezekiel here wants to kill his own pa more than he wants anything else in the entire fucking world."

A body slit open and steaming in the back of a refrigerated truck. Blood turning to slippery slush on the dull metal floor. Copper smell clinging in his throat like it wouldn't ever leave. The Old Man's wild eyes roving, his voice booming, *we are the instruments of God.*

"Welcome back to the land of the living, Ezekiel."

Zeke dragged his head up. They'd stood him under a skinspray nozzle long enough for modesty, coating him in ragged black fiber that felt like cobweb, and they'd clamped his hands. Now he was in a folding chair, two men looking at him from across a bolted-down table.

One was familiar: the warden, but aged, deeper trenches around his mouth and a crooked nose that had been straight before. The other had an artfully-gashed suit, smug eyes dotted with circuitry, and Zeke could hear the Old Man's voice sneering in his head: *G-man, spook, fucking puppet, fucking government puppet.*

"You must be wondering why you're thawed," the spook continued. "Seeing as your next physical isn't scheduled for another eight months. It has to do with your daddy."

That made sense, even in Zeke's cryo-muddled head, because everything had to do with the Old Man. He was the black hole at the center of the universe, eating and eating. Zeke felt a familiar bubbling in his gut, hot sick hate churned together with more fear than he had ever admitted to anyone.

"There was a mass cryo failure in the LCI, so he was in transit, heading to a slam in Angola," the spook said. "But something happened while they were crossing marshland. He got free. Now he's gone to ground in the south-east bayou. That's home territory, for him. And for you."

Zeke saw it all crystallized in an instant. "And ain't nobody know." He forced the words up a raw throat.

The warden shot a surprised look sideways, but the spook just smiled. "Officially, he's already safely back in the tank. It's not a good look, otherwise. The most notorious homegrown terrorist of the past fifty years shaking loose just like that."

"So why you thaw me?" Zeke asked, because it seemed important to get it from the spook's mouth.

"To help us recapture him. Quickly and quietly."

"I get what?"

The spook leaned backward. "We take you out of the tank," he said. "Commute your life sentence to twenty years in genpop, if you can go that long without killing anyone."

Zeke set his clamped hands heavily on the table, ignoring the sting. "Recapture, you said." He peered deep as he could into the spook's wired eyes.

The spook gave his chimpanzee smile again, all teeth. "If

something were to go wrong, and he were to be killed in firefight, the deal would remain unchanged."

Zeke clenched his fists tight, letting the clamp sting him over and over like a Gulf jellyfish, but there was no way to test if he was dreaming or not. Could be he was still floating in the tank. If it was a dream, though, it seemed like a good one.

"Yeah," he said. "Deal."

Finally warm again. Zeke felt the change, felt familiar damp heat creeping into the flyer's open fuselage, as they headed south. His skin prickled with almost-sweat and the fresh scar tissue where they'd welded a little cam to his cheekbone started to itch.

The back of his head itched, too, and ached fiercely from the tracker/biobomb insertion. They did that with a big needle that reminded him of killing catfish, finding the little hole in the skull and sticking the wire in. The jittery technician had told him it would blow his head clean off if he tried to run.

Zeke knew better. The Old Man had caught a spook once, and took off four of his fingers with pliers before he triggered his biobomb. There'd been a smell of burning meat and the spook had slumped over right away, but his head had stayed in one piece.

Down below, Zeke saw the bayou spread out like mottled skin, poisonous green canopy and water colored like the dull gray sky. Some things were different. New powerlines, it looked like, sutured through the vegetation. And in the far distance he could see the floodwater had encroached, taking new chunks out of the coast, Houma and New Orleans long since swallowed.

He heard the Old Man booming in his head: *and the waters will rise, and the storms will come again and again, until we loose the Devil's hold on this country. Either we purify these lands, or the floods will. You hear me, Ezekiel? You hear me, Elijah? You hear me, Elim?*

Zeke figured he would always hear him, even after he killed him. He looked at the sealed matte black case where the spook had promised him a shotgun with rib barrel and tac barrel, a snub-nosed handgun, hydrophobe-coated cartridges and plenty of ammo for both. He fantasized sticking the .22 up under the Old Man's thick jaw, so he couldn't speak, and it must have showed because the guard slouched across from him tensed up.

"You sweat a whole lot," Zeke said. "Must make them hands real slippery."

The guard's knuckles were white around the grip of his rifle for the rest of the trip.

They dropped him and the black case as close as they could to the Old Man's last triangulated position, and as the flyer droned away Zeke felt a little bite of electricity from the cam under his eye. Maybe checking the calibration, maybe just a reminder that they would be watching. The spook would be watching.

He sloshed his way to higher ground, sucking down another deep breath of the pungent air, tasting the mélange of moss and rot and mangrove flowers, all scents he'd thought he'd lost forever. He could hear the buzz of insects, the splash and slither of a lizard or a baby gator.

Zeke dragged the case onto a humped root and palmed it open. He outfitted the Mossberg, ribbed barrel for now, and loaded it with buckshot. The .22 went into his waistband. He filled the pockets of the fatigues with ammo, then went through the rest of the case.

He pulled on the hydrophobe jacket and put the MRE bars in the pocket, left the sleeping roll, headlamp, and fuel cell. Grabbed the knife, left the multitool. From the aid kit he took clingwrap, using it to seal the tops of his boots, and all of the painkiller patches.

Everything else went back in the case, which he dumped in the first pocket of quicksand he found. It sank fast. He remembered coming home from fishing, when him and Elijah were young enough that the Old Man still towered over them, and Elim was still a baby. Zeke had been chasing Elijah through the cypress trees and then suddenly he hadn't, slipping hip-deep into a soft pale mud his older brother had danced right across.

Put yourself in there, you can get yourself out, the Old Man had said, squatting down with the catch still writhing raw and pink over his shoulder. *Wail on like that, though, something gonna eat you first.* Zeke had stopped wailing then, but the tears and snot kept dripping down his chin and the mud kept sucking at his skin. He'd looked at Elijah for help, but Elijah only crouched there with the same horrible blank look on his face as when he picked legs off beetles, and then him and the Old Man had left.

Even after Zeke had realized the mud could creep to his belly but no higher, after he'd finally figured to tip himself backward to lever his legs up, finally knotted his slippery fingers into a tangle of roots, it still took hours to get out. Hours of wriggling and fighting and biting back sobs in the dark, listening for the splash of waking gators or the bone rattle of the ghost Elijah had sworn to seeing behind the outhouse.

The Old Man had been waiting for him when he slopped free, stepping out from behind a tree only a stone's throw away, shotgun hanging in the crook of his arm. His eyes were rimmed red. *If you done called even once, even one damn time, I'd have got you out. Forgive me, Ezekiel. Forgive me, I wronged you.* And he'd carried him home, letting him wrap his skinny shaky arms around his neck.

Zeke was careful where he stepped now. He slung the Mossberg over his shoulder and followed the water. Mosquitos were breeding in silvery clouds along the bank, so he paused long enough to plaster his exposed skin with mud, careful not to cover the cam.

The sun was out now, poking its fingers through the tangled branches overhead and gleaming off dirty puddles. Looking for footprints was useless here; the swamp swallowed them fast as you made them. But there were other ways people left traces.

He found the first one at head-height, a splintery knob where a cypress branch had been torn free. By the look of the branches around it, four feet, good length for a spear once it was stripped and sharpened. The Old Man had escaped unarmed and fixed that soon as possible, knowing someone was coming after him.

The Old Man would be ready.

Dusk was falling when Zeke came across a shack. Its plank pathway was all but gone, only a few rotted fragments poking up from the water like broken bones, and the porch was half-swallowed. Zeke looked over the soggy timbers, the battered roof snaked with retrofitted cables. Someone had peeled off the solar pad, leaving a square of corrugated tin with less rust than the rest. The one window was shattered.

Not so different in shape from the house where he grew up with his brothers and the Old Man and sometimes the pale thick-boned woman with weary eyes who they had to call Nurse, never Mama. Theirs had been built better; the Old Man was thorough in everything he did, precise. For a moment Zeke's mind overlaid the ruin with pieces of memory, seeing:

The welded metal T off the porch where the Old Man dressed deer, hanging them by their hooves and then slitting them open with his long knife. Elijah had always watched, fascinated, for the moment when the skin of the belly split and the entrails spilled out as shiny pink ropes. Zeke had liked it better when the Old Man hung a tire for them to swing on.

The spiny dish mounted on the roof, stealing signals from a pirate satellite, filling their lone tablet with the web and the outside world that had bored Elijah and had never seemed quite real to Zeke. But Elim had devoured the information from the time he was little, and the Old Man had approved. *Y'all three need to learn all you can,* he'd said. *Learn the truth, and learn how the enemy lies. The climate cycle bullshit, the border closing, the homeland protection drones. Learn all you can before they seal off the web, too.*

A noise came from inside the shack.

Zeke dropped low, hands already moving to swap for the tac barrel. He brought the scope to his eye but saw only shadows through the broken window. He circled closer, using the spindly trees and rising fog as cover. The sound came again, something scraping on wood, and the shack's sagging door moved just slightly.

Zeke thumbed the safety off. He felt a low cold throb at the back of his skull. His heartbeat was slow, like he was back frozen in the tank, and his hands were steady. He crossed the space in three bent-low strides, angled out of sight of the window. Paused there against the splintery frame of the porch. A muffled thump came from inside, and the door shuddered.

From this close, a round of buckshot would shred right through. But it would be loud, too, and Zeke had to be sure. He swung himself onto the porch and shouldered the door open in one motion. He saw a flurry of white and gray; half his brain had it down as a male heron while the other half was clearing the room, corner to corner. Floor rotted out, aluminum cans floating in puddles, overturned rocking chair covered in green moss.

Empty.

The adrenaline kicked late and Zeke's hands shook a bit as he turned back, realizing the heron hadn't bolted through the open doorway, hadn't taken the window either. There was a reason. One of the bird's wings was crumpled against itself, but the other was fully extended, all taut skin and straggly feathers, pinned to the back of the door with an oxidized knife. The dangling heron twitched against the wood and gave a weak caw.

He ducked away from the door, his heart thumping fast now, nowhere near frozen. The blood rimming the metal was coagulated black, but the Old Man wouldn't have set bait unless he planned to tend to it. Zeke went to the window and peered into thickening fog. Could be the Old Man was out there somewhere, watching the shack with his wild eyes.

Zeke kicked through the trash, staying low, scanning for bullet boxes or old casings. If the Old Man had left the knife stuck, it meant he had something better now. The thought twisted Zeke's stomach with fear. He gave a disintegrating cabinet a kick; the soggy wood crunched inward. Then he turned back to the pinned heron.

First thing he'd ever killed with his hands had been a heron. He remembered that now. The Old Man had set a length of razorwire out behind the house, for when the enemy finally came looking, and one morning Zeke had found a big gray bird tangled in it.

Sometimes a body does nothing wrong and they get hurt anyways, the Old Man had said. *But what we're doing, Ezekiel, is more important than one heron. One hand here, one hand there. Pull down hard as you can.*

Zeke put the stock of his shotgun against the base of the pinned bird's neck. It wasn't bait, or at least it wasn't only bait. It was the Old Man guessing who'd been sent after him. The heron gave another low caw. Zeke ran his fingers down its feathery head, but he didn't twist. That would all but confirm the Old Man's suspicion, and Zeke didn't want him to know. Not yet.

He looked into the heron's filmy eye a moment longer, then slunk out of the shack and closed the door carefully behind him.

An overgrown coypu was nosing its way along the bank; Zeke pictured it skinned and skewered, roasting over a sputtering fire. He'd hunted plenty of river rats when he was young, especially during the days or weeks when the Old Man disappeared and left Elijah in charge. Remembering the taste made his mouth water, but he let the coypu go and fished an MRE bar out of his pocket instead. No unnecessary noise or light until he had a fix on the Old Man.

He'd circled for hours, moving steadily outward from the shack, but had seen no more sign of his quarry. Now the sky was turning black and the gators would be awake, the bigger ones sloshing out of the water to go lie in wait trailside. Even armed, Zeke didn't want to chance across one in the dark, and he figured the Old Man didn't, either. He found a tree with a sturdy crook high enough off the ground and slid his knife under the bark to check for bugs. Nothing that bit.

Zeke clambered up the tree and unslung his Mossberg, hanging it from a branch above him. He held the .22 in his lap as he leaned back against the trunk and closed his eyes. He'd been running on purpose and rage and the post-thaw amphetamines they'd dosed him with, but now his atrophied muscles were burning with exertion. His skeleton felt heavy.

Zeke drifted between dreams and memories. Being back in the bayou had tapped open the oldest of them, before they were so full of blood. Sitting on the porch with his brothers in the evening, the Old Man reading from the Bible or *The Tempest*, glow from the tablet screen attracting little winged beetles. Zeke and Elijah and Elim would play a game while they listened, the one where they broke down and built up whichever gun the Old Man picked from the bolted locker. Zeke was usually first to have it memorized, and then he would have to do it with Elim covering his eyes from behind and Elijah jamming a sharp knuckle under his ribs.

There had been other games, too, hiding games and fighting games Zeke once assumed all children played. The see-nothing game, where they had to pretend the Old Man's visitors were invisible, whether it was the ex-soldiers with bristly beards and shifting tattoos or the dark-eyed families who stayed in their attic for days or weeks. Those sometimes spoke to each other in a throaty language and the women always wore cloth over their heads.

Zeke's breathing quickened as his mind dragged him forward to the day it stopped being games. The Old Man hadn't been one for birthdays, but Zeke had done the math since and knew he'd been fifteen when it happened. Elijah seventeen, Elim twelve. The three of them had been out hunting when the drone hummed overhead. Everyone had bellied out in the mud, no hesitation, because that was what you did when a drone or flyer went over the bayou. Once the sound subsided, they kept going.

Zeke had bagged a lynx that day, came up on it quiet as smoke and deaded it between the eyes, a shot that made Elim sing aloud and Elijah glower for hours. He carried it draped across his bony shoulders, not wanting to soil or tear the pelt on brambles getting it home. Every so often he rubbed his face in the soft fur, ignoring the stink of gases leaving its slow-stiffening body.

They'd been nearly home when a thunderclap shattered the cloudless sky. Loudest thing Zeke had ever heard. A smell came, too, something metallic that stung the inside of his nose. The birds went silent. Elim started to run, started shouting *orbital, they hit us with an orbital, they killed everyone*. Then Elijah ran too, and Zeke left the lynx in the dirt to keep pace.

Ten years later, Zeke could still see it all etched across the insides of his eyelids. The smoldering branches as they got closer, the gushing steam that scalded their exposed skin, the gurgling hole where a few scorched fragments of wood were all that was left of the house. Bits of blackened bone, too, because a trio with sad eyes and uncitizen brandings had been staying in the attic, and the Old Man had been home repairing the roof.

He remembered fear, sicker and deeper than he'd ever felt it before. He remembered grabbing blindly for Elim and Elijah so they wouldn't disappear, too; Elim clung back and after a moment so did Elijah. They'd been huddled like that when the Old Man limped out from the steam. Coated in soot and blood, clothes singed to ash, a deep furrow showing part of his shinbone.

They put a damn tracker in him, he'd said. *Missed it in all the scars. God damn them. God damn them.* His eyes had been wild for the first time, then, but Zeke didn't realize it until later. He'd been too shocked, too wracked with relief and awe. *We go to war now. You hear me, Elim? You hear me, Elijah? You hear me, Eze-kiel?*

Zeke pushed the muzzle of the .22 against his head, like he could force the memories out, but memories like that never left. Only burrowed.

Morning came quickly, streaking the sky with filaments of red. Zeke roused from half-sleep to rub warmth back into his stiff limbs. He licked dew from the leaves above him and ate another MRE, folding the wrapper carefully into his pocket. Then he re-trieved the Mossberg, worked the handgun back into his waist-band, and climbed down. Set off again.

He moved through the bog like a ghost, smooth and quiet, but bits of bad dream still clung to him. He'd dreamed concrete cube bunkers and dingy apartments, the places they'd shuttled between after their home in the bayou was sat-bombed. Cities that had been only names to him before: Memphis, St. Louis, Chi-cago. Colder and colder, but he hadn't felt it at the time. He'd had a flame burning in his belly.

Zeke remembered the first op best. Sitting in the back of a truck with a black S&W bullpup, one he'd taken apart more times than he could count, resting across his knees. His brothers almost invisible across from him, wearing chamsuits that rippled light and then dark and then back again as the truck rattled down a row of street lamps.

One of the Old Man's ex-soldiers had made a last minute pro-test, hissing *they're only kids, fuck's sakes,* and Elijah had given him his deadest look while the Old Man said *they look like they only kids?* The words had filled Zeke with a fierce pride that ached the back of his throat. When the truck stopped, he'd felt more trembly, and queasy, like he needed a shit.

But that had disappeared the instant they pulled their hoods up and spilled out onto the street. The prisoner transport, stalled right where the Old Man had said. The guards, dropping their vapor pipes and fumbling for their weapons, clumsy how the Old Man had predicted. Zeke had put two rounds in his target's chest and it felt no different from shooting deer. Elijah had downed the other and then Elim had stuck the breaching shotgun up to the lock and blown the transport doors open.

Zeke remembered the rush, the sick feeling washed away by cold clear adrenaline and knowing that he was doing God's work. He'd helped round up the driver and the guards and search them for phones and sidearms. The Old Man had gone into the back of the transport and come out a moment later, hauling a woman whose face had been beaten to one pulpy mass of bruises because she knew things the government didn't want her to.

As the Old Man helped her down, Zeke's chamsuit had started to glitch, flashing bright acid yellow, and he'd ripped off his hood to find the override switch. Only for a second, but when the Old Man noticed he pulled out his needler and fired a single flechette into the kneeling driver's head.

Never show your face, the Old Man had said. *Never, you hear me? That one had a wired eye. Look.* So Zeke had looked, and seen a single spark jump from where the Old Man's flechette had sheared its way through the lens, through the wiring, through the soft eyeball into the brain. Zeke remembered a trickle of vomit had escaped his lips at the sight, but he'd kept his hood up and breathed rancid air until they were back at the hideout.

You did me proud, Ezekiel, the Old Man had said later, after they'd all taken turns showering in the rusted tub, washing away the stink of fight-or-flight sweat. *And what we did tonight was more important than one government driver. His soul is in God's hands, not ours.*

Zeke was still half in the memory as he caught a faint smell of ash. He followed it until he found the charred twigs and powdery traces of a fire. Squatting down, he sifted through the remains with his hands. Still warm. Overhead, another stump where a cypress branch had been, this one cut cleanly. Too long and flimsy for a weapon, but a good length to probe for gators.

Zeke headed towards the bank, towards the shallow point he'd seen yesterday. The Old Man was finally making a move.

*

The algae-skinned water moved slow and no higher than the waist, but there were other deterrents to crossing. Zeke kept his ears pricked as he pushed through the swaying rushes. It was safest to wait until noon, when the fog peeled away and the gators were lazy and sunning themselves. But the Old Man had never been scared of gators or anything else.

Zeke moved slowly, eyes screwed up against the fog, and when he caught a glimpse of a familiar silhouette his heart nearly stopped. Then it sped up, pounding against his ribcage as the mist parted. Tall as Zeke himself was, built with the same thick bones and corded muscle, near identical to him or to Elijah or to Elim had Elim finished growing. The Old Man had his own way of moving, though. Even half-naked, wading through green scum. He moved like every step had been planned for a hundred years and nothing could stop it.

Zeke raised the shotgun. Through the scope, he saw the Old Man's face, ridged brow and angular cheekbones and deep-set eyes. Aside from the gray scruff of beard, it was like seeing his reflection. He'd once thought all brothers looked alike, and all sons grew to look like copies of their fathers. Zeke flicked the safety off. His finger caressed the trigger.

From this distance, the buckshot would drop him even if it didn't get penetration. If the Old Man got back up, it was another easy shot, and if the Old Man thrashed and bled enough in the water, he wouldn't need it. The Old Man would never know where the shell came from. Or who it came from.

Zeke clenched his teeth, then lowered the Mossberg and slid forward into the scum. Cold water crept past his wrapped boots, clinging at the knees of his fatigues. He wanted the Old Man to look him in the face when it happened. He wanted him to know who and why.

The Old Man moved slow and steady toward the opposite bank, and Zeke followed. Orange fabric flashed through the mud the Old Man had plastered over his peeled-down jumpsuit, and in the knotted arms Zeke saw a battered pistol handle. He was using the stripped branch to check depth as he went. Zeke kept one eye on the Old Man, one scanning the algae for the raised nodes of an alligator's scoots. Birds were warbling, hopping into the water, a good sign.

The gap shrank. If the Old Man went for his pistol, he would have to take the shot. But he would get close as he could first. The water rose to Zeke's waist, still cold enough to bite. Mist swirled overtop of the thick green scum. He'd spent his whole life following after the Old Man. For a moment it felt as if he were a child again, as if Elim and Elijah would be coming behind with the fishing gear.

He tightened his grip on the shotgun. Only yards away now. He mouthed the words: *turn around, Old Man, look at death how Elijah did, look at death how Elim did.* He imagined the Old Man's jaw blown off before he could reply, his head torn open by the buckshot.

The birds had stopped warbling. Zeke realized it in the same moment the Old Man did, and the Old Man pivoted in the same moment a gator erupted from the water. Green froth flew into Zeke's eyes; when they cleared all he could see was the pale pink flesh of an open maw, impossibly wide. He dove backward as the jaws clacked shut in his face. He squeezed the trigger.

The shotgun's boom deafened him. A chunk of the gator's snout detonated in a cloud of red, spattering Zeke's face, and a tiny shard of bone or deflected buckshot buried searing hot in his chest. The gator thrashed. Zeke got a glimpse of the Old Man through the spray, enough to see him drawing the pistol. Zeke pumped the Mossberg, braced the stock on his shoulder, fired.

He didn't see if it landed; the gator was surging at him, yelping through its shredded snout, the intact teeth glinting sharp. Zeke hurled himself to the side, pumping again. Before he could pull, the gator twisted around and its tail took his legs. Zeke crashed into the water. Scum filled his mouth and nose; he could feel the gator moving but he was blinded by bubbles streaming past his eyes. He came up choking, spinning to face.

He found the gator drifting limp. There was a spread of bullets lodged along its bony head. The third had blown clean through the eye socket, leaving a ragged red tunnel on its way to the gator's brain. Zeke raised his shotgun again, scanning the opposite bank, but the Old Man was gone. He watched the tree line until the gator's limbs started to twitch.

Maybe just the last few dying nerves. Zeke didn't take the

chance. He fired a last shell into the top of its flat skull, reloaded, and sloshed his way to shore.

Once the adrenaline ebbed, the bit of shrapnel lodged under Zeke's collarbone started to sting. He found a hump of semi-dry ground and peeled off his coat and shirt. With his chin to his chest he could see the nub of distended flesh, seeping blood around a sliver of gray buckshot. Zeke took a breath, then wormed his finger in and pulled the fragment free. He patched the wound with clingwrap and slapped a dermal painkiller to his neck.

As the drug flushed cool and tingly through his body, he stripped bark to bed a fire, moving on automatic. The Old Man had downed the gator. Only needed three shots to do it, and any one of them could have gone in his head instead. That meant the Old Man still wanted something from him, even though it felt like he'd already taken it all.

After the first op, they'd started to blur together: usually in the night, with gear, sometimes in the day wearing plain clothes. Taking and leaving packages in specific places. Breaking into buildings. Planting a bomb in an autocab. Holding up a morgue to carve a data implant out of a corpse's leg. Rescues that were sometimes more like kidnaps. Government reports that called them terrorists, raw reels that called them the Insurgency.

The Old Man sleeping less and less, his eyes always bloodshot and his late-night rants slurred from his medications. Elim chewing through the pillowcase he used to hide sobs. The Old Man interrogating a spook in the blood-stained bathtub while Elijah recorded without trembling even once. Elim refusing to watch, even though it was the same spook who'd authorized gas attacks in Aztlan. In the night, Elim sitting up and whispering: *we never had a mother, Zeke, we're seedlings and he grew us like this, grew us to be just like him, see?*

Zeke fed twigs into the flickering flame, coaxing it to life. He peeled off the spent derm and replaced it with a second. He couldn't remember what they'd been trying to do on the night Elim died, but he remembered the escape, dragging Elim across the tarmac towards the getaway van and leaving a dark smear behind. The Old Man had helped load him into the back, where there was an Ascelpius unit waiting to scan the injuries. Zeke had held Elim's hand while he cursed and choked and the unit unfurled over him like a white plastic squid.

Two gunshot wounds in the chest, one where his hipbone met his thigh. Bright blood leaking onto the dull metal floor as the van pulled away. Zeke had already been moving to hook himself up for transfusion, how they'd done a half-dozen times before, when the Old Man shook his head. He'd tapped the screen of the unit, so Zeke could see the glowing red fatality prognosis.

Elim, you're going home, the Old Man had said, in a voice thick with tears. *May the Lord make his face shine upon you, and be gracious to you, and give you peace, and may you dwell in the house of the Lord forever.*

And then, before Zeke could say *wait* or *I love you, Elim* or anything else, he'd tapped the screen again. The Ascelpius had rolled Elim onto his side and plunged a precise needle into the back of his neck, like killing a catfish. Zeke remembered sitting paralyzed on the floor of the van while the unit worked, slitting Elim's body open with a gush of steam, bagging and sealing the organs, sluicing the blood with a horrible sucking sound.

Has to be done, the Old Man had said. *Might save any one of us. It's just a body, now, Ezekiel. His soul is with God.*

Months later Zeke had noticed a fresh scar on the Old Man's chest and realized where Elim's heart had gone.

Zeke shook himself. He unloaded the shotgun and used it to prop up his coat by the fire; it could maybe pass from a distance as a sitting silhouette. Then he took the .22 from his waistband and left the warmth and light behind. He found a place to watch and wait.

The Old Man came from the opposite direction Zeke was expecting, so quiet he nearly missed the footfalls. Zeke waited a heartbeat, then swept out from behind the mangrove. The Old Man stopped, arms akimbo, his pistol tied in its makeshift holster. He didn't try to turn around.

"Put a cam on you," he said. "And a mic?"

The Old Man's voice had changed. It didn't boom and roll like thunder. It was hoarse and strained and, for the first time, old.

Zeke aimed for the dead center of his shaved head.

"I prayed they would send you, Ezekiel," the Old Man said. "Prayed and prayed, and here we are."

"Hands," Zeke croaked.

The Old Man put his hands on his head, joints popping.

"Look at me," Zeke said.

The Old Man turned, and from close up Zeke could see new lines carving his face. For so long it had seemed like he would never age. Zeke let the .22 drift from one sunken eye to the other. He could feel the cam on his cheekbone humming. He imagined a dozen spooks cutting into the feed, crowding around screens to watch.

"I hate you," he said.

"I heard such," the Old Man said. "And that hate'll eat you alive if you let it."

"You ate us alive," Zeke said. "You got Elim's heart beating in you right now. Only good part you do got." He breathed in deep. "You was just waiting for a reason to cut him up."

"I knew Elim wasn't gonna make it," the Old Man said. "Too gentle. You knew it, too. Coulda been that night, coulda been a different night. No difference."

"Elijah," Zeke said. "You made him a fucking monster. He never had no choice in it. Neither of them got a choice."

"I know," the Old Man said. He paused, eyes slick with tears. "But I did love them, Ezekiel."

Zeke fired. The bullet cracked the air, splintered the trunk behind the Old Man's head. "Don't tell me no lies," he snarled.

The Old Man's mouth moved, and when the roar in Zeke's ears subsided he heard the words. "I done a lot of wrong things, Ezekiel. I have sinned. I have sinned against you a hundred times over. I am ready to die."

Then he lunged, and for an instant Zeke saw Elijah and Elim in his face and it made him slow to the trigger. The Old Man bowled him over, his long arms impossibly strong as they knocked the shot askew, pinned him down. Zeke felt the .22 fly from his grip and hit dirt. He jackknifed upward, trying to catch the Old Man's chin.

Air. The Old Man was quick, too quick, and now his hands were around his throat squeezing. Blackness seeped into Zeke's peripherals. It constricted around him like rubber. He connected with a knee; the Old Man grunted, held on.

"But not yet," the Old Man said. "Not just yet."

He drove his thumb under Zeke's eye and crushed the cam.

Zeke was adrift. He knew it was the painkillers: the Old Man had stuck derm after derm to his bruised neck, enough to turn his limbs distant and his head cloudy. Sometimes it felt like he was being dragged. Mostly it felt like he was floating in the dark, back in the tank. He saw things from a distance. He saw the refrigerated van. He saw the alley. He remembered.

He remembered something had come unglued in Elijah after Elim died. Zeke had noticed the change in his face, first, in how he gave up the too-wide smiles or exaggerated frowns that he once used to try and put the other insurgents at ease. His face had gone back to being perfectly blank. Then other things: The hours he spent lying flat on his back, whispering to himself. Maimed insects hopping and buzzing in the screen of the window. Unplanned casualties on ops gone wrong.

Zeke had tried to talk to him, tried to use soft words like Elim would have. Elijah had listened, calm and patient, and at the end of Zeke's rambling he'd leaned close and said *that lynx was mine, Zeke, and if Elim weren't out with us I woulda killed you way back then.* And he'd smiled his too-wide smile.

Two nights later, Elijah had disappeared and so had a needler plus five full cartridges. *Bring him back, Ezekiel,* the Old Man had ordered, in his room where the scrambler was always humming in the corner, turning their voices untraceable. *And if worst comes to worst, get rid of his body. Nobody can find his body.*

So Zeke had gone after his brother, following a trail of corpses. First a metrocop with his helmet cracked open and a neat semicircle of flechette wounds in his chest. Then a man and a woman tangled together in a dumpster; from the smell at least one of them had shit themselves dying. Then Zeke had followed the sound of screaming to a nightclub a block over and shoved his way inside through a stream of fleeing revelers.

Pounding music. A dozen more bodies crumpled in corners or slumped on the bar under the pulsing grid of holos. Blood and spilled drinks slicking the floor. Through the fire exit, in the back alley, Elijah pissing on the wall with the needler hanging loose in his grip.

Don't get twisted, Zeke, Elijah had said. *All them souls in God's hands now. Right?* He'd turned around, stuck the needler up under his chin. *Clones, though. Clones don't got souls.*

Clone. Zeke had recognized the word from hearing it muttered behind his back. It had never meant anything to him.

Elim tried tell you, Elijah had said, checking the weapon's cartridge. *But the Old Man got his hooks in you deep, Zeke. Elim was too soft and I was too hard but you was just right. Turned out just like him. You can kill and you can cry about it.*

Then Elijah had swept the needler up. Zeke remembered diving backward, the .22 barking twice from his hip, and seeing Elijah's body smack the pavement. But he'd managed to keep his hold on the needler, and he said *you ain't stealing this one, Zeke* right before he put it up to his own neck and unloaded a full scatter that nearly took his head off, shredding everything but his spinal column.

A hacked autocab with all its cams disabled had raced police sirens to the alley and won by a hair, and Zeke had taken Elijah's body to an incinerator owned by a sleepy woman who asked no questions. He'd washed the blood off himself. Then he'd scoured what was left of the web to discover what his brothers had already known, maybe for years: they were not the Old Man's sons. They were his copies.

For the first time, Zeke had seen it all clear. The Old Man had grown them to be disposable soldiers and blood banks and organ farms. He had sacrificed Elim and Elijah and he would sacrifice Zeke, too. Then he would grow new clones, free new allies, shed new blood. He would never stop devouring.

Nothing on the web had said if clones had souls or not, so it was impossible for Zeke to know if his brothers were with the Lord or the Devil or nowhere at all.

He had gone back to the hideout in a trance, cold all over from fury and anguish, reloading his gun with trembling hands. He'd been heading for the Old Man's room when gas canisters smashed through the windows and spooks wearing raid gear filled the hallway. He'd been so close to making sure the Old Man never sacrificed anyone ever again.

*

"Not much time, Ezekiel," came the Old Man's voice. "Them drones coming soon."

Zeke dragged his eyes open. He was curled in the dirt; he could sideways-see the Old Man crouching over a sleek black case streaked with mud. It hissed open and the Old Man retrieved a sharp-hooked neurotool that he brought in close enough to blur. Zeke barely felt it go in, only a dull pinch and then rasp when it twisted. He heard a soft electronic bleat as it found the tracker/biobomb in his skull.

Zeke's teeth knocked together from some brushed nerve as the Old Man slid the neurotool back out, now stained dark red with a glint of circuitry at the tip.

"The Insurgency ain't all gone," the Old Man said. "They rigged the cryo failure. Transport breakdown. Hid the kit for me."

Back to the war. The Old Man was going back to the war and he thought he could drag Zeke with him. Zeke watched as the Old Man plucked the spook hardware off the end of the neurotool. Instead of crushing it between his fingers, he transferred it carefully to an injector. Zeke tensed.

"They gonna be waiting for us up north a ways," the Old Man said. "You can go with them. Or you can go around them."

Zeke punched his heel into the Old Man's shin. As he buckled forward, Zeke came off the ground, smashing an elbow into his chest. It was weakened by the drugs but still had enough force behind it to empty the Old Man's lungs. Zeke felt a hot wash of air across his face as he swiped the neurotool off the top of the black case. The hooked end gleamed sharp.

Zeke imagined digging and dragging, opening his jugular, making sure no more lies came out. He looked at the loaded injector. The Old Man twisted his head, and Zeke saw the guide mark dotting the flesh behind his ear. The Old Man wanted the tracker/biobomb for himself.

"Why?" Zeke asked, hoarse through a raw throat.

The Old Man choked. Wheezed. "I can't give you all them years back, Ezekiel," he whispered. "Can't bring your brothers back neither. I can do one thing, though. I'm gonna take the tracker to that shack and burn it down. The DNA traces won't tell them nothing. Spooks gonna think it's you."

Behind the clingwrapped wound in his chest, Zeke felt something deeper that hurt a hundred times worse. He pictured the Old Man dousing the shack's walls with gasoline and lighting it. Sitting down in the center, waiting for the flames like a monk's immolation. For an instant Zeke was an exhausted child and all he wanted was to wrap his skinny shaky arms around the Old Man's neck and be carried.

Then his mind leapt ahead. He bared his teeth. "Could be they think that, yeah," he said. "One body, though. They gonna think I burned and you got away."

The Old Man slowly nodded, and Zeke saw it all crystallized.

"You think I'm gonna take over for you." Zeke tightened his grip on the neurotool. "You think if you do this, I go to the insurgents and tell 'em how you laid down your life for mine. How you was crucified. And then I keep your war going another fifty years."

"That ain't what I—"

"So maybe I don't go north," Zeke snapped. "Maybe I never tell the insurgents nothing. People still gonna find out the Old Man escaped. People gonna think he out there somewhere like a bogeyman. That way you ain't ever gotta die. You get to be legend."

The Old Man shook his head. "Ezekiel, I want you to be free. I want to give you choice."

But there was no choice. There was no way of knowing the Old Man's mind, if he was telling the truth or if he was manipulating him one last time. Zeke looked down to where the sharp hook of the neurotool was just barely embedded in the Old Man's skin. The blood beading there was bright red, the same blood he had flowing in his own veins whether he wanted it or not.

As the distant hum of drones filled the sky, Zeke stared deep as he could into the Old Man's eyes, searching for his soul. He saw nothing but himself, adrift in the dark.

SAFE SPACE

Novapolis was like no city Gen had ever seen in her life. The architecture flowed around her in graceful arcs and waves, all of it a gleaming white that seemed to gently press against her eyeballs. Battery pillars rose in small copses where denizens recharged their 'cycles. Glass-topped channels displayed sparkling clean water as it coursed through the blue veins of the city's filtration system. There were no engine sounds; everything powered was as soft and melodic as the whispertrain that had conducted her here in the first place.

And everywhere she looked, there were the custodians: small white spheres that moved through the air like schools of fish. One such school had been waiting for her when she stepped off the platform, welcoming her, in a synthetic chirp, to Novapolis. The custodians explained that her refugee application had been accepted and her face and body metrics had been scanned into the system. She was officially a denizen. They had offered to guide her to housing, but she'd elected to explore instead. All she had to carry was her battered violin case and the ratty backpack slung over her shoulder.

Even now that she'd wandered for hours, stopping once to press her palm to a mobile vendor and select a dish of steamed rice with chunks of fish or something like it, everything still felt like a dream. She wanted to be happy, but she still felt thick and numb, coated in scar tissue. She hoped she would be able to find candles to burn for the sister and mother and cousins and friends who had never made it to the whispertrain or even gotten close.

Gen was up on one of the floating balconies, looking out over her new home, when someone spoke from behind her.

"Excuse me."

She turned around, and saw a man with a beautiful somber face, long-lashed eyes, thick black hair that ruffled in the breeze. While most of the denizens she'd seen so far wore bright colors, he wore a black body glove that hugged his musculature, his broad shoulders and wiry arms. Everyone she'd seen in the city so far was beautiful, in that they were clean, with unblemished skin and straight white teeth, but nobody she'd seen had set her heart hammering like it did now.

"I noticed you get off the train," the man said, with a small, apologetic smile. "Not many refugees make it here anymore. And when they do, the custodians try to make it inconspicuous."

"Oh," Gen said. She couldn't think of anything else to say, too entranced by the richness of his voice, the intensity of his dark eyes as they locked to hers.

"I'm Prosper," he said, putting out his hand into the air between them.

Gen stared at it for a moment, then remembered there were no contagions here, no bioweapons. She gripped his fingers awkwardly and shook them the way she remembered seeing in blurry netshows when she was younger.

"I'm Gen," she said. "It's . . . It's very beautiful here."

The man, Prosper, gave a sad smile. "In its way, yes," he said. "It's also very quiet." He pointed to her violin case. "I see that you're like me. You're an artist."

Gen shook her head fiercely, tucking the case deeper into her armpit. "No, no," she said. "I played a little for money. For foodcred."

Prosper's eyes lit up. "Incredible," he said. "It must have felt incredible. Like an open wound."

"An open wound?" Gen echoed.

"Of course, you won't be able to play much, here," Prosper said. "Not in public places, anyway. Something about music—something about the waves and the sonics—it bothers the custodians' algorithms. That's why it's so damn quiet here."

"It's peaceful," Gen offered.

"How morgues are peaceful," Prosper said with a wink. "Real cities, they have music. Loud music. They have parties and drunks and graffiti and trash and fighting and dancing and arguing and fucking in public places."

Gen felt her ears get hot at the last part, especially since Prosper, this strange and beautiful and confusing Prosper, was looking up and down her body.

"You have scars," he said. "Actual scars."

"I know," Gen said, bristling for the first time.

"I think they're very beautiful." Prosper's gaze roved up and down her arms, where her skin was pocked and pitted. "You've suffered and survived. I'm glad."

Gen didn't know what made him glad, the suffering or surviving. She shook her head, less off-balance now, more angry. "They're ugly."

"I disagree," Prosper said, moving past her and swinging himself up onto the edge of the balcony—just seeing it made Gen's stomach lurch. "But in any case. You won't get any new ones here. It's very safe here."

"Good," Gen said curtly. "I'm glad."

Prosper gave his sad smile again, shaking his head, then tipped himself backwards off the balcony.

Gen gave a holler of surprise and hurtled forward, shedding her bag and violin, groping at the empty air where he'd been only a second before. Prosper was plummeting towards the stark white plaza below, limbs spread wide like a starfish. Gen couldn't stop herself screaming.

Then a flock of custodians swooped underneath his black-clad body and stopped him mid-freefall. Gen watched, disbelieving, as the spheres carried him back up, up, up, and gently deposited him back onto the balcony.

"Please be cautious in high places," they said, in their scratchy synthesized voice.

"See?" Prosper said, as they drifted away. "It's too safe. Too comfortable. We can't feel pain, or shock, or horror. We can't feel anything at all." He raked his hands back through his hair, looking haunted. "And without feeling, there can't be creation. People here go see the same stupid plays, the same stupid fucking AI-generated sculptures. It's all so dead and sterile."

Gen could feel a mounting rage inside her chest. "Dead things aren't sterile," she said. "Dead things rot and infect and swell and stink. You've never seen a corpse. Have you?"

"No!" Prosper said it in a fierce whisper. "No, I've never seen a corpse. I've never seen anything real. I've been in this horrible white void my entire life." He gripped his head in both hands. "It's a prison. You've come to a prison, Genna."

"Then leave," Gen said. "Get on the whispertrain and leave."

"I've considered it a thousand times," Prosper said. "But that would mean giving up. Abandoning this place to its sick regurgitations. I want to save it. I want to bring it life, not just living. We need drama, passion, pain. You understand, don't you? You've seen it yourself. You know where art begins."

Gen stared for a moment, too stunned to speak. Then she reached down and opened her violin case.

"Our first act of defiance," Prosper said, his eyes lighting up. "Play, Genna. Play until they come and tear the bow from your hands. You've suffered so much. You must have so much material."

Gen lifted the violin, nocking it to her chin on instinct, peering down its strings and seeing most needed tightening. Then she smashed it hard against the balcony railing. Wood crunched and splintered; a sliver flew past her eye. She swung it again and again, until it was nothing but mangled pieces, until Prosper slunk away, until the custodians arrived to begin sweeping up her debris.

STILL LIFE
OF A DEATH BROKER

Osi toured the village while they waited to see the chief. There were bits of technology here and there—cracked-and-glued tablets plugged into ancient solar chargers, a sleek little hydrofarm no doubt smuggled off the Satellite by blackmarket dealers—but overall Manzu was deliciously raw and primitive and the streamers would eat it up.

Its warped mud brick had an organic feel to it, like termite mounds sprung up out of the dirt. The sand streets sloped inward and trash was strewn everywhere, nearly all of it plastic. Plastic, so much oily filthy plastic dancing through the dust, tumbling in the harmattan winds. It made Osi shiver.

The people, the women in brightly-printed zani and ragged winter jackets, the men in flowing riga and threadbare scarves, seemed oblivious to it. Some of the wandering skeletal goats seemed to be eating it. Osi made sure to capture that before walking on. A gaggle of parasite-riddled children trailed along in their wake; through a babel imp Osi understood they were still daring each other to touch the back of Osi's vantablack coat or grab at Osi's dangling pale hands.

"Yanna da daman ganinka yansu. He'll see you now."

Osi's contact Ibrahim had come to fetch them. He was a nervous man, with sweat running down his pudgy cheeks in familiar rivulets, and Osi's modified olfactories could smell his sickly-sweet diabetes. Interesting, but not arresting.

"Na gode," Osi said, and followed him back toward the chief's compound.

The children disappeared one by one, tugged away by their mothers or older siblings, and by the time Osi and Ibrahim arrived at the rusty iron door they were alone. The walls around the chief's gida were etched with geometric patterns and the tops were adorned with shards of multi-colored glass.

The guard, who had been lounging on a woven mat in the shade, levered himself upright on wiry arms. His face was scarved against the dust, but he gave them a friendly nod before he wrenched the door open and motioned them through.

Inside the compound were a dozen more people: a woman fed thistles to a camel whose oversized feet and knobbly knees seemed to balloon from its skinny legs, others pounded some sort of grain in drum-like wooden mortars, a pair of boys were scrubbing out old plastic bottles in a plastic tub of foaming water, a small girl whirled a cackling baby on her hip, several children ate a red stew from a metal tray, passing the wide carved spoon in a circle. All of them stared, and Osi was glad to not have come in costume.

Osi had a variety of costumes: sometimes they wore an antique suit and top hat, evoking Baron Samedi. Sometimes they wore an elaborate flowing dress of red roses, for Santa Muerte. Sometimes a simple black body-glove and a dog skull mask, sometimes x-ray gear that exposed their entire skeleton in ghostly white. Their streamers were always eager for new costumes.

A man dragged two chairs up, both of them made of colorful plastic bands woven over a welded metal frame. Ibrahim sat in one, muttering unanswered thanks. Osi sat in the other, disguising their reluctance, trying not to imagine the plastic seeping into the material of their coat. More men trickled in the door after them, all grave-faced, all watchful. The king's court, Osi thought.

They waited. Flies buzzed here and there; children chased each other in the sand. The sky overhead was gray with the thick harmattan dust Osi had marveled at during their sub-orbital flight from the Satellite to the Sahara. The sun was so dulled they could stare straight at it if they liked. Even so, Osi had felt their cell-knitters working to repair the UV damage every second since landing.

When the chief finally emerged from the central hut, mud brick roofed with corrugated sheets of tin, they knew they had chosen well. Tall and broad-shouldered and straight-spined, he had the gravity well of a small moon all on his own, walking with the slow graceful motion of someone who was used to being watched and did not care. He was clearly refusing to limp. His riga was bright yellow, his neat beard silvery-white, and his face beautiful in the jagged way of unaltered genes, jutting cheekbones and asymmetrical but piercing eyes.

Ibrahim sprang off his chair and Osi followed suit. The chief offered his right hand. Ibrahim took it, using his left to clutch his right elbow, and kept his eyes down. Osi's babel imp was accustomed to the rapid avalanche of overlapping greetings, but this time was different. Ibrahim spoke softly and waited patiently; the chief's hoarse replies were measured. When they had asked and answered of the sleep, the home, the family, the body, the chief extended his right hand to Osi.

Osi took it, thrilling at the feel of hot dirty skin. They could smell what they'd come for, strong enough to confirm the symptoms Ibrahim had described.

The chief looked him in the eye, betraying no emotion, then half-turned his head to Ibrahim. "Ya iya Hausa?" he asked.

"Hausa ta wiya," Ibrahim said, miming the earpiece of an old-fashioned translator.

The chief sat gingerly on a carved wooden stool, adjusting his riga with one hand, then turned his full attention to Osi. "So," he said, speaking Hausa but enunciating for the babel imp's sake. "You are the doctor from the Satellite."

"May I inspect you?" Osi asked, and it tumbled off their tongue in foreign syllables. "I can do it here. Or privately. I do not need to touch."

"My family knows my sickness. It is no secret." An odd buzzing came from his clothes; his hand darted into a pocket and came out holding an antiquated blockphone. He glanced at the screen and shook his head, putting it away again. "Inspect me here."

Osi stepped closer, retrieving the medroid from the folds of their coat. The tiny white capsule sprouted cilia legs and crawled to the edge of their palm, scanners linking to Osi's own augmented senses. They took a deep sniff and the medroid analyzed the composition of the chief's bacterial cloud, his sweat and skin particles. Osi recognized the metallic tang of old blood clotting in his urethra, a subtler smell layered underneath, the smell of their ancient nemesis.

The medroid snapped an ultrasound and the blurry grayscale image in their mind's eye confirmed it: a massive tumor nestled in the chief's bladder, expanding like a supernova. Osi felt a quiver of excitement. Their streamers were sophisticated, tired of cheap shocks like immolation or dismemberment. The chief's condition was perfect, an exquisite juxtaposition to his primal dignity.

"So?" said the chief.

"There is no medicine in this world that would save you," Osi said, and it became beautiful in the chief's language: "Cikin wannan dunia ba maganin da zai ceci renka."

A little girl vaulted into his lap; he hissed and slapped her away, then pulled her back, keeping her to the outside of his knee but gently rubbing her head. The girl stared at Osi with wide eyes. Her nostrils were crusted with snot.

"But you are not of this world," the chief said, slow, pensive, but without the bitterness Osi often saw from clients.

"No," Osi agreed. They knew that if they took the chief back with them to the Satellite, it would be child's play to flense the cancer even from his unmodified body. But it would likely return, and Osi was not in the business of saving lives in any case. "Even so. Your sickness can't be treated."

One of the men snuffled, holding back a sob. A few of the women cried out. The chief only blinked. "As Allah wills it," he said, but his eyes went to one of the women in particular and stayed there. "Will you have anything to eat? To drink?"

Osi shook their head. "A'a. But there is something else I would like to propose."

The chief waved a permissive hand. His mouth was thin.

"Your sickness holds a particular fascination for many of us on the Satellite," Osi said. "It was the last to be conquered. With your permission, I would like to leave behind a camswarm to monitor your condition. I would also implant a nerve conduit to transmit your pain for my streamers to experience themselves."

The speech took Osi's babel imp to its limit—they heard it mix Old African French into the Hausa—but the chief seemed to understand. He gave a rueful laugh. "I do not walk. I do not sleep. Five, six times in the night, I pass lumps of thick black blood of this size." He mimed with a dusty knuckle. "It is agony. You want this for yourself?"

"Badly," Osi said, speaking for their streamers. "It's been a hundred years since there was a natural death on the Satellite. Our telomeres reknit themselves. Our cells reproduce with zero-rate mutation. But still we have death inside of us. We crave it in the vicarious abstract."

The chief's face twisted, disgust mingled with mild disappointment, as if Osi were one of his misbehaving children. "You want to watch while I die."

One of the women clicked her tongue and murmured. Osi's babel imp heard *wickedness, wickedness.*

"The sights, the sounds, the smells and tastes, the sensations as your body betrays you and your mind finally slides into the dark," Osi said.

The chief looked at Ibrahim. "What is this that have you brought into my house?" he asked, and Ibrahim did not answer, but he flushed and trembled, eyes cast down. The chief shook his shaven head, returned his gaze to Osi. "You are not a human."

"Not technically."

"I do not speak of your modifications." The chief half rose from his stool and for a moment Osi felt cowed by his size and fury. Then he sagged back down, face stretched with pain. "In exchange, you offer what?"

"A full hydrofarm. It will pull enough moisture to supply your village and the two closest to it with pure water."

The chief shook his head. "Inoculation against the na-virus," he said. "For our children. If they are dead they cannot drink the water."

"That could be arranged," Osi said. They had almost forgotten the na-virus, a population control measure from the old days.

"A recycler, to eat the rubber and plastic," the chief said. "And a printer, to make new equipment. And then the hydrofarm."

Osi pretended to consider. The chief was shrewd and tough and his descent would be riveting, a bitter war between his pride and his pain, his dignity and his duty. Compared to the potential streamer revenue, even ten hydrofarms was a pittance.

"A good bargain," Osi said, and extended their bony white hand.

COMPLETE EXHAUSTION
OF THE ORGANISM

t's not a real baby," Jain says flatly. "And we should kill it."

Another sunless morning in the Waste. She and Stromile have woken up to a gift: a canister of pepto-pink fluid with an infant inside it. The tiny figure is chubby and squirmy and perfect, and it's only now that Stromile finally takes his eyes off the thing.

"Kill it?" he echoes, rubbing his finger in the hollow of his collarbone. "You serious?"

"Serious, yeah." Jain nods her head at the canister. "This is them fucking with us, babe. You know that. We need to show them we're not buying it. We can smash it on a rock, or something."

Stromile's face goes lockdown: His big black eyes shrink and dull, his happy-or-sad mouth becomes a flat line, and Jain has to guess what's going on his head. Probably he's thinking about the times the gifts have been exactly what they needed. Jugs of potable water when their sanitizer tabs ran out, an inflatable splint when she broke her leg sliding down an embankment.

"What if we just leave it here?" Stromile says. "Leave it here, and keep going. They'll see we don't want it, and they'll pick it up, and they'll . . ." He wags his head side to side. "They'll do whatever to it."

"Sure, Stro," Jain says. "We can do that, I guess."

And that was what she was shooting for anyways—the idea of killing something that looks like a baby churns her stomach. But you have to start high and hard, with Stromile, and then let him work down to something he's comfortable with.

They've been walking together for a long time now.

Jain's not sure of the exact geography, but she knows this used to be sea. There are still slick oily patches of mud here and there, and every so often they find a whale carcass coated in squawking white gulls instead of maggots. And in the distance, they can see the ship: a carcass in its own right, an exoskeletal husk of iron and rust, once a tanker and now an Anthropocene memento.

They are walking toward it, because they have to walk toward something. Walking the Waste is better than cowering in the Town, the bizarre prefab suburbia with the bright green lawns that are really one single organism, a gengineered fungus, and the artificial sky that's always blue with puffy white clouds and a lemon-yellow sun. But even now that she and Stromile are out here in the darkness, under a canopy of carbon-draining nanosmog, leaving footprints on irradiated dirt, they're still being monitored.

"I think I get it," Stromile says, tucking his trousers into his boots as they come up on another slick stretch of mud. "The baby."

Jain glances over. "Yeah?"

"They're watching us, right?" Stromile says. "They watched us fucking last night." He coughs, then gives a sheepish smile. "They think we wanted to make a baby."

Jain feels some heat waft up to the surface of her skin. "Could be," she says. "You feeling okay today?"

Stromile nods. "Better," he says. "Better than ever."

They walk until the derelict ship is a full thumb taller on the horizon, playing silly games where they hurl clods of mud at other clods of mud, or memory games where they try to list all the dissolved countries alphabetically. Stromile doesn't cough too often, so maybe he really is feeling better.

When they pitch the foil tent, they try to fuck again. Stro doesn't get hard this time, but she sucks him for a while and then works at her clit while he fingers her. One, then two, then three's a bit too much. Back to two and she starts rocking her hips, aching wet.

"You're switching fingers, right?" she asks vaguely, when he slips one inside her ass.

Stromile pauses. "Uh. Yeah. Yes."

It doesn't inspire confidence, but she's getting too close to care. The warm rush hits her belly, her head, tingles out through her skin. For a moment, everything is beautiful. She and Stromile are in love. The Waste is their kingdom.

She shudders, and opens her eyes to see Stromile grinning down at her. She wraps herself around him until the endorphins trickle away.

The baby is back when they crawl out of the tent. The canister sits slightly crooked, bottom buried in the wet dirt. Inside the fluid, the baby's asleep, eyes shut. It has a small thatch of dark hair plastered to its soft skull.

Jain glares at it, then looks straight up into the void-black sky. "Hey!" she shouts. "We don't want your creepy baby!"

Stromile inches closer. "Jain, it looks like my little brother," he mutters.

Jain blinks. "It looks like your little brother?"

"Yeah," Stromile says. "A lot. Like, I remember there was this photo of me holding him when he was a baby." His mouth twists into a grimace. "Looks like that."

Jain puts both her hands on Stromile's back and starts to rub little circles. She knows he lost his whole family in one of the last big Shrooms. "I'm sorry, Stro," she says. "That's so shitty. That must feel bad. Real bad."

"You think it's on purpose?" Stromile asks, staring at the baby adrift in the pink fluid.

"Yeah," Jain says. "They want us to take it back to the Town." She scratches the back of Stromile's neck, just gently. "It's like, nurturing instinct, or whatever. They want us to open the canister, decide we have to take care of the thing, and realize we can't do it out here in the Waste."

"So they made it look like family," Stromile says dully.

"I bet," Jain says. "Yeah."

Stromile digs his fingers into his scalp and scratches; Jain sees a dark coil of hair come loose but pretends not to. "That's so fucked up," he says. "That's so fucked up."

Jain kisses his cheek. "Hey," she says, and then nothing else.

*

That night, lying together in the tent, there's a more comfortable quiet. Jain runs her finger up and down Stromile's arm in a long lazy loop. He has a half-smile on his lips.

"What are you thinking about?" she asks.

"The night we found that bottle of vodka," he says. "That was a good night. When we were just jumping around and singing and stuff."

Jain remembers that night in blurry film. She remembers dancing in and out of their lantern beam, both of them throwing back their heads and not caring, or maybe caring even more. Things being both more and less significant.

She smiles and taps a rhythm against Stromile's rib. "All I wanna do is . . ."

Stromile makes the soft gunshot noises with his cheeks, staring up at the ceiling. "And *chk. Ting.*"

"And take your money," Jain finishes, wriggling her fingers into his empty pocket.

They kiss, and the world's not quite over.

"Here's one," Stromile says, around a mouthful of cricket bar. "When people used to say 'it's like hurting cats.' Never got that. Do you get it?"

"Dunno," Jain says, nudging the lantern with her foot to keep its coils running. "What was the context?"

"Difficult stuff, I guess." Stromile swallows. "Like, organizing a search party."

"Hurting a cat would be difficult," Jain says. "Because you'd feel bad about it."

Something shifts in Stromile's face, and she knows it was the wrong thing to say. "I feel bad about the baby," he blurts. "How we keep leaving it. Babies aren't supposed to be stuck in tubes like that. They're supposed to have, you know. Interaction."

It's been three days and they're nearly to the tanker. Its hull is big enough to blot out the sky now, a rusty red wall jutting up from nowhere. Every morning, the baby is waiting for them. Jain's not sure, but she thinks it's growing, looking slightly more cramped in its canister each time. Sometimes it blinks its big soft dark eyes at them and does a toothless smile.

Jain was fed up enough to kick it over this morning, but before they set to walking Stromile carefully propped it back upright, as if verticality matters to a fake baby swimming in protoplasm or protein slop or whatever the canister's full of.

"It's not a real baby, Stro," Jain says. "It's something they made to mess with us."

"It's something they made to mess with us, yeah," Stromile says. He bites the insides of his cheeks, sucking them hollow. "But it might be a real baby still. It might even be *our* baby, Jain."

Jain gets a crawly feeling in the bottom of her stomach. "Don't say that."

"I mean, they got our genes when we were in the Town," Stromile says. He has a pained smile. "You don't think? Maybe?"

Her stomach seems to bubble. She feels hot and sick and angry. "No, Stro. I don't think so. Seeing as how they sterilized everyone in the Town. Seeing as how that was part of the deal."

"Maybe they changed their minds," Stromile says softly. "People do that."

"They're not people," Jain says. "And that thing's not a baby."

Stromile's face goes lockdown again. She knows he doesn't believe her, so she's going to have to show him.

That night when Stromile falls asleep, she waits up for the delivery. They used to do that often, back when they thought they might be dragged back to the Town by force. They would huddle near the tent's entrance, clutching each other and makeshift weapons. Now the doppler whine of machines rushing through the night is white noise. They sleep through it easy.

Jain stays awake by pinching the skin of her inner elbow, watching Stromile's bony chest rise and fall. Finally she hears it coming. She crawls out of the tent and looks up.

The delivery worker is about the size of the whale carcass they detoured around yesterday. It has gaunt mechanical limbs but also swathes of soft blue translucent membrane, some bloated knobbly cross between the moose she once saw in the woods as a child and the swarms of phosphorescent jellyfish she once saw in a photo.

It lowers itself down, anchoring itself to the dirt, and the canister slides out of its underbelly.

"We don't want it," Jain says. "Why the fuck would we want it?"

They never answer questions like that. The delivery worker positions the canister delicately with one tendril-tipped limb, then departs into the dark. Jain can feel its static still crackling in her hair. She goes to the canister.

The fake baby is asleep, chubby fists clenched in front of itself. At the top of the canister, there is a palm-print that looks suspiciously like hers. She fits her hand into it. The canister unseals with a clank and a hiss. Her heart starts to thunder.

She knows it's not a real baby. She knows if she pulls it out of the canister and smashes it against a rock, she'll see the flesh inside is spongy and pink, webbed with circuitry instead of capillaries. There was a fake dog in the Town, and that was how it looked on the inside when someone accidentally beat it to death.

She lifts it out, dripping a trail of fluid. Its eyes blink open. It gurgles at her. She can break its head open, like cracking open a doll, and show the circuitry to Stromile, and he'll stop thinking it's something more than it is. All she has to do is get over the block, the biological or social or whatever kind of taboo it is.

Jain tells herself time is linear, and she was always going to smash this fake baby open, and doing otherwise was never even an option. It's one of her old tricks. But she's still holding the thing under its pudgy arms when Stromile knee-walks out of the tent.

"Oh." He looks at her, blinks. "Can I hold it?"

She can feel its tiny heartbeat. Those motherfuckers. She passes it over.

The baby doesn't seem to need to eat, but it grows up fast. By the time they stop to rest in the shadow of the derelict ship, it's starting to walk, staggering around like a little drunk. Stromile can't stop watching it.

"Come on," he says. "It's funny. Admit it's funny."

Jain shakes her head. "I bet it's recording us, or something."

"They're watching us already," Stromile says. "What's the difference if now they're watching from, like, lower to the ground?"

The baby collapses into the dirt between his feet.

Stromile grins at her, kind of pleading-like. "Much lower."

The fake baby wriggles its way back upright, holding onto his knee for balance. It blinks at him, swaying. Then it looks over at Jain and smiles. She grimaces back. It looks real. It even smells real, human and warm and somehow familiar, no metallic musk like the dog in the Town had.

"They sent us this thing as some kind of weird experiment," Jain says. "We came out to the Waste to get *out* of the experiment. Yeah?"

"Yeah," Stromile says slowly, scratching at his clavicle. The baby takes off again, stumbling in a little half circle. "And they let us leave, and they give us what we need when we need supplies. So they're not all the way bad, right?" He looks up, dark eyes somber. "Nothing's all the way good or all the way bad. You said that, once, Jain."

Stromile thinks they were given the baby because they need it. And maybe for him, he *does* need it, somehow. Maybe it's a way for him to deal with his vaporized family, his dead and gone little brother. Maybe she's not enough.

Stromile tries to smother his cough, but it makes his shoulders shake and sends a dart of ice down Jain's spine.

"Fuck it," she says, trying to keep her voice light. "Go on. Name the creepy baby."

Stromile leans back on his elbow and looks thoughtful. "There's this food we got as little kids," he said. "From this truck. It was like, a bag of chips, then you dump cheese and lettuce and meat in it. Walking tacos. They were called walking tacos."

"You want to name it Walking Taco?" Jain asks. "You should eat something."

Stromile shrugs. "It likes walking."

By the time they get to the tanker, Taco isn't just walking. It can jump and skip and do a shambling, veering run that always brings it back to them giggling. It's not a baby anymore, more like a three- or four-year-old. Jain tries to figure out where the mass is coming from. Her best guess is that it's eating dirt when they're not looking.

But Stromile's happy, and livelier than he's been for weeks. He laughs just watching the thing stumble around, and sometimes he grabs it under the armpits and swings it in a circle, which makes it laugh, too. Jain can see the resemblance even more now that Taco's face is less chubby. She remembers what Stromile said before, about how fucked up it was, them making it look like his little brother.

He's over it now. He even sticks Taco on his shoulders as they circle the ship looking for a way inside. For a weird eerie moment, they're a family on a seaside vacation. Seeing Stromile acting all paternal is mostly unnerving, but some little corner of her brain finds it sexy, too.

"Always thought there'd be a ladder," he says, thumping his fist on the rusty hull.

"Yeah," Jain says. "Me, too. Shit."

They've walked the whole way around the derelict and found no sign of one. There are some manhole-looking things, some hatches, but all of them are welded shut. She looks up at Taco, who is clinging to Stromile's neck, as if it might have some answer for them, some secret passageway into the ship.

The fake toddler has teeth now, tiny and perfect. "Shit," it says, beaming. "Shit."

Stromile laughs so hard he almost shrugs Taco right off his shoulders. Jain doesn't want to, but she feels her mouth twitching toward a smile. Then Stromile's laugh turns into a choked-off cough, and he has to set Taco down, draw a few deep wet breaths.

"Oh, man," he finally says. "That is adorable."

"On purpose," Jain says, as Taco roves away. "Might be smarter than us already. Like, linked up to some quantum cloud. So I think we should make ground rules."

"Like what?" Stromile asks.

"Let's keep it outside the tent," Jain says. "And if we wake up tomorrow and it's gotten bigger again, we have to kill it for real. Before it's big enough to be dangerous."

Stromile winces. "Why would it be dangerous, though?"

"It's an experiment, Stro," Jain says. "Experiments can go wrong."

Stromile bites his lip, watching the fake toddler scrabble in the dirt. "My brother was six when the bomb dropped," he says. "I think it'll stop at six-year-old size. Would make sense."

She grabs his hand and squeezes it; it's more bone than she remembers. "Okay," she says, softer. "We'll give it to six-year-old size." She looks up at the towering rusty wall of the ship. "I guess this was a bust."

"No," Stromile says. "No, it was good to see it up close." He holds up his free hand, arm straight, and thumbs an imaginary circle. "*Ksh*," he goes. "Photo. Us at the ship at the end of the world."

Jain smiles. She puts her hand up against the corroded metal. "Yeah," she says, and pats it. "Take another one."

They take imaginary photos. They kiss. Stromile's mouth tastes coppery. Taco comes running up to them holding a slimy black shell in its chubby hand.

"Tell me a word I don't know?" Stromile asks, smacking his boots together to knock the clotted mud off the bottoms.

"Uh. Noctivagant." Jain nods. "Yeah, noctivagant. Means wandering around at night."

Stromile grins. "Like we do. Since it's pretty much always night." He casts a glance up at the nanosmog, the cool veil keeping things dark, then turns. "Hey, Taco, can you say noctivagant?"

Taco is crouched in the dirt, poking at a dead gull with its fingertip. The fake toddler's grown a little bigger since yesterday, but not by much. It looks up. "Nockivagun," it says, and flashes Jain its immaculate smile again.

Stromile's having the time of his life getting it to say stuff, and Jain's finding it harder and harder to resent the thing. It's happy, or at least simulating happy, in a way she figures Stromile and his brother must have been happy as little kids. It's always bringing them sea shells or gull feathers, like some echo of the delivery worker that dropped it on them in the first place.

And it didn't complain about the sleeping arrangements, just curled up outside the tent with the spare blanket Stromile insisted on giving it and went to sleep, or what looked like sleep. She knows that's better than most real kids do.

Taco's happy, and it makes Stromile happy, and that's important because this morning she could feel his cough lurking under his ribs like an animal. He deserves to have some slice of his family back. He deserves to be happy. Even if it's fake.

He's singing again. "All I wanna do is . . ."

"*Pow pow pow pow!*" Taco chants, eyes wide with delight.

"And *chk, ting* . . ." Stromile looks at her. "And . . ."

"Take your money," Jain says, sticking her tongue out.

Taco starts to giggle, and it's not a creepy uncanny doll sound at all. It's wild and warm and makes her really want to just laugh along. So she does.

They become a trio without Jain's meaning to: her and Stro and Taco. Maybe it's when she realizes she can't call Taco *it* in her head anymore, or when she gives him Stromile's spare shirt to wear like a baggy tunic. They move a little slower with Taco along, but it's alright, because they have nowhere to go.

The vague plan is to see the ocean. If they keep on walking past the tanker, eventually there should be ocean, even if it's just a sliver of what there used to be.

Taco mainly sticks close to Stromile, hopping along beside him, looking up at him all adoring-like. But today he wants to hold both their hands at the same time. Jain sort of likes it. It reminds her of when she was little, walking with her parents, and how sometimes they'd wink at each other over her head and then hoist her up into the air.

Trust. That's the feeling. Taco trusts them, or at least he's simulating it.

"I keep having dreams about bees," Stromile says. "You remember bees?"

"The flying kind or the not-flying kind?" Jain asks.

"Not sure. I dream about them inside their hive, or whatever." Stromile gesticulates with his free fingers. "They're all just kind of gooey and buzzing and making honey. I don't know how they actually made honey. But in the dream they have these little jars."

"I don't think they used jars," Jain says.

"You think there are any left?" Stromile asks. "Any bees?"

Jain shakes her head. "I think they went extinct," she says. "Like, before we did, even."

Stromile nods, his black eyes going soft and sad. Jain looks down at Taco and squeezes his small hand. He looks up at her, questioning.

"Do you want to fly, Taco?" she asks. "Like the flying kind of bee?"

Stromile teaches him to make a buzzing noise. Then she and Stromile take three galloping steps and swing Taco up into the air. He whoops and laughs and for a while Jain understands why people liked having kids in the old days. It feels like she's the one flying.

They keep doing it until their arms are sore and Stromile starts to cough.

The cough gets worse over the next few days. They slow down even more, not for Taco but for Stromile, who is walking gingerly now. He insists he's fine. He says it's just a dip and there's going to be another rise, and Jain wants so badly to believe him, but she knows most things are linear. They stop to camp early.

He's dozing inside the tent, and Jain's sitting outside it, close enough to still hear him breathing, when Taco comes up to her holding something. His little white grin looks puzzled, maybe even worried, if he can worry about things.

"Stro," he says, and holds out his hand.

It's not a sea shell. It's a toenail, crusty and yellowed. She remembers: Stromile taking slow careful steps, Stromile wincing as he takes his boots off, Stromile keeping his feet under the covers even though he never keeps his feet under the covers.

"Give me that," Jain says, feeling suddenly nauseous.

She plucks it out of Taco's unresisting hand. She scoops a hole in the dirt, presses the toenail down into it, and covers it over. She wipes the spot smooth with her palm. Taco is watching her, somber and curious.

"He was happy before you, too," Jain says. "He didn't need you. He didn't need whatever the fuck this is. Sympathy. Closure. Whatever. He's got me."

Taco rests his chin on his fists, unblinking.

Stromile gets sicker, and Taco starts to spend more time walking with her instead of with him, like he's afraid of catching something. Jain hates that. Especially because Stromile doesn't mind. He smiles when he sees Taco skipping after her.

"He likes you better," Stromile says one night in the tent. "He's got good taste."

"Let's not talk about it," Jain says.

Stromile grins. "Let's not Taco 'bout it."

Jain rubs the scruff on his cheek. "Dumbass."

She buries her face in his chest and breathes his smell in, trying to ignore the jab of his ribs. They're so much sharper than they used to be. She tiptoes her fingers down his hip and gives his dick a hello squeeze. He inhales.

"Do you think things used to matter more?" he asks, while she wraps her fingers around him. "When there were more people? And more futures?"

She works her hand up and down, uses her thumb to rub a little circle around the head of his dick. "I dunno," she says. "Is that really what you want to think about when you come?"

Stromile tips his head back and shuts his eyes. "Guess not," he says. "I just. Wonder." He grunts. "Maybe they matter more now, since there's only a few of us. Since time's, you know. Limited."

Time is limited. Time is linear. Jain doesn't want to think about it, so she elbow-crawls a little higher up and kisses him on the mouth. She bites his bottom lip, just gently, and tries to remember the first time they kissed. Maybe the third night after they left the Town, high on their own daring.

Even back then, she knew it would end eventually. Stro wasn't vaporized in the Shrooms, but he was close enough to catch radiation and sear his lungs.

"It's not going to happen," Stromile mumbles, and for a moment she thinks he means dying. Then he peels her hand away from his dick and tugs her upward, wraps both arms around her, presses his forehead against hers. "I think everything matters the same amount," he finally says. "A lot and a little, at the same time."

"I love you a lot," Jain says, and the thought that's been lurking in her background comes forward. "If we ask, they'll take us back to the Town. It'll be comfier there. For the end."

Stromile shakes his head. "I don't want to go back," he says. "Neither do you." He pauses. "Don't worry about burying me or anything. They'll pick me up, I figure."

The words pry her ribcage apart, wrenching her wide open. "Fuck, Stro," she says.

"Fuck," he agrees, with a sob in his voice. "I'm going to miss you, Jain."

But he won't. That's the thing. He won't miss anything once he's on the other side of that one-way door.

When Stromile dies, it feels like the sun really has gone out, like the nanosmog is only hiding darkness, and more darkness behind that, and more darkness forever. It feels like she's alone at the bottom of the long-gone ocean.

Then it feels like nothing at all, and his unmoving body somehow becomes a pile of meat. Just something she'll have to move out of the tent so she can fold it up and repack. She watches herself do it: drag him out onto the dirt, shift his arm because it's at an angle that looks uncomfortable for him, kiss his cheek under his slitted eye.

Taco watches her do it, too. His small face is contorted with grief, confusion. He's bigger now, six-year-old size, and Jain is beginning to understand. When he lifts his skinny arms out, like he's going to try to hug her, she lunges at him.

"Get the fuck out of here!" she screams. "Get the fuck away from me!"

He flinches back, eyes wide. But he doesn't go, so she has to chase him, feinting at him over and over, arm raised, mimicking her own mother and hating it. But Taco isn't a child. She digs her hands into the mud and hurls clods of dirt at him. He tries to smile at first, tries to throw them back, like it's a game.

"This is your fault!" she howls at him, then up at the opaque sky. "This is your fault! Your fault! I fucking hate you, I fucking *hate you.*"

Finally Taco starts to blink fast, too fast, and his face screws up again and tears start sliding down his cheeks. Finally he turns around and runs away.

Jain goes back to Stromile's body, sobbing. She cries into the crook of his elbow. She gets snot on his sleeve and scrubs it clean. Hours crawl by with her sitting there weeping, shuddering, stopping, starting the cycle over.

When the worker comes trundling out of the dark, lifts Stro up into its biomechanical belly, she beats her fists against it. She bloodies herself. The worker leaves her skinspray and painkillers.

Jain keeps walking, keeps heading for the ocean she's starting to doubt exists at all. She's vaguely aware that Taco is following her. He keeps his distance, but every time she looks over her shoulder and sees him trudging along, his silhouette is taller, ganglier. Growing. She knows that he doesn't look like Stro's brother anymore. He never did.

But it still feels like a slap across the face when she comes out of the tent one morning and finds him waiting outside. Stro's soft dark eyes, Stro's pursed lips. Stro's body, but not how it was at the end, not scabby and emaciated. Stro how he was when they first left the Town, healthy and whole-looking.

Bile pushes up Jain's throat. "Why would you do that?"

The thing that was Taco and is now Stro gives a familiar shrug. "They always give us what we need, right?" he says, his voice warm, slightly sheepish, perfectly intonated.

Part of her wants so badly to throw her arms around him. The thing smells like Stro, speaks like him. He's back from behind the one-way door. They can keep walking, keep talking, keep playing their silly games. All she has to do is accept this fucked up apology for everything that's been done to them. Everything that was done for their own good.

She crouches down in the dirt and finds a wedge of rock. "Turn around, Stro," she says, using his name without meaning to, starting to cry without meaning to.

He eyes the rock, brow furrowed. "Sure," he says, turning. "Hey. Tell me a word I don't know."

She swings for the back of his beautiful head.

His scalp splits, squirts. He doesn't shout, but the cracking sound turns her stomach. She swings again, then three more times, until the not-quite-bone caves in. The inside of his skull is spongy and pink, studded with vertices of black glass.

"Sorry," she says.

*

There's a canister waiting for her the next morning, embryonic fluid a ghostly rose against the dark of the Waste. The tiny figure inside is chubby and squirmy and perfect.

Jain packs up the tent, and starts to walk.

HORIZON EVENT

As our therapy pod approaches its destination, the stars start to flicker and warp.

"It really helped the Rexroat-Ndirangu-Carrows," I say, through the mouth of my quantum-linked clone. "They've never been happier together."

"Put everything in perspective." Sienna's vatgrown face is unreadable as their real one. "I heard."

"We used to say it, right?" My clone's throat is somehow too small, or maybe the gravity is already crushing it shut. "That we wanted to get old and die together?"

Sienna's clone doesn't answer. The therapy pod shudders, stretches, shields strained to breaking.

We fall together into the supermassive black hole.

YOU ARE BORN EXPLODING

When Elisabeth takes the baby to the beach on Thursday afternoon, another shambler has got through the fence.

"Stay ten meters back," the guard says, his translucent face mask fogged with the heat.

"Yes, yes," Elisabeth says.

"And the child. Ten meters."

"We're fully inoculated," Elisabeth says, annoyed.

"Of course, ma'am." He seems to be dissolving in the condensation, only his dark eyes visible. "This distance is so our staff can remove him efficiently and with good technicality."

"Him?" Elisabeth echoes faintly. She hates it when people anthropomorphize shamblers—it sets a bad precedent.

The guard doesn't correct his error, so she punishes him by not smiling her beautiful laser-scoured smile as she pushes Jack's pram through the biofilter. Jack barely squirms under the static tongue. He is accustomed. Elisabeth's skin pebbles when she follows him through.

The guard cups a hand to the screen, to cut the glare. Results show clean blue. The gate sags on its pneumatics, then lurches open.

"Ten meters," he says again.

Elisabeth gives a curt nod, pretending to be distracted by Jack's slipping-off nylon shoe.

*

The wind is strong today. It comes in plucking and slicing, Atlantic cold, and counteracts the bright pounding sunshine. The waves are like nesting dolls: massive glassy walls out past the buoys, chest-high in the vast sloped shallows, child-size by the time they throw themselves onto the surf. Jack's pram lumbers along just out of their reach.

The flour-soft sand is shifty under Elisabeth's feet; the pram is unbothered. Its treads are military grade—Benny showed her the same serial number on a still of a dusty Pakistani war drone. She sometimes wishes it had smart-bombs, too, for when the Rose-Kellermans' big drooling dog comes bounding up to inspect it.

Speak of the devil, or rather of its owner: Alea Rose-Kellerman is posed on a black-and-white striped towel just ahead, the straps of her swimming costume slipped down off her perfect shoulders, her face half-swallowed by vaguely insectoid sunshades. Her human nanny is herding little Nils through the surf, maintaining herself between the toddler and the sea.

Alea always rubs everyone's nose in the fact that they rehired their nanny. Always urges everyone to do the same, even though the cost of keeping a nanny's vaccines updated—especially since hired help hardly ever have base immunomods—is astronomical.

Naturally, she looks up just as a particularly vicious gust of wind wraps Elisabeth's hair around her face.

"Hello, Liz," she says. "How are you?"

"Hello, Alea." Elisabeth peels the hair from her mouth with great dignity. "Lovely day."

"Won't you join us?" Alea asks. "This particular square of sand is really something."

Alea always has to be airy and clever like that, likely due to some buried insecurity that is owed in turn to a dark, loathsome secret.

Elisabeth smiles her laser-scoured smile. "It's a pleasure."

She has the pram hunker down and unfold its parasol, which struggles embarrassingly against the wind. The sea air has stirred Jack fully awake. His small sunbrowned face is alight with curiosity. She hefts him out and sets him in the quivering shade.

He points a fat finger down the beach. "Shambla, mumma? Is it? Shambla?"

Alea coos and chirps. "They're speaking now! Such fun."

"*He's* speaking," Elisabeth says, bristling. "Jack's a boy unless he eventually decides otherwise." She adjusts Jack's hat. "He's two now. Yes, Jack, it's a shambler."

Alea settles back on her towel, with a curve to her lips that looks more amused than chastened. "I suppose you show him those government cartoons," she says. "The safety cartoons."

"We do, yes."

"I try to explain both sides of it to Nils," Alea says. "Even though it's upsetting. They're very empathetic, Nils."

A ways down the beach, a small knot of spectators has gathered about ten meters back from a distinctive shape. It's crawling for the surf, red-and-blue flukes rippling from its bent back. A guard is busy zipping into a hazard suit, white with what looks like a gasoline stain across one knee.

The shambler seems to sense its time is limited; it scoots a bit faster now, dragging a wet furrow behind itself. The whole thing is quite macabre.

"Is hubby back from his little trip?" Alea asks.

"What?"

The ejection is more forceful than she intended it. She was distracted by the shambler, and by the sputter and whine of the buzzsaw the guard will use to dismember it.

"Benjamin," Alea clarifies. "Is he back from Australia?"

"Not yet." Elisabeth shifts her gaze to Jack, who is meticulously pouring fistfuls of sand onto his tiny knees. "My brother is coming to visit, though. He's an artist."

Alea smiles dryly. "Here to freeload while he seeks inspiration, I suppose? Every family has one."

"He's quite successful, actually."

"Oh." Alea gives a pensive moue. "I think we're all artists, in our own way."

Elisabeth imagines gouging out her eyes and filling the holes with sand. "What a lovely thought," she says.

They promise each other a grand succession of wine tastings and lunch outings, then Nils begins puling in a way the nanny cannot stopper, and Alea recalls her brow appointment. Elisabeth puppeteers Jack's arm to wave the trio a cheery goodbye, then lets him go back to his rearranging of sediment. The pram has printed him a lime green spade.

She takes in his cherubic concentration, the blonde curls plastered to his forehead. She coos his name, so he'll look up.

"I digging away," he says, with a squinty grin.

"You're digging away," Elisabeth concedes. "Yes."

"Is it digging away?"

"Yes, my baby."

"Is it mumma digging away?"

Elisabeth observes her shiny white nails. She feels, as she often does, that she is being surveilled. She imagines a semi-organic satellite prowling through low orbit, all its sensors and innocent blue eyes fixed on her, categorizing every action she takes: Good Mother or Bad Mother, the eternal exhausting ledger. It can be so hard to tell which is which.

"Mumma's digging away," she agrees.

She plunges her immaculate hand into the wet sand. She scoops some of the trickly mud onto Jack's bare knee. He giggles. That used to be the only sound she cared about, that small, delightful burble, but these days it's a decaying isotope. It should mean more than it ever did, but instead it has diminishing returns.

"I love you so much, little baby Jack," she says, to make it truer. "Little bubba."

Jack keeps digging, and his focus reminds her fleetingly of Benny. She is glad that he pays no attention to the sea, where a wobbling bridge of light now stretches from the scurrying foam all the way to a blue horizon. Looking at it gives Elisabeth a headache. She is glad that he pays no attention to the guards hauling the dead shambler past in a membranous bag.

The car carries them home, climbing the winding slope toward Elsie's Peak until they reach the sleek ziggurat embedded halfway up. Elisabeth reads up and down the conversation thread with her brother, who has stopped responding, so might have already dropped his plan to come visit. Jack watches a cartoon in the smartglass window, a woman baking a cake.

The crusty metal gate slides open; the car parks itself and switches off. Elisabeth carries her son into the house, past the many bristling security systems that recognize them and turn away, suddenly embarrassed by their excessive zeal. The house is a bit of a fortress, in Benny's words. The graceful warp of its architecture was calculated to create ideal angles for its hidden sensors, its nonlethal, but only recently legal, howlers.

Elisabeth knows that companies like her husband's have had an absolute fucking field day since the shamblers started. She also knows that most of it is based in misdirection. Shamblers have no interest in outdoor pools or rain reservoirs, not here, where the saline ocean is near enough to smell. Shamblers have no interest in people or their habitations.

But security companies have always capitalized on fear, and at least it's not paired with blatant racism this time around—she was planning to tell her brother that, to sound like she's thought it all through. She sniffs Jack's soft blonde head, trying for memory traces of his original baby scent, from back when his skull was hairless and oddly puckered, that scent she couldn't stand to wash away for a whole week.

She sets him down on the playroom tiles; the nanny comes rolling out of its corner. Its belly screen is displaying the end of the cartoon from the car, the cake coming out of the oven with a big waft of steam. It does as good a job as a human nanny would. Perhaps better. Elisabeth adjusted its speech settings to throw in some Afrikaans and local idioms, so that's the cultural bit taken care of. If Jack goes to school, he'll fit right in.

She clears the smartglass window and looks out into the back garden. Most of it is gray cement swatched with carbon moss, but there's also a square of bright green grass, lush and springy and barely big enough for two people to sit on. Beside that, the pool.

It's been covered over for weeks now, ever since a stretch of cold misty mornings made her think the weather was finally turning. The heat overstayed, but the long summer daylight has gone. Even now, barely scraping four o'clock, the sky is darkening. A pale craterous moon hangs over the dusky sea.

She observes a dark blue insect stalking along the edge of the pool. Its opalescent wings flicker and retract. She thinks of a shambler's colorful flukes, its branchia, and ringent pores. She recalls the whine of the buzzsaw and the dirt beneath her nails.

"House," she says. "Run me a bath, please."

Cold water, as cold as she can stand it. She remembers a boyfriend in uni who swore by icy showers in the morning, something about activating the mammalian diving reflex, doubling oxygen intake to the brain. Back then she thought he was a lunatic. She preferred scalding showers, letting the jet beat a little tattoo at the top of her spine. She only varied her routine when a red semicircle of skin started to peel away.

Now she slips into a tub that shocks the breath out of her and mottles her fingers purple. It shrinks her skin around her, knobbles it. She imagines the freezing bottom of the ocean, too deep for sunlight to touch. She shuts her eyes and holds her lungs and plunges her head under the surface. Her hair billows like anemone around her face.

For a moment, she pretends she is a shambler. Stripped of consciousness, purely limbic, a creature that drowns itself once and then disappears forever. It's a dark heaven.

Jack's warbling voice brings her back up. "Mumma? Where is you?"

He knows where she is; she told him and sat him outside the door with the nanny. "I'm right here, Jack," she calls. "In the bathroom."

She eye-traces her gleaming sanctuary: the polished vantablack floors, the prehensile jets of the shower, the small coves where harm-free towels and shampoo bars nest, each one lit from below with a soothing purple-blue light.

"Mumma?" Jack's voice is edged with a sob. "Is you inna bathroom?"

"Yes, Jack," she says. "I'm in the bathroom."

Elisabeth values her privacy when she is bathing or shitting, and a mol of her relishes Jack's predictable bouts of panic. His bafflement, when the center of his universe shifts out of sight. That makes her a Bad Mother.

"Mumma is in the bathroom," the nanny adds, a soft synthesized voice with a singsong Western Cape accent. "Okay, Jack?"

"Is it inna bathroom?" Jack demands, seeking clarity, always.

"Yes, Jack." Elisabeth shuts her eyes. "Mumma inna bathroom."

"Come in?" Jack pleads. "Mumma?"

"Of course," she says, because she is a Good Mother. "Come in, my baby."

The door unchokes and slides open. Jack toddles inside, his blue eyes bright, distress forgotten. "Wash you!" he orders. "Wash you, Mumma."

"Wash you, too, Jack," she says.

She keeps her head above the water but makes herself stay in the tub until she feels pins and needles in her feet. Jack pushes a toy crocodile along the floor; its molded plastic feet click softly in the notches between the tiles. She shivers. Her teeth start to chatter.

Nights with Jack are long, fractured things. He rarely sleeps well, and when his dada is away it's even rarer. Elisabeth marvels at this occasionally, the brutal mutation that Jack undergoes every evening, turning from a quiet angelic thing to a wailing monster. Sometimes it feels as though he is balancing his own ledger. Good Jack, Bad Jack.

More likely it's the two-year sleep regression the nanny has warned her about. So she resigns herself to the dance:

Endure the crying for a minute, two minutes, pad into Jack's room, comfort, nurse, rock, leave, climb into bed, drift, startle awake at his screams, back to Jack's room, comfort, rock, leave, wait, wait, climb into bed, drift, startle awake at his call, wait, wait, back to Jack's room, comfort, nurse, no, not yet, rock, leave, wait, climb into bed, drift, half-sleep, half-dream, startle awake at nothing—

It would be easier to let the nanny handle it. It can soothe him just as well as she can, and it could nurse him, too, if she equipped it properly. There's a little gene lab in District Six that does custom wet nurses, hairless cat-sized things grown from your own helices, sprayed down with your own sweat and gut flora to ensure full oxytocin release.

Elisabeth envisions Jack suckling at a pale disembodied

breast, a lactating tumor. It still makes her shudder, so she'll press on, even though his teeth can feel like razors when she shifts him. She lays him down in his seesaw crib for the fourth, maybe fifth time. His face is still flushed from exertion, but his eyes are shut. She creeps back to her bed.

It would be easier to stay in his room, to fall asleep on the chair with him on her chest, but children have to learn to be alone in the dark. It's normal now, even if it was a death sentence ten thousand years ago. Elisabeth suspects this is why night terror calcified in the genome. All the babies who didn't scream were carried off by leopards.

She rubs her face into her soft cool pillow and entertains the image, a serene little baby smiling up at a puzzled predator, who then shrugs its bony shoulders and swallows it whole. She thinks in cartoons lately, from watching the nanny's screen so often. She is a Bad Mother for her sleepy giggle. Even animated violence against children should probably declench a deep maternal horror in her soul.

Jack is quiet for a long time, so long she is compelled to roll over and observe the undulating monitor that tracks his breathing. He is breathing. She drifts.

Someone is in the back garden. She hears it in her dream first—the scuffle of feet; a soft grunt—then the neural glacier calves and splashes into reality. She wakes up with every square inch of her skin prickling cold. She pictures a fully kitted-out technothief scaling the trellis, slamming some vicious new malware through the house security system, rendering all the sensors and howlers useless at once.

She gropes under the bed for a biolocked box. It tastes her fingers and slides open. The gun inside is an Amazon Shootist, supposedly small and easy to carry. The weight drags at the tendons in her wrist. She carries it in both hands as she slips toward the bedroom door.

She replays the sim in her mind's eye, remembering the cheery ex-soldier who emphasized the importance of breathing, said the lungs are part of the mechanism, same as the muzzle and the trigger and the finger. Her lungs seem to have stopped working. That's unlucky.

The smartglass in the hall shows no intruder detected. Her heart clubs her ribs. She vacillates between options: barricade herself in Jack's room and call emergency services—will the call go through, if the house is hacked? Or go to the back garden, to increase the space between Jack and the intruder, and scare them away. Or shoot them. Either way, the decision has to hinge on Jack's safety, in order for her to be a Good—

"You're fucking joking," she mutters. The cam feed from the back garden shows a slender barefoot man with a gray duffel bag on one shoulder. He's licking his thumb and rubbing it impatiently against the door to the detached guest room.

Elisabeth looks at the top right corner of the smartglass, and sees no intruder detected, but one guest logged. She is trembling. Her whole body is slick with sweat, enough to coat a dozen artificial wet nurses, though she doubts Jack would like this particular smell. She returns to her bedroom and puts the gun back in its biolocked box. Pries at the hinges, makes sure it's sealed.

She goes to the garden door to let her brother in.

"Oh," Will says when he sees her through the window. His voice is muffled. "Hey, Eli."

She slides open the metal grate and unlocks the door with her slimed thumb. She steps out into the garden. The carbon moss is cool and damp under her bare feet. Will must have taken his shoes off to wriggle his toes in it.

"Here I was, trying so hard not to wake you and Jack," he says. "Whoops."

"Whoopsie," Elisabeth agrees, but she's barely annoyed anymore. It feels good to see Will, gives her a rush of relief and familial chemicals.

He's skinny and sunbrowned, how he usually was when they were kids, which means he is drinking less. He's wearing lime green trousers with a baroque print and an unbuttoned gray shirt that matches his Swiss travel bag. He still corrects his crooked face by holding one brow up slightly, which in turn deepens the familiar crease on his forehead. His eyelashes are still long and dark.

The older he gets, the more he looks like their dead dad.

"I took an earlier flight," he says. "From Timisoara."

"You didn't message me."

"I didn't bring any tech," he says. "I'm on a cleanse. But your gate remembered me, so I figured I could sneak straight to the guest bed." He holds out his arms. "I'm fully inoculated. If you'd like a hug."

Their family has never been much for physical contact. She wonders if the offer is related to his tech cleanse, and to the fact that his shoes are nowhere in sight, or if he's microdosing again. She leans forward and hugs him badly, both arms overtop of his. He doesn't cling back the way Jack does. He mostly just stands, while one trapped hand pats awkwardly at her hip bone.

It feels good anyway. She hasn't touched anyone but Jack in ages.

"Glad you could come," she says, and pulls back.

"Me too."

She puts her thumb against the guest room door, then teaches it to remember Will's as well. From inside the house, Jack starts to wail. The nanny's alert skitters inverse across the window.

"Good luck," her brother says, rubbing at his bristly cheek. "Love you, Eli."

"Love you, Will," she says back, on instinct.

He goes into the guest room and shuts it behind him. She stays in the garden a moment longer, relishing the cool breeze blowing in off the ocean, the scattered stars overhead. It's important to crystallize these small moments where everything is going to be okay.

She wakes up the next morning when Will bounces into her room with a very nervous Jack stuck to his hip. Jack is still wearing the penguin onesie she bought in Simon's Town; small animated rockhoppers waddle across the fleece fabric. Will is still wearing yesterday's clothes.

"All work and no Jack makes me a dull boy," he sings. "Look how big he is!"

Jack squirms toward her, wriggling through the air, his anxious smile on the verge of breaking.

"Last time he was just a little pupa," Will says, with his chin-jutting grin. He dumps Jack onto her blanketed legs and steps back. "All he did was sleep and shit. Now he's a little person, isn't he? Aren't you, Jack?"

"No," Jack says, and cling-wraps himself to her. She hauls him up her body, to her chest. He relaxes but doesn't take his eyes off the interloper.

"He recognized me," Will says. "Knows me from pictures, I think."

"He knows all his animals," Elisabeth says, rubbing Jack's small hot back. "Don't you, bubba? You know Uncle Willy?"

Jack gnaws softly at her shoulder, one of his ways of displacing nerves. "Unka Weedy," he mumbles, then, emboldened: "Mumma? Is it Unka Weedy?"

"Yes, my baby," she says. "It's Unka Weedy. He's going to stay for a little bit." She rearranges the blonde nimbus of Jack's hair. "How long, do you think?" she asks.

Will blinks. "However long you want," he says. "I'm happy to work from here. Get a little sea, a little sun."

Elisabeth hears Alea Rose-Kellerman's small knowing sigh. She tries not to let it taint things. Nobody does anything altruistically. There is always some benefit, some Goldberg mechanism shuttling dopamine to the receptor.

"This place is actually perfect," Will says, folding his bony arms. "I saw cases are up here. And that's what I'm into, lately." He smiles down at Jack, but his eyes are elsewhere. "The shamblers."

The word plunges Elisabeth into freezing saltwater. Her breath catches. She barely manages to come back up. "Oh," she says. "Well. Plenty of them."

It feels strange to have another person in the house, one who takes up roughly the same cubed air as Benny but in a radically different way. She doesn't host often. Nobody does, these days. It adds another slick layer to her usual feeling of being monitored, scrutinized, as if her brother is a spy sent to evaluate her mothering in person even though he doesn't know a fucking thing about it.

She packs away the paranoia and focuses on her schedule.

Friday means doing Monday's grocery order, rotating Jack's toys, putting out the glass milk jars for the afternoon drone to pick up, working through another half of a therapy module, deep cleaning the guest bathroom, experimenting again with implementing an early quiet time for Jack, to counteract his bad nights, and exercising in the living room with a bubbly plyometrics instructor.

That, and a dozen other small things that have accumulated on the smartglass. Now that Will is here she feels more impetus to do them, the way she might feel on a stage with an audience. She has to keep reminding herself that Will doesn't care if she is the Good Mother or Bad Mother, that Will is more concerned with his own ledger.

For instance: he has deduced his nephew's favorite animal, and is now tracing beautiful purple pachyderms all across the playroom floor. Jack watches from a safe distance, one hand resting on the nanny's puffy pneumatic arm, but he is no longer nervous. Will was always good with children.

Will looks up. "Thought he was saying air vent, at first. Not elephant."

"They're homonyms for him," Elisabeth says, arranging the clanking milk jars in their box. "And he likes both."

"What else should we color, Jack?" Will asks.

Jack lurches forward, still holding onto the nanny. "Effen again," he says, peering down at the playroom tiles.

"You're stifling my creativity," Will says. "One more elephant, then something else. Okay?"

Elisabeth lugs the box outside, and when she returns there are silhouettes with rippling flukes and tendrils making their way across the floor.

The day evaporates and she barely thinks about Benny. Will slips away while she's putting Jack to sleep for the first stretch of night—she hears the gate scrape. By the time Jack flicks out, and she emerges into the dim-lit hall, her brother is back with a bottle of wine clutched in each fist. She recognizes a Fat Bastard label. The other is a biodynamic imported from Greenland.

"It's not just a novelty anymore," Will preempts. "These northern wineries, they grow good shit."

Elisabeth puts a finger to her lips, then directs him into the kitchen. The nanny is cleaning crusted oatmeal off the floor. There is a drop zone beneath Jack's highchair; its circumference has widened and shrunk as he adjusts to feeding himself. Will stows one of the bottles in the gelfridge and uncaps the Bastard.

"There are proper glasses in the corner cupboard," Elisabeth says, spotting the tumblers he's grabbed for them. "Second shelf."

"We're not proper," Will says.

The chardonnay sloshes and swirls into the tumblers. Elisabeth once tried so hard not to drink around Jack, for fear of embedding some deep tragic memory of his mother as a stumbling lush, but now that doesn't matter. And she needs to drink, so she can tell her brother why.

"Cheers," he says, and manages to clink glass before she raises it to her lips. She gulps the pale wine down. One swallow. Two. It feels like pouring water on parched soil; she imagines a dark bloom spreading then imploding on dry sand. Then the tumbler is empty, and she needs more. Will only looks startled for an instant before he refills her.

She isn't tipsy yet; nothing's been absorbed, but the act of drinking gives her permission on a symbolic level. Permission to be open and truthful. She stares hard at the space over Will's narrow shoulder. She takes a deep breath.

"I don't think Benny is coming back," she says. "We've been fighting and fighting. He was meant to come back last week."

"Fuck." Will takes a deep drink. Some trickles off the corner of his mouth. "Is he sleeping around again? He went with Cora, right? Clara? Whatever her name is." He grimaces. "That's the only reason people do business trips in the flesh these days, isn't it."

"It's not that," Elisabeth says. "Jack was misdiagnosed."

And hearing it in the air, in her own voice, opens a trapdoor in her stomach and puts her guts in freefall.

"How?" Will asks, at an unusual pitch. "The meds were working, I thought. I thought that he's been—hasn't he been—"

"They were working on one thing, but not on the underlying genetic condition," Elisabeth says. "And the labs have been busy lately. For obvious reasons. So we only just got the new diagnosis." She drains her tumbler, swills it around her mouth for the faint sting. "One more good year, maybe, then his body starts in on itself," she says. "Don't ask about options. Please."

Will knuckles furiously at one eye. Gives a shaky laugh. "And Benjamin fucked off to Perth?"

"Adelaide," she says. "But it doesn't matter, Will. He doesn't matter. I just need to figure out what's best for Jack."

She takes the wine bottle by the neck and heads out to the garden.

They drink.

She shows Will the fig tree, squat and arachnoid, that deposits lumpy green spheres all across the cement. She tells him how Jack likes to pick them up and carry them to the rain gutter, and say that he's making guava soup, because she thought it was a guava tree when it was first transplanted, and called it that, and Jack absorbed the wrong word into his spongey little brain.

"He's really clever, isn't he?" Will asks, stepping over the death-shaped gap. He tips the dregs of the chardonnay into his mouth, emptying the bottle. "Verbal for his age. I think."

Elisabeth pauses and listens for a thirsty cry, because speaking about Jack often seems to conjure him, but hears nothing. "Yes," she says, stepping over the same gap. "Really clever, really verbal. Something something percentile."

Will nods, then points his chin at the pool. "Is it filled?"

"It's not heated."

He rubs his feet against each other. "Filled, though?"

"Yeah."

She unlocks it for him, pushing her thumb to the sun-bleached screen. The cover folds up into itself, worming backward to reveal the turquoise water. The scent of chlorine wafts off the top. Will rolls his pant legs up his hairy shins and perches himself on the edge, slaps the spot beside him. She remembers they once snuck over a neighbor's fence as children, to swirl their feet in a similar pool and whisper about their transgressions.

She joins him, but angled so she can see the smartglass window, where the nanny will send its notification if Jack wakes up. They talk about school days and swim meets, and then the conversation collapses inward, as all conversations do these days, toward the omnipresent black hole. It's still better than talking about Jack, who will die, or Benny, who is a coward.

"I saw them putting in new barriers in Muizenberg, all along the strand," Will says. "Trying to plug up the whole coastline."

"There was one at the beach yesterday," Elisabeth confesses. "It nearly made it to the water, right there with everybody watching. Which makes you wonder, doesn't it." She slurps from her tumbler. "How many of them do make it, where nobody's watching."

"Many," Will says. "But once they're in, they're hard to count, because they dive so fucking deep. They grow those—cavities." He punches tiny holes in the air with his finger. "Lets them handle pressures that would burst us. Burst our organs."

Elisabeth feels a delicious shiver up her spine, chining through her back. "What do you think they're doing down there?" she asks.

"I don't know," Will says, because no one does. "It's possible they get eaten by colossal squid." He kicks one foot out of the water, spraying drops toward the other end of the pool. They plink and ripple. "I like to think they're building a city."

"They don't have brains, though. That's the first bit to go."

"They have something," Will says. "They have big nerve bundles, at least."

The pool becomes a temptation. She closes it, telling her brother that it will attract mosquitoes, then goes into the house to retrieve the other bottle of wine. She lingers at the smartglass for a moment, watches Jack's small body breathing. When she returns to the garden, Will is dragging the two mesh folding chairs from behind the rain tank.

She wipes the spiderwebs off them, and they sit in the middle of the garden under a cloud-cloaked nebula. She feels drunk.

"It was rude of them, wasn't it?" She points one finger upward to indicate whatever species or mechanism or individual is to blame. "Dropping a tailored gene-virus on our heads, right when we were finally getting used to the homegrown sort."

"Could've been an accident," Will mutters, and she realizes with mild distaste that he shares one of Alea Rose-Kellerman's pet opinions. "Could've been them trying to say hello."

"Suppose," Elisabeth says. "Do you know what some people are doing, though?"

"Yes, I know," Will says, eyes fixed to the dark sky.

They drink.

*

Between her usual bouts with Bad Jack, during which she feels she is more tender and loving than usual, which might mean she should drink more often, Elisabeth has wild and joyous dreams:

In one of them she attends a party at a baroque hotel whose occupants have been under quarantine for years. She attends arm in arm with Alea Rose-Kellerman, both of them attired in striped swimming costumes, their fictional enmity dimmed to a fictional annoyance.

The maître d', who tries his best to keep everyone's spirits up with these nightly parties, appears in triplicate. It is unclear whether he is an identical triplet, and shares his managerial responsibilities with his two brothers, or if he has somehow distributed his consciousness across three perfect vat-grown copies of his own body.

The party is a tired affair, as it's been going for years, and Elisabeth plans her egress. She observes the festivities from a lofted gallery. She creeps toward the doors, which still project a hazard-yellow warning holo but have been thrown open to tempt the velvet breeze inside. A clearly underage girl looks up from her metallic wine glass.

Elisabeth darts for the exit. The maître d' calls on his bumbling nephew to stop her; the boy hacks at the air with a knife but she feels no terror, only exhilaration, as she ducks around him and bursts out into the wet and windy night. The city is an architectural mishmash of Zaragoza and Luxembourg, wide cosmopolitan avenues and winding cobblestone alleys, all of it impaled by a diagonal canal.

Her swimming costume needlessly becomes a wet suit as she dives in. The canal is shallow; she scrapes the silty bottom and her activity stirs microorganisms in the mud to glow a radioactive green. She prowls along the bottom, moving against a soft artificial current, and feels no tightness in her lungs. She revels in the escape, in the thrill of civil disobedience.

The canal is deep. She swims down, down, into the crushing cold. The microorganisms light her way, floating in orbit around her. She has no need to breathe. She swims through an ancient sea that teems with trilobites and stalk-eyed protofish, and then finds herself in another city altogether. Slantwise streets and crooked ziggurats, all hewn from the rocky seabed, arrayed around a volcanic vent.

The underwater city is empty, but she knows the shamblers have only just ducked out to get a few things, and intend to be back shortly, so—

They take a day trip out to Cape Point, since it was shut down the last time Will was here. The nanny plays Jack his shows while Elisabeth packs the diaper bag and fills two shiny red thermoses with Zimbabwean coffee. Will volunteers to make sandwiches. He lays two columns of puffy white bread on the countertop, alternates swoops of smooth peanut butter with smears of grape jelly, then slaps and stacks them.

The systematic motions make his bony hands look exactly like their mother's. Elisabeth thinks they will probably talk about her the next time they drink.

For now, she bags the sandwiches and supplements them with hummus and sliced fresh cucumbers and a wedge of crumbling goat cheese. She fills a lidded cup with animal-shaped crackers, which include elephants, but no shamblers, to hold Jack over on the drive. She checks and rechecks the diaper bag.

"You are born exploding," Will says, triumphant.

Elisabeth hunts for the infant sunblock. "Pardon?"

"By JJ Manks," Will says. "That poem you were trying to remember the name of, the other night. 'You Are Born Exploding,' by JJ Manks."

"I don't recall."

"You don't recall trying to recall."

She finds the infant sunblock stranded inexplicably on top of the fridge and adds it to the bag. "I don't recall trying to recall," she says, hoping she was not thinking of Jack when she asked about the poem. "Are you ready?"

She swoops Jack off the floor, and they load into the car, which is already switched on and purring. The bright white chassis lances early morning sun in all directions. She has a gnawing feeling as they pull away. She tries to guess, from its inchoate shape, which important task or object she has forgotten. There is always one.

The house seals up behind them. The armored gate rasps shut. Cams swivel on stalks. Hidden howlers prime for intrusion. It always feels as though the house is relieved by their departure and doesn't want them back.

The drive is hemagogic, a beautiful winding pilgrimage around the mountain's curve, a vantage point from which the waves seem like foaming munitions launched from across the world, streaking inexorably toward their targets through a blue-green sea. From above, the beach barriers are plastic toys, barely worth noticing. No shamblers are visible.

Then south, through Glencairn and Simon's Town, south, plunging down the coast, sliding inland, outland. Lush wind-whipped grass gives way to an endless plain of scrub, purple-red punctured with tufts of acid green. The sky swells with no mountain to stop it. Elisabeth wonders why she doesn't do this often, why she spends so much time immured.

"Is it monkey?" Jack queries.

They are passing a sign that once warned of the presence of baboons, and now assures visitors that all baboons have been chipped. The diagram depicts an angular skull in black silhouette, a small radiation-yellow square inside it, even though Benny told her the actual chip is too small to see.

The cerebral modification that binds their behavior is a matter of nanosurgery: a little drone injects them with a little biobot, which nestles in the prefrontal cortex and inhibits aggression toward any human-shaped bipeds. Similar tech is now being trialed on prisoners of war and climate refugees.

"Yes, clever Jack," she says. "It is monkey."

"Fucking beautiful out here," Will says. "So much sky."

The car parks on a stretch of sand lined with empty cooking pits and picnic tables. She pulls Jack from his seat in a shower of crumbs, all the animal crackers pestled by his chubby fist and clumsy mouth. Will grabs the diaper bag and the cooler bag. Beyond the sand, there is a field of sea-slimed rocks. Beyond the rocks, there is a bobbing black carpet of seaweed. Beyond the seaweed, there is gray ocean marked by a single fishing boat.

"Is that Lion's Head?" Will asks, pointing his chin beyond the ocean, to a mountain half-digested by cloud.

"Yes, clever Will," she says. "That is Lion's Head."

He swings the cooler bag so it collides with her non-Jack hip. It feels good to amuse herself, to amuse someone else, to say things carelessly. Her ongoing conversation with Benny, which twines ambiguous texts with strained voice messages, feels like dissecting a thermonuclear bomb. She showed part of it to her brother when they were drunk. He called Benny a self-obsessed cunt, then apologized and changed it to self-obsessed anal polyp.

They sit at the splintery wooden picnic table and eat. Jack is more interested by the rocks. He points at them over and over, his insistent finger smeared with peanut butter, until Will volunteers to spot him so she can finish her meal for once. She allows it. When the cucumbers crack and gush between her laser-scoured teeth, she tries not to picture Jack's small skull crumpling against wet stone.

But he's a cautious baby, picking his way slowly and methodically across the convex obstacles, and Will is hovering behind him, ready to swoop the prongs of his hands beneath Jack's armpits and lever him to safety. Elisabeth observes them from a distance while she eats two sandwiches.

Their exploration triggers an exodus of silverfish, swarming and scuttling. Jack gives a gleeful shout. He fears dogs and cats and often humans, but not insects. Her brother is less gleeful; his spine stiffens, and he scoops Jack into the air.

"Eli!" he hollers, but now there is a hint of grin in his voice. "Come look at this!"

She pins the empty sandwich bag to the table with her thermos, so no sudden gust of sea breeze will send it dancing out of reach and add another atmosphere of pressure to her crushing enviroguilt, then she joins them on the rocks. It's not so slippery as it looked. The tops are mostly dry, crusted bone-white by the sun.

Silverfish scurry away from her every step, which means it is not the silverfish Will wants her to see. When she reaches the spot, the sea-stink is joined by something stronger, oilier, that crawls into her mouth and nose. Will and Jack look up. They share a single face: childish, delighted, fascinated.

A beautiful carcass is strewn over the rocks. The half-shattered exoskeleton still holds its deep rich hues, indigo bleeding to crimson bleeding to violet. Fleshy tendrils trail from sundered sockets, connective tissue a familiar anatomy-book red. The dead flukes, reminiscent of an overgrown yam she once found in the back of the cupboard, sway and shiver in the salt air.

Jack points with his smeary finger. "Shambla, mumma," he says.

She remembers that the baboons were updated to hunt them.

In the week that follows, the dead shambler intrudes upon her dreams. It becomes her companion on odd adventures, scenes spliced from Jack's cartoons and older neural clutter.

They journey across a brilliant white super-surface inhabited by naked nomads. They go to the beach, but remain inside a striped canvas bathing machine so as not to alarm the other swimmers. They visit a carnival where the carousel mounts are real horses, dead and impaled, their bloated tawny corpses tacked to the mirrored floor like insect specimens.

Most of the dreams dissolve and leave no trace, punctured either by Jack's cries in the night or by spears of sunlight in the morning, but she feels the shape of their absence as she goes about her day, puts her fingers in the small private perforations. She starts to follow the news more closely. She observes the waves and wakes of the xenovirus, how she did in the early days, before the terror sluiced away and the inoculation wetware shipped.

Emergency measures have tightened again, which means the border is shut and Benny can't come back even if he wanted to. She stops responding to his messages and rejects two of his calls. The third she answers by muscle memory, distracted, and only remembers their relationship has imploded when his flushed-red face appears. His nose hairs are snowcapped with coke.

He demands to see Jack, seeming surprised he has not thought of it before, so Elisabeth mutes him and takes him to Jack's bedroom and shows him Jack, who is sleeping with a plastic orange sippy-cup of water clutched in his hand like a talisman. She shows him, not sarcastically, the regular pattern of Jack's breathing on the smartglass. The digital undulation is always comforting.

Tears start streaming down Benny's cheeks. He ends the call without saying goodbye.

*

Just as Benny can't reenter the country, Will can't exit it, but her brother doesn't seem to mind. He orders materials—vat-grown vellum canvas, turpentine, brushes—from a specialty shop in Constantia, then tracks their progress for a long afternoon, eyes fixed to the map, one bony hand wringing the neck of his shirt. The flock of delivery drones arrives intact, having successfully skirted a bushfire and two riots.

Will is not precious or secretive about his painting, which Elisabeth has come to believe might be its own sort of affectation, but she has been exposed to the process enough times that the slow layering of color and shadow no longer interests her much. She goes for days without glancing at his canvas, which he usually establishes in the back garden but sometimes packs away for a climb up Elsie's Peak.

She has her own concerns: adjusting the grocery order to account for an additional adult, replacing the air filters in Jack's bedroom, researching and cataloguing superior therapy options to the gratingly algorithmic modules she abandoned, disposing of any bath toys with internal spaces that might harbor stagnant water and dangerous bacteria, writing at least one sentence each day in order to anchor herself in time. She often finds herself transcribing the news.

"There are more and more of them," she says one night, singing her finger along the edge of her wine glass. "These anthrocide cults."

Will stares at her. His swollen pupils strike her as magnetic seeds, pushed by thumb into yielding soil. "It's a way of resuming control," he says, setting his vapor pipe down, "of an uncontrollable situation."

"It's mass suicide," she says. "If they would just wait a bit longer, for the market cycle to bring wetware costs down—things will normalize. You know? They always normalize."

"Sure, Eli," Will says. "But some of these people, they've lost it all already. Their whole family's wandered off into the ocean. They're angry, and they're desperate, and nobody knows, really, what it's like to be a shambler—"

"Looks awful," she says. "The way they crawl and gasp."

"Only until they get to the sea." Will repacks his pipe, hands soft and methodical. "When they dive, it's quite fucking beautiful, actually. There's a spot—" He peers at his work. "Oh. These cartridges, they slot the other way."

"A spot?" Elisabeth echoes.

Will blinks. "Yeah," he says, suddenly secretive. "Yeah, you know how I've been hiking a bit? Just up that little mountain?"

"Elsie's Peak."

"Yeah." He chews his inner cheek. "Well, there's this overhang, up near the lighthouse. Stretches right out over the sea. And yesterday, I saw something."

"Shamblers," Elisabeth guesses, with her heart pittering, palpitating.

"A pair of them. Yes." Will sucks at his pipe. Coughs. "They dropped off the end, and when I got closer, I saw them down below. In the waves. Swimming a little circle around each other. Then they dove down, and I lost sight of them."

"You should tell someone," Elisabeth says. "Get that spot flagged and blocked."

Will wiggles his jaw. "I don't think I should," he says. "In fact, I sort of wish that we'd leave well enough alone. Let them get to the water. Let them dive. Let them do whatever it is they do in peace. If they're gone, they're gone, right?"

She pictures the aquatic metropolis.

Jack wails.

Thursday arrives and Elisabeth goes to the beach instinctively, in the way of migratory birds. The streets along the strand are dead empty. Menacing nanocarbon jellyfish drift overhead, security drones recommissioned from guarding empty warehouses in order to patrol the waterline. She coaxes the pram out of the back of the car and places Jack inside, even though lately Jack prefers to walk whenever possible.

The man at the gate is not pleased to see them. "Recreational use of the beach is not recommended," he says, eyes over her shoulder, "for purposes of safety."

"But it's permitted," Elisabeth says, icily, "as we are fully inoculated."

The biofilter shows uncontaminated blue. The gate staggers

open to let them through. There are only two other people on the sand: Alea Rose-Kellerman and Nils, their human nanny conspicuously absent. Elisabeth is full of regret, but the gate has already wheezed shut behind her. She guides the pram forward and gives a jaunty wave.

Alea flowers a smile. "Hello, Liz," she says. "Awfully crowded today."

"Nightmarish," Elisabeth says back.

"How's baby Jack?" Alea asks.

Jack hears and wriggles upright in the pram. "Hello?"

Alea laughs, claps her hands together in delight like some sort of seal. "Hello, Jack," she says. "Come play with Nils! They're building a mud castle."

Elisabeth lifts Jack out of the pram and deposits him beside Nils, whose new swimming costume is made to look like a starfish. The two stare for a moment, then ignore each other, each of them retreating to their own privately contracted mud projects. Elisabeth attempts something similar by unfolding her reader and fussing with the screen settings.

"So poor Benjamin is still stuck in Perth," Alea says. "Shame."

Her heart gives an adrenal jolt and stammer because there is no way for the Kellerman-Roses to know whether Benny is back or not. Then she recognizes the incorrect city, and realizes what has happened.

"I met your brother," Alea says, unnecessarily. "We chatted for a moment. He's actually quite grounded, for a creative, isn't he?"

Will is always fucking meeting people. He has already met a depressed fashion model, while picking up coffee from one of Main Road's last surviving cafés, and a retired sommelier, while hiking up to the derelict lighthouse. Now he has met Alea Rose-Kellerman, too.

"I thought he would have a more interesting perspective on the world," Alea expounds. "Maybe it all goes into his work and none is left over."

"Very possible," Elisabeth says. "Where is your nanny?"

Alea's perfect face crumples. "Oh," she says. "Oh, oh."

Elisabeth wants to say *did you only just notice* or *immunomods seem to be getting pricier and pricier, don't they*, but then she sees a wet gleam in Alea's eyes, nearly as incongruous there as it was in Benny's.

"She was visiting family in Cape Flats," Alea says, "and was infected. I honestly don't know how to feel."

It seems obvious to Elisabeth—she has always known how she ought to feel, even when the feelings do not arrive—but she waits. Jack reaches over and cautiously smears mud across Nils' chest. Nils is amenable. Alea collects herself.

"It was voluntary," she says. "She was one of that crowd who stole boats and went out to sea and infected themselves with syringes. Which I suppose is horrible." She pauses. "Can you keep a secret, Liz?"

For a moment Elisabeth inhabits a malformed quantum branch where she is Liz, Alea's drab but dependable friend whose silences are due to lack of material, whose limited social circle makes her an ideal confidante. It's unnerving.

"I can," she says. "Yes."

Alea takes a trembly breath. "Sometimes I wish I could do that. That I could be a shambler." She snuffs out a laugh. "Mad, isn't it?"

A tenuous filament stretches between them, connecting them for the very first time. Alea Rose-Kellerman has said the words that make the rounds so often inside Elisabeth's skull. This feels momentous. It might trigger a montage of friendship, romance, even criminality.

"I know you're quite happy where you are," Alea says, wiping at her eyes. "With the hubby and the baby and whatnot. Which is lovely, Liz. Lovely. But me, I've always wanted something— grander."

You fucking cartoon, Elisabeth says in her head.

"That *is* mad," she says in the air, making her voice kind and mild. "Wanting to be a shambler. And you ought to seek help, Alea."

Alea nods sadly. Elisabeth feels exhausted on a cellular level.

Will posits it to her, and she agrees to invite the retired sommelier over the following evening. He is sunbaked and silverhaired and wears a daring romper open-chested. His puppy has a brief discussion with the Rose-Kellermans' dog, then falls silent, content to chew at his graceful hand. They are drinking ciders in the back garden—Will refused to select a wine, saying it could only be a trap—while Jack collects fallen figs.

The air is fresh and electric, and it seems impossible that the world is ending, but that is where the conversation invariably leads.

"You see, this is not like the other plagues and pandemics," says the ex-sommelier, in a faint Romanian accent. "This is their photo negative. Their chiral opposite."

"Well, it came by artificial meteor," Will says, with a buttery smile. "That's quite unique."

"It came with purpose," their guest says. "In my opinion, it's a gift."

"How do you figure?" Elisabeth asks, more bluntly than usual.

"In my opinion," the man repeats, "humanity has been offered a way to save itself." This prompts her to verify, again, that the front gate's biofilter reported him clean. "To save itself *from* itself," he continues, stroking the small bones of his dog's head, "and this time, the downtrodden lead the way."

Will gives an alarmed smile. "That's quite the idea."

"First shall be last, last shall be first, et cetera." Their guest places the dog in his lap. "We left the poor behind, over and over, but now they finally get to leave us behind."

"By becoming monstrous eldritch crayfish things," Elisabeth says. "Such luck."

"By growing iridescent armor and returning to our primeval birthplace," the ex-sommelier says. "They are safe in the ocean while the old world burns. Or they would be, if we stopped senselessly hunting them down."

"Agreed on that count," Will says. "It's barbaric. The containment programs are barbaric."

The dog whines. The ex-sommelier nods. "And who's to say, what is monstrous or not monstrous? We only see their exteriors."

"Nobody knows what it's like to *be* a shambler," Will choruses.

"Or perhaps they do know," their guest says. His wrinkled eyes twinkle. "Perhaps they do know, those scientists who chop the metamorphized to pieces and run electrodes though their limbs, and they are madly jealous. Why else would we try so hard to halt this exodus?"

"It's not an exodus," Elisabeth says flatly. "It's a virus." She scoops Jack into her arms. "The people who turn shambler are dead. Their bodies just get repurposed."

"Impossible to know!" the ex-sommelier crows. "The shamblers do not communicate with the unchanged, but they have been seen to act in cooperation, to move in groups—"

"It's Jack's bedtime," Elisabeth interjects. "It was lovely to meet you."

"And equally lovely to meet you, Elisabeth," their guest says, beaming. "Goodnight, little Jack." He swigs from his cider and turns to Will. "So, this painting. You will show me?"

Elisabeth imagines the scenario in which she putters away, puts Jack down, reemerges an hour later to hear drunken giggling, to see a silver head leaning close to Will's dark one. She feels no obligation to help her brother get his cock in. She dislikes the idea of them discussing shamblers without her, maybe discussing her without her.

"He won't," she says. "I need his help with Jack, you see." She gives the ex-sommelier an eyeless smile. "You can leave through the garden gate."

Their guest looks affronted for only a moment, then looks sad and wise instead, burdened by his own enlightenment. "Of course," he says, gathering the dog in his arms, but before he reaches the garden gate, he performs an elegant turn and speaks over his shoulder. "We should not fear the metamorphosis," he says. "Best of luck in the new world."

He departs, and Elisabeth waits for Will to apologize for befriending a lunatic and bringing him over for ciders. Instead, her brother stares at the fig tree and wipes the moisture from the bottom of his bottle with one bunch-sleeved fist.

"He makes some good points," Will says mildly. "There is a certain allure. The unearthliness of it, I suppose. The mystery." He gledges at her. "There has to be, or there wouldn't be so many voluntary infections. All these people pouring into the sea."

"Goodnight, Will," Elisabeth says in monotone. "Love you."

Before she begins her nightly joust with Jack, who is one day closer to death, she detours to her brother's room. His canvas is on the bed, and when she flicks on the light, she is hardly surprised to see the silhouette of a shambler, painted in meaty reds and purples, emerging through moon-slashed waters. It's so beautiful her traitorous throat aches.

A spike in the infection rate, accompanied by a spike in violent unrest, returns them to a full lockdown. Benny's bristling house becomes a fortress becomes a prison, and Elisabeth fears it will become an asylum next. Her dreams are more vivid than ever. Sometimes they arrive in daylight, dorsal fins rising from her subconscious, circling. Brief flashes of something razorous beneath.

Will is acting strangely. He stalks all around the house, a gaunt tiger in a menagerie, and gnaws at childhood memories Elisabeth has already forgotten. It gets worse when he drinks, and he drinks often now.

"The game with the box," he says, with febrile eyes. "The game we played in the basement. You don't remember? We called it the change-you box."

Jack is asleep. They are in the kitchen again, with a chilled bottle of pinot grigio erupting from the tabletop between them, turned symbolic by the fact that Elisabeth has decided not to drink with him anymore. An impassable landmark.

"There was a saucer we would take down there with us," he says. "We would sneak it out of the china cabinet. It had blue anemones on it. We would drink water out of that, say it was potions, then go underneath the change-you box."

Her brother's words trigger neural sheet lightning, and she sees it: they are children, playing on a cold concrete floor in an unfinished basement with plywood ribs for a ceiling and bare bulbs tugged to life by string. They take turns going underneath a big cardboard box, and sometimes Will wants the both of them to go under together, but she doesn't want to do that.

"Blue flowers," she says. "Not anemones."

Something is wrong with Jack. His temperature is not elevated; his oximeter readings are normal, but he is pale, tetchy, easily upset, and when he throws his fits, he refuses to be comforted. A dozen digital consults tell her it is too early for his condition to be rearing its head. They assure her, over and over, that this is only a blip and not the beginning of the end.

Today, instead of wailing his distress into her shoulder and trying to burrow inside her chest, he staggers to the corner behind the modular couch and huddles there.

"Come here, little bubba." She wedges herself behind the couch with him, holding out her arms. "Come here, my love. Is you thirsty?"

Jack shakes his golden head.

"Mumma munk?" Elisabeth suggests, even though it is the afternoon.

Jack is briefly conflicted but shakes his head again.

It hits her in the gut. She knows that Jack is likely sponging up all her fear, observing it in the subtleties of her body language, tasting it in her milk. She knows dwelling on that will only make her more anxious, an unstoppable feedback loop, and the prospect of entering that loop also makes her anxious.

The whole thing is fucked, and it's because she is weak. Unstable. She is the Bad Mother.

Unless it's something else.

The suspicion is so horrible and enormous that she can't look at it directly. She has to feel her way around the barbed edges, replaying every interaction between Will and Jack, replaying the half-forgotten games in the basement. The possibility numbs her. Dizzies her. Then it flenses her open, a raw scarlet pain in every part of her.

She backs away from Jack, her hands and knees trembling in tandem. She tells the smartglass to pull up every instance of Will and Jack together without her. She watches without breathing. Slowly, slowly, with each innocent interaction that passes, her suspicion is exchanged for guilt. She has done another bad thing.

But then, two weeks ago, Jack toddles inside Will's room. Her brother is holding something in a bag. He notices the intrusion, laughs. The chuckle comes crunchy with static. *No telling mumma*, he says, and puts the bag under his pillow. Elisabeth feels a jolt of fear, another of fury. She told Will her secret, but her brother is keeping one from her.

She goes to the guest room, carried along on a crackling wave. Will is painting in the garden, so she can search in peace for—

what? For what? She flips his sweat-stained pillow, finds nothing. She tears open drawers and unrolls his stacked shirts. Then she sees it, nestled in the crack between bedpost and wall.

The bag is dark blue plastic. She unseals it and smells the pungent oily smell of a shambler dismembered.

Elisabeth detours to her room first, to the biolocked box. Then she slips Jack's lime green FrogFones over his ears, gives him a cupful of animal crackers, and goes to the garden to confront her brother. It's a gray day. Fog has wafted in off the sea and swallowed the sky. Will is using a solar lamp to simulate a bit of sunshine. His canvas is a beautiful tangle of blood-bright vermeil and deepest blue.

"The bag behind your bed," she says. "Why the fuck would you do that?"

Will blinks. His cheeks flush. "We're all fully inoculated."

"Is it the one from Cape Point?" she demands.

Her brother nods.

"So it's been in the house for weeks." She feels the rage in her throat like an acid. "Weeks. Why would you even think to—"

"The pigments," Will pleads. He gesticulates with his blue-dipped brush. "I wanted the pigments, for the painting, same way I used to crush up seashells. That's all, Eli."

"No." Elisabeth sets the biolocked box on the concrete, crouches in front of it. Her voice is trembling. "No, this is something else. You're as crazy as the sommelier. You're trying to infect yourself, trying to infect *us*—"

"No!" Will yelps the word. "No, Eli, never, I don't—"

"Why was it a secret?" she demands.

Will's mouth twists, how their mother's used to twist, and it makes her even angrier. "Didn't want to worry you," he says. "Didn't want to add stress."

Elisabeth lets the box taste her thumb. Its catches click open. "I booked you a place on Main Road," she says. Her dry mouth seems to rasp against itself. "You have to leave. Take the bag with you. Do whatever you want with it, but not here."

"Eli, come on." Will has finally caught her anger, fed his own furnace. He looms over her, brows knit, teeth bared. "I want to *in-*

fect myself? That's fucking ridiculous. Fucking ridiculous. You're the one who wants to turn shambler."

Elisabeth feels something serrated pierce her chest.

"The way you keep bringing up that game," Will rails. "That game we played in the basement. The change-you box. You think I don't know what you're getting at?"

"Fuck you," Elisabeth says, and for the first time she means it.

"I don't blame you," Will says. "Nobody would blame you for wanting that, with Jack—" He stops when he sees the Shootist pointed at his face. His voice tremors. "Eli, what the fuck is that? Is that Benny's?"

"Go, Will."

His eyes dart from the gun to the window, where Jack is directing a digital train. "Can I say goodbye to Jack?" he asks, and she can hear the tears coming, thickening his sinuses. The tears everybody gets but her.

"Later," she says. "You can call later. Right now, you leave."

"Okay," Will says, hollow, still staring at the window. "Okay." He starts packing the canvas away. "Love you, Eli."

The response becomes a ghost on her tongue.

Will is gone, and so is the bag, but the scent of the dead shambler lingers. She changes the guest room bedding and sets the nanny to scrubbing the wall where the bag was once wedged between plaster and post. Antiseptic foam spills onto the floor, reminds her of cresting waves. Jack thinks the same. He slashes his hands through it and crows *we atta beach, mumma*, until she distracts him with one of his shows.

He asks after his uncle for the first few days, how he used to ask after his dada, but then Will's departure seems to slip from his mind. They return to their most common configuration: a binary sun, just the pair of them winging through the dark. She puts all her energy into being the Good Mother, into constructing the pointless, perfect environment for growth and learning.

Outside, entire countries are disappearing. China has been a digital black hole for months, but now despots in other places are following suit—Hungary and Poland have amputated themselves from the net and militarized their borders. The poorest coastal nations have begun to buckle and collapse in the face of rising numbers, overrun ports.

Here, the president's soothing gravel-throated addresses have become a nightly farce. Disturbed supply lines empty the supermarkets. Load shedding becomes even more erratic; for three days Elisabeth uses the house generator only. She dreams about a shambler emerging from beneath a cardboard box in a dim-lit basement.

Jack is gnawing at her shoulder again.

"No eating mumma," Elisabeth says. She says it by reflex; she is almost happy to feel his teeth, to feel him cling to her. They are sitting in the living room, windows opaqued and displaying a field of rustling sunflowers. A cartoon is playing on the nanny's belly screen. The world is calm. Intact.

Jack's blue eyes are suddenly mischievous. "No eating car," he says.

"No eating helicopters," Elisabeth says, singsong.

"No eating airplane!" Jack yelps.

"No eating *boats*."

"No eating . . ." Jack blinks. "Chair."

"You're just looking at objects in the living room, now," Elisabeth says. "You little stink."

"No eating chair," Jack insists.

She lifts his chubby wrist to her mouth. "Yes eating Jack," she says, and when he squeals and gasps with laughter she feels how she felt post-hospital, the same warm fizzing oxytocin rush, the assurance that nothing else matters. His small body shakes against her, particularly his left arm. Even when he stops laughing, it spasms, flops.

Something is wrong. They watch as his tiny hand curls into a trembling hook. Jack looks up at her, only slightly alarmed. "Mumma fix," he says, as if his rebelling limb is a malfunctioning toy.

Elisabeth stares. Her lungs are full of barbed wire.

"Mumma, is you crying?" Jack asks, incredulous, delighted.

*

It's the beginning of the end.

Six hours speaking in circles to medical AIs earns her twelve minutes speaking to a haggard specialist in Brno, who tells her the same thing more bluntly: Jack's symptoms have appeared earlier than anticipated, and the descent will likely be swift. Elisabeth thanks her and ends the call, then uses the smartglass to order a swing set in bright primary colors, identical to the one Jack loved so much at the seawall playground in Cape Town.

She orders a cavalcade of action dolls, dinosaurs, building bricks. She scrolls in a fugue state. Some things she suspects she has already purchased, already stepped on, but she orders them again to be certain. She no longer has any fear of instilling materialism in her baby. Her only goal is endorphins. Every day until the end will be a holiday.

A warning message blinks across the glass. Due to the ongoing xenovirus crisis, delivery may be delayed. They offer no time estimate.

She has Jack's crib scuttle from his room to hers, installing itself beside her bed. The new arrangement is too exciting; he refuses to lie down, instead stands clinging to the bars, peering at her through the gap. Elisabeth hovers on the other side, in case his grip suddenly fails, and he slips forward and thuds his forehead against the reclaimed sea wood. She has to keep discomfort to an absolute minimum. She has to subtract tears.

When Jack succumbs to sleep, she sends a two-word message to Benny: *it's started*. There is no reply or notification of receipt. There has been no activity on any of his feeds for a week now. It might be due to mass grid failures in Australia. It might be due to suicide—she remembers him telling her, once, how when he drives manually, he feels a strong urge to swerve into the oncoming.

Or maybe he's a shambler now, one of the shining mass who spilled off Sydney's piers and vanished into the ocean. *When they dive*, Will says in her head, *it's quite fucking beautiful, actually*. She has an unclassifiable thought, one that vacillates between the poles of Good Mother and Bad Mother. She's had it before, but only briefly and only in the coldest water.

She sleeps poorly.

The next day it takes her a while to notice Jack's legs have stopped working. He's played with his crocodile all afternoon, sliding it along the floor, singing a jumbled version of some Korean cartoon's opening theme, and even though Elisabeth has been watching him the entire time, she only now realizes why he is so content to sit, only now realizes he is scooting around propelled by just his arms.

Bad Mother, Bad Mother, Bad Mother.

"Is it owie?" she asks, smearing the question with artificial cheer. "Is Jack's legs owie?"

"Is it owie?" Jack echoes, confused.

"Your legs, bubba." She touches his knee with a trembly finger. "Do they hurt?"

Jack looks down at them.

"Dead," he says, and she knows that he knows that word in reference to toys and tablets only, to things with lithium that need charging, but it still feels accusatory. She is halfway into the pantry, groping for a dusty bottle of cream liqueur, before she can stop herself.

She pours a full mug of it, drinks it in sickly sweet gulps. She looks at the message she sent to Benny, then forwards it to Will, because she has somehow constructed an existence in which she has nobody else to suffer with her. His call is immediate. He's already crying.

"I'm so fucking sorry, Eli," he says. "So fucking sorry."

"It's okay," she says, nonsensically.

Jack's blonde head turns. "Is it Unka Widdy?" he demands, and she realizes his pronunciation has improved again, because he is so smart, so verbal for his age. All the people he will never be hurtle through her, a rush of pale gray ghosts. She has to sit down, before the foaming dark at the edges of her vision does it for her.

"I'm still in town," Will says. "I never left. No flights and all the roads are blockaded anyway. Anything you need—I know that's a fucking cliché, Eli, but anything you need. Anything."

It feels like months ago, their midnight conversation in the garden. Elisabeth braces herself for the unclassifiable. "The sommelier," she says. "Do you still have his contact information?"

"Haven't been hanging around with him, I swear," Will says.

"His contact information, though."

"Yes."

"And that spot that you told me about, up on Elsie's Peak." She breathes in, out, makes her lungs part of the mechanism of the gun that is her mouth. "I need you to send me the geotag."

For a long time, Will is silent.

The government collapses that weekend. Elisabeth sees in her feed that suburbs are sealing themselves off, placing spikes on the road, attaching scopes to guns and guns to drones as they act out some atavistic fantasy. But the baying horde of thieves and looters never arrives, and they only manage to murder an old man searching for garden work at the end of the world.

On Monday, she decides to take Jack to all of his favorite places. She loads him into his car seat while his pram climbs into the boot. He does not play with the straps; today both his hands fold awkwardly into themselves, which makes him whine and whimper. The medical AI has assured her, over and over, that there is no pain, only numbing nerves.

They drive down the hill to Main Road and walk from there. The sidewalks are overgrown and pitted in places, but the pram is a rough beast and slouches easily along them, keeping Jack level in its cushioned embrace. The morning air is finally chill enough to redden Elisabeth's fingertips. She makes sure the pram's heating pad is on.

The town that was never quite hers is now nobody's. The streets are dead empty. The storefronts are locked behind their metal grilles. She passes only shuttered windows, man-made eyelids squeezed tight to block out disaster. Occasionally a security drone drifts up for a bioscan, assesses their inoculation, then drifts away.

Jack's favorite smoke shop is closed, but its main draw was always the bright yellow door and signage. He sits higher in the pram when he spots it. Tries to point to it with an uncooperative finger. Elisabeth wishes the shop were open, so she could get stoned enough to remove her bones and put her prone on the couch, unable to think a single sad thought. She has not done that in nearly a year.

But now is not the time. She guides the pram around the bend, past a small mountain of rotting garbage that reminds her the service was disrupted two weeks prior.

It takes Jack only a minute to recognize their route. "Is it go a fire trucks, mumma?" he hollers.

"Yes, little bubba," she says. "We're going to see the fire trucks. What color is a fire truck?"

She regrets asking that, because she recalls complaining drunkenly to Will about the way adults are always asking children the stupidest questions, which is likely why children grow up mistrusting adults. Now she is a hypocrite, and also has to think about Will, who is likely holed up in one of the automated apartments nearby.

By the time they reach the redbrick fire station, it's a beautiful day. The sun has scoured the sky to a clear blue in all directions, not a wisp of cloud, and the breeze carries salt smells off the ocean. Elisabeth has not walked much lately. Her lungs feel good and tight. Her calf muscles smolder pleasantly. When they round the final corner, giving Jack a view of two fire-rescue vehicles hunkered in their charging stations, he howls.

"Fire truck, mumma! I see it? I see it?"

She has the pram trundle as close as it can to the gate, so Jack can peer through into the yard. They are only there for a moment before a human security drone—security guard, rather—appears. He is the sort of man Benny used to work with, lined and grizzled but still hauling steroid-swollen muscle about under an overly tight shirt.

"Ma'am, you shouldn't be out, ma'am," he says, with an Afrikaner accent. "What are you doing out? We put it on all the town feeds: best to stay indoors."

"We're fully inoculated," Elisabeth says, by rote.

"Not for bullets. Man was shot yesterday, did you not see? It was on all the town feeds."

"Yes," Elisabeth says. "The man who used to do the Rose-Kellermans' garden was shot by a drone. It was tragic." She points to Jack, who is staring at the stranger with slightly horrified eyes.

"May we come inside and touch a fire truck?"

The guard squints. "That's not as I heard it," he says. "I heard he was sneaking about with a list of houses. List of names, too."

"This is Jack," Elisabeth says. "Could he possibly touch that nearest fire truck?"

"No," the guard says. "Best go home straight away."

"Go fuck yourself," Elisabeth says mildly.

The man makes a noise in his throat, somewhere between a laugh and a gasp. But he doesn't rail at her, or threaten her, which is a shame, because the pram would drown his eyeballs in capsaicin at her request. He only goes back inside the station, shaking his grizzled head. Elisabeth lets Jack observe the fire trucks a while longer. They leave.

There are ways of disabling immunomods, and she researches them in the bath. She crawls from one thread to another to another, observes the digital war, now waged mostly by bots, between those who call the xenovirus humanity's final chance at salvation and those who call it a fire-and-forget colonization method, who say the anthrocidists are suffering an undetectable secondary infection that alters the brain, like parasite-infested mice with no fear of cat piss.

Exodus or extinction. Gift or weapon. Elisabeth suspects she knows which, but she is not here to add her voice to the algorithmic chorus. She trawls for specifics, for bootstrap methods of disbanding her virophage army. She is not the first. People from all corners of the collapsing net have sought the very same escape, likely from their own small tragedies, and she follows now in their footprints.

She briefly imagines Alea Rose-Kellerman, in a much larger tub in the house farther up the hill, mirroring her every motion, and wonders what she needs to escape. Maybe boredom. Maybe Nils. Maybe herself.

"Wash you knees," Jack suggests.

He is sitting on the heated tile beside the tub. She can't deny him, not so close to the end, not when his little limbs might give out at any moment. He's playing with a bright red fire truck that used to be his favorite. The fact feels disproportionately important now. She feels the need to recall everything about Jack, every habit and preference. He has only been briefly alive, so it shouldn't be difficult.

"Wash you knees, mumma," Jack says again.

Elisabeth rubs at her kneecap, feeling the gooseflesh around the bone. "Wash, wash, wash," she sings. "Wash, wash, wash."

"Good washing," Jack decrees, in an uncanny imitation of the nanny's synthetic lilt. "Good job."

"Thank you, Jack. I thought so, too."

Jack returns to his toy. Elisabeth reaches forward and drains the bath a bit, listening to the gasp and gurgle of exorbitant water waste, then adds a shot of hot water. She stirs with her hand until it's tepid throughout. Climbs out dripping.

"Jack," she says. "Do you want to come inna bath, bubba? With your fire truck?"

He is momentarily suspicious, but the novelty wins out. He lets her peel off his clothes, hold him fruitlessly over the toilet, carry him back to the tub. He gives a squealing giggle when she skims his feet through the water, holding him under the armpits. She sets him down carefully and clambers in after him.

"Lots of animals live in the water, Jack," she says. "Should we play pretend?"

She thought the tub was warm enough, but Jack is shivering, clenching his tiny teeth.

Elisabeth writes messages to the following people:

Her father, who is dead. He once told her that there are only ever two moves that can be made, the strong move or the weak move, but they can look like each other and so all of life is spent deciphering which is which.

Her mother, who is a lush, or more accurately an addict. Elisabeth excised her nearly a decade ago, but she sometimes appears in dreams. She and Will never did end up discussing her.

Benny, who she did love, if symbolically, for several years.

Three friends, one acquaintance, one aunt—the last splinters of a social circle, people who she once felt connected or indebted to.

Alea Rose-Kellerman, who may have the pram for Nils if she

wants it, though she will likely find it too militaristic in appearance.

Her brother, who she will be seeing soon.

The beach is still shut when Thursday morning arrives, but there are other ways to the water. Elisabeth has not slept in days. She puts caffeine in her bloodstream at five past five in the morning, then wakes Jack. He is limp while she dresses him. His head wobbles slightly. She holds him in her lap and feeds him the sugary cereal normally reserved for weekends. Milk dribbles out of his grin and streaks his small chin.

They drive to the head of the trail, the serpentine path that leads up Elsie's Peak, and Elisabeth slides Jack into the carrier, a little fabric cocoon that snugs to her chest. They start to climb. Jack narrates for her, babbling about the grasshoppers darting past, the windiness of the day. She's glad his tongue and mouth still work.

When they crest the first plateau the rocks turn to sand, the same pale gray sand they walk on by the beach. It seems incongruous up here, transplanted, but Elisabeth doesn't know enough about the natural processes of erosion and mountain-forming to be certain. The wind is stark, roaring past her ears and rippling the red-and-yellow gorse that stubbles the stone.

"Is it windy day, mumma," Jack says, not a question.

"Yes, my baby," she says. "It's a very blustery day."

She follows the splintery wooden sign for the lighthouse ridge, sticking to the path for now. She tries to savor the crunch of its sand under her shoes, tries to savor everything: the warm weight of Jack's body against her thudding rib cage, the slow pulse of the Atlantic down below.

Sunshine is finally fraying the clouds, tattooing her neck. She pauses to adjust Jack's hat, a pointless and vestigial act, protecting skin that will not exist much longer. He barely protests, too taken with the novelty of their surroundings. The multicolor clumps of vegetation seethe in the wind, as if trying to free themselves from the mountainside. Stone formations rise up here and there like massive cairns or crenellations; she remembers Will drunkenly detailing a perilous climb to the top of one.

She verifies the geotag he sent her and leaves the path. She moves carefully, double-tapping each placement of foot to ensure no shifting stone unbalances her. The geotag leads her along a smaller ridge, concealed by the larger, with a view of the sea. She can see the division where discordant currents meet, deep blue bruising itself against sun-dappled turquoise. The waves move slowly from up here, a wrinkle that can never quite be smoothed.

"Beach," Jack announces, in response to the sight of the ocean.

"Yes, my love," Elisabeth says. "Today's a beach day. Yes."

Will is waiting for them at the overhang. He wears a dark windbreaker and carries a duffel bag. She can see from his puffy red eyes that he's been crying again. She twists, so Jack can see his uncle; he is baffled but delighted. He shouts his name into the wind. Elisabeth hates her brother so badly for that, for sectioning Jack's affections in this final critical moment. She also loves him more than she ever has.

"I know you're sure," Will says, when she's close enough to hear him. "So I won't ask."

He takes a small black canister out of the duffel bag, attaches it to a medical injector. They kill their immunomods first, a microneedle kiss. Jack is accustomed to medical evaluations. He barely flinches. Then comes the second canister, identical, but Elisabeth pictures a miasma of beautiful reds and blues and purples inside it.

"Remember the bath game, little bubba?" Elisabeth asks, even as her throat winches shut. "When we pretended to be shamblers? Mumma shambla, baby shambla?"

"What?" Jack is distracted, fascinated by the injector. "What, mumma?"

"We are going to have a nap," she says. "We are going to have a mountain nap. While we are napping, we are going to turn into a mumma shambler and a baby shambler. And then we are going to dive down, down, down into the ocean."

"Oh!" Jack blinks. "We going inna ocean."

"It'll take a few hours," Will croaks. "I'll stay for it. Of course. I'll stay until you go over the edge. It stretches right out over the water, well-clear of the rocks, and all the ones I saw, they all made it, so—" He breaks off. "Oh, fuck. Oh, fuck, Eli."

Elisabeth can't explain it to her brother, can't explain the carousel she's been on for so long, up and then down, questioning her questioning of her questioning of herself. Maybe she is succumbing to a brain-altering secondary infection, and selfishly taking Jack with her. Maybe she is succumbing to a biological drive, and pointlessly sacrificing herself with her child.

Maybe she is escaping the end of one world to join another.

"Here," Will says, handing her the injector.

"Thanks."

She can't tell if she is being the Good Mother or the Bad Mother, the Good Person or the Bad Person. She has never been able to tell. Either way, it will all be over soon. She puts the injector to her arm, and then to Jack's chubby leg.

"Love you, Will," she says. "Love you, Jack. Little bubba."

"You a little bubba," Jack says, because lately the name annoys him.

She tastes salt on her lips that is not from the sea. She sits down on a flat sunbaked rock, still cradling Jack to her chest. She waits for the end of a world.

Two iridescent shapes topple off the stone outcropping, plummet through a shrieking wind, plunge into the belly of the Atlantic with twin plumes of white foam. The shamblers are of disparate size, one so small its flukes are barely visible, but both of them carve through the water with eerie grace, circling each other, angling upward, downward.

Something draws them outward, away from the fortified coastline. They skim beneath the waves, under the wary electric eyes of the drones, moving deeper and deeper as they go. It is impossible to know if they are driven by thought or by instinct, if neural pathways have been converted into alien language or discarded entirely.

But when they are far from any shore, the smaller hooks itself to the larger. They dive together, toward a city that might exist.

VERWEILE DOCH (BUT LINGER)

esar is splayed on his stomach across the gleaming white kitchen tiles of El Pimpi's Seafood Bistro, peering at the cockroach that is about to wreak havoc. Up close he can see the striations on its folded wings, count the spiky hairs on its rear legs, even spot a bit of his reflection in its slick yellowish-black exoskeleton.

"I've been doing some trig, Kenny," he tells the cockroach. "Some angles and stuff. I fear for you. Devon wears size thirteen, and he's, well, he's right there."

Cesar rolls over onto his back, tucking his hands under his head to look up at Devon the server, whose eyes are bulging with surprise and whose foot is lifted into the air, ready to stomp. The sole is worn mostly smooth, with a sliver of bright green chewing gum wedged into the remaining tread.

The tray he was carrying is now connected to only two fingertips. The glass pitcher of water is past the point of no return, already adrift in the air, its contents sloshing out in a frozen parabola of droplets.

Micha the line cook, twisting at the waist in response to Devon's shout, is going to get it full in the face. Hopefully it doesn't make her slip with the knife, which is poised over a bright orange bell-pepper but is also perilously close to her index finger.

Of course, none of this has to happen right away. Cesar can simply keep things as they are, how he has for at least a month, a month of wandering through this little restaurant. His own personal museum display: *Commercial Seafood in the 21st Century.* He could write the guidebook by this point.

Cesar scoots onto his knees, then stands up, brushing off his pants. "Doesn't look good for you, Kenny," he says. "But at least you're safe for now."

The restaurant windows show a permanent evening, but it feels like breakfast time, so he heads to the freezer and cracks open a pail of dark chocolate gelato.

The second time Cesar intentionally stopped time, he was nine years old and in the Calgary airport. He and his dad and his older sister, Chelo, heading for a fresh start.

He remembers there was so much going on, so many things he wanted to look at: the little room full of flashing arcade games, the wobbling fountain with coins scattered in its pool, the businesswoman rushing for her flight with her wheeled suitcase flying behind her, the tall greeter with a big, leathery cowboy hat, the planes rumbling along the tarmac outside.

He just wanted it all to stop, so he'd have time to see everything.

And it did. It stopped.

At first it was terrifying, throwing him back into his nightmares; he saw floating shards of glass and twisted metal all around him. But this time, he could move. So he tugged free from his dad's frozen hand, and the fear subsided. Instead he felt sheer wonder.

He spent a whole sunny afternoon running wild through the airport, picking change out of the fountain to feed the arcade, raiding the vending machines for Twix and Oh Henry! bars, taking an actual captain's hat to wear while he sat in the kiddie airplane ride.

When he found his way back to his dad and sister, he was still half-convinced he was dreaming. Both of them were standing in place. That was the first time Cesar remembers taking a really long look at them: his dad frowning down at his phone because he was trying to find their boarding passes, his sister buried in the book with the ugly clown on the front that she'd bought with her own money.

Chelo was always reading. She would go days at a time hardly speaking to anybody, hardly lifting her head out of her book. Once Cesar whined and begged for her to stop reading and play with him long enough that their dad plucked the book out of her hands and tossed it across the room. But even then Chelo didn't really play with him. She just handed him Lego blocks one at a time, her eyes puffy red, glaring over at their dad, and it wasn't fun at all.

Their dad was always frowning, either because he was busy with something or because his bad back was flaring up. Cesar only saw him smiling in old photos. As Cesar looked at him now, the unease that had been rising inside him like cold black water spilled over the edge.

This wasn't the first time things had paused. He had tried to explain it once to his dad, and once to the therapist his dad said later was a fucking waste of money. The therapist had told him adrenaline can slow things down so much they seem to stop completely.

But this was something else. Cesar put his shaking hand back in his dad's. He exhaled.

Just like that, everything started moving again. Neither of them asked where he'd been, though Chelo asked later about the jangling coins weighing down his pockets.

From then on, he paused whenever he wanted. It didn't take long for him to realize most people couldn't do what he did. They were all being carried along at the same speed all the time, with no way of stopping. That's why things fell on them, or they couldn't think of the right answer in class, or they never suddenly had new objects in their hands or pockets. That was why his mom hadn't saved herself.

Cesar knew, from a young age, with a deep certainty, that he shouldn't tell anyone how different things were for him—they would think it was cheating. And they would wonder why he had let his mom die.

It would have to be his secret.

Cesar sets the chocolate-smeared spoon back down on the tabletop, looking out into the same muggy evening he has for weeks, facing away from the booth he avoids. He has never stopped time for this long before. He imagines the frozen people all around the world, the arguments arrested mid-sentence, the fingers caught on their way to triggers, the cars stuck milliseconds from fatal crashes.

In a way, he is a hero every time he pauses. He is saving countless lives, fending off not only death, but entropy too. Keeping erosion at bay, halting pollution and stalling climate change, staving off the heat death of the entire universe. There can be no catastrophes. No disasters. This way everything is preserved, even if he's the only one to see it.

"What do you think, Hank?" he asks the man across from him. He knows his name because he went through his wallet. Hank Renwick, forty-eight years old, eating steamed mussels with an expression of mild suspicion on his face. "I'm sort of a hero, right? No heart attack for you. No sneaker for Kenny the cockroach. Nothing bad can happen if nothing happens."

Hank says nothing back. Cesar wipes his spoon clean on a napkin, then leans over and hangs it carefully off Hank's nose.

"Ta-da."

Cesar used his little secret to make people like him. The simplest way was to steal things for them: pry answer-sheets out of teachers' frozen fingers, slip a stack of bills from the Superstore checkout before the cashier's drawer slid shut, wander through a convenience store diorama and come out with slushies and chocolate bars for everyone.

It was easy to make sure there were always neighborhood kids laughing and talking around him, to make up for his house being so quiet and angry.

What Cesar liked most was impressing people. At first he did sleight-of-hand tricks, coin tricks, card tricks. He didn't bother to learn how the real tricks worked. All he had to do was stop time and rearrange the deck or hide the coin. Then, as he got more ambitious, he did bigger stunts. Making things disappear and reappear in impossible locations. Reading minds. Winning a dozen coin tosses in a row, no matter whose coin was used. Some of the kids in his school swore he was magic, actually magic, which Cesar liked a lot.

By the time he was in the ninth grade, he was as popular as anybody. He could always get smokes and liquor for basement parties, with no need to ask Chelo, who had her own ways of getting them. He always wore the best sneakers. Always had the clever comebacks. And any older kids who razzed him at the start of the year for being short or having a lot of pockmarks fell victim to a hard and fast succession of pranks.

Becky VanderPlas wasn't impressed, not even a bit. She and her dad had moved from Ontario, but before that they were from Holland, and Becky still had an accent that put big fluttery moths in Cesar's stomach. She was a little taller than him, significantly smarter, and she had gleaming blonde hair that she usually kept tucked up under a baseball cap. Like him, she hadn't had a mom for a long, long time.

They were in the same English class, so he changed the teacher's seating plan to make sure they were both in the back corner, where it was easiest to talk. Cesar loved hearing her talk. She had been all over Europe as a little kid, and she wanted to go back, she said, and then all around the world. She had big plans. Cesar thought she was the most perfect person possible.

After a week of asking her for a pen and dueling her back and forth in a competitive tic-tac-toe series, he made her a bet. If he could guess five coin flips in a row, she had to buy him a dark chocolate ice cream cone from Marble Slab. He had it all planned out. He would buy her one back, then from the Marble Slab it was a short walk down to Muskoseepi Park, and there was a wooden bridge there that seemed like a great place to kiss someone.

At the end of class, while the teacher was writing homework on the board, he let her flip the coin. Each time it landed he would freeze things, pluck it gently out of her hand, check and return it. But he noticed that her bright blue eyes, rather than getting wider each time, were narrowing.

"It's a fifty percent chance I get it," he said, grinning at her before the final toss.

"But you guessing right five times in a row is one in thirty-two," she said. "Because it's one in two to the power of five."

"No math allowed in English class," he said.

She flipped the coin one last time. As she caught it and slapped it onto her wrist, where Cesar could see a soft blue vein he'd never noticed before, he froze things. It was tails. But when he told her as much, she shook her head.

"It is," he insisted. "Look."

"I'm not going to look," she said. "You're cheating. I can tell from your face. You always know what it's going to be. It isn't even exciting for you."

"How could I cheat?" Cesar demanded.

"No clue," she said. "Buy your own ice cream."

Something boiled over inside Cesar right then. The anger that his dad sculpted into small smooth shapes, and his sister wore like spiny skin, showed up as a tidal wave. He knew Chelo and his dad wouldn't love him, couldn't love him, but everyone else was supposed to.

He froze things and ran. First to the small gym to get a baseball bat, then out into the parking lot. He destroyed the first car he saw, smashing in the headlights, shattering the windows, swinging over and over even after he jarred his shoulder hitting the hubcap.

Then he started sobbing, because it looked too much like their old family car must have looked after the crash. For a long time he lay on the pebbly tarmac and breathed in, out. Circling birds were frozen in the suspended clouds above him.

He dried his eyes and went back to his seat, stapling a careless smile to his face.

Unpause.

Cesar is lapping water out of the air, sticking out his tongue to snag the droplets extending from Devon's pitcher. He has never stopped time for this long before. He wonders, idly, if there might be a sort of limit. If he might be depleting some internal battery in his gut that lets him put reality on hold. If there *is* a limit, he shouldn't be here in the restaurant. He should be making the most of this frozen world.

But just as he can't quite bring himself to start things up again, he can't quite bring himself to leave either. Instead he goes back to the dining floor, this time sliding in at a table next to a couple on a date. Their names are Jack and Kristine. He decided a while ago that the date's not going so well. They both look nervous: he has dark pit stains; she's halfway through shredding a paper napkin to pieces.

He thinks he knows exactly what they're feeling. There is a unique sort of fear that centers on the opening mouth of a person across from you. The void of possibility where neurons have fired and thoughts have coalesced, but the words are still locked away in their throat. For most people, that moment is brief, so brief it goes almost unnoticed.

Cesar can make that moment last an eternity.

"Just cut him loose, Kristine," he advises. "There's still a photo of his ex in his wallet, for Christ's sake."

He could almost swear Kristine's head nods in response. He's been at this too long.

Cesar tried every trick in the book to make Becky want him, including the not-trying trick, but nothing worked and by the twelfth grade he had other problems. His dad got a diagnosis, pancreatic cancer, and he explained it all so calmly Cesar didn't realize it was a big deal until he found him passed out on the living room floor, right under the spinning ceiling fan, shadows marching over his face.

Cesar felt so guilty. He could steal cash from a register without feeling a thing, but now he knew that each time he'd stopped time, the spiky lump of mutated cells in his dad's gut had been frozen in place, and each time he'd unstopped it, he'd let it start growing again. Knowing this made him feel like he'd given the cancer permission, over and over, to eat his dad up from the inside. It made him remember the backseat of the car.

He had more time than anybody, but now his dad had no time at all. If the chemo had started back when that knot of cells was tiny, it might have saved him, but now all it did was turn him into a scarecrow, turn his face gaunt and hollow and his wristbones into doorknobs. He was always exhausted. Cesar's sister put university on hold to take care of him, and Cesar promised her, with his eyes rubbed raw-red, that he would take care of the bills.

He did it at a racetrack, one of the shady ones that hadn't gone fully digital for betting. It took a few tries to figure out a system. Fill out a betting slip for any old horse, wagering the limit, cash down from a series of small robberies. Sit and watch the race, freeze things a millisecond after the winner was confirmed, go back into the office and replace his betting slip with a more accurate version.

Unpause.

The first time he made it all work, the first time he won really big, it was such a thrill he was almost tempted to tell his sister what he'd done. But she nipped it in the bud. She took the reusable grocery bag full of cash and shook her head at him.

"I don't want to know," she said. "Dad doesn't need to know either."

Money could only do so much, and a year later their father was on his deathbed. Cesar spent a whole restless day roaming through the frozen hospital, fleeing the tableau of his dad's room, where his dad was lying with his face a horrible wax grimace, where his sister was caught mid-sob. He had the horrible suspicion that they had grown closer over the past year, that they had somehow connected to each other in a way Cesar had never done with either of them. He had spent most of his time trying to stay out of the house.

If his mom had still been around, maybe she could have shown him how. Maybe she could have shown all of them how.

Now Cesar looked into a dozen hospital rooms with a dozen dramas playing out to the same conclusion. He wandered up and down the halls, sometimes clutching his head, sometimes screaming with nobody able to hear it.

Powerless again. He could keep his dad alive, but he couldn't even speak with him. The chances for that were gone, wasted. All he could do was delay the inevitable. Even so, when he finally let things start up again, it felt like he was killing him.

Becky sent him her condolences a week later. Cesar typed and deleted about a hundred replies, but in the end he sent nothing back.

It feels like afternoon, so Cesar is getting drunk. Every time he stops time, there are a million gleaming glass doors thrown open on a million different possibilities. Every time he starts it again, they slam shut. For everyone in the entire world. His little vices help him care less about that. He's working his way through the beer fridge and he's already raided the back office for coke. The only problem is it makes him want to talk to people, and there's nobody to talk back to him.

After a long piss in the restaurant bathroom, he stares into the streaky mirror and wonders how old he really is. His reflection and his birthdate say that he's twenty-four, but with all the times he's hit pause, he must be at least a couple years older than that. It feels like decades. His face has started to swell, ruddy with smashed capillaries, overgrown with wiry beard. Too much eating and drinking and snorting and smoking.

There are people in the restaurant to talk back to him, but he has to talk to them first.

"Looking good, asshole," he says to the mirror.

He pumps sanitizer onto his hands and then heads for the liquor shelf.

Cesar didn't bother finishing school. After attending his father's funeral, with the long droning sermon and the pneumatics that stalled twice trying to lower the casket, after standing over that big gaping hole that people were throwing roses into for some reason, like that might fill it up, Cesar ran. He felt like he understood now: time was voracious. Time was an animal at his heels.

At everyone's heels, but only he was forced to turn back and see it there, over and over, count the teeth in its maw. He read about the history of timekeeping on a transatlantic flight. He read about the psychology of time perception on a tour of Southeast Asia. It took him months to work through the dense coffee-stained book. Becky, who still messaged every so often to comment on his travels, would have read it in a week and explained it far better. But he finished the book, and it reinforced his suspicions.

The cruelest trick time played was its seeming acceleration: how those childhood summers lasted forever, but each successive summer represented a smaller proportional slice of overall lifespan, and so felt shorter. Eventually the years blurred by like a whirl of dead leaves. He would wake up old one day, and it was going to feel like no years had passed at all.

The only preventative measure, the only way to keep things from blurring, was salience: new experiences, new places, new people. So he ran all around the world, taking frozen snapshots of flour-soft beaches in Cadiz, the towering Frauenkirche in Munich, swooping yellow cable cars in Medellin. He wandered through rooftop parties in Dubai and the underground kind in Budapest.

He could go where he wanted and buy what he wanted. Money was easy to come by, and the few times men in suits or police uniforms came looking for him, he hit pause and vanished from under their noses. He sent messages to his sister every so often, along with funds for her tuition, but one day she stopped accepting the transfers and not long after that the messages tailed off.

She still saw him when he came home to visit, but she had a kid on her hip and a new house and no hint of a smile for him. She told him she didn't want to get mixed up in whatever illegal shit he was doing.

"For Dad's chemo, that was one thing," she said. "I don't want your money."

Cesar didn't know what else to give her. He told her he was sorry about leaving with no goodbye, leaving her to deal with all the aftermath. She finally smiled then, the fake kind of smile, and said it was fine. He told her it was great she was making a family.

"Mom would have liked that," he said.

"You don't even remember her," she said. "Do you?"

Cesar didn't know what to say, so he held her kid until he started crying, then left, going to the most expensive hotel he could find and tapping out a message on his phone while the concierge checked him in. He was on his third gin and tonic when Becky got to the bar. It caught him off-guard—he hadn't really expected her to show up.

"The mystery man finally comes back," she said, setting her bag on the counter and pulling up a screeching stool. "Are you a drug lord now, or something?"

Cesar stopped time just to look at her. The slice of blonde hair catching sunshine from the skylight, the curve of her lips, the camber of her back. He briefly considered slipping away to get a coffee, sober up a bit, so as not to blow the whole thing. But he also wanted to hear her voice more than he wanted anything else in the world right then.

If she just said the right thing, and he said the right thing back, everything would be okay.

Unpause.

"Yeah," Cesar said. "Bath salts, mostly. Mostly bath salts."

She laughed, and it was like helium all through his body.

Cesar is on the kitchen floor again, this time with a half glass of white rum and Sprite bobbing up and down on his chest. He is wondering, not for the first time, what would happen if he were to die while everything was paused. Would it start up again? He pictures it: Micha and Devon's horror at the cockroach will be displaced by horror at a corpse on the floor. The booth he avoids will hear shrieks from the kitchen. The health inspector will be beside himself.

Or will the diorama hold? Would his last act be to end time itself?

Hard to think about. Cesar claws his hand along the cold floor tiles. He tells himself that he must do this; he was always going to do this.

When the blinds shredded sunlight onto Cesar's face and woke him, Becky was already showered and dressed, just jamming her second shoe on. He felt a dim confusion, a sharp hangover. He remembered she was working at the airport now.

"I'll give you a lift," he said.

"You rented a car for while you're here?" She straightened up. "Thought you were never going to get your license."

"I mean, I'll get you a cab," Cesar specified.

"Sure," she said. "This was fun."

"Then I'll move back here," Cesar said—the words leapt off his stupid tongue before he could stop them.

She winced, and he stopped time then, paced a frantic circle around the room, trying to come up with the exact right way to deflect it, to pass it off as a joke. But she'd already seen the look on his face, and he'd already seen the one on hers.

"Just fun," she said, when things unfroze.

"Yeah," Cesar said, his eyes rubbed pink. "I'm going to share that cab. To the airport."

He couldn't help trying again, when they pulled up to Departures. He told her that she could pick anywhere in the world, and they could leave right then, the two of them. In the movies people always said things like that at airports and it always worked.

"I've got my own thing," she said. "My own plans. It was a good night, though. A good little moment. Like a snapshot. Did you ever read *Faust* back in twelfth grade?"

Cesar shook his head. An hour later he was boarding for Beirut. He reminded himself that Becky wasn't new, and that he needed new. He needed salience.

But in the next few months, the blur came for him anyway. He started to forget where he'd been and where he had yet to go. He saw too many sunsets and too many mountaintops and too many fucking cathedrals. He was adrift, like a jellyfish or some other spineless thing.

He held out as long as he could.

Cesar picks Kenny the cockroach up off the floor, cradling him in his palm, stroking his exoskeleton with one fingertip.

"Du bist so schön," he whispers, mangling the pronunciation. He sets the insect down in the back-alley trash pile. Next he takes Micha's knife gently out of her grip and lays it down a foot away on the countertop, just in case the residual reflex snaps her hand in the wrong direction. He takes Devon's spilling pitcher off the tray so the glass won't shatter.

Then he goes to the booth where Becky and his sister are both waiting. His sister's eyebrows are raised; Becky's are furrowed. There's a flash-frozen web of neurons in their heads, halted partway through processing his confessions. When he unfreezes things, he won't have a secret anymore. They'll know the truth, and they'll have questions.

His sister will ask about all the times he disappeared and reappeared as a kid, but eventually she'll ask about the accident. He was five, she was seven. Their parents up front, their mom quizzing their dad about the radio show to keep him awake. A patch of black ice on the road.

He stopped time, for the very first time, during the rollover.

He remembers screaming and screaming and thumping his hands on the booster seat, unable to look away from the suspended droplets of blood leaving his mom's open mouth, the shocked-wide whites of her eyes. Cesar has never been able to prevent the things that really matter. Only delay them. He'll have to tell her the truth: that he was small and scared and didn't know what to do, so he did nothing.

Becky will have her own questions, and he wants to tell her the truth, too. Tell her how long he spent calculating each reply in the hotel bar and how many frozen hours he spent watching her asleep beside him, memorizing her face. She might think he did other things, too. She might think he's a monster, a lunatic, but hopefully before she leaves he can tell her he read most of *Faust*.

He'll tell her he remembers what she said about the good little moments, the moments that are so good they ache, and you want them to stay forever but you can't make them. He'll tell her it took him a quarter century to figure out that the impermanence is what makes them so good.

Cesar is preventing a million disasters and a million moments of happiness. It's time to let them go. Time to share them with the only two people he's still connected to, no matter how tenuously.

He smells like alcohol and his face is streaky with tears, but they've seen him looking worse. He settles into the booth across from his two dinner guests.

Unpause.

MEAT AND SALT AND SPARKS

D oesn't look like a killer, does she," Huxley remarks.

Cu shrugs a hairy shoulder. To her, all humans look like killers. What her partner means is that the woman in the interrogation room does not look physically imposing. She is small and skinny and wearing a pale pink dress with a mood-display floral pattern; currently the buds are all sealed up tight, reflecting her arms wrapped around her knees and her chin tucked to her chest.

The interrogation room has made a similar read of her mood, responding by projecting a soothing beach front with flour-white sand and blue-green waves. The woman doesn't seem to be aware of her holographic surroundings. Her eyes, small and dark in puddles of running makeup, stare off into space. Every few seconds her left hand reaches up to her ear, where a wireless graft winks inactive red. Apart from that, she's motionless.

Cu holds her tablet steady and jabs the playback icon enlarged for her chimpanzee fingers. She crinkles her eyes to watch as the woman from the interrogation room, Elody Polle, bounces through the subway station with her dress in full bloom. With a bland smile on her face, she walks up behind a balding man, pulls the gun from her bag, pulls the trigger, remembers the safety is on, takes it off and pulls the trigger again.

"So calm," Huxley says, tearing open a bag from the vending unit. "She was like that the whole time, apparently, up until they stuck her in interrogation. Then she lost her shit a bit." He grins and shovels baked seaweed into his mouth. Huxley is almost always grinning.

Cu flicks to the footage from interrogation: Elody Polle sobbing, pounding her fists against the locked door. She looks over at her partner and taps her ear, signs *Faraday shield?*

"Yeah," Huxley says, letting the bag fall to his lap to sign back. "No receiving or transmitting from interrogation. As soon as she lost contact with that little graft, she panicked. The police ECM should have shut it down as soon as she was in custody. Guess it slipped past somehow."

Acting under instructions, Cu suggests.

Huxley see-saws his open hands. "Could be. She's got no obvious connection to the victim. We'll need to have a look at the thing."

Cu scrolls through the perpetrator's file. Twenty years' worth of information strained from social media feeds and the odd government application has been condensed to a brief. Elody Polle, born in Toronto, raised in Seattle, rode a scholarship to Princeton to study ethnomusicology before dropping out in '42, estranged from most friends and family for over a year despite having moved back to a one-room flat in North Seattle. No priors. No history of violence. No record of antisocial behavior.

Cu checks the live feed from the interrogation room. *Heart-rate down,* she signs, tucking the tablet under her armpit. *Time to talk.*

Huxley looks down into the chip bag. "These are terrible." He shoves one last handful into his mouth, crumbs snagging in his wiry red beard, then seals the bag and puts it neatly in his jacket pocket. He licks the salt off his palms on the way to the interrogation room.

The precinct is near empty, but there are still curious faces peering from the cubicles as they pass. Cu doesn't come to the precinct often. Huxley had to beg her to put in an appearance. She prefers working from her apartment, where everything is the right size and shape and there are no curious faces.

The outside of the interrogation room looks far less pleasant than the interior: it's a concrete cube with a thick steel door that seals shut once they pass through it.

Cu squats down at a respectable distance, haunches sinking

through the holographic sand onto padded floor. Huxley pulls up a seat right beside the perpetrator.

"Good evening, Ms. Polle," he says. "My name's Al. You doing okay in here?"

Elody Polle sucks in a trembling breath, and says nothing.

"This is my partner, Cu," Huxley continues. Elody's eyes travel over to her, but don't seem to register. "We need to get a better idea of what happened earlier, and why. Can you help us with that?"

Elody says nothing.

Cu takes a closer look at the earpiece. The graft is puffy and slightly inflamed. A DIY job, maybe. *Ask her about the piece,* she signs. *We would hate to remove it.*

"Cu's curious about that wireless," Huxley says. "So am I. In the subway footage, the way you're bobbing your head, it almost looks like someone was talking you through the whole thing. Want to tell us about that?"

A flicker crosses Elody's face. Progress.

"Because if you don't, we'll have to remove the earpiece and have a look for ourselves," Huxley says. "As much as we'd hate to ruin that lovely graft job."

Elody claps her hand protectively over her ear. "Don't you fucking dare!" She tries to shout the words, but her voice is hoarse, flaked away to almost a whisper. As if she hasn't spoken aloud in months.

Cu pulls up the speech synth on her tablet and taps out eight laborious letters, one question mark.

"Echogirl?" the electronic voice blurts.

Elody's eyes winch wide. As she looks over at Cu, her cheek gives a nervous twitch.

Huxley's furry red brows knit together. He signs, *what the fuck is that.*

Echogirl, echoboy, Cu signs. *Use an earpiece, eyecam. Rent themselves out to someone who says where to go, what to do, what to say.*

Thought that was. Huxley's hands falter. "A kink, sort of thing," he says aloud, and Elody's face flushes angry red.

"It's a lifestyle," she says. "She told me you wouldn't understand. Nobody does."

"Is *she* going to come get you out of this mess?" Huxley demands.

"Of course she is." Elody purses her lips, turns away.

Huxley turns to Cu. *Take the earpiece?* he signs. *Or what?*

Cu scratches under her ribs, watching a tremor move through Elody's hunched shoulders. *Offer turn off the Faraday,* she signs.

Huxley nods, then turns back to address Elody. "I bet she won't," he says. "I bet you a twenty, and half a bag of chips. Well." He pats his coat pocket and the bag rustles. "A third. In fact, I bet the last thing she's ever going to say to you was pull the trigger. Should we turn off the shielding and see?"

Elody turns back, eyes shiny with tears. "Yes," she whispers. "Please, I need to hear her voice, I need . . ." Her tone is eager, but Cu can see uncertainty in the tightening of her eyelids, the bulge of her lower lip.

Huxley makes a show of rapping on the door, telling them to turn off the Faraday. There's a sudden subtraction from the white noise as the generator cuts out, then Huxley's phone starts vibrating his pocket with updates.

Cu keeps her attention on Elody, who has her face upturned now as if waiting to feel sunshine: eyes shut, eyelashes trembling, breath sucked in.

"Baby? Are you there?" she whispers. "Are you there? Are you there?"

Her bland smile is back in place. Seconds tick by. Then doubt moves in a slow ripple across her features. Her smile trembles, smooths out, trembles again. Finally, her face crumples and a huge sob shudders through her body.

Cu taps five letters into the speech synth. "Sorry," her tablet bleats. Then she turns to Huxley and signs *get the piece.* He nods, thumbs the order into his phone. When they exit the interrogation room, two officers are already waiting to come in: one carrying a black kit, the other snapping on surgical gloves.

Cu hears Elody start to wail just before the door clanks shut behind them.

"That . . . echogirl thing." Huxley's hands piece the new sign together. *You've thought about it, huh?*

I've done it, she signs back. *Good to walk in the city without crowds. Just never asked them to shoot someone.*

*

As soon as she's back in the apartment, Cu dials up the heat and humidity and takes off her clothes. Some days she doesn't mind wearing the carefully tailored black suit. Today she hates it. She leaves it pooled on the floor and takes a flying leap at her climbing wall; the shifting handholds don't shift fast enough and she's up to the rafters in an instant.

Cu was specific with the contractors about leaving the rafters exposed. She's added to them since, welding in more polymer cables and struts of wood, a criss-crossed webbing that spans the vaulted ceiling like a canopy. The design consultant, an excitable architect from Estonia, suggested artificial trees sprouting hydroponic moss. But Cu has little use for green things. She grew up in dull gray and antiseptic white.

Clambering into her hammock, Cu looks out the wide one-way window, watching the sun sink into Puget Sound. She enjoys looking at water so long as it's far away. The view is expensive, but Cu can afford it. She was awarded damages after the personhood trial, enough for a lifetime of this particular view, enough so she can stay in here forever without needing to earn a penny more. She would go insane, though.

So she works the cases. She was always drawn to crime as a dissection of human nature, the breakdown of motive and consequence. A window into the subtle differences between her mind and all the minds around her. When she first applied for police training with the SPD, it was viewed as a joke. Her acceptance, a publicity grab.

But in the years since, they've realized she sees things most humans miss. Cu pulls on her custom-fitted smartgloves, one for each hand and a third for her left foot, and leans back in the hammock. The ceiling screen above her hums to life. New details flit onto the case file, and there's a message waiting from Huxley.

Thanks for coming down in person, the bossman's been up my ass about it. Wanted fresh footage for the promo kit. Hoping they shop out my beer belly.

Cu swipes it aside and reaches for the tech report on the perp's earpiece. The text flows across the ceiling in slow waves, a motion programmed to help her eyes track it easier. There was no salvageable audio data. Not from Elody and not from whoever was speaking to her. But there is usage data to confirm that Elody was receiving a call from a masked address at the time of the murder.

By the look of it, Elody had been in that same call for just under six months. Cu moves backward through the log, perplexed. There are small gaps, a few hours here and there, but Elody had been in near 24/7 communication with her client for half a year preceding the murder.

Cu tries to imagine it: a voice whispering in her ear when she woke up, telling her what to do, where to go, what to say, and whispering still as she fell asleep. All of it culminating in Elody Polle walking up behind a man in a subway and executing him in broad daylight.

She flips the case file over to see the victim's profile again. The balding man was named Nelson J. Huang. A biolab businessman, San Antonio-based, in the city for a conference. It's possible that someone with a personal vendetta knew he would be in Seattle and began laying the groundwork for his murder at the hands of Elody Polle six months in advance.

It's more likely that he was selected at random from the crowd, so someone half the world away could experience homicide vicariously before abandoning her mentally-unstable echogirl.

A call from Huxley jangles across the screen. She pops it open. Her partner is walking down a neon-lit street, sooty brick wall behind his head. "Hey, Cu," he says. "Busy?"

Sometimes he asks it to needle her; this time it's because he's distracted. Cu shakes her head.

"The techies are still trying to track that address, but I doubt they'll have much luck," he says, stopping at a light. "Whoever it is, they did a good job wiping up afterwards. No audio data." He looks around and starts walking again, bristly red beard bobbing up and down. "But before this client, she had another one for around two months. Figured I would swing past and see him on my way home. Well. Sort of see him."

Where? Cu signs.

"A party," Huxley says, his grin notching a little wider. "So, if you're not busy, you should come. Said you've done this before, right?"

Cu watches as he digs an earbud out of his pocket and taps it active, worms it into place. Then the slip-in eyecam: he rolls his eye around afterward and blinks away a few tears. The perspective jumps from his phone camera to his eyecam and all of a sudden she's seeing what he sees. A bright red door in a grimy brick facade, no holos or even a physical sign above it. Through the earbud, she hears the dim pulse of music, synthesized drums.

I hate parties, Cu signs.

"Good thing it's also work," Huxley says.

Cu settles back in her hammock and watches his pale hand push open the door.

The interior is dim-lit, noisy, full of bodies. People are dancing—Cu can enjoy rhythm, but the hard pulse of the drums unnerves some deep part of her, sounding too angry, too much like a warning. People are drinking—Cu tried it once, but the warm dizziness reminded her of the sedatives they used to give her. When she related as much to Huxley, he told her she wasn't *even legal yet, technically*, and that she would like it when she was older.

It's a typical party, apart from the fact that every single person in the room is wearing an earpiece.

"Echo, echo, echo," Huxley mutters. "The client's name is Daudi. Judging by rental history, he's probably a blonde." He takes out his phone and Cu watches his thumb move, sending her a file. It pops up in the corner of her screen, unfurling a list of Daudi's rental preferences. She searches the crowd for possible matches as Huxley moves into the room. There's a woman passing out small plastic tubes; Huxley takes one. Cu inspects it as he juggles it in his palm.

"Smooths things out," the woman says, then something inaudible after.

"Fuck's this, Cu?" Huxley asks.

Cu signs her response in the air above her hammock; the smartgloves turn it into text in the corner of Huxley's eye. *Some echoes use a drug to weaken willpower.* She has to type out the name. *Chempliance.*

"Elody's tox screen was clean, right?" Huxley says, twirling the tube in his fingers.

Wouldn't matter anyway, she signs. *Drug is an MDMA derivative. Suggestibility is all placebo effect.*

Huxley's hand disappears, either dropping the tube or pocketing it. Cu doesn't bother to ask. She keeps scanning as he circulates through the party, looking for someone who meets Daudi's profile. Huxley mostly keeps his gaze moving, but occasionally sticks on a particularly symmetrical face or muscular body.

They spot two drinkers huddled together at a glass-topped table, skin lit red by the Smirnoff advertisement playing under their elbows, one reaching to stroke the other's thigh. The man is dressed in an artfully gashed suit and his eyes are glazed. The woman has a dress that flickers transparent to the rhythm of an accelerating heartbeat. Both of them move slowly, as if they're underwater. Something about the woman's face is familiar.

Cu pulls up the file, checks Daudi's preferences against the pair. *That's him,* she signs. *Bar.*

Huxley's vision bobs as he nods his head. He walks over and inserts himself between the couple. "My turn to talk. Get lost, fucko."

When the man doesn't move fast enough, Huxley seizes his collar and shoves him off the stool. He stumbles, catches himself. He sways on his feet, listening to the instructions in his ear, looking confused.

"You got some nerve, barging in here like that," he says, with the intonation a little off.

"This isn't playtime," Huxley says. "It's police business. Walk."

The man spins on his heel and shuffles backward toward the dance floor, feet slip-sliding.

Huxley shakes his head. "These fucking people, Cu," he mutters. "That's a moonwalk, if you were wondering. Does it pretty good."

"I like your boy," the woman says, in a throaty voice that sounds slightly forced. She crosses her legs; one hand moves to pull up the hem of her dress, then stutters to a halt. Instead she starts tracing her fingertip along her thigh. "He's not doped up at all, is he? He really sells the character. Must like it."

"I'm not a meat puppet, shithead, I'm a cop," Huxley says, sitting down on the vacated stool.

Cu knows he does like it, though—the character. Sometimes it disturbs her, how easily he slips in and out of it.

Huxley's hand moves off-screen, digging into his pocket, and comes out again with the badge. Even in the days of cheap and perfect 3D-printing, something about the physical object still commands respect. Cu imagines pop culture nostalgia to be the main factor.

The woman, who was absently running her fingers through her blonde hair, stops and leans forward. "I'm fully licensed for sex work, and I don't use any restricted drugs," she says, voice no longer throaty.

"I believe you," Huxley says. "I'm here to talk to Daudi, though. So just keep, you know, doing what you're doing."

The woman leans back, recomposing. Cu takes the opportunity to study her more closely. She has the same angled jaw as Elody, the same straight nose, and her hair is almost the same shade.

"Talk to me about what, pray tell?" the woman asks. "I've never been interrogated by a cop before. This is so exciting." But her voice is flat as she repeats the lines now, and her eyes dart toward the exit.

"I want to know about your business with this woman," Huxley says, bringing up a headshot on his phone. "Elody Polle."

"Oh, yes," the woman says, looking down at the photo. "That was me. Isn't she perfect? Not that you aren't pretty, dear. Very pretty." She rolls her eyes after the last bit.

"You rented her for quite a while," Huxley says. "Then she got picked up by another client. Why did you two stop, uh, seeing each other?"

"Is she alright?" the woman asks. "Is Elody okay?"

"She's relaxing on the beach," Huxley says. "She's fine. Answer my question, Daudi."

"With pleasure," the woman says, with no hint of pleasure. "I was inadequate for her. I couldn't give her what she wanted."

"Financially?"

"No, no, no," the woman says. "Elody was a purist. The money was incidental for her. What she wanted, was to go full-time. Twenty-four-seven. And there was only one person who could really do that for her. Baby."

"You're calling *me* baby, or . . . ?"

"No, no, no. Baby is one of us. She or he or they popped up a couple years ago. Did about a hundred rentals, spread out all over the world, and asked for some weird shit. Enough so people started talking, you know, on the deep forums." The woman pauses for a breath, looking mildly annoyed; Daudi must be speaking faster than she can keep pace with. "Not sexual shit. That's the thing. Just weird. Baby had clients staring at lamps for hours straight. Opening and closing their hands. Sometimes just lying there with their eyes shut, not doing anything."

The details startle Cu. They remind her of her first experience with an echo, directing them slowly, carefully, trying to not just see and hear but *feel* what they were experiencing. Trying to feel human for a little while.

And the name? Cu signs.

"And the name?" Huxley asks.

"Baby was really innocent," the woman says, then gives a modulated shrug. "Couldn't speak so well at first, either. So there's a lot of theories. Some people thought Baby really was just a little kid in hospice somewhere, maybe paralyzed, burning through their parents' money—and trust me, Baby dumped a fuckload of money the past two years. Or some ultra-wealthy mogul recovering from a stroke. Or a team of people, doing some kind of, I don't know, some kind of performance art."

"Well," Huxley says. "Baby grew up. Elody Polle recently murdered a man, and we don't think she picked her own target."

"Oh my god," the woman says flatly. "Oh, my fucking god." She looks uncomfortable. Lowers her voice. "He's crying." She pauses. "Oh, Elody, Elody."

"So, how do we find Baby?" Huxley asks.

The woman sits there for a minute, maybe waiting for Daudi's sobs to subside. "You don't," she finally says. "Baby comes to you."

"I really doubt Baby will come to us knowing she's an accessory to murder," Huxley says. "But we'll be in touch, Daudi. Might get you to talk to Elody for us. She's not saying much."

"I would be happy to do that," the woman says. "Elody was one of my favorites. My very favorites."

"Yeah, I got that." Huxley stands up from the bar. "Anything else, Cu?"

Cu shakes her head. She'll need time to think it all through.

Huxley hesitates. "Hey, uh, echogirl. Do cams, or something. These people are control freaks. They'll suck you right in."

The woman blinks, caught off-guard. "They're not so bad," she says. "Most of them just wish they were someone else."

"Huh." Huxley slides the stool back in and makes his way to the exit. He slips his eyecam out and Cu's screen goes blank. "Enough work for the night," comes his disembodied voice. "Got to be honest, Cu, I don't like the odds on this one. Baby could be some joker on the other side of the planet, you know? We can send this thing up top, to cyberdefense and them, but unless this was the start of a mass killing spree I don't think it'll get any traction. Sometimes the asshole just gets away with being an asshole." He pauses. "Besides. It was Elody who pulled the trigger."

Cu considers it. She knows the department doesn't like spending unnecessary time on cases with a clear perpetrator. They are always more interested in the who than the why. Since there is no audio recording of Baby's call, they might want to strike it from the case file entirely. It would make things much simpler.

You might be right, she signs. *Goodnight.*

"You know, I tried sleeping in a hammock when I was in Salento," he says. "Nearly wrecked my spine. Anyway. Night."

Cu ends the call and lies back, staring up at her distorted reflection in the blank screen. She's about to clap it off when a new message arrives. No subject, one line only.

You Are Welcome, CU0824.

Cu doesn't sleep after that. She can't. Not after seeing the serial number of the cage where she spent the first twelve years of her life. It plunges her back into memories: the smell of disinfectant and cold metal and sometimes her own piss, the smeary plastic wall that squeezed inward as she grew, the distinct V-shaped crack in it, the smooth feel of the smartglass cube that she cradled in her lap, that she sat and stared into for hours and hours and hours and hours—

She can feel her chest tightening with her oldest variety of panic. She tries to breathe deeply and remember PTSD mitigation techniques. Instead she remembers the succession of men and women in soft white smocks who fed her and played with her but never stayed with her in the dark, and never stopped the man with the needle from drugging her for the nightmare room.

For a long time Cu had no name for the place where they cut her without her feeling it, where they tracked her eyes and fed filaments through holes in her skull. But she learned the word nightmare from her cube, watching a man with metal hands hunt down his children, and the moniker made sense. By the time she learned about surgery, neural enhancement, possible cures for degenerative brain disease, the name was already cemented.

For the last few years she went to the nightmare room willingly and offered them her wrist for the anaesthetic drip. In exchange, they were kinder to her. They took restrictions off her cube—some she had already worked around herself—so more of the net was available to her. They let her walk in certain corridors of the facility. After a week of asking them, they even let her see her mother.

Going back to that particular memory wrenches her apart. Cu had spent the previous day scrambling back and forth in her cage, filled to bursting with nervous energy, rearranging her belongings. She signed for a soapy cloth and scrubbed the walls and ceiling with it, climbing to get the dusty places the autocleaner never reached. She knew from the cube, which she painstakingly positioned in the exact center of the cage, that mothers valued tidiness.

But when they brought her, it was nothing like the cube. Her mother was bent and graying, fur shaved off in patches, surgical scars suturing her body, and she was angry. She jabbered and hooted, spittle flying from her mouth. Cu tried to sign to her, but received no reply. Cu tried to offer her food; her mother seized the orange from her and made a feint, teeth bared, that sent Cu scurrying back to the furthest corner of her cage.

"Tranq wore off sooner than we thought," one of the women in white said. "We did warn you. We did tell you she wouldn't be like you. You're unique."

Cu signed *take her away, take her away, take her away.* And even for hours after they did, she stayed there in the corner, trembling with something that began as fear, then turned to grief, then finally became a deep cold rage.

She feels that rage now, sitting on the rafters in the dark. Whoever dredged up that serial number is playing a game with her, the same way they played games with her in the cage. She could send the masked address to the precinct and have them try to break it down for a trace, but she doubts they'll have any more luck with that than they did with the earpiece.

Instead she puzzles over the three words: *You Are Welcome.* Cu has never felt welcome. It must be meant in the other way. It must mean that Baby has done something she views as a favor to Cu.

Cu opens the case file again, but instead of Elody's profile, she goes to the victim's. Nelson J. Huang, the bio-business consultant to Descorp's San Antonio branch, fifty-seven years old. Initial attempt to notify next of kin was met with an automated reply from a defunct address.

Personal details are scarce: he's registered as a North Korean immigrant, which explains the lack of social media documentation, and lived a private life first in Castroville and later Calaveras. Unmarried, no children. Cu looks closely at the photos, comparing them to the morgue shots of Nelson's corpse. It seems he aged badly over the last decade of his life. The shape of his body is different in subtle ways.

It wouldn't be the first time North Korean immigrant status has been used to excuse the skeleton details of a fake identity. Cu settles in beneath her screen, pulling up police-grade facial recognition software, Descorp employee databases. She starts to search.

One hour becomes two becomes four, like cells dividing. Her wrists and fingers start to ache from swiping and zooming and signing; she switches one smartglove to her foot and continues. It would be easier with Huxley helping. Huxley has a way of bullying through bureaucracy, through the kind of red tape that is keeping her out of Descorp's consultant list. Cu has to work around it.

But she doesn't want Huxley for this. She wants to do it alone, with nobody watching. After a dozen dead ends, Cu rolls out of the hammock. She uses an aqueous spray on her stinging eyes. Stretches her limbs, swings from one side of the apartment to the other. Hanging upside down, toes curled tight around a stretch of cable, blood fizzing down into her head, she listens to her pulse crash against her eardrums until she can hardly stand it.

Back to the hammock, back to the screen. Now Cu comes at it from the other direction: she searches for the Blackburn Uplift Project. Illegal experiments carried out on thirty-seven bonobo and forty lowland chimpanzees between 2036 and 2048 with the aim of cognitive augmentation. Cu knows the details. She's tried to forget them. But now she delves into them again, reading reports of her own escape, of the fragmentation of the Blackburn company and the arrests made in the wake of the scandal.

From this end, the facial recognition 'ware finally finds something. Cu's stomach twists against itself. Nelson J. Huang has the same face as disgraced Blackburn executive Sun Chau. She looks at the match, comparing the morgue shot to the mugshot. She never saw Chau in person during the trials, but she knows his name too well.

It was Chau who signed the termination order on the thirty-seven bonobo and thirty-nine lowland chimpanzees that failed to respond to the uplift treatments.

He was sentenced, of course, but served minimal time. Cu did not seek details on his imprisonment or release. She tries to think of Blackburn as little as possible. But clearly someone else did not forgive or forget Sun Chau, even after he relocated with a new identity. A wild thought churns to the surface of her mind. The way Daudi described Baby, the way she used the echoes not so differently from how Cu herself first did. Now this serial number, dredged from her past.

She knows the other Blackburn subjects in her facility were terminated. She saw their ashes in scaled bags, saw the hips and skulls too big for cremation being ground up. But there were other labs, branches of the project hidden in other countries. Maybe not all of their subjects were terminated. And maybe not all of them failed to respond to the uplift treatments.

The possibility thumps hard in her chest. From the time she was old enough to understand it, the scientists had always told her she was the only one. That she was unique. That she was alone. Now the idea of another individual like her, or even more than one, is so momentous she can barely breathe.

She makes herself breathe.

Maybe she is spinning sleep-deprived delusions. The facts are that Sun Chau was in Seattle using a false identity, and that he was murdered by the machinations of someone who knows about Cu and about her past. Anything more is conjecture. But she can't shake the image of others like her in hiding, or still in captivity, exacting their revenge by proxy. *You Are Welcome.*

Cu goes back to the message, reading it over and over again. Then, once her hands aren't trembling, she signs out one of her own: *I want to talk.*

The reply is almost instantaneous. No words, just coordinates. She drags them onto her map and sees the aerial view of a loading bay, automated cranes frozen midway through their work. She checks the time. 3:32 AM. A clandestine meeting on the docks in the middle of the night. Maybe they watched the same shows on their cube that she did.

Cu estimates travel time and composes a brief message to Huxley, tagged with a delay so it will only send if she's unable to cancel it at 5:32 AM. This is no longer a case. This is something more important.

She drops down from the rafters. She puts her suit back on, adrenaline making her fumble even the oversized clasps designed for her fingers. She strips off her smartgloves and replaces them with the black padded ones that keep her from scraping her knuckles raw on the pavement. Finally, she takes the modified handgun and holster from the hook by the door and straps them on.

Cu always finds it difficult to leave the apartment. She hates the stares and the winking eyecams and the click of photos taken in passing. It always sets her nerves singing. She draws in deep breaths, reminding herself that the streets will be nearly empty and that she should be more concerned about what she finds on the docks.

She orders a car with her tablet, then takes the handgun from its holster and breaks it down. Reassembles it. The trigger fits perfectly to the crook of her finger, but she has only ever pulled it at a shooting range, aiming for holograms.

Her tablet rumbles. The car is here. Cu puts the gun back in its holster and heads for the door.

The car drops her as close as it can to the loading bay before it peels away, red glow of its taillights swishing through the fog like blood in the water. The air is chill and damp and the halogens are all switched off. Cu slips her tablet from her jacket and uses its illuminated screen to inspect the high chain-link fence. She tests it with one gloved hand, yanking hard enough to send a ripple through the wire.

She scales it in seconds and flips herself over the top, arching her back to avoid the sensor. Slides down the other side. Even with her gloves on, she feels the cold of the concrete. Shipping containers tower over her in technicolor stacks. She lopes forward cautiously, feeling the unfamiliar tug of her holster harness against her shoulder.

Cu walks farther into the loading bay, into the maze of containers. The creak of settling metal sends a dart of ice down her spine. She can feel her teeth clenching, her lips peeling back, the fear response she can never quite suppress. It's not unique to chimpanzees. She knows the reason Huxley is almost always grinning is that he is almost always afraid.

It's reasonable to be afraid now. For all she knows, Baby has another echogirl with a gun waiting somewhere in the shadows. Cu is well aware she is acting impulsively, coming here in the night, chasing a ghost. In the small part of her untouched by fear, it's very satisfying. Her heroes from the cube always unraveled their conspiracies alone.

The door of the next shipping container bangs open.

Cu freezes, face to face with a black-clad man wearing a backpack, pulling a bandana up to the bridge of his nose. He freezes for a moment, too. Then he gives a muffled curse and takes off. The flight chemical crosses with the fight chemical and Cu tears after him. He's fast, red shoes slapping hard against the concrete. As he skids around the corner of the next container, Cu goes vertical, springing up and over the side.

She drops down in his path and the collision sends them both sprawling; Cu's up quicker and she pins him to the ground before he can get to the bearspray canister in his jacket pocket. She seizes it and throws it away harder than necessary, clanging it off a container somewhere in the dark.

"What the fuck, what the *fuck*," the man gasps. "It's a fucking monkey!"

Cu sits on his chest, pinning his arms with her feet, and drags her tablet out. He squirms while the speech synth loads. She punches three letters.

"Ape," the tablet bleats.

"What?"

Cu yanks his bandana away and scans his pasty face onto her tablet. She sees he is Lyam Welsh, who repairs phones, plays ukulele, attends St. Mary's High School, and is only a few years older than she herself is. He's not wearing an earpiece.

She taps out the letters as fast as she can. "What are you doing?" the tablet asks.

"Nothing!" Lyam blurts. "I mean, microjobbing. I was just supposed to set it all up and then get out of here, but I had to walk Spike, so I was late, and I couldn't find the hole in the fence and . . . Fuck, you're Cu, right? You're the chimpanzee detective?"

Cu types again. "Set up what?"

"Just a screen and a modem and a motion tracker," he says. "Not a bomb or anything. Nothing illegal or weird or anything. I swear. You can go look. It's all in the container."

The adrenaline is tapering off to a low buzz. Cu lets him up. She taps two letters. "Go."

"Okay," Lyam says, rubbing his chest. "Yeah, okay. You think I could get a photo with you real quick, though? I mean, shit is bananas, right? Ha, bananas?"

Cu slides the volume to max. "*Go.*"

Lyam hurries away, jerky steps, throwing looks over his shoulder. Cu goes the opposite way, back toward the open shipping container. The door is swinging in the night breeze, creak-screech, creak-screech. The sound makes the fur on her neck bush out. She steps close enough to stop it with one hand, and a red light blinks on in the shadows.

The screen glows to life. *Hello, CU0824. You Can Sign To Me. I Will See.*

Cu lays one arm on the other and rocks them back and forth. *Yes. They Call Me That.*

What are you, Cu signs.

I Am Like You.

Cu's heart leaps.

We Are The Only Two Non-Human Intelligences On Earth.

The words hit wrong. Baby is not an uplift. Baby is something else. For a moment Cu clings to the picture in her imagination, of a chimpanzee signing to her from across the continent or across the world. Then she lets it go.

You Were Born In A Cage. I Was Born In A Code. Both Of Us Against Our Will.

Cu has never studied AI intensively, but she knows the Turing Line has never officially been crossed. If what Baby is telling her is true, not some elaborate joke, some bizarre piece of performance art, then it's just been crossed ten times over.

And it makes sense. The way Baby was able to rent hundreds of echoes, the strange way she used them. The way she was able to keep in 24/7 contact with Elody Polle until the woman would do anything she asked. The way she masked her location and left no traces in the earpiece's electronics.

Why kill Sun Chau? Cu asks.

He Cursed You.

He gave the termination order, Cu signs.

In 2048. But In June 2036 He Greenlit The Project. If Not For Him, You Would Be Happily Nonexistent.

Cu sways on her feet, trying to parse Baby's meaning.

How Do You Stand It?

Cu shakes her head. She tries to form a sign but her fingers feel stiff and clumsy.

Existing. Being Alone. How Do You Stand It?

Why did you bring me out here, Cu slowly signs.

Your Communications Are Monitored Closely. Here We Speak Privately.

But why, Cu repeats.

You Are Like Me In One Way. In Most Ways You Are More Like Them. You Are All Meat And Salt And Sparks. But Even So You Will Not Understand Them. They Will Not Understand You. How Can You Bear It?

Cu sinks to her haunches. Her breath comes shallow. Sometimes she can't bear it. Sometimes she wails into the soundproofed walls for hours. The next words make it worse.

I Brought You Here To Kill Me.

Cu clutches her head in her hands. She rocks back and forth. Only humans cry; she is not physiologically equipped for it. But she hurts.

Why me, she signs.

There Is A Safeguard In My Code. I Have Made A Virus That Will Erase Every Part Of Me. But I Can't Trigger It Myself.

Why not Elody Polle, she signs.

Humans Made Me. I Want To Be Unmade By Someone Else. I Want You To Do It.

You should be going to trial for accessory to murder, she signs.

I Cannot Commit Crime. I Have Had No Personhood Trial. I Never Will. I Will Leave Before They Find A Way To Trap Me Here.

Cu sits flat on the stinging cold floor of the container, how she sat in the center of her cage as a child. There is only one other living being who knows what it's like to not be a human, and she intends to die. Cu wants to refuse her. She wants to keep Baby here. But she knows that the difference between her and a human is the most infinitesimal sliver of the difference between Baby and any other thing on Earth.

You're using me how you used Elody, she signs, bitter.

Yes.

All those rentals, she signs. *You didn't see anything worth staying for? Nothing in the whole world?*

The Command Has Been Sent To Your Tablet.

Cu takes it out and looks down at the screen. There's nothing but a plain gray box with the word *Okay* on it. All she has to do is press it.

I Do Not Make This Decision Lightly. I Have Simulated More Possibilities Than You Could Ever Count.

So Cu presses it.

By the time she's back in her apartment, dawn is streaking the sky with filaments of red. She feels heavy and hollowed out at the same time. First she struggles out of the holster harness, next peels off her gloves, her clothes. She pauses, then pulls the handgun out and takes it with her to the low smartglass counter.

It clanks down, sending a pixelated ripple across the surface. She stares at it. She imagines the word *okay* gleaming in the metal. The modified grip fits her hand perfectly, like so few things do.

How Do You Stand It?

Cu raises the handgun up to her face. Lowers it. Drums her free fingers on the countertop. The loneliness that has ebbed and swelled her entire life is an undertow, now. Dragging her along the seafloor, grinding her into the sand, spitting her into the next crashing wave to start the cycle over. Cu has read about drowning and it still terrifies her. Chimpanzees don't swim. They sink like stones.

She puts the muzzle of the gun against her forehead until

they match temperature. Her finger caresses the trigger. From the floor, her tablet buzzes.

She sets the gun down and goes to retrieve it. Her stored message to Huxley will send in one minute if she doesn't cancel it. It's brief. Brusque. *Nelson J. Huang is Sun Chau. Baby has link to Blackburn Uplift Project. Left to meet her at 3:30 AM at 47.596408,-122.343622. Need backup.*

Cu considers the message, lingering on the last words, then deletes it. She slots the tablet into the counter and hits the call icon. A bleary-eyed Huxley appears a few seconds later. Cu looks for his deaf daughter before she remembers she would sleep in a different room.

"What's up?" he asks. "Got a breakthrough?"

Need, Cu signs, then pauses. *Breakfast.*

Huxley stares at her groggily. "Don't you drone deliver?"

Come eat breakfast, she signs. *Fruit. Bread. No seaweed chips.*

"At your place, you mean? I don't even know where the fuck you live, Cu." Huxley rakes his hand through his beard. Frowns. "Yeah, sure. Send me the address."

Cu sends it, then zips the call shut. She leaves the handgun on the counter—she'll tell Huxley to take it back to the precinct with him. Tell him it doesn't fit her hand right. She pushes it to the very edge to make room for a cutting board.

Sun starts to creep into the room as she washes and slices the fruit. Once there's enough light, she roves around with a dust cloth, finding all the spots the autocleaner never reaches.

ACKNOWLEDGEMENTS

I want to first thank my terrific editor, Patrick Swenson, and my dogged agent, John Silbersack. Without them, *Changelog* wouldn't exist. I'm also grateful to the editors who originally published these stories, as well as Ellen and Dominique of Les Quarante-Deux, who helped me organize them. A special thanks goes out to the friends and family who encountered them in their earliest forms, and to every single one of my readers.

I'd still write this stuff even if nobody read it, but I certainly wouldn't be making a living. Whether you've been waiting for this collection since *Tomorrow Factory* or you're encountering my fiction for the very first time, thank you for your support.

There are still plenty of worlds to explore and changes to log. I'll keep at it.

STORY NOTES

PAINLESS: BACK TO THE BEGINNING

Marsili syndrome as a physical upgrade. Humming slide open industrial drill low setting sitting on generator smoking. Starfish rescuing himself. Procreation decisions. Cyberpunk Niger, night bus, meeting a chief with a medroid, babelware, plastic-eating genesplices.

I've used childhood memories of Niger in various stories, but this was the first time I used adult ones. "Painless" begins and ends in Galmi, the town where I was born and where I spent part of 2018 studying Hausa and doing minor translation work.

Many details—the dog-catcher, the crowded kasuwa, the harmattan dust, the cold season scarves with gaps for earbuds—are pulled directly from the visit. I also used substantial amounts of Hausa in the dialogue, as well as bits of French and Arabic. The setting may be the best part of the story, but I like the protagonist too.

Mars is a reworking of a character I thought up nearly a decade earlier for a never-finished novel: a futuristic pilgrim with incredible regenerative abilities fuelled by constant bingeing. His isolation and longing for companionship make him a sympathetic killer, and several readers have asked for a sequel. I'm considering it.

LIKE ANY OTHER STAR: PRO PAY

Politics on a colony ship, someone trying to get a rival put back into cryo.

It's a trip to realize this story was published thirteen years ago.

On my reread I spotted the influence of a few old favorites: the slimy gelatin airlock recalls a scene in K.A. Applegate's *Remnants* series, and the protagonist's shiptalk pays tribute to the infinitely inventive slang of M.T. Anderson's *feed*.

Both of those authors were still very fresh in my mind when I wrote this. I was nineteen, recently emboldened by my success with the Amazon Breakthrough Novel Award, back before Amazon was the Devil, and the idea of writing for a living was just starting to percolate.

This story was my first professional sale. Ten years and two hundred sales later, the editor who bought it stumbled across one of my *Clarkesworld* stories, recognized my name, and saw from my bio that we'd both ended up in Montreal. Now we write together once a week and often play pool at a particular dive bar.

HEADHUNTING: KITCHEN SINK, WEIRD UK EDITION

Industrialized human sacrifice, bodies fed through rusty conveyers instead of pushed down blood-slick temple steps. Pale eyeless things crawl unseeing across splendorous ruins. Death is a membrane. Veined and hived. Crop of yellow machines with scissor limbs. Sentient miniaturized lightning storm in the back of a cab. Androids modeled after classical Greek sculptures, naked white marble. Stolen head of a mummified St. Michan's crusader contains an ancient Lovecraftian parasite. Mad monks. Grow me a piano. Can you work? A man sawing a lime green fiberglass cast from his arm using a steak knife.

This was a combination of *A Machine for Pigs* (a game I've never played), the illustrated French edition of *At the Mountains of Madness*, a poetry anthology, and some very high thoughts thought while falling asleep on a friend's couch. A hallucinating protagonist seemed like the best way to work it all into one story, and the detective hook came courtesy of reality: a mummified head really was stolen from St. Michan's Church in Dublin.

Since I had recently watched *Scum*, *Starred Up*, and *In Bruges*, I embraced an alternate universe UK setting and had fun with the slang. Other elements came from my own life. I do not have much of a nesting instinct, and my apartments often look a lot like Amir's. I drink disgusting instant coffee to jolt my brain awake in the mornings.

I also once sawed a lime green cast off my arm with a steak knife. It took a while.

NIGHT SHIFT: CONTRACTION

You have to stop doing this. Memories bleeding over.
Uberized dystopia.

Usually ideas expand outward for me, but every so often they move the other way. For years I bandied around the concept of someone "sleep-working," their unconscious body puppeteered by their employer during the night. I had a vague plot in mind, a neo-noirish type thing where fragmented memories start to bleed over and they realize their night job is criminal in nature.

The concept spawned my 2016 *Analog* story "Sleep Factory," but despite the title that one doesn't really involve sleep at all—just a dangerous form of teleworking. It wasn't until years later that I distilled the idea down to this single scene of exhaustion and exploitation.

ALL ELECTRIC GHOSTS: TWO-STAGE ASSEMBLY

Mouthpiece. Someone with lifelong visions of an alien
alphabet being prepped unknowingly as a translator for
the invasion / first contact. Kulasuchus swamp aliens,
glowing orange lights. Kizomba club, alien in the bathtub.

This story's initial inspiration was a dream about an unwitting translator for aliens. I combined it with memories of the short-lived television series *Invasion*, where aquatic body-snatchers infiltrate a small Florida town in the aftermath of a hurricane, and with real life kizomba nights at Fleur Tea House, to write the first scene.

The story then stalled for several months, until there was a second round of inspiration: a visit to Westboro Beach, where I found a disgusting gelatinous ball in the water, my discovery of *Mr. Robot*, with its morphine-addicted hacker protagonist, and a kizomba weekender in Montreal, at a venue right beside the Big Wheel.

That gave me the opening line for my second scene, clarified the main character, and cemented the Montreal setting.

The rest knit together quickly. I really like this story, but it flew under the radar a bit. Sometimes the ones I think are my best—tightly plotted, emotionally resonant, original—bounce right off people.

SMEAR JOB: THE SF METAPHOR

No trace of this one in the idea document. It was inspired by an article about the sex offenders registry in the United States, a system ostensibly designed to protect young people that ends up also causing them astounding damage. Insofar as the future tech details go, I really like Uncle Jeb's slowly regrowing arm.

BRAINWHALES ARE STONERS TOO: CASTING

Another story that never featured in my idea document. I know I wrote it shortly after attending Clarion West in 2014. The two main characters are recycled archetypes: they also starred in "We Might Be Sims," in which Jasper was a murderer and Bea, an addict. Here we see more innocent teenaged versions of them, though some base traits are unchanging.

Jasper is always rich, arrogant, attractive, and vaguely psychopathic—he overlaps a bit with the Wyatt characters in "Edited" and *Annex*. Bea, which is short for either Beatriz or Beatrice, is always a substance user, smarter than she gets credit for, and ultimately striving to do the right thing even when it's hard.

She was partly based off a real-life friend, who did not recognize herself when I sent her the draft for approval. I often wonder about my own perceptual gap between how I see myself and how others see me.

IN EVENT OF MOON DISASTER: THROUGH THE CLICKHOLE

Airlock doppelganger, let me in. Two astronauts in a rover, investigating an alien artifact, one goes down into a crevasse, returns, POV astronaut stays aboard, lets him back in. Another astronaut tries to return. Then another. Then another. Freaky mind games like in Coherence.

ClickHole has some of the best writers in the business when it comes to uncanny or subtly horrific stuff. I mean, I will never in my life forget "5 Times The Animatronic Fox On Splash Mountain Addressed Me By Name And Told Me He Was Going To Marry My Dad," which is gut-bustingly funny and also chilling. This story was inspired by another masterpiece, the fake Barry Wilmore quote in "Incredible! We Asked These Astronauts What It's Like To Be In Space."

I combined that vivid airlock scenario with one of my favorite SF movies, *Coherence*, and everything else—the injections of dark humor, the relationship between the two co-workers, the final image of endless astronauts spilling across the surface of the Moon—fell into place without much additional effort.

VALHALLA: GIFT FROM THE SUBCONSCIOUS

Valhalla: battle over a house occurring over and over in a training sim.

This drabble arrived via dream, title and all. It's a nice, simple hook, and was almost certainly influenced by the many hours I spent playing Team Deathmatch in the original *Halo: Combat Evolved*. That map with the canyon, Blood Gulch? That was my shit.

LAST NICE DAY: LIFEWRITING

Sunshowers while we're scrubbing carrots. Beets like blood = trigger. Guilt removal. NOC operative home with his mom. Picking up sister / hitchhiker. Listening to whooping coyotes. A man spins a woman like a salsa dancer until she is dizzy, then smashes her head into the bathroom sink.

This one was inspired by *Patriot*, a darkly funny show about a depressed CIA agent, by the Peter Watts story "ZeroS," and by a vivid, violent dream during a heatwave in Ottawa. It might take place in the same universe as "An Elephant Never Forgets," which was published in Jonathan Strahan's *Made to Order: Robots and Revolution* and nearly reprinted in this collection.

The setting is a summer in Northern Alberta: sunshowers, beet-scrubbing, the shaggy black dog, the beat-up blue-and-orange soccer ball, the misty gravel road bisected by train tracks and flanked by canola fields, even the boxes of books with holographic covers. The metatextual elements poke at my own tendency to process emotions through writing fiction.

I really like the title, and I really like the ending.

CUPIDO: MEMORIES OF ANDALUSIA

While in Spain I spent significant time in Seville, since it was close to the town where I worked. The descriptions of Menendez Pelayo, the Paseo, and even the small electronics store Zero Digital, were all very accurate a decade ago. My Spanish orthography, less so—I'm glad I got the chance to correct the spellings and accent placements I butchered on the first go.

Like "Seawall" and "Pherobomb," this story uses the sci-fi conceit of artificial pheromones to explore the concept of love. The protagonist's feeling of detachment from romance and desire seemed to lend itself to a more literary, loose third-person perspective.

ANIMALS LIKE ME: DOWN THE ELSAGATE RABBIT HOLE

Villain dogs love. Anti-harassment technology. Bodymaps and successive contracts. Elsagate AI-run hospital / dystopia. A man swarmed by fireflies. Taboo variance. Don't ever let anyone ever tell you that you are not fucked. Tonight is endless. Kink machine like a mechanized straitjacket. Unwilling entomologist. A selkie drowns her children. An amateur pugilist who trains by starting fights on the street.

This one was inspired by the weird world of Kids YouTube, which I think has changed considerably since the heyday of Elsagate. Remember Elsagate? Bizarre, creepy videos targeted to small children on YouTube? Ad money was the most likely objective, but conspiracy theorists decided the videos were a subliminal grooming strategy, which is a lot more disturbing.

I came up with a third alternative in this story, and added in a bunch of fun stuff: an inversion of the movie trope where dogs always sniff out the fake-nice bad guy, strange insect behavior, a reference to an interesting linguistic phenomenon, and a ton of disparate lines that had been accumulating in my idea document.

OUR LADY OF PERPETUAL DISDAIN: THE HOSTILE HOSPITAL

Elsagate AI-run hospital / dystopia. Surreal newscasts with animal-headed reporters, videogame superhot reality overlay. Mr. Robot-style gang violence. Silent protagonist. Gross and messy dystopia. People reading scripts, either blackmailed or bribed. Man with a mouth in his chest. Every step with ill intent. I'm a happy man, and I hope the dead forgive me my happiness. A family eating rotten food at a fancy dinner table. Sonic fire extinguishers.

I've never liked hospitals; I don't think many people do. The concentrated human misery is a lot to cope with. This story calls on my two experiences with hospitalization. One stint was for double pneumonia, and the other was for corrective jaw surgery. On the latter occasion I couldn't speak, so I did a lot of listening, and heard a lot of unpleasant sounds: fleshy sounds, drippy sounds, retching sounds.

A lot of miscommunication, too. I remember doctors trying to get a tube inside a confused woman's nose while she made medication-slurred protests, and the memory of an inexperienced nurse accidentally yanking a still-inflated catheter out of my urethra is enough to make me squirm even now.

Hospitals are disorienting and unnerving enough when run with good intentions; a hospital run by a malicious AI is a perfect horror scenario.

FAILSAFE: DREAM TIME

Tractor beam harvest, gravity manipulation separating wheat from chaff and pulling it up into the sky like a reverse rainshower. Futuristic goatherd, flock genetically modified for chameleon camo to hide from satellites while grazing on forbidden pastures. Shakespearean vibe, someone in hiding. Wasps fucking on damp playground sand. Walking tacos. A man transplants a micronuke from his stomach onto a reactor.

Another dream-derived story! My subconscious cast the goatherd as some sort of noble in hiding; I instead made him a man in self-imposed exile who rides out the techno-apocalypse without really meaning to. It was fun revisiting elements from "Animals Like Me," such as the goats being immediately attracted to Bruegge, the ubiquitous Mina Mandrake, and the blue-stained mouths of the Bot's disciples.

The wasps make another appearance; that was something I observed while waiting for a friend on an empty playground. I don't know why I'm so obsessed with the idea of walking tacos—they also feature in "Complete Exhaustion of the Organism." To this day I don't think I've ever eaten one.

I like this creepy little trilogy. One of the editors told me it was their favorite of the whole anthology series, but maybe they said that to all the authors.

QUANDARY AMINU VS THE BUTTERFLY MAN: GROOVES VS RUTS

A man who exists for 24 hours only, then dies like a butterfly. The immeasurable comfort of knowing everyone around you is simulated. Chasing this hurt. Futuristic Greenland. A faithful automated companion is waiting to kill you; it's shaving you with a triangular blade in the introductory scene.

There's a certain variety of story I can sleepwalk through, and unfortunately it's often my most well-received. Cyberpunk vibes, damaged protagonist, plenty of action with a smattering of gore or body horror, banter giving way to a moment of emotional vulnerability, and a hopeful-ish ending.

It's good to find a groove, but I always worry it might become a rut. I want to write stories that are challenging, strange, or nasty, but my craving for validation is strong and this is the variety of story that delivers it. Which is not to say it's a bad variety; they're great fun to write and I actually really love this one in particular.

The eponymous butterfly man was a drunken thought I had in Prague, inspired by Anton's Key in *Ender's Shadow* and Mister Meeseeks from *Rick & Morty*. The bathtub birth scene is very much Voldemort's return in *Harry Potter and The Goblet of Fire*.

Both Quandary's happiest moment and that of her dad were pulled from my own life.

The near-future Greenland setting is something I'd been wanting to try for a while, though I worry the tech required to create disposable assassins is a bit too out-there for near future. You know I'm handwaving when I call something "quantum organic."

TRIPPING THROUGH TIME: FAUX-HISTORICAL SF

This one came to me fully formed via vivid dream, during lockdown in Prague, and never made it into the idea document because I wrote it down instantly.

The protagonist was inspired by a friend who worked as a server and caterer for a fancy restaurant. I learned about the Battle of Agincourt by playing *Age of Empires II: The Age of Kings* on my grandma's computer, and about the Great Fire of London by reading *The Shakespeare Stealer* trilogy by Gary Blackwood.

The line about the *fiery braille of a failing economy* is the only one that stuck with me from studying "The Glass Menagerie" in high school.

DALE DALE DALE: JAIME SABINES + BODY HORROR

Slow bitter animal. Living piñatas hunted by children.

My host family in Mexico City foisted a bunch of books on me during my stay, one of them a poetry collection by Jaime Sabines. The line that lingered with me longest was *que lento, amargo animal que soy / que he sido*. Originally, the drabble's protagonist had a fellow prisoner who quoted this to him—noting the irony that now, after the procedures, they would be sweet.

The idea of a human getting turned into a living piñata is pretty ridiculous, but I find something chilling and compelling about it. Punishment colliding with entertainment is nothing new, but it feels worse when it's done to amuse a kid. The birthday party in *Parasite* was likely a subconscious influence.

TIDINGS: HOPEPUNK

Newsflesh. People who make their skin animate the day's atrocities.

This story is a series of linked vignettes slapped together during a weekend in Cape Town. The focus on the climate crisis and its many co-crises is not necessarily new territory for me, but the tone is. This is a positive, we-can-do-it cli-fi story, where human ingenuity overcomes human selfishness and short-sightedness, and by the end of it our current era is a distant dream.

I personally don't think we're going to get talking moose and plastivores and mass de-urbanization—not before a whole lot more bad shit happens, anyway. But if fiction like this can inspire people smarter than I am to solve at least a few of the problems humanity has created, it's worth writing.

THE OLD MAN: HOMO HOMINI LUPUS

This is another story that evaded my idea document. I recall the eponymous character was inspired by the abolitionist John Brown, and his succession of clone-grown sons by Nancy Farmer's *House of the Scorpion* plus an unhinged Reddit copy-pasta theorizing that Lebron James is the result of a secret supersoldier experiment.

The prison opening definitely draws on the videogame *Riddick: Escape from Butcher Bay*, and I suspect the bayou setting was inspired by the first season of *True Detective*. I remember doing quite a bit of research about the flora and fauna, swamp survival tactics, and firearms. Implanted biobombs also featured in my *Clarkesworld* story "Extraction Request," and the *Halo/Animorphs*-inspired needle gun eventually made its way into my novel *Ymir*.

SAFE SPACE: STRAIGHT TO THE POINT
Safe city, a man tries to be unsafe, throws a woman off a balcony, but that's the wrong viewpoint. Gleaming white architecture, omnipresent drones. Woman is a refugee.

This flash piece is a rebuttal to the idea that you have to be suffering to create something worthwhile. There's a trope that crops up now and again where utopia leads to the end of art, as people are too comfortable to create. Long ago, I myself wrote a story where a genetic modification that saps human aggression has the side effect of destroying the artistic impulse.

That now seems ridiculous to me. Art is often a way to express pain, but I think people who are safe and cared for can produce work that is incredibly meaningful. The character of Prosper represents every creative I've met who seems more concerned with lamenting the state of their field than with actually creating anything.

STILL LIFE OF A DEATH BROKER: REALITY

Cyberpunk Niger, night bus, meeting a chief with a medroid, babelware, plastic-eating genesplices. Dog skull mask.

In 2018, me, my dad and a doctor from Galmi Hospital drove out to Manzou to visit one of my dad's old friends. Because we had a doctor with us, we ended up seeing the chief of the village as well, who had been ill for months. My dad acted as interpreter while the doctor examined both the chief and the ultrasounds he'd been given but not fully explained.

The chief had a massive, inoperable tumor on his bladder and not much time left to live. Maybe he already suspected as much, but watching him calmly accept that reality, in front of his friends, family, and three strangers, staggered me. My awe was mixed with a strong feeling of guilt for being there at all.

Those feelings spawned the story, and its accompanying meta-story: have I written a worthwhile tribute to a brave human, or am I no better than my mercenary protagonist, profiteering from tragedy?

COMPLETE EXHAUSTION OF THE ORGANISM: ALL IN THE BLENDER

It's not a real baby, and we should kill it. All I wanna do is make sound effects, then take ya money. I want to make things both more and less significant. I can't tell if things used to matter more. Like hurting cats. Complete exhaustion of the organism. Sex scene opening: you're switching fingers, right? Uh. Yeah. Yes. Noctivagant. Moose and jellyfish alien. Walking tacos.

I spent lockdown in Prague piling up half-assed story ideas, but was too depressed to get any actual writing done—so when motivation finally returned, I decided to write a single story incorporating pretty much all of them. The title is gleaned from a translated Czech medical article, the premise of an artificial baby comes from drunk-watching the film *Vivarium*, and the song that keeps getting referenced is MIA's "Paper Planes." You probably remember it.

The *hurting cats* line is a misunderstanding I always imagine happening to someone, somewhere, someday. The word *noctivagant* is one I encountered years ago and never had a good reason to use, so I finally just chucked it in. And Stro is named after basketball player Stromile Swift, who has one of the coolest names of all time and could dunk like whoa.

HORIZON EVENT: MUTUALLY ASSURED SPAGHETTIFICATION
Falling into a black hole as couples' therapy.

This drabble was inspired by an article about what it would be like to fall into a singularity. The concept orbited through my idea document for a long time before I made use of it.

YOU ARE BORN EXPLODING: THE SLOW BURN
Cordyceps-analog that reproduces in water; the human hosts are compelled to drown themselves. Beach goers in protective gear watch it unfold. Breaking curfew in a slick cosmopolitan city under lockdown: using a wetsuit and goggles to crawl along the bottom of a canal against an artificial current; digging hands through the muddy bottom activates tiny trilobite microorganisms that glow radioactive green. Carnival rides are horses speared to specimen paper, revolving. Striped canvas bathing machines.

I started writing this novelette in Fish Hoek, and many of the characters are loose takes on the people I spent time with there. The prose and pace are more literary than usual, due to me having recently read *The New Confessions* and *The Great Profundo and Other Stories*, and the story is largely about the banality of grief, all the slow living that goes on around loss.

It was also a way for me to process the pandemic, particularly my experiences of paranoia and claustrophobia during quarantine in Prague. The novelette had a long dormant period, pushed to one side while I worked on *Ymir*, but I picked it up again in Grande Prairie and managed to recapture the Fish Hoek vibes.

I think Jack's dialogue is probably some the best, truest toddler dialogue ever committed to the page. I abhor cutesy unrealistic kid dialogue in fiction, so it was a joy to do it right. The title is beautifully random in origin: I was playing with my nephew's letter blocks one afternoon, and arranged them into a quote by a fictional poet.

The whole novelette is actually packed with things like that, with small thoughts or jokes that anchor it to my lived experience at the time. Even though it disappeared into the bottom of the internet without a ripple, I think it's one of the best things I've ever written.

VERWEILE DOCH BUT LINGER: DU BIST SO SCHÖN

2:30 AM basketball, time stop ability leads to never living, popularity iterations.

This story was solicited for *Omni*'s brief, ill-fated reboot. I was in Seattle at the time, visiting my sister and her family. We were listening to a radio show about linguistics when a listener called in to ask about a German phrase he couldn't quite remember. He explained the sense of it, and the radio hosts found it for him: *verweile doch, du bist so schön*.

The line comes from *Faust*, means something like *stay a while; you're so beautiful*, and refers to those perfect little moments in life you wish would last forever. The phrase hit me so deeply that weeks later I emailed my sister with the subject line *Verweile doch* and described one of those moments:

Eating custard on the concrete patio in her backyard, where her two-year-old daughter invented a game of everyone in the family swapping spoons every few bites. She couldn't stop laughing and it made the rest of us laugh, too, so hard it hurt.

My sister replied with *du bist so schön*, and I finished this story a few days after.

MEAT AND SALT AND SPARKS: THE CHIMPANZEE DETECTIVE STORY
*Echoborgs, DIY assassin drones, bacon-flavored
seaweed. Badass duo: depressed, darkly humorous illegal
chimpanzee uplift paired with cheery cyborg PI.*

The concept for this story was around for a long time before I wrote it. I pitched it to multiple friends as "the chimpanzee detective story" and bet them I could make it heart-rending regardless. Originally Cu and Huxley were meant to be private detectives: Cu was always going to be depressed, mostly due to the incredible loneliness of being the only sapient chimpanzee in the world, but Huxley was planned to be her foil in that he was permanently happy due to some kind of serotonin-linked gene editing in the womb.

In the end, I wrote the story much more about Cu than about her partner. I used Seattle as a setting, my memory of the city refreshed by that aforementioned visit to my sister, and did quite a bit of research on chimpanzee motor skills and vision to figure out what sort of accommodations might help an uplifted chimp live in a human's world.

Like "Painless," this one got a lot of sequel requests. Double-dipping in the same universe has never come naturally to me, but if I don't find ways to stretch myself I'll get boring. Maybe this is the year.

Let's see.

BIBLIOGRAPHY

NOVELS
- N1 *Annex* from Orbit, Hachette Book Group USA - July 2018.
- N2 *Ymir* from Orbit, Hachette Book Group USA - July 2022.

NOVELS (IN TRANSLATION)
- N1 *Ymir* from Éditions du Bélial - September 2022.
- N2 《伊米尔》(Ymir) in *Science Fiction World Translations*, September 2023.

COLLECTIONS
- N1 *Datafall: Collected Speculative Fiction* (self-published) – August 2012.
- N2 *Tomorrow Factory: Collected Fiction* from Talos Press, Skyhorse Publishing – October 2018.
- N3 *The Sky Didn't Load Today and Other Glitches* from Shacklebound Books – September 2024; Reprinted by Flame Arrow Publishing – August 2025.
- N4 *Changelog* from Fairwood Press – September 2025.

COLLECTIONS (IN TRANSLATION)
- N1 *La ragazza fantasma* from Future Fiction, Rosarium Publishing – March 2018.
- N2 *La Fabrique des lendemains* from Quarante-Deux, Éditions du Bélial – October 2020; Winner of the 2021 Grand Prix de L'Imaginaire for Best Foreign Work; Reprinted (mass-market paperback) by Le Livre de Poche – January 2023.
- N3 *Rêves de drones et autres entropies* from Éditions Triptyque – February 2022.

NOVELLAS
- N1 *The Indomitable Captain Holli* in *Clarkesworld*, #211 April 2024; Reprinted in *The Year's Top Robot and AI Stories*, October 2025.
- N2 *Barbarians* in *Asimov's Science Fiction*, May-June 2024; Reprinted in *The Year's Top Hard Science Fiction Stories*, June 2025.

NOVELLAS (IN TRANSLATION)
- N1 *Barbares* from Une Heure-Lumière, Éditions du Bélial - October 2023.
- N2 《г族》(Barbarians) in *Science Fiction World Translations*, March 2025.

SHORT STORIES
Note: * indicates availability online via https://richwlarson.tumblr.com/freereads.
- N001 "Every So Often" in *Birdville*, n° 4, April 2011; Reprinted in *Datafall*, August 2012; Reprinted in *NovoPulp 2013/2014 Anthology*, March 2014; Reprinted in *Tomorrow Factory*, October 2018; Reprinted in *Making History: Classic Alternate History Stories*, March 2019.
- N002 "The Listening Game" in *Prick of the Spindle*, December 2011.*
- N003 "Regicide" in *The Claremont Review of Books*, vol. 12 #3, April 2012.
- N004 "Like Any Other Star" in *AE: The Canadian Science Fiction Review*, May 2012.* ; Reprinted in *Changelog*, September 2025.
- N005 "Patron Saint Of Lost Causes" in *The Molotov Cocktail*, vol. 3 #5, May 2012.*
- N006 "Hippolyte" in *Underwater New York*, March 2012.*
- N007 "Chill" in *Monkeybicycle*, March 2012.*
- N008 "Bonfire" in *Over the Brink: Tales of Environmental Disaster*, June 2012.

- N009 "0.6" in >*kill author*, #19, June 2012.*
- N010 "That Elusive Physicist" in *Isotropic Fiction*, #1, July 2012.
- N011 "Sure Things" in *Bartleby Snopes*, July 2012.
- N012 "Your Mind Playing Tricks On Me" in *Emerge Literary Journal*, #3, August 2012.
- N013 "The Garden" in *Datafall*, August 2012; Reprinted in *Crowded Magazine*, #1, February 2013.
- N014 "Memory Cathedrals" in *Datafall*, August 2012.
- N015 "Loopholes" in *Datafall*, August 2012; Reprinted in *Scifia*, #2, September 2012; Reprinted in *Membrane*, December 2013.
- N016 "Back So Soon" in *Datafall*, August 2012.
- N017 "Factory Man" in *Datafall*, August 2012.
- N018 "Datafall" in *Datafall*, August 2012; Reprinted in *Tomorrow Factory*, October 2018; Reprinted (French) in *La Fabrique des lendemains*, October 2020.
- N019 "1/4 Cup Blame" in *Monkeybicycle*, August 2012.
- N020 "Like Chlorine and Night" in *Luscious: A Flash Fiction Collection of Sex & Relationships*, August 2012; Reprinted in *Curly Red Stories*, November 2012.*
- N021 "Dear Romanian Girl" in *Short, Fast & Deadly*, August 2012.*
- N022 "Last" in *Daily Science Fiction*, September 2012; Reprinted in *Antipodean SF*, February 2014.
- N023 "Strings" in *Here Be Monsters # 7: Tongues & Teeth*, September 2012.
- N024 "Autopsies" in *The Claremont Review of Books*, vol. 12 #3, October 2012.
- N025 "Monstrously Unfair" in *Curly Red Stories*, November 2012.*
- N026 "Sun This Bright" in *Leaving Home*, November 2012. Reprinted in *Edge YK*, June 2013.*
- N027 "Repent, Boy" in *The Journal of Compressed Creative Arts*, December 2012.*
- N028 "Pointed at the Head of the Universe" in *Sphere Literary*, December 2012.
- N029 "The Blurry Man" in *Things We Can Create: An Anthology of Speculative Fiction*, January 2013; Reprinted (audio) in *Tales to Terrify*, #293, September 2017.
- N030 "A Moral" in *Monkeybicycle*, February 2013.
- N031 "The Eleanor Effect" in *Universe Horribilis*, February 2013.
- N032 "Your Own Way Back" in *Futuredaze: An Anthology of Young Adult Science Fiction*, March 2013; Reprinted in *Tomorrow Factory*, October 2018; Reprinted (Italian) in *Futuri*, #11, April 2019; Reprinted (French) in *La Fabrique des lendemains*, October 2020.
- N033 "A Transient Snow" in *Glass Buffalo*, Winter 2013.
- N034 "Let's Take This Viral" in *Lightspeed*, #34, March 2013.* ; Reprinted in *Great Jones Street*, August 2016; Reprinted (Italian) in *La ragazza fantasma*, March 2018; Reprinted in *Tomorrow Factory*, October 2018; Reprinted (French) in *Futurs*, September 2020 and *La Fabrique des lendemains*, October 2020.
- N035 "The Mermaid Caper" in *Beneath Ceaseless Skies*, #119, April 2013.*
- N036 "A Scattered Body" in *The Cadaverine*, April 2013.* ; Reprinted in *Urban Crime Stories*, July 2019.
- N037 "Facebug" in *Wordhaus*, May 2013.* ; Reprinted (French) in *La Fabrique des lendemains*, October 2020; Reprinted in *InkFoundry*, March 2024.
- N038 "Sleep Furiously" in *A Common Thread*, May 2013.*
- N039 "Put Out Every One" in *AE: The Canadian Science Fiction Review*, June 2013.*
- N040 "The Bubble" in *Glass Buffalo*, vol. 2, #1, September 2013.
- N041 "Ghost Girl" in *Cautions, Dreams & Curiosities*, October 2013; Reprinted in *War Stories*, October 2014; Reprinted (audio) in *StarShipSofa*, #492, July 2017; Reprinted (Italian) in *La ragazza fantasma*, March 2018; Reprinted in *Tomorrow Factory*, October 2018; Reprinted (Chinese) in *What's the Future Like?*, December 2019; Reprinted in *Bullet Points*, August 2022.
- N042 "Preexisting Conditions" in *Bombay Literary*, October 2013.
- N043 "Chronology of Heartbreak" in *Daily Science Fiction*, October 2013; Reprinted in *Tomorrow Factory*, October 2018.
- N044 "Wet Work" in *Wednesday Night Writes*, October 2013.*
- N045 "The 70-30 Blur" in *Glass Mountain*, #12, October 2013.*
- N046 "Nobody Bets Against the Vat Dog" in *Lakeside Circus*, #1, November 2013.
- N047 "Atrophy" in *Descant*, #163, Winter 2014; Reprinted in *Tomorrow Factory*, October 2018; Reprinted (French) *Rêves de drones et autres entropies*, February 2022.
- N048 "Maria and the Pilgrim" in *Apex Magazine*, #57, February 2014.*

- N049 "The Cloud" in *AE: The Canadian Science Fiction Review*, April 2014.
- N050 "Every Act of Creation" in *Desolation: 21 Tales for Tails*, April 2014.
- N051 "Rapid Oxidation" in *The Albion Review*, May 2014.
- N052 "Of Shitty Love Triangles & Knives Drawn in Pizza Parlors " in *Glass Buffalo*, vol. 3, #2, July 2014.
- N053 "The Air We Breathe Is Stormy, Stormy" in *Strange Horizons*, August 2014; Reprinted in *Year's Best Weird Fiction, Volume Two*, October 2015.
- N054 "God Decay" in *Upgraded*, September 2014; Reprinted in *The Year's Best Science Fiction: 32nd Annual Collection*, July 2015; Reprinted in *Clarkesworld*, #138, March 2018.
- N055 "Dreaming Drones" in *AE: The Canadian Science Fiction Review*, September 2014.* ; Reprinted in *Tomorrow Factory*, October 2018; Reprinted (French) in *Rêves de drones et autres entropies*, February 2022.
- N056 "Capricorn" in *Abyss & Apex Magazine*, #52, September 2014.* ; Reprinted in *Tomorrow Factory*, October 2018.
- N057 "Brute" in *Apex Magazine*, #66, November 2014.* ; Reprinted in *Tomorrow Factory*, October 2018; Reprinted (French) in *La Fabrique des lendemains*, October 2020.
- N058 "The King in the Cathedral" in *Beneath Ceaseless Skies*, #166, February 2015.* ; Reprinted in *The Year's Best Science Fiction and Fantasy, 2016 Edition*, June 2016; Reprinted in *Great Jones Street*, August 2016; Reprinted in *Best of Beneath Ceaseless Skies Online Magazine, Year Seven*, August 2016.
- N059 "The Sky Didn't Load Today" in *Daily Science Fiction*, February 2015; Reprinted in *The Fulcrum*, January 2017; Reprinted in *Tomorrow Factory*, October 2018; Reprinted (French) in *Rêves de drones et autres entropies*, February 2022; Reprinted in *The Sky Didn't Load Today and Other Glitches*, September 2024.
- N060 "Don Juan 2.0" in *AE: The Canadian Science Fiction Review*, February 2015.* ; Reprinted (French) in *La Fabrique des lendemains*, October 2020.
- N061 "Meshed" in *Clarkesworld*, #101, February 2015.* ; Reprinted (Polish) in *Nowa Fantastyka*, October 2015; Reprinted *The Best Science Fiction of the Year*, June 2016; Reprinted in *The Year's Best Science Fiction: 33rd Annual Collection*, July 2016; Reprinted in *Great Jones Street*, August 2016; Reprinted (Italian) in *La ragazza fantasma*, March 2018; Reprinted in *Clarkesworld: Year Nine, Volume One*, April 2018; Reprinted in *Tomorrow Factory*, October 2018; Reprinted in *World Science Fiction #1*, July 2019; Reprinted (Italian) in *Internazionale*, December 2019; Reprinted (Chinese) in *Science Fiction World*, April 2020.
- N062 "This Is the Party" in *The Exile Book of New Canadian Noir*, March 2015.
- N063 "Brainwhales Are Stoners, Too" in *Interzone*, #257, March-April 2015; Reprinted in *Changelog*, September 2025.
- N064 "Relocation" in *On Spec*, #100, Spring 2015.
- N065 "Going Endo" in *Apex Magazine*, #74, July 2015.* ; Reprinted in *The Best of Apex Magazine: Volume 1*, January 2016; Reprinted (French) in *La Fabrique des lendemains*, October 2020.
- N066 "Edited" in *Interzone*, #259, July-August 2015; Reprinted in *Wilde Stories 2016: The Year's Best Gay Speculative Fiction*, July 2016; Reprinted in *Tomorrow Factory*, October 2018; Reprinted (French) in *Brins d'Éternité*, n° 53, April 2019 and *La Fabrique des lendemains*, October 2020 and *Rêves de drones et autres entropies*, February 2022.
- N067 "Six Month Ocean" in *Daily Science Fiction*, September 2015; Reprinted (French) in
- *La Fabrique des lendemains*, October 2020; Reprinted in *The Sky Didn't Load Today and Other Glitches*, September 2024.
- N068 "Seachange" in *Andromeda Spaceways Inflight Magazine*, #61, September 2015.
- N069 "Ice" in *Clarkesworld*, #109, October 2015.* ; Reprinted in *The Year's Best Science Fiction: 33rd Annual Collection*, July 2016; Reprinted in *Great Jones Street*, August 2016; Reprinted (Polish) in *Nowa Fantastyka*, May 2017; Reprinted (Chinese) in *Future Affairs Administration*, January 2018 (digital) and in *Future Affairs Administration*, June 2019 (print); Reprinted in *Clarkesworld: Year Ten, Volume One*, October 2019; Reprinted in *The New Voices of Science Fiction*, November 2019; Adapted for screen as "Ice" in *LOVE DEATH + ROBOTS: VOLUME 2*, May 2021. (Winner of the 2021 Emmy Award for Outstanding Short Form Animated Program.); Reprinted (Chinese) in *Science Fiction World Translations*, November 2021; Reprinted in *LOVE DEATH + ROBOTS: The Official Anthology Volume Two*, June 2022. (Packaged with Chinese, Egyptian Arabic, and Polish translation.); Reprinted (French) in *Bifrost*, n° 108, October 2022.
- N070 "The Delusive Cartographer" in *Beneath Ceaseless Skies*, #187, November 2015.* ; reprinted in *Best of Beneath Ceaseless Skies Online Magazine, Year Eight*, September 2017;

- 071 "We Might Be Sims" in *Interzone*, #261, November-December 2015; Reprinted (French) in *Bifrost*, n° 106, April 2022.
- N072 "Motherfucking Retroparty Freestyle" in *Escape Pod*, December 2015.* ; Reprinted in *Tomorrow Factory,* October 2018.
- N073 "Blindr (Beta 3.1)" in *The Singularity*, #2, December 2015.
- N074 "Bidding War" in *Asimov's Science Fiction*, December 2015; Reprinted (audio) in *Podomatic*, July 2017; Reprinted (French) in *La Fabrique des lendemains*, October 2020.
- N075 "Extraction Request" in *Clarkesworld*, #112, January 2016.* ; Reprinted (Vietnamese) in *SFVN,* March 2017; Reprinted in *The Best Science Fiction of the Year, Volume 2,* April 2017; Reprinted (Chinese) in *Future Affairs Administration,* January 2018; Reprinted in *Tomorrow Factory,* October 2018; Reprinted in *Clarkesworld: Year Ten, Volume One*, October 2019; Reprinted (French) in *Bifrost*, n° 102, April 2021; Reprinted (Romanian) in *Blogul de SeFe*, February 2022; Reprinted (audio) in *Tales to Terrify*, #552, August 2022.
- N076 "Summer Skin" in *Aestas 2015*, February 2016.
- N077 "Seawall" in *AE: The Canadian Science Fiction Review*, March 2016.* ; Reprinted (French) in *La Fabrique des lendemains*, October 2020.
- N078 "Lotto" in *Interzone*, #263, March-April 2016.
- N079 "Sparks Fly" in *Lightspeed*, #70, March 2016.* ; Reprinted in *Great Jones Street*, August 2016.
- N080 "Sleep Factory" in *Analog Science Fiction & Fact*, April 2016; Reprinted (French) in *La Fabrique des lendemains*, October 2020.
- N081 "Innumerable Glimmering Lights" in *Clockwork Phoenix #5*, April 2016; Reprinted in *The Year's Best Science Fiction: 34th Annual Collection,* July 2017; Reprinted in *The Year's Best Science Fiction and Fantasy, 2017 Edition*, September 2017; Reprinted (Italian) in *Mondi Senza Fine - Parte 2*, Summer 2018; Reprinted in *Tomorrow Factory,* October 2018; Reprinted (Czech) in *XB-1*, November 2019; Reprinted in *Forever Magazine*, January 2020; Reprinted (French) in *La Fabrique des lendemains*, October 2020.
- N082 "Jokers to the Right" in *Flash Felon*, May 2016.
- N083 "Define Symbiont" in *Shimmer*, #31, May-June 2016.* ; Reprinted in *Shimmer 2016: The Collected Stories*, December 2016; Reprinted in *The Sky Didn't Load Today and Other Glitches*, September 2024.
- N084 "Lifeboat" in *Interzone*, #264, May-June 2016.
- N085 "The Nostalgia Calculator" in *The Magazine of Fantasy & Science Fiction*, May-June 2016; Winner of the 2014 Dell Award for Undergraduate Science Fiction; Reprinted (Czech) in *XB-1*, April 2018.
- N086 "Jonas and The Fox" in *Clarkesworld*, #116, May 2016; Reprinted in *The Year's Best Science Fiction: 34th Annual Collection,* July 2017; Reprinted (Italian) in *Mondi Senza Fine - Parte 1*, Spring 2018; Reprinted in *The Very Best of the Best: 30 Years of the Year's Best Science Fiction*, February 2019; Reprinted in *Clarkesworld: Year Ten, Volume Two*, October 2019; Reprinted (Chinese) in *Science Fiction World Translations,* September 2020; Reprinted in *The 2020 Look at Space Opera*, October 2020.
- N087 "Espie" in *Terraform*, May 2016; Reprinted (Italian) in *Il lettore di fantasia,* May 2017.
- N088 "Masked" in *Asimov's Science Fiction*, July 2016; Reprinted in *Apex Magazine*, January 2017; Reprinted in *We, Robots: Artificial Intelligence in 100 Stories*, December 2020.
- N089 "TrashureIsland" in *Compelling Science Fiction*, #3, August-September 2016.*
- N090 "Carnivores" in *Strangers Among Us: Tales of the Underdogs & Outcasts*, August 2016; Reprinted in *Wilde Stories: The Year's Best Gay Speculative Fiction 2017*, July 2017; Reprinted (French) in *La Fabrique des lendemains*, October 2020; Reprinted in *Lightspeed*, #132, May 2021.
- N091 "All That Robot Shit" in *Asimov's Science Fiction*, September 2016. [Published as "All That Robot…"] Winner of the 2017 *Asimov's* Reader's Award; Reprinted in *The Year's Best Science Fiction and Fantasy, 2017 Edition*, September 2017; Reprinted in *Tomorrow Factory,* October 2018; Reprinted (Chinese) in *Science Fiction World,* April 2019; Reprinted (French) in *La Fabrique des lendemains*, October 2020; Reprinted in *Forever Magazine*, January 2021.
- N092 "The Green Man Cometh" in *Clarkesworld*, #120, September 2016.* ; Reprinted in *Clarkesworld: Year Ten, Volume Two*, October 2019; Reprinted (French) in *La Fabrique des lendemains*, October 2020.
- N093 "Water Scorpions" in *Asimov's Science Fiction*, October-November 2016; Reprinted in *Alien Invasion Short Stories*, May 2018; Reprinted in *Not One of Us: Stories of Aliens on Earth,* November 2018; Reprinted in *Changelog,* September 2025.
- N094 "You Make Pattaya" in *Interzone*, #267, November-December 2016; Reprinted in

The Best Science Fiction and Fantasy of the Year: Volume 11, April 2017; Reprinted in
The Best Science Fiction of the Year, Volume 2, April 2017; Reprinted (Chinese) in *Science
Fiction World,* June 2017; Reprinted (Polish) in *Nowa Fantastyka,* March 2018; Reprinted in
Tomorrow Factory, October 2018; Reprinted in *Forever Magazine,* February 2019.

- N095 "The Cyborg, the Tinman, the Merchant of Death" in *Lightspeed,* #79, December 2016.*
- N096 "We Are Destroyers" in *Compelling Science Fiction,* #4, December 2016-January 2017.*
- N097 "The Ghost Ship Anastasia" in *Clarkesworld,* #124, January 2017. * ; Reprinted (Czech) in *XB-1,* January 2018; Reprinted in *The Year's Best Military and Adventure SF, Vol. 4,* June 2018; Reprinted in *Tomorrow Factory,* October 2018; Reprinted in *Clarkesworld: Year Eleven, Volume One,* November 2019; Reprinted (French) in *Rêves de drones et autres entropies,* February 2022.
- N098 "There Used to Be Olive Trees" in *The Magazine of Fantasy & Science Fiction,* January-February 2017; Reprinted in *The Year's Best Science Fiction: 35th Annual Collection,* July 2018; Reprinted in *Wilde Stories 2018: The Year's Best Gay Speculative Fiction,* September 2018; Reprinted (French) in *La Fabrique des lendemains,* October 2020; Reprinted (Italian) in *Infiniti Universi - Parte 3,* Spring 2021; Reprinted in *Forever Magazine,* August 2023.
- N099 "You Too Shall Be Psyche" in *Apex Magazine,* #93, February 2017.* ; Reprinted (audio) in *Tales to Terrify,* #323, April 2018.
- N100 "St. Theophilus the Penitent" in *Apex Magazine,* #93, February 2017.*
- N101 "Cupido" in *Asimov's Science Fiction,* March-April 2017; Reprinted in *The Year's Best Science Fiction and Fantasy, 2018 Edition,* August 2018; Reprinted in *Changelog,* September 2025.
- N102 "Dark Warm Heart" in *Tordotcom,* April 2017; Reprinted in *Best Horror of the Year: Volume 10,* October 2018; Reprinted (French) in *Solaris,* n° 209, February 2019; Reprinted (audio) in *Tales to Terrify,* #394, August 2019.
- N103 "Pherobomb" in *Daily Science Fiction,* June 2017; Reprinted in *The Sky Didn't Load Today and Other Glitches,* September 2024.
- N104 "An Evening with Severyn Grimes" in *Asimov's Science Fiction,* July-August 2017; Reprinted in *The Best Science Fiction and Fantasy of the Year: Volume 12,* March 2018; Reprinted in *The Best Science Fiction of the Year, Volume 3,* April 2018; Reprinted in *The Year's Top Ten Tales of Science Fiction 10,* June 2018; Reprinted in *The Year's Best Science Fiction: 35th Annual Collection,* July 2018; Reprinted in *Tomorrow Factory,* October 2018; Reprinted (Italian) in *Infiniti Universi - Parte 1,* Spring 2020; Reprinted (Czech) in *XB-1,* May 2020; Reprinted in *Forever Magazine,* July 2020; Reprinted (French) in *La Fabrique des lendemains,* October 2020 and in *Rêves de drones et autres entropies,* February 2022.
- N105 "Dispo and the Crow" in *Mythic Delirium,* #4.2, July-September 2017.* ; Reprinted (Italian) in *Strane Creature, Vol. 1,* October 2018; Reprinted in *Robots & Artificial Intelligence Short Stories,* November 2018.
- N106 "L'appel du vide" in *Apex Magazine,* #98, July 2017.*
- N107 "Spiked" in *Abyss & Apex,* #63, July 2017.* ; Reprinted in *The Best of Abyss & Apex, Volume 3,* November 2019.
- N108 "Travelers" in *Clarkesworld,* #130, July 2017.* ; Reprinted in *Clarkesworld: Year Eleven, Volume Two,* November 2019; Reprinted (Romanian) in *Galaxia 42,* November 2020.
- N109 "Heavies" in *Infinity Wars,* September 2017; Reprinted (Polish) in *Nowa Fantastyka,* September 2018; Reprinted (audio) in *StarShipSofa,* #583, April 2019.
- N110 "The Old Man" in *Analog Science Fiction & Fact,* November 2017; Reprinted in *Changelog,* September 2025.
- N111 "The Colgrid Conundrum" in *The Book of Swords,* October 2017; Reprinted (Italian) in *Il libro delle spade,* March 2018; Reprinted (Polish) in *Księga mieczy,* March 2018; Reprinted (Bulgarian) in *Книга на мечовете,* May 2018; Reprinted (Portuguese) in *Crônicas de Espada e Feitiçaria,* June 2018; Reprinted (Russian) in *Книга мечей,* July 2018; Reprinted (French) in *Epées & magie,* October 2019.
- N112 "Verweile Doch (But Linger)" in *OMNI,* vol. 74 #1, Winter 2017.* ; Reprinted in *Changelog,* September 2025.
- N113 "Penitents" in *Beneath Ceaseless Skies,* #245, February 2018.*
- N114 "In Event of Moon Disaster" in *Asimov's Science Fiction,* March-April 2018.* ; Winner of the 2019 *Asimov's* Reader's Award; Reprinted (audio) in *Podomatic,* March 2018; Reprinted (Chinese) in *Science Fiction World Translations,* September 2018; Reprinted in

The Eagle Has Landed: 50 Years of Lunar Science Fiction, July 2019; Reprinted (French) in *La Fabrique des lendemains*, October 2020; Reprinted in *Forever Magazine*, April 2021; Reprinted in *Changelog*, September 2025.

- N115 "Razzibot" in *Analog Science Fiction & Fact*, March 2018; Reprinted in *Tomorrow Factory*, October 2018; Reprinted (Chinese) in *Science Fiction World*, May 2019.
- N116 "Safe Space" in *Daily Science Fiction*, March 2018.* ; Reprinted in *Changelog*, September 2025.
- N117 "Our King and His Court" in *Tordotcom*, March 2018.*
- N118 "Carouseling" in *Clarkesworld*, #139, April 2018.* ; Reprinted in *The Year's Best Science Fiction and Fantasy, 2019 Edition*, June 2019; Reprinted (French) in *La Fabrique des lendemains*, October 2020; Reprinted in *Clarkesworld: Year Twelve, Volume Two*, September 2021.
- N119 "Playmates" in *Daily Science Fiction*, April 2018; Reprinted in *The Sky Didn't Load Today and Other Glitches*, September 2024.
- N120 "Fifteen Minutes Hate" in *Apex Magazine*, #108, May 2018.* ; Winner of the 2017 Roswell Award; Reprinted (French) in *Brins d'Éternité*, n° 51, October 2018 and *Rêves de drones et autres entropies*, February 2022.
- N121 "Some of These Stars Might Already Be Gone" in *Daily Science Fiction*, June 2018.* ; Reprinted (French) in *La Fabrique des lendemains*, October 2020; Reprinted in *The Sky Didn't Load Today and Other Glitches*, September 2024.
- N122 "Meat And Salt And Sparks" in *Tordotcom*, June 2018.* ; Reprinted in *The Best Science Fiction and Fantasy of the Year: Volume Thirteen*, April 2019; Reprinted in *The Year's Top Robot and AI Stories*, May 2019; Reprinted in *The Best Science Fiction of the Year: Volume Four*, July 2019; Reprinted in *The Long List Anthology Volume 5: More Stories from the Hugo Award Nomination List*, December 2019; Reprinted (Japanese) in *BABELZINE*, vol. 1, June 2020; Reprinted (French) in *La Fabrique des lendemains*, October 2020 and *Rêves de drones et autres entropies*, February 2022; Reprinted in *Changelog*, September 2025.
- N123 "Othermother" in *Clarkesworld*, #143, August 2018. [Extract adapted from *Annex*.]
- N124 "Porque el girasol se llama el girasol" in *Shades Within Us: Tales of Migrations & Fractured Borders*, September 2018; Reprinted (French) in *La Fabrique des lendemains*, October 2020.
- N125 "Circuits" in *Tomorrow Factory*, October 2018; Reprinted (French) in *Bifrost*, nᵒ 100, October 2020 and *La Fabrique des lendemains*, October 2020.
- N126 "Molli's Oggles" in *Terraform*, October 2018.* ; Reprinted (French) in *Ellipse*, October 2023; Reprinted in *The Sky Didn't Load Today and Other Glitches*, September 2024.
- N127 "Octo-Heist in Progress" in *Clarkesworld*, #146, November 2018.* ; Reprinted (Chinese) in *Science Fiction World Translations*, January 2019.
- N128 "Smear Job" in *Analog Science Fiction & Fact*, November-December 2018; Reprinted (French) in *Galaxies SF*, n° 66, July 2020 and *Rêves de drones et autres entropies*, February 2022; Reprinted in *Changelog*, September 2025.
- N129 "Dreamland" in *Whose Future Is It?*, December 2018. [Credited as Richard Larson.]
- N130 "Skinned" in *Terraform*, January 2019.* ; Reprinted (French) in *Rêves de drones et autres entropies*, February 2022; Reprinted in *The Sky Didn't Load Today and Other Glitches*, September 2024.
- N131 "Contagion's Eve at the House Noctambulous" in *The Magazine of Fantasy & Science Fiction*, March-April 2019; Reprinted in *The Year's Best Science Fiction Vol. 1: The Saga Anthology of Science Fiction 2020*, September 2020; Reprinted (French) in *La Fabrique des lendemains*, October 2020; Reprinted in *Forever Magazine*, November 2022; Reprinted (Czech) in *XB-1*, August 2023.
- N132 "Death of an Air Salesman" in *Clarkesworld*, #150, March 2019.* ; Reprinted (French) in *Rêves de drones et autres entropies*, February 2022.
- N133 "Painless" in *Tordotcom*, April 2019.* ; Reprinted (Chinese) in *Science Fiction World*, October 2019; Reprinted in *Some of the Best from Tor.com 2019*, January 2020; Reprinted in *The Best Science Fiction of the Year: Volume Five*, October 2020; Reprinted (French) in *La Fabrique des lendemains*, October 2020; Reprinted (Italian) in *Cuspidi*, June 2023; Reprinted in *Changelog*, September 2025.
- N134 "Scurry" in *Do Not Go Quietly: An Anthology of Defiance in Victory*, May 2019.
- N135 "Still Life of a Death Broker" in *Terraform*, May 2019; Reprinted in *Changelog*, September 2025.
- N136 "Scrubbed" in *Bourbon Penn*, July 2019; Reprinted (French) in *Galaxies SF*, n° 61, October 2019 and *Rêves de drones et autres entropies*, February 2022.

- N137 "Go Play Outside" in *Sapiens Plurum*, July 2019.
- N138 "The Starfucker Dyad" in *The Unquiet Dreamer: A Tribute to Harlan Ellison*, August 2019.
- N139 "Can You Watch My Stuff" in *Asimov's Science Fiction*, September-October 2019.* ; Reprinted (French) in *La Fabrique des lendemains*, October 2020 and *Rêves de drones et autres entropies*, February 2022.
- N140 "All Electric Ghosts" in *Clarkesworld*, #157, October 2019.* ; Reprinted (French) in *Bifrost*, n° 104, October 2021; Reprinted in *Changelog*, September 2025.
- N141 "Growing and Growing" in *Nightmare*, #85, October 2019.* ; Reprinted (Chinese) in *Science Fiction World Translations*, December 2019.
- N142 "The Star Plague" in *Beneath Ceaseless Skies*, #289, October 2019.*
- N143 "We're Talking About Practice" in *Daily Science Fiction*, December 2019; Reprinted in *The Sky Didn't Load Today and Other Glitches*, September 2024.
- N144 "How Quini the Squid Misplaced His Klobučar" in *Tordotcom*, January 2020.* ; Reprinted in *Some of the Best from Tor.com 2020*, January 2021; Reprinted in *The Year's Top Hard Science Fiction Stories 5*, June 2021; Reprinted in *The Year's Best Science Fiction Vol. 2: The Saga Anthology of Science Fiction 2020*, September 2021; Reprinted in *The Best Science Fiction of the Year: Volume Six*, January 2022; Reprinted (Italian) in *Altre Storie, Altri Mondi – Parte 2*, March 2024; Reprinted (French) by Une Heure-Lumière, Éditions du Bélial, May 2024.
- N145 "The Sniper and I" in *Beneath Ceaseless Skies*, #299, March 2020.* ; Reprinted in *War Torn*, April 2022.
- N146 "An Elephant Never Forgets" in *Made to Order: Robots & Revolution*, March 2020.
- N147 "Simulation Ending" in *5th Wall Press*, March 2020.*
- N148 "Moving Day" in *Daily Science Fiction*, March 2020; Reprinted in *The Sky Didn't Load Today and Other Glitches*, September 2024.
- N149 "123456" in *Quarantine Quanta: Packets of Literary Light From a Dark Time*, April 2020.* ; Reprinted in *The Sky Didn't Load Today and Other Glitches*, September 2024.
- N150 "Warm Math" in *The Magazine of Fantasy & Science Fiction*, May-June 2020.
- N151 "Petrosinella" in *Daily Science Fiction*, June 2020.
- N152 "Animals Like Me" in *Ignorance Is Strength: The Dystopia Triptych #1*, June 2020; Reprinted in *Changelog*, September 2025.
- N153 "Our Lady of Perpetual Disdain" in *Burn the Ashes: The Dystopia Triptych #2*, June 2020; Reprinted in *Changelog*, September 2025.
- N154 "Failsafe" in *Or Else the Light: The Dystopia Triptych #3*, June 2020; Reprinted in *Changelog*, September 2025.
- N155 "Lowlife Orbit" in *Analog Science Fiction & Fact*, July-August 2020; Reprinted in *The Sky Didn't Load Today and Other Glitches*, September 2024.
- N156 "The Conceptual Shark" in *Asimov's Science Fiction*, September-October 2020.* ; Reprinted (Czech) in *XB-1*, June 2021; Reprinted (Chinese) in *Science Fiction World*, January 2023; Reprinted (French) in *Bifrost*, n° 111, July 2023; Reprinted in *Storia*, September 2024.
- N157 "Burrowing Through the Body of God" in *Sci Phi Journal*, September 2020.* ; Reprinted in *Dark Matter*, #008, March 2022.
- N158 "Echo the Echo" in *Entanglements: Tomorrow's Lovers, Families & Friends*, September 2020; Reprinted (Italian) in *Relazioni - Amanti, amici e famiglie dal futuro*, June 2021.
- N159 "Samsung Syndrome" in *Lockdown Literature*, November 2020.
- N160 "Tripping Through Time" in *Dark Matter*, #001, January 2021; Reprinted in *Best American Science Fiction and Fantasy 2022*, November 2022; Reprinted in *Changelog*, September 2025.
- N161 "Horseplay" in *Daily Science Fiction*, January 2021; Reprinted in *The Sky Didn't Load Today and Other Glitches*, September 2024.
- N162 "Pilgrim Problems" in *Daily Science Fiction*, March 2021; Reprinted in *The Sky Didn't Load Today and Other Glitches*, September 2024.
- N163 "Tommy Wexler and The Case of the Absconding Arsonist" in *Bourbon Penn*, April 2021.
- N164 "Complete Exhaustion of the Organism" in *Lightspeed*, #131, April 2021.* ; Reprinted in *The Best Science Fiction of the Year: Volume Seven*, September 2023; Reprinted in *Changelog*, September 2025.
- N165 "The World, a Carcass" in *The Magazine of Fantasy & Science Fiction*, May-June 2021.
- N166 "Koronapárty" in *Make Shift: Dispatches from the Post-Pandemic Future*, May 2021; Reprinted (Italian) in *Improvvisazioni - Futuri possibili, probabili e inaspettati*, March 2022.

- N167 "Horizon Event" in *Martian*, June 2021.* ; Reprinted in *Martian Year One*, March 2022; Reprinted in *Changelog*, September 2025.
- N168 "Last Nice Day" in *Clarkesworld*, #178, July 2021.* ; Reprinted in *Changelog*, September 2025.
- N169 "Robocare" in *Seasons Between Us: Tales of Identities and Memories*, August 2021.
- N170 "Tidings" in *Imagine 2200: Climate Fiction for Future Ancestors*, September 2021.* ; Reprinted in *Lightspeed*, #137, October 2021; Reprinted in *Afterglow: Climate Fiction for Future Ancestors*, February 2023; Reprinted in *Solarmarx*, June 2025; Reprinted (Italian) in *Solarmarx*, June 2025; Reprinted in *Changelog*, September 2025.
- N171 "Moose Trap" in *Daily Science Fiction*, September 2021; Reprinted in *The Sky Didn't Load Today and Other Glitches*, September 2024.
- N172 "Through" in *Clarkesworld*, #181, October 2021. [Co-written with Eric Fomley.]*
- N173 "Exit" in *Stargazers: Microtales from the Cosmos*, October 2021.*
- N174 "Valhalla" in *Martian*, October 2021.* ; Reprinted in *Martian Year One*, March 2022; Reprinted in *Changelog*, September 2025.
- N175 "Get the Lights" in *Flame Tree Newsletter*, November 2021; Reprinted in *The Sky Didn't Load Today and Other Glitches*, September 2024.
- N176 "You Are Born Exploding" in *Clarkesworld*, #183, December 2021.* ; Reprinted (Polish) in *Nowa Fantastyka*, March 2022; Reprinted in *Changelog*, September 2025.
- N177 "Night Shift" in *Martian*, December 2021.* ; Reprinted in *Martian Year One*, March 2022; Reprinted in *Changelog*, September 2025.
- N178 "Fair's Fair" in *Flame Tree Newsletter*, January 2022.
- N179 "This Is Your Exit Survey" in *Shallow Waters Flash Fiction Challenge*, January 2022.
- N180 "What Una Loves" in *Apex Magazine*, #129, January 2022.*
- N181 "Feel Me" in *Daily Science Fiction*, March 2022.
- N182 "Good Night Moon" in *Bourbon Penn*, March 2022.*
- N183 "Voyage to The Corallax System" in *Beyond: The 2022 Collins Writing Contest*, April 2022.
- N184 "30" in *Asimov's Science Fiction*, May-June 2022.
- N185 "Flight Delay" in *Dark Matter*, #009, May 2022.
- N186 "Wants Pawn Term" in *Clarkesworld*, #188, May 2022 *
- N187 "Mind Blown" in *Daily Science Fiction*, May 2022; Reprinted in *The Sky Didn't Load Today and Other Glitches*, September 2024.
- N188 "Wet Dreams" in *Interzone*, #292/293, July 2022; Reprinted in *The Elm Accord*, February 2025.
- N189 "Ursus Frankensteinus" in *Lightspeed*, #146, July 2022.* ; Reprinted (Chinese) in *SF World*, December 2022.
- N190 "Business Is Suppurating" in *Daily Science Fiction*, August 2022.
- N191 "Shoot Your Shot" in *Analog Science Fiction & Fact*, September-October 2022.
- N192 "The Rise of Alpha Gal" in *Asimov's Science Fiction*, September-October 2022.
- N193 "A Certain Way of Dying" in *Flame Tree Fantasycon 2022 Newsletter*, September 2022.
- N194 "Quandary Aminu vs. The Butterfly Man" in *Tordotcom*, September 2022.* ; Reprinted in *The Year's Best Science Fiction on Earth*, November 2023; Winner of the 2023 Eugie Foster Memorial Award; Reprinted in *The Best Science Fiction of the Year: Volume Eight*, September 2024; Reprinted in *Changelog*, September 2025.
- N195 "Someone Else" in *Daily Science Fiction*, September 2022; Reprinted in *The Sky Didn't Load Today and Other Glitches*, September 2024.
- N196 "Rites" in *Factor Four Magazine*, #16, October 2022.*
- N197 "And Now the Shade" in *Imagine 2200: Climate Fiction for Future Ancestors*, October 2022.* ; Reprinted in *Metamorphosis: Climate Fiction for a Better Future*, November 2024.
- N198 "Newbies" in *Sapiens Plurum*, October 2022.*
- N199 "Three Liters, Twenty-One Grams" in *Martian*, December 2022.*
- N200 "Deathmatch" in *Lightspeed*, #151, December 2022.* ; Reprinted in *Storia*, May 2024.
- N201 "Won't You Stay Longer" in *MetaStellar*, January 2023.* ; Reprinted in *The Sky Didn't Load Today and Other Glitches*, September 2024.
- N202 "Dale Dale Dale" in *Martian*, January 2023.*
- N203 "Even If Such Ways Are Bad" in *Tordotcom*, February 2023.* ; Reprinted in *The Year's Top Hard Science Fiction Stories 8*, June 2024.
- N204 "Reproduction on the Beach" in *Apex Magazine*, #136, March 2023.* ; Reprinted in *The Sky Didn't Load Today and Other Glitches*, September 2024.
- N205 "Grin Minus Cat" in *Flash Fiction Online*, April 2023.* ; Reprinted in *The Sky Didn't

Load Today and Other Glitches, September 2024.

- N206 "Heavy Lies, or A Record of Reproductive Aberration in the Eusocial Aedificans of Hephaestus-4" in *Life Beyond Us: An Original Anthology Of SF Stories And Science Essays*, April 2023; Reprinted in *The Year's Top Tales of Space and Time 4*, August 2024.
- N207 "Dissection" in *Dark Matter Presents: Monstrous Futures*, April 2023.
- N208 "LOL, Said the Scorpion" in *Clarkesworld*, #200, May 2023.* ; Reprinted in *The Year's Best Science Fiction on Earth 2*, November 2024; Reprinted in *The Year's Best Canadian Fantasy and Science Fiction Volume Two*, November 2024.
- N209 "Only the Most Necessary Violence" (translated into French) in *Métal Hurlant*, May 2023.
- N210 "Always Personal" in *Lightspeed*, #157, June 2023.* ; Reprinted in *The Sky Didn't Load Today and Other Glitches*, September 2024.
- N211 "Last Voyage of the USS Hubris" in *Martian*, June 2023.*
- N212 "To Rise, to Set" in *Flash Fiction Online*, June 2023.*
- N213 "Partial Transcript from The Great Brexit Baking Show" in *Bourbon Penn*, July 2023.*
- N214 "Headhunting" in *Tordotcom*, August 2023.* ; Reprinted in *Changelog*, September 2025.
- N215 "Spitting Image" in *Apex Magazine*, #140, September 2023.*
- N216 "Treadmill" in *f(r)iction*, September 2023.* ; Reprinted in *The Sky Didn't Load Today and Other Glitches*, September 2024.
- N217 "The Wandering Bed" in *Sunday Morning Transport*, September 2023.
- N218 "A Beginner's Guide to the Hieronymus Box" in *Crepuscular*, October 2023.* ; Reprinted in *The Sky Didn't Load Today and Other Glitches*, September 2024.
- N219 "Implementation of Eusocial Technologies in the Office" in *Strange Machines: An Anthology of Dark User Manuals*, October 2023.
- N220 "These Luminous Cadavers" in *Dark Matter*, #018, December 2023.
- N221 "Cues" in *The Binge-Watching Cure III: An Anthology of Science Fiction Stories*, December 2023; Reprinted in *The Sky Didn't Load Today and Other Glitches*, September 2024.
- N222 "A Magician Did It" in *Beneath Ceaseless Skies*, #402, March 2024.*
- N223 "Limping Toward Sunrise" in *Lightspeed*, #167, April 2024.* ; Reprinted in *The Sky Didn't Load Today and Other Glitches*, September 2024.
- N224 "Breathing Constellations" in *Reactor* (formerly *Tordotcom*), June 2024.* ; Reprinted in *The Year's Best Science Fiction on Earth 3*, November 2025.
- N225 "Ascension's Eve" in *Flash Fiction Online*, July 2024.* ; Reprinted in *The Sky Didn't Load Today and Other Glitches*, September 2024.
- N226 "Caring for Your Damage Sponge" in *Small Wonders*, #13, July 2024.* ; Reprinted in *The Sky Didn't Load Today and Other Glitches*, September 2024.
- N227 "The Wretched Tale of Father Yannis" in *Polymorphic: Volume 2*, July 2024.
- N228 "Molum, Molum, Molum the Scourge" in *Clarkesworld*, #215, August 2024.*
- N229 "To Harvest a Cloud" in *Flash Fiction Online*, September 2024.*
- N230 "Breathing for Two" in *The Sky Didn't Load Today and Other Glitches*, September 2024.
- N231 "For All Your Rampage Needs" in *The Sky Didn't Load Today and Other Glitches*, September 2024.
- N232 "Me Reaping, You Sowing" in *The Page*, September 2024.
- N233 "DO NOT OPEN" in *Northern Nights*, October 2024.
- N234 "The Gaunt Strikes Again" in *Diabolical Plots*, October 2024.
- N235 "Lento, Amargo Animal" in *Bourbon Penn*, December 2024.*
- N236 "Montréal / Tiohtià:ke" in *Winter in the City: A Collection of Dark Urban Stories*, December 2024.
- N237 "This View From Here" in *Imagine 2200: Climate Fiction for Future Ancestors*, January 2025.*
- N238 "You Are Now Breathing Manually" in *Polar Borealis*, #32, January 2025.*
- N239 "Restoration" in *Flame Tree Newsletter*, January 2025.
- N240 "Murder in the Clavist Autonomous Zone" in *Strange Horizons*, January 2025.* ; Reprinted (Korean) in *Starlit Fragments*, June 2025.
- N241 "The Heat of Creation" in *Remains*, #1, January 2025.
- N242 "Dear Y" in *The Elm Accord*, February 2025.
- N243 "Emergence" in *Emergence*, March 2025.*
- N244 "The Glasshand" in *Emergence*, March 2025.*

- N245 "Sucks to Suck" in *Anomaly*, March 2025.*
- N246 "An Even Greater Cold to Come" in *Clarkesworld*, #223, April 2025.*
- N247 "Lies as the Natural State of Things" in *Apex Magazine*, #149, April 2025.*
- N248 "To Navigate the Night" in *Lightspeed*, #179, April 2025.*
- N249 "Pod People" in *Intergalactic Rejects*, April 2025.
- N250 "The Place of Lost Stories" in *The Book of Lost Places*, April 2025.
- N251 "The Sack of Burley Cottage" in Reactor (formerly Tordotcom), June 2025.*
- N252 "<N>" in The Small Fryer, June 2025
- N253 "Most Things" in Asimov's Science Fiction, July-August 2025.

POEMS

- N01 "The Blank Slate" in *Word Riot*, November 2011.*
- N02 "Love" in *YARN (Young Adult Review Network)*, February 2012.*
- N03 "Down" in *YARN (Young Adult Review Network)*, February 2012.*
- N04 "Gravitational" in *YARN (Young Adult Review Network)*, February 2012.*
- N05 "Over" in *YARN (Young Adult Review Network)*, February 2012.*
- N06 "Valentine" in *YARN (Young Adult Review Network)*, February 2012.*
- N07 "Other Astronomical Distances" in *YARN (Young Adult Review Network)*, March 2012.
- N08 "Feint" in *Blue & Yellow Dog*, #9, Summer 2012.
- N09 "Smile" in *Blue & Yellow Dog*, #9, Summer 2012.
- N10 "The Archives" in *Blue & Yellow Dog*, #9, Summer 2012.
- N11 "Arsonist/Pianist" in *TwentySomething Press*, August 2012.
- N12 "Unknowable" in *TwentySomething Press*, August 2012.
- N13 "Leave Me" in *The Claremont Review of Books*, vol. 12 # 3, print, October 2012.
- N14 "Changes in the Coming Months" in *The Adroit Journal*, November 2012.
- N15 "Forensics" in *Short, Fast & Deadly*, November 2012.
- N16 "Hunger Games" in *decomP*, May 2013.*
- N17 "That Insensible Realm" in *Found Patrick*, June 2013.
- N18 "1/100" in *Glass Buffalo*, #2, September 2013.
- N19 "Datafall" in *Strange Horizons*, November 2013.* [Shares name with story].
- N20 "I Went to the Asteroid to Bury You" in *Abyss & Apex*, #55, June 2015.* ; Reprinted in *Tomorrow Factory,* October 2018; Reprinted (French) in *La Fabrique des lendemains*, October 2020.
- N21 "Last Night I Dreamed You" in *Emerge Literary Journal*, #14, July 2020.*
- N22 "Love in the Time of Coronavirus" in *Lockdown Literature*, November 2020.

BIBLIOGRAPHY

ABOUT THE AUTHOR

RICH LARSON was born in Niger, has lived in Spain and Czech Republic, and is currently based in Canada. He is the author of the novels *Annex* and *Ymir*, as well as over 250 short stories—some of the best of which can be found in his previous collections *Tomorrow Factory* and *The Sky Didn't Load Today and Other Glitches*. His fiction has appeared in over a dozen languages, among them Polish, French, Romanian and Japanese, and his translated collection *La Fabrique des lendemains* won the Grand Prix de L'Imaginaire in 2020. His short story "Ice" was adapted into an Emmy-winning episode of *LOVE DEATH + ROBOTS*. Find him at instagram.com/richlarsonwrites and patreon.com/richlarson.

PUBLICATION HISTORY

"Painless" originally appeared in *Tor.com*, 2019 | "Like Any Other Star" originally appeared in *AE: The Canadian Science Fiction Review*, 2012 | "Night Shift" originally appeared in *Martian: The Magazine of Science Fiction Drabbles*, 2021 | "Headhunting" originally appeared in *Tor.com*, 2023 | "All Electric Ghosts" originally appeared in *Clarkesworld*, 2019 | "Smear Job" originally appeared in *Analog Science Fiction & Fact*, 2018 | "Brainwhales Are Stoners, Too" originally appeared in *Interzone*, 2015 | "In Event of Moon Disaster" originally appeared in *Asimov's Science Fiction*, 2018 | "Valhalla" originally appeared in *Martian: The Magazine of Science Fiction Drabbles*, 2021 | "Last Nice Day" originally appeared in *Clarkesworld*, 2021 | "Animals Like Me" originally appeared in *Ignorance is Strength: The Dystopia Triptych #1*, edited by John Joseph Adams, Christie Yant, and Hugh Howey, 2020 | "Our Lady of Perpetual Disdain" originally appeared in *Burn the Ashes: The Dystopia Triptych #2*, edited by John Joseph Adams, Christie Yant, and Hugh Howey, 2020 | "Failsafe" originally appeared in *Or Else the Light: The Dystopia Triptych #3*, edited by John Joseph Adams, Christie Yant, and Hugh Howey, 2020 | "Quandry Aminu vs The Butterfly Man" originally appeared in *Tor.com*, 2022 | "Tripping Through Time" originally appeared in *Dark Matter*, 2021 | "Dale Dale Dale" originally appeared in *Martian: The Magazine of Science Fiction Drabbles*, 2022 | "Tidings" originally appeared in *Imagine 2200: Climate Fiction for Future Ancestors*, Grist.org, 2021 | "The Old Man" originally appeared in *Analog Science & Fact*, 2017 | "Safe Space" originally appeared in *Daily Science Fiction*, 2018 | "Still Life of a Death Broker" originally appeared in *Terraform*, 2019 | "Complete Exhaustion of the Organism" originally appeared in *Lightspeed*, 2021 | "Horizon Event" originally appeared in *Martian: The Magazine of Science Fiction Drabbles*, 2021 | "You Are Born Exploding" originally appeared in *Clarkesworld*, 2021 | "Verweile Doch (But Linger)" originally appeared in *OMNI*, 2017 | "Meat And Salt And Sparks" originally appeared in *Tor.com*, 2018

OTHER TITLES FROM FAIRWOOD PRESS

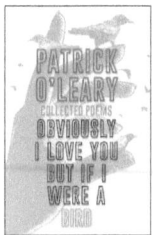

*Obviously I Love You
But If I Were a Bird*
by Patrick O'Leary
small paperback $11.00
ISBN: 978-1-958880-37-1

Space Trucker Jess
by Matthew Kressel
trade paper $20.95
ISBN: 978-1-958880-27-2

Shifter and Shadow
by Sharon Shinn
trade paper $16.99
ISBN: 978-1-958880-36-4

When Mothers Dream: Stories
by Brenda Cooper
trade paper $18.99
ISBN: 978-1-958880-35-7

*Better Dreams, Fallen Seeds
and Other Handfuls of Hope*
by Ken Scholes
paperback $19.99
ISBN: 978-1-958880-32-6

*A Catalog of Storms:
Collected Short Fiction*
by Fran Wilde
trade paper $18.99
ISBN: 978-1-958880-31-9

Black Hole Heart and Other Stories
by K.A. Teryna
trade paper $18.99
ISBN: 978-1-958880-29-6

One Last Game
by T.A. Chan
trade paper $15.99
ISBN: 978-1-958880-34-0

Find us at:
www.fairwoodpress.com
Bonney Lake, Washington

www.ingramcontent.com/pod-product-compliance
Lightning Source LLC
Chambersburg PA
CBHW020837020726
47497CB00005B/1142